Heat Wave

Melissa Gunn

Cover design by Getcovers.com

Heat Wave

ISBN 978-0-473-62229-9 (Paperback POD)

ISBN 978-0-473-62231-2 (epub)

ISBN 978-0-473-62232-9 (kindle)

ISBN 978-0-473-62230-5 (Hardcover POD)

CONTENTS

This one's for Tabby

CHAPTER ONE

FREYA ARRIVES IN YORK

The odour of hot steel assaulted Freya's nostrils in waves as she stepped off the train into York station. The smell was accompanied by a hint of soot, warm asphalt, and a strong suggestion of impatience and a lack of facilities. Burnt coffee overlaid the whole. Wrinkling her nose, she lugged her suitcase behind her, bumping it with difficulty up the stairs which led to an overbridge crossing the tracks. The cat cage in her other hand was just as unwieldy, but much lighter. Halfway up, she switched hands, as the suitcase handle bit unbearably into her palm. There was a discontented yowl.

"Sorry, Mr Fluffbum," she answered the yowl. "Not long now."

Or I hope it won't be long. Why did I pack so much stuff? This thing weighs a tonne. Still, it's not as though I could have left anything behind in my student flat. No-one else was staying on.

Despite the heavy luggage and unpleasant odours, Freya felt a frisson of excitement as she ascended the stairs. She was now officially an adult, graduated, moving to a new city and a new job on her own - well, on her own apart from her cat - and with nothing to mark her as anything but mundane. She nodded to herself at the thought.

Yes, I can be a normal person here. Whatever that is. She hauled her suitcase up another step. Only a trickle of other passengers had disembarked, and none stopped to help her with her unwieldy luggage. As she reached the top of the stairs, arm muscles burning from the effort, she felt like she had ascended into an oven, the cavernous domed barn overhead seeming to catch the unseasonal heat instead of shielding her from it.

She paused to push tendrils of dark blond hair off her face and give her arms a break. But as sweat sprang up on her forehead, she wished she hadn't bothered to stop.

This is the north of England; it's not supposed to be hot.

Freya flapped at her face to try to generate a breeze, but it didn't make much difference.

Just keep going. It's got to be cooler soon.

She bent down to check on her cat.

"Not long now, Mr Fluffbum. You'll like the new apartment. It's got a huge back yard according to the pictures - pretty much in the country. I expect there will be lots of mice."

The cat's eyes glowed yellow in the darkness of the cat carrier, then blacked out as he blinked.

"Yeah, I'm looking forward to it too. We've been in a city too long." Resolutely, Freya picked up both cat cage and suitcase and set off again.

Freya was halfway across the overbridge when another train squealed to a halt below her. A surge of people erupted from its doors, and a minute later, Freya was surrounded by a buffeting wave of humanity. Or no, not quite humanity. As she tried to continue her luggage-encumbered crossing of the overbridge, she found herself surrounded by a ring of brown-haired young men, all about the same height as her. They maintained a constant chatter around her, even as she looked for an exit. Trying to assess the situation, she noticed short, dense beards, furry forearms, long curved nails. Their eyes darted around, faster than human. One man was fiddling with some sort of fidget toy. Or maybe that was just his keys. Nostrils flared around her; someone let out an excited whoop. They looked similar enough to be brothers. The clues all added up to one thing.

Oh, no. Weres, she thought. *Not again. Still, they've got no reason to bother me.*

But their conversation became more specific to Freya. She shivered and tried to increase her pace, hampered by the surrounding bodies.

"She smells like new blood, Harry. Gonna invite her to join us?"

"Depends if she's willing, dunnit?"

"Maybe, maybe not."

"Willing's more fun, though. I like fun."

"I like her hair, it's nearly our colour."

It is not, Freya thought. Her hair was not nearly so brown, though it had never been as blond her sister's, either. *Just nondescript. Neither one thing or another.* She'd always wished it was blond like her sister's or black like her friend's hair.

"Why don't we just ask her if she'll come?"

Sounds like as good an opening as I'm going to get.

"Excuse me, gentlemen. You're in my way. Would you mind moving aside?"

OK, that was pathetic. Come on, Freya, be forceful.

Around her, heads cocked to one side, a couple of men nudged each other with their elbows. One appeared to nominate himself as a spokesman.

"We're off for a drink, want to join us?" He sounded cheerful, not too pressing.

Maybe I'm imagining the threat here, thought Freya. *They could just be very enthusiastic human youths.*

"No thanks, I have an appointment," she said aloud.

"Aw, come on. The pub's just round the corner, it won't take long," said the spokesman.

Freya shook her head firmly.

"Sorry, I'll be late." *Or at least I'll arrive in the dark to a place I've never been. Worse than late.*

The group pressed in closer around her, forcing her to stop. More voices joined the first. It seemed hotter than ever with so many bodies so close.

"Just one drink, yeah?"

"Are you a toff or something, think you're too good for us?"

"Be a sport, lady. No harm no foul, yeah?"

Freya began to feel panicked. How had her arrival turned sour so fast?

Someone's hand touched the arm holding the cat cage. Someone else tugged on her ponytail, before sliding a hand down her side towards her butt. Her back was still protected by her rucksack, but this was too much.

"No! Get away from me!" she shouted, dropping the handle of her suitcase, rather more carefully setting down the cat cage, and applying her elbows and knees to whatever soft parts she could reach. Where were station security? What about all those other people who'd got off the train? Freya realised with a sinking heart that with so many people packed around her, she probably couldn't even be seen by anyone outside the circle.

"We're just being friendly," a voice leered in her ear. She whipped around, trying to catch the speaker with an elbow.

"Not my style of friendly," she panted. Someone caught her by the rucksack, and another caught her upper arm, preventing her from moving. She tried to kick out, and was briefly rewarded as one of her assailants staggered back, clutching at his groin. However, her triumph was short-lived as another body took his place. She was trapped.

CHAPTER TWO

A STRANGER TO THE RESCUE

"There seems to be an absence of gentlemanly behaviour in this station," observed a new voice, formal and slightly accented. Standing nearly a foot taller than the group of men who surrounded her, a large man was looking over the huddle with distaste. He wore dark clothes, well-tailored garments that highlighted muscular limbs and a broad chest. Dark red hair was brushed smoothly back from his face, showing broad cheekbones and eyes of some indeterminate colour. He looked to be a couple of years older than her. It was probably only her imagination that the heat in the station intensified as he approached.

Why do rich people always seem to have smooth hair? Freya wondered irrelevantly. Not that she had any evidence that the newcomer was rich, but he did have an aura of power that she associated with wealth. She patted her own rather wavy dark-blond hair (*not brown, definitely not*) self-consciously. After the tussle with the were-whatever-they-weres, it was anything but smooth. *Definitely not wealthy, me. Maybe it's just that he doesn't have to fight his way through a train station.*

She found her eyes dwelling on him anyway.

This is not the time to be dwelling on muscular men. Focus on getting away from the weres.

"Who are you saying in't a gentleman?" asked the spokesman gruffly, patting his own clothes down with his free hand. "We're just inviting this here young lady to have a drink with us."

There was a general widening of space around Freya, and she breathed a little more freely.

"She does not appear to be thirsty," said the newcomer dryly.

"Sure, she is, anyone would be in this heat."

"I'm really not," said Freya mendaciously, firmly shaking the hand off her arm.

The ring of men looked at one another and back at the red-haired man, and shuffled back a step.

"Right you are, then. Enjoy your day, miss." The group of men streamed past her down the stairs to the main station. She felt one of them pat her bottom as he passed, and she twisted aside indignantly. Baffled by the sudden change of behaviour from her attackers, not to mention their abrupt language transition - they sounded like servants from some period drama, now - Freya was left alone on the overbridge, looking at her apparent rescuer with some concern.

"Thanks," she said.

"No thanks is required. It is my pleasure to ensure that beautiful women are not molested in this city."

Okaaay. What do I say to that? What about the not-beautiful women?

Inclining his head formally to her, the man strode off after the departed group.

I guess I don't have to say anything, then. Just as well, I don't know whether to thank him or tell him off for being an archaic so and so.

Freya reclaimed her suitcase and her cat cage. She peered anxiously at the black and white cat within.

"Are you OK, Mr Fluffbum?" she asked the cat. There was no answer, just wide eyes glinting light back at her. "Yeah, I know. Not the way I expected this to go either," she said. Freya patted herself down to make sure nothing was missing, and started on the long, bumpy descent down the stairs. It hadn't been a pleasant encounter, but as far as attacks by weres were concerned, she'd experienced far worse in the past. Freya wondered what sort of weres they had been. She mentally added up the clues. Short, sleek brown hair, fairly playful - at least at first - and working as a group. *Hmmm...* She paused at the base of the stairs to pull out her phone. Her hand needed a break from the suitcase anyway. A quick search for mammalian pack hunters gave her a shortlist.

They hadn't seemed particularly canine despite operating as a group. Maybe were-mongoose? No, otters, I think. Those cute little ones, that live in groups at the zoo, not the big river otters. Though those guys weren't cute. Were-otters. That's a new one for me.

Shrugging off the incident as best she could, she exited the station at last, and having deposited half her luggage in a locker, began the search for the correct bus to her new accommodation. A new life lay before her; she'd finished university and landed a real job. Freya was determined that roving packs of were-otters notwithstanding, she was going to try being a mundane human being for a change. In the past, she'd been hampered by her heritage as a demigoddess, with were-foxes providing unpleasant interludes. But there seemed no reason for her to use the small powers she had as an eponymous descendant here in York. She was going to be employed as a scientist working on plant diseases. Surely that was as far as anyone could get from being a demigoddess? It sounded so ordinary. Boring, even. Freya could hardly wait.

CHAPTER THREE

A COUNTRY HOUSE

Freya eyed the two-story building with some trepidation. It was a lot more remote than she'd been expecting, for a house only a few minutes by bus from the city. Although it had other dwellings flanking it on either side, they were separated by large stretches of land swathed in grass and dotted with trees. A large, dark yew tree offered welcome shade by the short driveway that led to the house.

No point in standing here, no matter how pleasantly shady it is. It's time to brave the dragon - I mean, landlady.

Freya stiffened her resolve, and picking up Mr Fluffbum in his cage, wearily began pulling her suitcase along the gravelled drive. It bumped annoyingly from side to side as the small wheels encountered larger rocks. Still, this was the last leg of the trip to her new life, she could stand an irritating suitcase. She reached the stone steps that led to the door. A metal boot scraper was fixed to the top step, but its gleaming metal surface suggested it hadn't seen mud in a long time. It was an odd contrast to the door, which was dark green and battered, with a horseshoe affixed to it as a doorknocker.

As the unexpectedly loud echoes from the knocker died away, Freya stood as far away from the door as the steps allowed, wondering what to expect. There hadn't been many photos online, but the low rent and pet allowance had encouraged her to apply as soon as she'd had confirmation of her new job.

The door swung inwards with a creak, and a rather dishevelled blond woman was revealed, holding a glass of wine in one hand. Wisps of hair framed her face, falling out of a messy bun. She wore a salmon-coloured tank top over cut-off jeans, and her feet were bare.

"Oh, hello then. You must be Freya. Come in and take a load off, it's far too hot to be walking around. Is that the cat, then?" Without waiting for Freya's answers, the woman ducked down and held out a hand to Mr Fluffbum, who looked up at Freya through the bars of the cat cage before deigning to sniff the woman's hand.

"Oh, and I'm Angie, a 'course," she added as an afterthought. "Come in and let him explore. Want a glass?" She waved her own glass at Freya, the liquid slopping dangerously close to the brim.

Not a dragon at all, it seems. She seems totally mundane, thank goodness. If a little sozzled.

Freya repressed the urge to take a step back.

"No, I'm good. Maybe later?" she said.

"Course, love, course. Now come in and I'll give you the tour." Angie stepped aside to allow room for Freya to enter. "Here, I'll bring your suitcase up. That must have been a challenge on the bus."

Well, thought Freya, *sozzled or not, at least she seems to care. And she sure doesn't reek of power.* A quick glance at Angie's forearms reassured her that she wasn't likely to be domiciling with a were of any sort.

"Thanks," she said aloud. "That'd be great."

She approached the university labs early the next morning. A bus had taken her from near her new lodgings to a stop just outside the campus. This part of the university was mostly postgraduate labs and research centres, so there was less of the usual bustle of students here. A few vehicles were parked outside the big buildings and a rack of bicycles was mostly full. Signs directed her to a reception area, where she spent several minutes signing documents to get her work ID card. It was all reassuringly human, right down to the ten pages of rules she had to read and sign before being allowed into the main building.

"There you go, love," said the receptionist. "Canteen's off to your left, and here's a map to help you get you to your lab. Good luck!"

Freya stepped out with a will. It was time to start her new life.

CHAPTER FOUR

BAT WOMAN

"Furl your wings a moment please, bat-woman."

The voice came from behind Freya as she walked along the long driveway towards the bus stop after work. Embarrassed, Freya pulled in the edges of her cloak and tried to walk a bit closer to the edge of the narrow concrete path. It was really too hot to wear her cloak this afternoon, but the morning had been chilly and it was easier now to wear it than carry it. Besides, she enjoyed the flare and billow of the cloak as she walked. To her surprise the man who'd caught up with her didn't pass by, but instead fell into step beside her. With a start, she recognised him as her anonymous rescuer from the train station. She wished she could think of something intelligent to say. Instead, she stammered.

"It's really a cloak. Not like bat wings at all, they only have skin for wings." *Why did I say that? Now I sound like an idiot.*

The man laughed at her, teeth gleaming. The afternoon sun lit sparks in his red hair.

"You must be in the biology section then, to know such things?" He had an unusual accent, very precise in his enunciation. Freya couldn't identify it.

"Yes, I've only been here a couple of weeks. Well, you saw me when I arrived at the station, I guess you know that. I keep getting lost on my way through the building here, all those long white corridors look identical. But then I turn a corner, and have to swipe my card to get through some doors and they won't let me through because I'm in the wrong place. It's maddening! I hope I get used to it soon." *Am I talking too much?* Freya wondered. *I am talking too much.*

The man nodded, and it took Freya a moment to realise he was responding to her comment, rather than to her unspoken thought.

"Yes, I am sure you will. But it does take time. Perhaps you will find *me* by accident one of these days. I am Stefan, geologist. You will be on the wrong side of the building if you find my lab. But maybe that will not be a bad thing. Look for my name on the doors. See you when you next get lost!" With those words, he quickened his pace and crossed the drive into the car parking area. Freya watched him stride past the grassed areas where she had seen black rabbits frolicking in the evenings, the last couple of weeks. She didn't know what to make of the encounter. Had she been invited to make friends, or jeered at?

At that moment, she heard the roar her bus made as the driver used engine braking to slow down before the stop. She had to break into a run to reach the bus stop in time, her cloak flapping once more as she raced along the shrubby driveway to the road where the bus was drawn up under tall trees.

"Wait, I'm coming!" she yelled, waving her arms as she ran. Too late. With another roar, the bus jerked into motion just as she reached its rear end. Banging her hand against the side of the bus in frustration, she stopped running - only to be surprised when the bus stopped and waited for her, the driver opening the doors.

"Sorry love, you're a bit late today." The bus driver was unusually polite as Freya scrambled on and fumbled out her ticket. She hadn't realised that she'd been noticed. But then, she was the only one getting on the bus at this time. Perhaps it wasn't so surprising. She staggered to the back seat, lurching as the bus took off once more, speeding up as though to make up for lost time, before the brakes were slammed on again to take a tight turn down a small country lane. She clung to the seat in front of her to avoid being flung forward down the aisle. Freya was enjoying her new job in a big university lab complex on the edge of the countryside - far from the sea and its dangerous deities - but the local transport certainly left something to be desired.

CHAPTER FIVE

ENTER THE CHILLI GUY

F reya inadvertently worked through the usual lunch hour the next day. There was only a thin scattering of people left in the canteen when she hastened there. She viewed the price list for the remaining food in the canteen with dismay.

"A tenner for lunch? Isn't there a cheaper option?"

"Of course, love, you can just have the vegetables for a fiver." The server was unsympathetic as she gestured to a pile of dark green cooked leaves and partially dried-out yellow-crusted mashed potatoes. "Not that there's much of them, mind, the weather gods aren't helping anyone."

Though it was cool in the air-conditioned building, the heat wave that had met Freya in York still hadn't given way to the more usual grey skies. Freya's boss was taking bets on how long it would last.

"I'll take the vegetables, I guess," Freya sighed.

Was that reference to the weather gods co-incidental or deliberate? Surely it was just a chance phrase.

She scanned her phone to transfer the money, and took the plate she was given. Freya looked around. The policy analyst who worked in the office next to her lab was sitting at a nearby table. His grey hair covered by a cap, always clad in rumpled dun-coloured clothing, he hadn't struck Freya as an obvious choice of companion. Unexpectedly, he waved her over. He was never talkative, bolting his food as though it would be snatched away if he ate too slowly. Feeling stuck, she joined him, sitting in the chair opposite. He nodded acknowledgment of her presence, but continued to eat.

Freya resolutely took the first bite of what was possibly spring greens.

Ugh. Not spring greens - at least, not in any form I've ever tried them. Or want to again. She chewed on. *If I get this mouthful down, I can leave the rest. Maybe the other vegetables will taste better.*

Her morose chewing was interrupted.

"Spices. That's what this food is always missing. We could learn a thing or two from the Mexicans, I reckon."

Freya could only stare. This was the longest sentence she'd ever heard from the taciturn analyst.

"Er... yes?" she ventured.

"Yeah. I went to Mexico once, when I was young. Best food ever. Real taste. Not like this stuff."

Freya was astonished. Who knew that the policy nerd could actually venture forth a conversational gambit, for a start? And what a surprise that he'd been abroad - and liked it. He gave the impression of being a traditionalist stay-at-home person. Maybe she'd judged too much from his nondescript clothing and ancient cheese-cutter cap.

"How long were you there for?" she asked.

"My brother and I went for three months. Before the storms got so bad in the Atlantic. I still dream about that food. Amazing sauces. Spice like you wouldn't believe. Hot and sour, with chillies and limes. I've got a few chillies growing at home, but it's not the same." The analyst paused. "Do you like chillies?"

Freya answered diplomatically.

"It's alright, I suppose."

"It's my favourite thing," he said. "I make bottles of chilli sauce to get me through winter. But I get told off when I bring it to work. Apparently, it breaks the quarantine rules. Shame. The food here needs spicing up."

Freya had to agree with him. Spices would definitely improve the taste of her lunch. Though chilli wouldn't be her first choice. Or her second...

"They overcook the greens, too," she said. Her nameless greens were a case in point.

"Oh, I don't mind that, really. If only we had spices, I could live with it. Spices were the basis of empire, you know. How the mighty have fallen, eh?"

"We have plenty of basil, oregano, that sort of thing."

"Oh yes, things we can grow here, cool climate stuff, but not the rest of the palate. Are you old enough to have tasted real cinnamon? Or nutmeg? Rainforest spices, the taste of heated lands. Not as good as chilli, of course, but they had their own special place." He was gazing into the middle distance, now. He tasted the air a couple of times, snakelike.

Creepy. This guy is waxing poetic over spices? I thought he was into policy, not food.

"Surely it's all in the way you cook food," she argued. "Mingling flavours and stuff. And we still have chocolate. And half the stuff in the supermarkets is flavoured with cinnamon."

The policy analyst - what was his name, even? - managed to look offended as he shovelled mashed potato into his mouth.

"Fake essence is what they use in the supermarket," he said once his mouth was clear. "Chemistry lab stuff, not the real thing. And it's all very well cooking food well, but you have to have the right ingredients, too. I will give you; chocolate is one of them. Goes well with chilli."

"That's hard to imagine." Freya shuddered inwardly at the idea of mingling her favourite food with her least favourite spice.

"Look, tell you what. I'll show you. I have a group of people coming over to see my chillis later in the summer. You come too, and see what I mean. I'll have some of my favourite dishes prepared."

"Er..." Freya wondered how she could refuse without giving offence, but failed to come up with a way. "Thanks?"

Maybe I can figure out something by next week.

"Good. I'll drop an invite in your pigeonhole."

The analyst finished the few scraps of food lingering on his plate, stood up, and left to deposit it in the waiting racks of dirty plates.

Freya finished her unappetising meal of overcooked carrots, aged mashed potatoes and unknown greens, alone, pondering the unexpected conversation.

CHAPTER SIX

A LACK OF SPICES

Back in the lab she raised it with Kylie, another lab worker who had been showing her the ropes.

"I had lunch with what's-his-name. The chilli guy. Policy person. Whatever. He was saying we used to have a lot more spices. Do you know anything about that, coming from abroad and all?"

Kylie hailed from Australia, though with her brown hair and darkly tanned skin she didn't fit Freya's idea of a typical Australian. Well, maybe the tan fit. Of course, Freya hadn't met many Australians - world travel was enough of a challenge that not many made it this far.

"Oh, you got cornered by Phillip, did you? He gets everyone sooner or later. No one suspects he has anything to say, and then, boom! It's chilli this, and how can we survive without spice the other. He's a bit odd, but he's usually right about policy stuff." Kylie passed Freya an empty box for pipette tips, ready to be filled. It was the sort of mind-numbing job that drove Freya crazy with boredom, but it had to be done at least once a day.

Why did I think a job in science was going to get me out of all the boring jobs? Oh, that's right, I was aiming for boring. Boring and paid.

"Well, it wasn't exactly boom. I mean, it wasn't very dramatic. But what about the spices?" she asked.

"Oh yeah, that's true enough. Only old geezers like him talk about it though. Although I guess in a place like this, we should know all about it really. I mean, it's plant diseases that are half the problem."

"And the other half?"

"Come on, Freya, you live in the world, don't you? Would you bother putting something expensive on a ship these days? I mean, chances of a bad storm are like, a hundred and fifty percent between here and the equator. And it's not like the sky's full of planes the way it used to be. I had to save for years before I could afford to get here."

"Oh, I know *that*. I guess the thing that surprised me most is that someone like Phillip would express opinions."

"You always have to watch the quiet types." Kylie winked, making her statement into a joke.

Did the chilli guy just want to invite me to his party, or is there something more going on? Freya wondered, as she started on the tedious task of filling each empty hole in the pipette tip box with a reusable, sterilisable plastic tip. Their lab went through several boxes a day, and refilling the boxes after they'd been through a glorified dishwasher was a task everyone loved to hate. "Come with me to his get-together, then. See what the quiet type gets up to at home. I'd rather have someone as backup, anyway," she added, half under her breath.

"Ooh, you have an invite to one of the chilli guy's famous parties? Count me in!" said Kylie.

For a moment Freya was sure that Kylie's ears twitched forward. *No, I must have imagined it.* "Seriously, you want to go?" She couldn't imagine the analyst's get-together being a desirable gathering.

"You bet. I've been hearing about Phillip's parties since I got here. And I haven't had an invitation."

"Alright, then. Assuming Phillip doesn't mind an extra. You ask him, alright? And you have a car, don't you? You can drive us both there. I'll let you know when I get the invite."

If everyone's so keen to go, I guess I should check it out. And maybe Kylie will be a friend. I could do with one here.

"That's awesome, Freya. I can't wait," Kylie said, dumping a fresh load of clean pipette tips onto Freya's bench.

"Thanks ever so," Freya said, eyeing the pile wryly.

CHAPTER SEVEN

AN EVENING WITH ANGIE

That evening, Freya once again related her day's encounters to Angie, as she'd begun to do in response to Angie's frequent requests for a bit of a chat of an evening.

"I don't think he's handsome, exactly." Freya felt she should be clear on this point.

"Go on, you've been talking about this Stefan person for fifteen minutes already."

"Er. Yes. He's just different from anyone else I've met, that's all." Despite the confusing combination of his aura of power, attractive features, and his unusual figures of speech, Freya found Stefan an intriguing figure. She wondered if he attended the weekly pub gatherings on Friday after work. She hadn't been to one yet, as she'd been busy moving her things from a locker near the station to her new room - a task that relied on clear skies, as she didn't own any waterproof mode of transport.

"Could be worth talking to," was Angie's opinion - not that Freya expected any other point of view. Angie worked as a nurse and had a husband who was away most of the week, and she thought pretty much anyone was worth talking to. This meant that Freya spent more time talking to Angie than she had expected when she was accepted for the rental. Freya was finding it a novelty to have someone so interested in every detail of her daily life. Angie extracted every speck of information about Stefan, then announced that it was wine-o'clock, and did Freya want to join her?

"Depends on the vintage," said Freya with a laugh. Over the last week, Angie had invariably produced English wine in a cardboard cask.

"Only the best around here." Angie grinned, and sure enough, pulled out the same cardboard cask. "To semi-handsome oddly accented men," she declared, raising her glass. Freya laughed, and raised her own. There were worse ways to end the day.

"So, any other interesting things happen today?" Angie asked.

Freya explained about her lunch with the policy analyst.

"Ooh, I've heard about him. You should go, no question. He's a real kingpin around here, or so I hear."

"Really? He doesn't look like one. Or act like it either."

"Well, he wouldn't at work, would he?" Angie took a large gulp of her white wine. "I've heard rumours about the chilli king though. Half of them probably aren't true, but I bet you could do worse than go to that party. You might find out something interesting. Or make some useful contacts, that's always important, or so they tell me. It's not something I have to work at in my job."

"I'm not really very good at networking," Freya said.

"All the more reason to go. Besides, I want to hear about what his place is like. That'd give me some good gossip on the wards. Not that I gossip, of course." Angie winked.

"All right, all right, I'll go!" Freya was a bit annoyed that Angie seemed more interested in the chilli guy than in Stefan. *She'd* rather think about Stefan. He was much better eye candy than the chilli guy, at any rate. Even if he was odd.

CHAPTER EIGHT

FRIDAY PUB GATHERING

Friday afternoon saw Freya in the beer garden of her lab's preferred pub for the first time, nursing a half pint of cider at a wooden table and hoping the afternoon would end before it got to her round. She didn't begrudge buying a round in general, but this week she was cash-poor, having sunk most of her money into the deposit for her new room. She needed to get paid - but of course, since she worked at a university, everyone was paid two weeks in arrears, and then only if the paperwork had gone through a week beforehand. All things considered, she'd be lucky if she got paid in the next two months.

Freya found herself looking for Stefan's face amongst her colleagues, and was slightly irritated with herself for being disappointed by his absence. She had more or less got the hang of getting to her own lab from the front desk each morning, getting lost less often as the days went on. However, that meant she hadn't accidentally-on-purpose located the geology lab either, as she'd half-hoped to do. She sighed, and discovered she'd drained her cider. Looking around, she saw that everyone else's glasses were empty too. Her nearest neighbours had already stood a round. *Oh well, nothing else for it...*

"My round, what's everyone drinking?" she said brightly. Her lab-mate, Kylie laughed.

"If you're buying before you've gotten paid, they can all drink lime and soda. Don't worry, I'll get this one. You can owe me, next time." Freya felt a sharp spurt of relief. She'd made the offer, and that counted, socially. She'd had to learn such niceties when she got to university. Her Mum had not encouraged pub visits, and the society that went with them.

At least I've passed that test. Human, see, just like the rest of them - or at least making a good appearance of being one. When Kylie went to order the next round, she followed to help carry the drinks.

"Thanks, Kylie. I owe you one."

"No dramas," said Kylie in her distinctive Australian twang. "Stefan did the same for me, the first week I was here. Government payroll sucks big time. But we all know how it works." Together Freya and Kylie picked their way back to the table their lab group occupied.

"Cheers, then!" Freya raised her glass in salutation, feeling supported by her workmate, but still somehow isolated. She was almost sure that she was the only demi-goddess at the table, probably in the room. She wondered how many other demis were out there, and if she'd ever know when she met one. That was a supernatural sense she didn't have - she had to rely on the cues she'd been drilled in, growing up. Her mother had told her that her sensing ability might grow in with time, but if not, she was to treat everyone as fully human. She was still waiting for that sense to appear. Some days she felt lonely, isolated, being unable to reveal her true self. Today, though, she let herself relax in the company of her unsuspecting, presumably all-too-human workmates. She'd wanted to see what it was like to be a mundane. This, apparently, was it.

"Cheers." Kylie clinked her pint glass against Freya's.

Freya sat back and observed her fellows. There was a broad cross-section from her lab present, many of whom she wasn't yet familiar with. She caught herself looking for Stefan again, then told herself she wasn't doing so.

Focus. This is the time you're supposed to be networking, being social. She'd learnt that lesson at uni too, a lesson others hadn't seemed to need.

"Does Stefan come here often?" she asked Kylie in a low voice, hoping she wasn't giving away her interest too obviously.

"Most weeks, except just lately. Why, are you hoping he'll cover the next round?"

Freya laughed. No, she hadn't betrayed her true interest.

A snippet of conversation at the table beside hers caught her attention. The speaker was someone Freya didn't know, an older woman with olive skin. Her companion was a blond woman she'd seen in the canteen.

"...heard she was just on her way home the usual way, when she was attacked," said the older woman.

"Do they know who did it?" asked the blond.

"Not yet. She told me the police didn't believe what she told them, so that won't help."

Freya focussed on the odd conversation, forgetting to reply to Kylie's joking question.

"What did she tell them, then?"

"She told me she saw a giant dog out of the corner of her eye. Next thing she knew she was bleeding on the road and her wallet was missing. I had to print her a new ID card."

A touch on her arm brought Freya back to her neighbours.

"Earth to Freya, are you there?"

Reluctantly, Freya returned her attention to Kylie.

"Sorry, what?" She didn't want to lose track of that conversation, but she couldn't ignore Kylie.

"I asked if you wanted some crisps. I'm going to go order some."

"Oh, sure. Yes. Please."

"Look after my drink, then, will you?"

Kylie walked back to the bar, and Freya returned her attention to the conversation at the other table. To her disappointment, the topic under discussion had moved on to the merits or otherwise of real ale. The olive-skinned woman was walking towards the exit. Kylie returned, opening a bag of crisps wide and placing them on the table for general sharing. She helped herself to a generous handful and gestured for Freya to do the same.

"Kylie, have you heard anything about someone from work getting attacked?"

Kylie was usually up on local gossip. Freya wasn't sure how she managed it, because she almost always saw Kylie hard at work in the lab, not out and about chatting to people.

"Oh, yeah. One of the women from accounting, I think. She'd probably upset someone by telling them they were over budget and would have to cut back."

"Sounds harsh."

"I'm kidding, Freya!"

Oops, missed that cue. Pay attention, Freya.

"I know," Freya lied, "I just wondered what really happened."

"So do the police. Me too, if I'm honest. No-one needs a predator around." Kylie gave an exaggerated shudder. "Better make sure we don't go home alone, eh?"

Later, Freya accepted a lift home rather than take the late bus the way she had planned to - it would have been churlish to refuse the offer, not to mention risky. But she missed having the quiet time on the bus to process the day's happenings.

CHAPTER NINE

STEFAN APPEARS

Giving Kylie a cheery wave as she closed the car door, Freya turned towards her driveway and gave an involuntary shriek. Beside the giant yew that towered over the drive, a tall figure lurked. The pub discussion about predators sprang to the front of her mind. Freya's heart pounded uncomfortably fast as she considered her choices. Run? Nowhere to run to, unless you counted empty fields. Fight? She had never been much of a fighter, preferring to avoid conflict. By default, she froze, feeling like a rabbit in the headlights. The dark figure stepped forward, and out of the deep shade took on a veneer of familiarity.

"*Stefan*? What are you doing lurking in my driveway like a stalker?"

Stefan chuckled, moving into her personal space as he did so. Freya started to back up. She might find him intriguing, but after the evening's tales, she was not in an especially receptive mood. She abruptly realised that her place of refuge was in the other direction, past his looming figure, and stopped backing. He began to talk, somewhat to Freya's relief. A talking, looming male was much better than an attacking, looming male.

Come on, Freya, this is the handsome Stefan. There's nothing to fear from him, Freya told herself. *No giant dogs here. And he didn't attack, he just startled you.* She fanned her suddenly hot face with her hand.

"There is no need to worry. I have been trying to clear the roads of a menace. You have heard of those attacks, yes? I too. And I am not one to leave a cowardly attacker of the weak with free range in my home territory. I have not yet found him however, and so I wait here to make sure that you are not victimised by this nuisance."

His words echoed her thoughts, his odd phrasing distracting her from her spurt of fear. Freya felt that she should say something, but couldn't think what. She shifted her weight and found her voice.

"Er, great. I heard something about that at the pub this evening. Um. For a moment I thought you were a lurker, you gave me such a fright."

"My apologies for frightening you so. As you see, my motive was quite the opposite."

"Thanks, I guess. So, I'll just be going in then. Er. Excuse me." She stepped sideways in an attempt to show Stefan that he was in her way. The edge of her cloak brushed him and to her relief, he stepped aside.

"Onwards, brave maiden, to your sweet place of rest. See you in the geology wing soon, yes?"

"Yeah, maybe," muttered Freya. She didn't quite run inside, but it was a near thing. Stefan in the hallways and corridors at work was attractive. Stefan stepping unexpectedly out of the bushes outside her home was disturbing.

Safely ensconced in her room, Freya pondered Stefan's strange actions. He hadn't actually threatened her in any way - in fact he had been protective if his own account was to be believed.

But how did he know where I live?

Maybe she should find out more about him before she pursued any notions of attraction. It took her a long time to fall asleep that night.

CHAPTER TEN

AN INVITATION TO DINNER

Freya wasn't sure what she would do with herself, next time Stefan appeared in her vicinity. While she'd been interested in making his acquaintance previously, she wasn't so certain that would be a good idea now. The decision was taken out of her hands at lunchtime soon afterwards, when Stefan appeared at her table with a laden lunch-tray.

"Good day to you. I trust your rest was unbroken by nefarious strangers over the weekend?"

Seriously? thought Freya. *Why do I meet so many people with archaic language patterns?*

"Er, yes. I mean, no, it wasn't."

"Ah, good to know. You have spent time in this area before? You know the hazards?" Stefan asked.

Freya frowned at him.

"What hazards do you mean? Stray sheep?"

"Ah, you are not a local here, I take it. It is good to know of the people who live in this area, before you run abreast of them unprepared."

Freya looked sharply at Stefan. What was he hinting at? What sort of people should she be worried about? Was he actually a supernatural of some type, warning of other supernaturals? Demi-gods could be harder to pick than weres. But maybe there were simply lots of odd people in the area.

"Tell me what I should know, then," she invited, "so I am prepared. I assume you aren't a local either." She picked at the salad remaining on her plate. Today's vegetable offerings had clearly been affected by the continuing heat, the lettuce wilted and bitter and the broccoli showing signs of bolting.

Stefan looked around them, perhaps calculating the distance to their nearest neighbour in the canteen. He took a large bite from his dish of stew and chased it with a mouthful of bread.

"Here is not so good," he stated after swallowing. "Meet me in the city, for dinner. Your bus goes there, if you stay on it all the way."

Freya wasn't sure what to say – she hadn't expected a dinner invitation. It was a bit creepy that he knew what bus she took - but then, he'd seen her catch it the other day, hadn't he?

Should I be going out with someone unknown, if there are attacks happening? But Stefan's not unknown, and he helped me out at the train station.

She decided to take the plunge and do it anyway – after all, if Stefan was some kind of demi, she'd need time to observe him to figure out what type. She sat silent for a few moments, thinking. Stefan didn't seem to mind, eating his meal with good appetite. They were joined by Kylie before Freya had decided what to say. Kylie slid into the free chair on the side of their short, square table.

"Gidday, Stefan. I didn't know you knew Freya, here."

Stefan looked at Kylie with a strange expression on his face. Was it dislike? Fear? Or perhaps longing? Freya couldn't decide.

"We are only just beginning to know one another, I think," he said.

"Checking out the new blood, are you?" Kylie was openly derisive this time.

I thought Kylie said Stefan had helped her out when she was new. She doesn't seem so keen on him now. Freya wondered if there was some untold history between them. That might explain the flicker of emotions that crossed Stefan's visage as he looked at Kylie's challenging expression. In the end, he glanced away, seeming ill at ease.

"Stefan rescued me from a bunch of over-enthusiastic young men at the station when I first arrived," interjected Freya, trying to dissolve the conflict. "I'd have lost my luggage otherwise." *Or had to go for an unwanted drink.*

"Good to know you haven't lost your touch for rescuing people, Stefan. I hope you're at least as much of a gentleman to Freya here as you were to me," said Kylie. Her sarcastic tone removed a lot of the complimentary aspect of her comment. "Something similar happened to me in my first week in the job, here, Freya. Bit of a coincidence, don't ya think?"

"It is fortunate that I have been in a position to help both of you beautiful ladies, is it not?" said Stefan smoothly.

"Just peachy," drawled Kylie.

Freya decided she'd had enough of this conversation with its metaphorical concealed daggers.

"Kylie, if you want to tell me something, just say it. I'm not good at picking up on hints. And Stefan, you were asking me about dinner. I'll go." Without Kylie there, Freya might have simply declined. But something about being told not to do something made Freya want to do it anyway.

"I am most happy to hear that," said Stefan.

"I'll talk to you back in the lab, Freya," said Kylie. She stood up and walked away stiffly. Was she angry? Upset? Freya wished she was better at reading faces. Had she offended her new friend? It seemed like it.

Freya turned back to Stefan.

"I've only been to one restaurant in the city. And that was before I moved here," she said. *That time Aisha and I visited Karim.* Freya tried not to feel bitter at the reminder of Karim, her friend's brother. He had seemed so determined to see more of her, the first year he had moved for university, but that hadn't lasted. She wrenched her attention back to the present.

"Never fear, dear lady. I have an extensive knowledge of the local restaurants. We shall go to the best, depending on what your tastes dictate, of course. Tell me what flavours you enjoy."

Well, that's straight to the chase! He certainly doesn't waste time.

"So long as there's a good selection, I don't mind," she temporised. "Anything would be better than the options here. But I haven't got a lot of money yet, so perhaps a cheaper option would be good."

"We are all working at academic rates, yes? You may be assured that dinner will not be breaking the bank."

Freya was a little reassured that he didn't immediately suggest paying for dinner himself. She liked to maintain her independence. And if she took the bus to the city, she'd have a definite end-time, as she would have to catch the last bus home. She found herself becoming intrigued by the idea of a night out in the nearby walled city. She had not been confident to explore it much on her own yet, although the last few years of self-defence classes had helped her to overcome some of her fear of groups of strangers.

"All right, then. I'll meet you at the bus stop after work. Thursday?" A week night would also mean an earlier night - just in case she needed an excuse to leave.

"Most assuredly a good day to go. Until Thursday it is." Stefan took his empty lunch tray, and depositing the remains in the compost receptacle across the canteen, he walked out. Freya addressed herself to her own remaining lunch in a state of some confusion. Was it a really a good idea to go to dinner with Stefan? Especially when Kylie seemed so antagonistic towards him. If he actually was some sort of demi like her, shouldn't she find out? Even if she was trying to pass herself off as a mundane. Another part of her was flattered that the attractive-looking Stefan was showing interest in her, no matter how odd he seemed.

In the lab after lunch, Kylie avoided meeting Freya's eyes, scurrying from the lab bench to the samples freezer and back repeatedly.

Finally, Freya decided to broach the topic herself.

"What's with you and Stefan, Kylie?" she said.

Kylie hunched over the sample she was working on.

"Ancient history," she said. "Don't mind me. Go on and have fun with Stefan."

Freya frowned. Whatever was bothering Kylie, it didn't seem like it was such ancient history that she was over it.

CHAPTER ELEVEN

ANGIE WANTS GOSSIP

When Freya recounted her conversation with Stefan to Angie that evening, Angie had no doubts.

"Woohoo, dinner date already," she hooted. "That calls for a celebration!" Going to the cupboard, she brought out an actual glass bottle. "I've got just the thing!"

"No, no," said Freya, laughing at Angie's enthusiasm. "It's not a dinner date as such - at least I don't think so. He said he'd tell me about the local hazards. He didn't want to talk about it at work, which is a little concerning, now I come to think of it. What if some of the hazards are there?" She frowned. "It all seems very normal so far. Students doing their thing. People telling me what to do. Lots of middle-aged people who've done their jobs forever. Like that chilli guy. To look at, you'd think he'd be a meat and three veg eater, but he was waxing lyrical about Mexican food."

"Oh, the chilli king. You shouldn't judge people so much by appearances, Freya. I mean, look at me. If my hair was still dyed pink the way I had it in my teens, you'd probably think I was a right cracker. Whereas now, you'd never know, right?" Angie was wearing her usual random out-of-uniform selection of clothes, topped off tonight by a fascinator in rainbow hues.

Freya laughed, which she suspected had been Angie's purpose.

"Fair call. I'll try not to be so judgmental."

"Good, because I want to know more about that party you've been invited to. When is it?" Angie twisted the top off the top of the bottle. "You know, I wish we still had corks for this sort of thing," she said, before pouring a generous measure of wine into two glasses. "Shame the cork trees are gone."

Freya shrugged. She'd never paid attention to wine corks, though the loss of the cork oaks was something her Dad had complained about when she was a kid, and had perhaps influenced her interest in plant diseases.

"The invite turned up at work today, and it's not till August."

"Oh, that's a pity. I'll have to wait on my gossi- I mean, the girls at work will be disappointed not to get to hear about it yet."

"My heart bleeds for them." Freya raised her eyes heavenward, and sat down on her now-customary chair with her glass.

"I'll pass on your sympathy. So, if I can't have the chilli king this week, tell me more about the infamous Stefan. Where is he going to take you?" Angie asked, settling herself comfortably.

"I don't actually know where we're going. You know I haven't spent much time in the city, so I couldn't suggest anywhere. I'll have to tell you afterwards."

"I can't wait to hear about it. I'll wait up if I'm not on shift!"

"You're incorrigible," Freya smiled. Angie was a little over-enthusiastic at times, but it was hard to resist being drawn in by her ebullience. "Don't wait up, though - I'll be taking the bus."

CHAPTER TWELVE

DINNER DATE

Thursday rolled around all too soon. Freya found it hard to concentrate at work that day.

"Hey, Freya," Kylie asked at some point. "Was it you who loaded the centrifuge with these empty tubes?"

"Oops, sorry." She reloaded the equipment in question with the tubes she'd meant to use. A few minutes later, another plant pathogen was on its way to being decoded. Freya couldn't decide if she was nervous or excited about the evening to come.

Clocking out time came at last, but Freya had to make sure the lab was tidy before she left. She'd had so many accidents today, there was a lot of cleaning up to do. Finally, she could delay no longer without missing the agreed-upon bus.

After the cool of the air-conditioned lab, the heat hit her like a wall when she walked outside. She shed layers of clothes as she walked, hanging the discarded clothing over one arm, which immediately grew uncomfortably sweaty.

I wish this heat was over already. What happened to having just two weeks of proper summer in Britain? We really appreciated it then.

The heat seemed to intensify as she walked. Most people had already departed for the day, so the path out to the bus-stop was empty. However, as she approached the stop - hidden from lab buildings that made up the university complex by a small copse of trees - she saw that Stefan was waiting for her. Despite it being the end of a long, hot day, he looked well-groomed, his clothing accentuating his broad shoulders and long legs.

I wonder if he works out, to keep those perfect muscles? Freya couldn't help but admire his form as she approached.

She didn't usually see him at the bus stop, so she had assumed he was more of a car person. More people owned cars, out here in the country. It was very different to the city where almost everyone took the bus, train or other public transport. Her own family had always been staunchly against using cars. Freya had often thought that probably because they couldn't afford one, they'd made it a point of principle. However, Stefan hadn't suggested using a private vehicle, and she was happier using a public mode of transport with an unfamiliar person - no point in providing entrapment opportunities. She wondered briefly if she was more paranoid than the average person.

"Ah, well met, Freya of the evening," called Stefan.

Freya couldn't tell if his tone was mocking or cheerful. *OK... I know he speaks oddly. Work with it...*

"Where are we going tonight?" she asked as they walked side by side toward the business end of the bus stop. She was hyper-aware of his presence beside her, but determined to act casual.

"I have made a booking at the fine establishment of the Red Dragon. I have not actually eaten there before, but it has excellent reviews. I am sure you will love it."

Freya chuckled nervously. Stefan's tone was confident. *How can he be so sure of what I do and don't like? He doesn't know me yet.*

"That's actually the one restaurant I'd been to. It was good, so that's OK. I didn't think they took bookings, though."

"They were happy to do so when I called. I will enjoy seeing you revisit a favourite memory."

And that's just a little odd. Should I be going to dinner with this person? Her thoughts were interrupted by the approaching roar of the bus. *Too late to back out now. Besides, he's very good looking. And what other chance would I get to go out on the town?* Freya allowed herself to surreptitiously admire the breadth of his shoulders and the curve of his cheekbones.

The bus was an old style model, not yet replaced with a quiet electric version. Stefan motioned for her to enter first, and she tagged on to the bus with her phone as she entered. The bus driver raised his eyebrows as Stefan followed her in.

"Going somewhere nice then, love?" he asked.

"I hope so!" she replied. The bus driver never sped off without her these days.

She selected a seat by the window. Stefan slid into the seat beside her, and they were off with a lurch as he sat down. The noise of the bus made conversation almost impossible, so Freya arrived in the central city without any further useful information - though substantially warmer, since the old bus did not have air-conditioning. She was sure it was nothing to do with Stefan's thigh touching hers on the journey.

"Do they send buses here from the capital, when no-one wants to use them anymore?" she wondered aloud.

"I assume it is simply the same bus that did this route fifty years ago, and they have not bothered to update it," said Stefan.

They left the bus station with alacrity - the heat seemed concentrated there. Together, they walked towards the bridge over the river Ouse - happily not swollen by rains today. If anything, the water level was lower than it should have been. It had been a long, dry spring, aging onto a hot, dry summer. No doubt the vintners in the south were celebrating. The olive groves would appreciate the heat, too. Here in the North of England, the unaccustomed heat was less welcome. Freya noticed a number of young men lying on the river banks without shirts, the pink of their skin seeming to grow redder even as she watched. Or maybe they were simply blushing under her amused gaze. Stefan seemed to be trying to get her attention. *Does he object to me looking at those men?* she wondered with surprise. *He's probably got a better chest than any of them, anyway.*

Freya hoped that the oppressive heat of the day would ease a little as the evening wore on. She'd automatically worn light cotton trousers for her day in the mostly-air-conditioned labs (computers and DNA rated cooling systems, unlike people), and ever since leaving her work building, she'd been overheating. She wished she'd thought to bring a dress for the evening. Then she'd not only be cooler, she'd also feel as though she was having a proper night out.

Too late now.

Freya felt the cool breath of the river with relief as they crossed, and paused on the bridge to enjoy the breeze. She hadn't summoned a water deity in years, not since going away to university. Water deities reminded her of Tammy, her lost sister. But as she gazed at this wide river, she found herself wondering what form the local deity would take if she did summon it.

No, better not think of it. I don't even know if Stefan is a demi or not, yet. And besides, most of the river deities I've met always want to talk... not what I need to complicate the night with.

She'd also read that the Ouse was once a tidal river, connected to the sea. A lock downstream meant that was no longer the case - and therefore any deity she might call was certain to be bad-tempered as a result of the imposed constraint. Freya shook her head at herself, and looked over the bridge at the city.

The ancient buildings of the Shambles area still stood despite the increasing number of floods that hit the centre of the city. Freya supposed that the stone buildings had a lot to do with that. And a city built at the confluence of two rivers was bound to experience flooding. Maybe they were just used to it.

Leaning on the stone balustrade, Freya plucked up the courage to ask Stefan about the dangers he had mentioned at work.

"So, tell me about the hazardous countryside of Yorkshire," she said, half-joking. It was hard to imagine the sleepy countryside surrounding the city as dangerous.

Stefan looked around and leaned over the edge of the bridge as though checking underneath it, before answering.

"There are a few different dangers that you should be aware of. For example, have you heard that wolves have now been released into the moors?"

"Sure," Freya said. "But we're a long way away from the moors here - and even at work we're a good distance off."

"Good, that is a good start. The other hazards... are more difficult to explain. Perhaps I should start with poetry."

Oh, no! thought Freya. *Not a poet!* She knew she shouldn't be so biased, but she'd never had a good experience with a self-proclaimed poet. Stefan must have caught her expression, because he chuckled.

"No, no, not my own poetry. The poetry of one of your old masters. Donne, I believe. The line I am thinking of is something like, 'be you born to strange sights, invisible things to see'. I am not getting it quite correct, but that is the essence. The point is, are you yourself born to strange sights? I believe that this may be the case."

Freya sighed. So much for a mundane existence. She had clearly not disguised her demi nature nearly as well as she thought. First outed by Aisha, back at school, and now by Stefan. Oh well, if he had guessed, it probably didn't matter too much if she acknowledged it.

"Yes, I guess you could say that. I've seen plenty of strange sights, though probably not invisible ones - I mean, that's just impossible. Or it means that the person writing can't see them. True invisibility isn't a thing, even with those new camouflage cloaks they use in the movies."

I'm talking too much again, aren't I? She wasn't sure what to make of the expression on Stefan's face, but realised she was trying to impress him with her knowledge.

"Ah, good. I am correct. And you may have realised that I too am born to strange sights, though not in this country, naturally. Still, the seeing of invisible things, or *unexpected* things, can be dangerous. That is part of what I wanted to warn you about."

"Oh. That doesn't sound good." Freya's stomach clenched, remembering some of the dangerous beings she had interacted with in the past - a past she had hoped was behind her.

"Indeed, it is far from good. Perhaps I should speak clearly. There is a monster roaming the countryside. A beast, if you prefer. He - for it is a he - has been preying on lone females in the most vile way possible. I spend my nights tracking this monster, for the public good. Also, this is my territory at present, and I do not like competition in my territory. But I have not yet managed to close on the beast, for he is cunning."

"Well, thanks for the warning. I heard someone talking about an attack, last week. But what am I supposed to do about that?" Freya asked doubtfully. She was slightly worried by Stefan proclaiming he had territory, too. Most humans didn't see the world that way - at least not consciously. A monster roaming the land was more than a trifle worrying, too. Freya enjoyed her alone time in the countryside. However, Stefan answered cheerfully.

"You have two options. Perhaps three, depending on your abilities. First, you can pretend that you never heard my warning. Carry on with your life in whichever way you choose. Live with the consequences. Second, you can heed my warning. Keep yourself safe, don't go out alone. Avoid smaller gatherings. Stay quiet and sheltered."

"So, basically, live a normal life and get into trouble, or forget any chance of living well, shut myself inside and be bored to death instead. Or get annoyed by big, loud groups. I can't say that either option sounds appealing," said Freya.

"In that case, perhaps we should explore the third option. Over dinner - we will miss our booking if we do not go now."

Suppressing her irritation that Stefan didn't get straight to the point, Freya followed as he led the way to their dinner destination.

"Come, this way. There is no direct route, of course. This city leaves much to be desired in its geography," said Stefan.

Leaving the river, they followed a confusion of small laneways and alleys cut through by wider streets. As they stepped out onto the cobbled streets of the old town - for the restaurant was inside the walled section - Freya looked around with interest. It was a while since she'd had a chance to explore this city. She'd last been here visiting her friend Aisha's brother, Karim. She wondered where Karim was now. Back in Egypt, presumably. His degree had been completed before hers, and while she and Aisha had kept in touch, Aisha's emails rarely mentioned her brother. Freya's own fledgling relationship with Karim had quickly cooled to mere friendship, and they had not communicated much after an incident that Freya preferred to forget. Before that though... Freya smiled, remembering an earlier outing. She, Karim and Aisha had toured the city on foot, visiting the places Karim directed them to. They'd laughingly obliged him in a tour of the local archaeological museum, since he was an archaeology student, and had skipped a lot of the more typical tourist haunts. Some they'd included however - in fact, that had been the time she'd visited the tavern she and Stefan were going to tonight. It claimed to be one of York's oldest pubs - some said it had York's oldest food too, but Freya was fairly sure that that honour went to the themed offerings at the nearby Viking centre. Those same Vikings had brought Freya's ancestors to this country. Freya shook off the thought. She was determined to enjoy the rare opportunity to eat at a restaurant. As a student she had never had much money for dining out. And growing up, she couldn't remember ever eating out - her financial circumstances had actually improved when she became a student, eligible for loans and allowances.

As they resumed their journey into the walled city, Freya felt the day's heat leaching off the stone buildings and exuding off the asphalt roads like a wolf's hot breath. She felt as though some unknown enmity accompanied the heat, a panting fury. Perhaps Stefan's warnings were playing with her imagination. After all, he hadn't been at all specific.

They reached the old building that was their destination at last. After the dire revelations on the way, Freya had rather lost her appetite.

CHAPTER THIRTEEN

DINNER AT THE RED DRAGON

L ooking up at the ancient tavern, Freya noticed something.

"I love the cat on the wall. I'd forgotten about that."

Stefan smiled benevolently at the black cat sculpture she had noticed climbing up the black and white external walls. That struck Freya as a good sign. A person who liked cats, even cat sculptures, was surely sensitive. Freya smiled at Stefan.

Inside, the ancient oak beams were as black and battered as on her previous visit, the carpets still worn and red. She gladly selected a cool drink. A half pint of cider, locally brewed. She didn't want to lose any inhibitions tonight. She was already on edge. She wanted to enjoy a meal out, and find out if Stefan attracted or repulsed her - and if he was in fact a demi of some kind - but she was too keyed-up to do either right now.

"Well, what's option number three?" she asked once they were seated at a small wooden table by a thankfully open window. There was a fireplace in the room, stacked with bright paper flowers instead of flames. They still seemed to emit heat. Freya let her gaze rest on those while she waited for an answer. It was easier than trying to hold Stefan's gaze, which was intense, his light hazel eyes seeming to contain sparks of red light.

It's just a reflection of the carpet, she told herself.

Stefan took a sip of his own drink - some sort of ale, by the look and smell - and settled back into his chair, seeming perfectly at ease.

"Yes, well as I mentioned, the third option depends on your abilities. Are you capable of defending yourself, for example?" His voice was serious.

"Well, yes. To an extent. I've taken nearly every self-defence class in existence. I even took sword classes at uni - although those were usually wooden swords." Freya wanted Stefan to know that she was not incapable, or some sort of damsel in distress. She had worked hard at those defence classes, spurred on by her past encounters with weres.

"This is good. A good beginning. The next question is, do you have any unusual... abilities? Those strange sights we discussed earlier?"

Freya took a deep breath.

"I'll tell you mine if you tell me yours."

To her surprise, Stefan laughed, a great booming guffaw that made the other patrons turn and stare. She took a sip of her cider and tried to avoid their eyes, but couldn't help but be reassured by his laughter.

"Fair enough, fair enough," he said, when he finally stopped laughing. He brushed his overlong auburn hair out of his eyes. "Why should you trust me, after all?"

"Why indeed?" was Freya's semi-serious rejoinder. It was hard to resist the laughter of someone who was genuinely amused, she thought. Even when she didn't get the joke.

"Well, lovely Freya. Perhaps I should tell you a little more about myself before we discuss option three. You know that I do not originate from this country. In fact, I have been here a few years, but before that I was raised in Iceland. Yes, land of the puffin-eaters."

"What? I didn't know people ate puffins!" Freya was horrified at the thought.

"There are not enough puffins left for anyone to eat anymore, but it is a traditional delicacy. But of course, Iceland is famously the land of ice and fire. I am not partial to ice - that is a part of why I am here and not there - but I have long held a fascination for volcanoes. So, for me it was a wonderful place to grow up, at least in summer. But when I was still young, I discovered that the world is not quite what it seems. In short, I encountered my first frost giant. I was somewhat surprised, for I had always thought they were mere stories to frighten children with. And we do have a strong fairy-story tradition in Iceland. You know of this perhaps?"

Freya shook her head automatically - though of course her mother had spoken of the huldufólk in her theology lessons. Frost giants, too.

"Ah, it is a shame. But to the point, the frost-folk and those who follow the ways of fire do not mix well, and I accidentally crossed this frost-giant. Or perhaps it was not an accident, but the actions of a headstrong boy." He grinned disarmingly, as though inviting her to laugh of at the actions of the boy he had been. "It matters not. The result was that I came here to study, and be fairly free of those folk, and here I remain, at least for now."

Freya nodded slowly and sipped her cider again.

"You follow the fire. Makes sense for a geologist, I suppose. Do you study volcanology?" Freya immediately felt silly for asking this, since there weren't any volcanoes in this country, but Stefan beamed.

"In a way, yes. I study how we can get energy from the magma that lies beneath us all. And of course," he added nonchalantly, "I call the internal fires to where I want them."

Freya couldn't quite stifle her gasp. Here was a demi-god with inherited power beyond her dreams, sitting in the pub with her. The thought of calling up magma from the earth was so far removed from her own teenage experiments with water summoning, she couldn't imagine it. She wondered uneasily how that sat with the broken powers that modern-day demi-gods tended to possess. Stefan obviously saw the fear on her face.

"Fear, not, dear maiden," Stefan reassured in his odd vernacular. "I am very careful with my calling, and I do most of my actual experiments far from here, when the magma lies closer to Jörð's crust."

Freya managed a smile.

"That's another name for Gaia, right? How reassuring," she said, only a little sarcastically.

"Indeed, it should be. And you must be more aware than the average person to realise that. So now, I have bared my all - at least, I have told you my history and my abilities. I would very much like to hear yours."

Freya breathed out slowly. How much should she tell?

"I suppose you have given me a life story," she temporised, not feeling comfortable with baring her soul to a relative stranger. "Mine... well. I spent most of my childhood moving from one house to the next, always along the coast. We were always having our houses destroyed. You know, sea level rise, storms. That sort of thing. I don't know why we didn't move inland. My Dad did. I haven't seen him in years. I had a sister. She... left. My Mum - well, she's out there on the coast still, trying to keep an eye out for my sister. I suppose the family has a sort of water affinity, but my Mum's more of a plant person. I'm not really sure what I am. Er. Other than a descendant of Freya-the-goddess, that is. I have done a few things with water, or streams, really. I always wanted to work with plants, even though I can't grow them, and also to get away from the sea. So, I came inland to university, got a degree, got a job, and here I am. That's about it, really." As usual, Freya left out the were attacks that had marred her teenage years. Not to mention the wind demi who had saved her life a time or two. And her small half-were nieces and nephews.

All right, so I don't want to share my whole life-story.

Stefan was leaning forward over the small table between them, his eyes intent upon her.

"I am most pleased that you are not aligned with the frost-folk," he said.

Why is he so worried about frost-folk? They're just as bad - or good, I suppose - as volcano gods.

"I find myself wondering what hidden abilities you have, as yet undiscovered. Have you any idea?" Stefan asked.

Freya decided to lighten the mood.

"Well, I never miss a bus," she joked.

Stefan smiled back, his eyes crinkling at the corners.

"This is not a skill to be sniffed at."

Freya found herself drawn in by his smiling eyes, despite her fear of his declared powers. Had she really thought he was 'not quite' handsome?

"Excuse me, are you ready to order now?" The waitress was back at their table, tapping impatiently on the menu.

"Oh, sorry," said Freya. She hastened to make a selection from the paper menu in front of her, which she had hardly glanced at so far. She was pleasantly surprised by the variety available to her, but chose the first plant-based item on the menu, trying to quell the waitress's ire with promptness. Stefan was more leisurely in his approach, and asked for the specials of the day. While he conversed with the waitress over the relative merits of the dishes, Freya tried to re-centre herself. She wasn't usually swept away by emotions, and she felt as though she were standing at the top of a rain-slippery slide with an unseen end. What would happen if she let herself slip?

When at last Stefan had selected something, Freya returned to the 'third option' again, which he had so far avoided discussing. Surely it was noisy enough in here that no-one else could hear a sensitive discussion? After all, they'd already been openly discussing demi-abilities. She rubbed her ears before she asked. Maybe later they could go outside again.

"So, what is this mythical third option, then? Given that half the reason I took the job here is so I got to have time in the countryside by myself, I'd quite like to know how I can maintain that."

Stefan put his chin in his hand as he looked at her seriously.

"Well, now. It is a difficult thing to keep what you want, and still be safe. But with your background, perhaps it is possible. My thought is to take you with me, out on the road. Perhaps you will have more luck than I at locating the beast. It could be like the hunting teams of old, with your abilities complementing mine. What say you?"

Freya looked at Stefan, taken aback. She'd never seen herself as a hunter of any sort.

"Er. Well. Locating, sure. But I'm not into hunting things. Figuring out plant pests, finding hidden water sources, that's more the sort of thing I'm good at."

Stefan nodded encouragingly. "Perhaps we can see how our partnership works, then. A trial run, if you will."

"I suppose."

"You wound me with your lack of enthusiasm. But there, perhaps I should be grateful that you are at all in agreement. Here, a toast to a trial run!"

He raised his glass; out of politeness as much as agreement, Freya raised her own and drank.

"Good, good. If we are to trial this partnership, I will need to show you the region I have covered thus far. Perhaps we survey it after our meal. Speaking of which, here it is." Stefan turned his attention to the waitress who had reappeared and was juggling plates. "My compliments on the speed of your service, we had but barely ordered, and here is our food already. I am most impressed."

"Here's your cutlery." The waitress was clearly *not* impressed. She finished placing plates, plunked a cup containing a selection of eating implements into the centre of the table and turned away to serve the next table.

"So much for the delightful service I was assured of at this establishment. Ah well, she is no doubt worked off her butt, as I believe the saying goes."

Freya snorted cider out through her nose, and hastily blotted herself with her napkin. *Great first date move, Freya. Lucky this isn't really a date.* She wasn't sure if she was glad or sorry about that. Stefan inspired a confusing range of emotions.

"Er, yeah. Something like that." Freya picked a fork out of the cup and used it to spear a leaf from her salad. She followed the leaf with a hot potato chip. "The chips are good, anyway."

Stefan smiled.

"That is all right then." He applied himself to the piece of meat that the waitress had placed in front of him. Freya supposed it was a steak, but she had never been entirely sure about the specific names of pieces of meat. It hadn't been a topic of education in their plant-based household. Even after they took in her sister's were-fox kits, meat was just meat, cut bigger or smaller according to the size of body it was feeding. It was never for her, though, only for the were-foxes. Her mother had refused to have meat in the house at first, but it turned out that the kit's digestive systems didn't cope with an all-plant diet. The family had adapted reluctantly. Freya had spent a lot of time after school catching grasshoppers for the kits, to reduce the amount they had to spend on special were-fox food. Freya watched Stefan uneasily as he ate the steak with obvious enjoyment. He noticed her watching him.

"Is there a problem, fair maiden?"

Freya dabbed at her face with her napkin,

"Oh, it's nothing."

"But you look disturbed about something. Surely there must be a problem."

Freya wanted to crawl into a dark corner. She'd obviously shown her feelings too much without realising it.

"I'm a vegetarian, that's all."

Stefan's eyebrows climbed up his forehead.

"I would not have guessed it; you look so healthy."

Freya's embarrassment vanished in a surge of annoyance.

"That's such a typical ignorant meat-eater comment!" she snapped.

Stefan laughed.

"I am sorry to cause you offence. Had I known I would have chosen a different meal for the evening. But surely no lasting harm is done?"

"I suppose not." Freya poked at her salad uncomfortably.

"Please, do not waste the meal. So much effort has been put into it."

"Oh, I know. Those cute edible flowers and all. I'm amazed they have any left, it's been so hot. I actually do hate to waste food. I mean, that's why I applied for my job, you know. I spent so much time foraging for food as a child, I wanted to try and improve our food security so that others have enough to eat."

Stefan chuckled again.

"You are an excellent advertisement for your department. Keep talking, tell me more."

Freya had to laugh too, a little reluctantly.

"OK, I may have said something like that in my interview. But it *does* have the benefit of being true."

Stefan laughed. "The best possible way to pass an interview, then."

The awkward moment passed. They talked of the university and other uncontroversial topics for a while.

"D'you know, I had lunch with someone the other day who told me he grew his own chillis," said Freya.

"Ah, you must have met the inimitable Phillip. I'm surprised he didn't try to sell you a bottle of chilli sauce."

"He probably saw my expression when he asked if I liked hot sauce." Freya dipped a chip into the unspiced bean mix that came with her fried potatoes.

"That would be a first for Phillip. He is not renowned for paying attention to the faces of others. I understand he runs a chilli library from his home. I believe he is a purveyor of seeds to other enthusiasts."

"Hidden depths from the policy analyst. Who knew? It seems like a difficult crop to grow in the north of England, though." She took a large mouthful of salad, and then felt obliged to cover her mouth while she got the stalks arranged tidily into her mouth. "Sorry." She felt like a guinea pig, hastily chewing through green stems until they were small enough to swallow.

Stefan waved a hand magnanimously.

"Think nothing of it. And as for chillis in the north, I believe he has a whole range of the things in a hothouse."

Freya felt rather stupid. After all, her own mother was still employed in a greenhouse. She hastily took another bite to cover her embarrassment, and once again had to cover her mouth. *Note to self. Don't order a salad if you want to eat in public. Especially if you have a hot date.* She considered a moment. *Volcano demigod. Maybe he's literally hot.* She waited for him to comment on her gaffe, but Stefan continued talking regardless, so perhaps it was OK.

"In fact, it is possible that we should visit Phillip and his hothouse. I believe the surrounding area may be an excellent place to search for the beast. But not tonight. He must be prepared for an invasion of his privacy. Otherwise, he may match my fire with that of a one-million-Scoville Naga pepper."

"That sounds painful, aren't Naga peppers one of the hottest in the world?"

"Indeed so. Most assuredly it would be painful. I am keen to avoid the Naga pepper, so we will arrange a meeting with him before we visit."

It seemed to Freya that it took an age for her to get through her salad, but she managed it in the end. Stefan had devoured his piece of meat in substantially less time, but he didn't seem to mind talking while she ate. He helped himself to chips from her plate from time to time, which she felt awkward about at first, but then grateful for. The meal was rather larger than something she'd make for herself at home. As she took the last bite, he leaned forward confidentially.

"Do you *like* desserts?"

Strange thing to get confidential about, thought Freya.

"Oh yes, I've got a bit a sweet tooth, really. That's partly why I chose the salad, to balance out anything unhealthier I might have."

"Ah, very typical of the female of the species. Whereas I prefer to maintain a savoury diet. Chocolate, for example, I find holds no appeal."

"You're on your own there. Chocolate is my saviour."

"In that case, I will request the dessert menu for you. Perhaps they have a cheese course I could partake of." As he said so, Stefan scanned the room for waitstaff. The grumpy waitress from earlier appeared as if by magic, already bearing small printed dessert menus.

I wonder if she's some sort of demi. Probably a Demeter, they always like food.

"Would you like some afters?" she asked.

"Indeed so. Freya, if you would?"

Freya hastily scanned the menu, hoping to find something both small and chocolate flavoured. She was in luck.

"Can I have the chocolate tart, please?" She was almost hungry again already, imagining the smooth chocolate filling in a crisp pastry base. She looked up and realised that Stefan was watching her with a slight smile. Freya glanced away, cheeks burning.

"Sure you don't want the apple? It's a healthier choice than chocolate, and local, too," said the waitress.

"Thanks, but I'm really wanting chocolate." *Maybe she's a Pomona demi, after all. They all love apples. And I'll eat unhealthily if I want to.*

"And for you, sir?" The waitress's *sir* seemed forced, but it clearly pleased Stefan, for he smiled broadly.

"I will take a cheeseboard if you have one."

"We've got Wensleydale or cheddar."

Stefan's smile blinked off.

"That seems insufficient. Is there nothing from the continent?"

"Sorry, sir, that's all we've got. The trade barriers are still in place."

"In that case a glass of port will suffice."

Freya watched the exchange with some concern. Should she take back her dessert order? She'd really been looking forward to a dessert made by someone other than herself. And chocolate, no less. Even if it was probably smuggled in, Freya couldn't resist chocolate. Stefan noticed her furrowed brow, for he reached over and stroked her hand. His touch sent an almost electrical thrill through her.

"There is no need to be worried. You will have your chocolate, and I will drink my port, and then perhaps we can investigate what else the city has to offer. We will leave investigations further afield for another time."

Freya relaxed and began to enjoy the evening at last. The tart, when it came, was delicious - rich, smooth and creamy. She offered some to Stefan, who waved it away.

"No, no, I truly would rather see you enjoy it."

"Oh well, if you're sure. All the more for me." She savoured another spoonful of the chocolate filling, leaving the crust untouched. *Why spoil the best part of the dish with inferior pastry, anyway?* Good chocolate was definitely something she'd not had enough of, growing up on a diet of charity food and foraged edibles. She sat back at last with a satisfied sigh, licking her lips to ensure that no embarrassing splodges of chocolate remained. "That was great. Thanks for bringing me out here."

"It was my pleasure." Stefan's gaze lingered on her lips for a moment before he rose. "Shall we move on?"

Freya wiped her lips with her serviette uncertainly. *I'm sure I got all of the chocolate off. Didn't I?*

CHAPTER FOURTEEN

YORK WALK

F reya walked beside Stefan through the streets of the old city. They'd left the restaurant after splitting the cost of the meal, and now wandered through the streets.

"I've never visited the Viking centre. It was too expensive for me last time I was here," said Freya as they passed the centre in question. Freya was enjoying herself now, glad that she'd made the decision to come out with Stefan, regardless of any plans he had for hunting.

"It is a tourist honeypot, but I could take you there sometime if it would please you."

Freya shrugged.

"Maybe. I don't know if I need to know what the Vikings did here. It was all rather violent, wasn't it?" Freya didn't want to know about ancient violence. There was too much violence in the recent past.

"No more than anywhere else. People are all alike in that way. The Vikings were more dirty than anything else." Stefan didn't seem bothered.

Freya shivered. Time to change the subject.

"Did you have anything else in mind tonight? I'd like to catch the 10:30 bus, but we have a bit of time yet."

The long evenings of summer meant that there was still plenty of light, slanting golden through the hot streets.

"Perhaps it is best to walk for a little first, while we formulate a plan."

"Sure, it's a nice enough evening." Freya was enjoying the feeling being out and about with someone who could be a friend. She had been feeling rather lonely since moving to York. Nice though her landlady was, it wasn't the same as going out with friends. It would be a little more relaxing if she could shake the habit of looking for demi-traits in everyone she passed, but the years of training her Mum had given her stuck fast. The man across the road with bulging muscles well-displayed by his tank top was either a Herculean or a smith-god descendant. The irritating person who passed by too fast on a motorbike just as they left the Shambles a few minutes later was clearly marked as a Wodenite - a Woden demigod - by the black ravens on the back of his leather jacket. Freya glanced hastily away, remembering an early encounter with a Wodenite. There seemed to be more demis in York than Freya had expected. She thought sadly that it seemed unlikely that she would be able to maintain her cover as a mundane for long - even Stefan had picked up on her differences.

"You seem a little tense," said Stefan.

"No more than usual. So, what sort of plan were you thinking?" She glanced over at Stefan, appreciating the effect of the golden light falling on his face, picking up the contours of full lips and straight nose. His dark red hair almost glowed. They crossed the street, dodging a larger than usual array of electric cars. *Focus on the cars, Freya. A night out is no fun if you end up in a hospital bed.*

"My thought was that together we could walk or drive the roads of the Riding, until we encounter my en- the beast. Then disarm him, and discover his purpose."

"Just like that? There's a lot of roads." Freya paused outside a coffee shop, distracted by its advertisement 'genuine Australian coffee beans'. "Do they actually grow coffee in Australia?"

"Not as far as I am aware, but you are the biologist, are you not?" Stefan paused with her.

"Coffee is a bit outside my realm. I know people love it and it's plagued by diseases, but I've focused on things that grow here. Except chillis, I guess." She shrugged and started to move on. "Coffee counts as someone else's problem. Even though it's endangered by a whole host of different issues."

"Ah, but I am one of the 'someone else's'. Wait a moment while I get a sample of these Australian beans. I am most curious." Stefan ducked into the shop, which was still bustling despite the late hour. Freya opted to wait outside where there was at least the chance of a breeze. The crush of people inside didn't appeal, even in Stefan's company. Fortunately, it wasn't long before Stefan emerged, clutching a paper cup. They resumed walking, dodging the crowds.

"The Australian beans were only available as iced coffee. Perfect for a hot evening, or so I am told." He took a long pull from his cup and grimaced. "An interesting taste, certainly. I suspect Australian coffee beans are on special for good reason."

"I'll tell the lab; someone might want to analyse a sample."

"They can have mine."

"That bad, is it?" Freya grimaced sympathetically.

"Indeed." Stefan disposed of his cup as they passed a rubbish bin.

"I guess the lab won't get that sample after all."

"I did not wish to carry it all evening."

"I wish I'd thought to get an iced chocolate, that'd be perfect just now," said Freya.

"It is probably just as well that you did not. If their Australian coffee is a good example of their wares, then their chocolate would not be worth the paper it was served in."

Despite Stefan's pronouncement, Freya couldn't help but look back regretfully. They turned onto the wide Castlegate road, heading towards Clifford's Tower, an ancient hill-fort within the city, crowned by a stone tower, rising above the river-flats.

"Oh well, lucky save, then. I'll have to be satisfied with the smell of chocolate in the air instead." A local chocolate-making factory provided that smell in abundance. It was making Freya more desirous of chocolate, rather than less.

"That is probably the better option. But you wanted a plan. Perhaps with your biological skills you can help me attenuate the areas in which we look."

The corners of Freya's mouth twitched upwards. They reached the base of Clifford's Tower, its steep grassy sides deflecting a breeze from higher up.

"Cool air," she nearly hummed. "Let's go up."

Stefan nodded. "It looks like an excellent place to view the area. We should ascend, by all means."

The thought flickered through Freya's mind that perhaps they had not come at random to this spot, but she pushed it aside. They had been discussing tourist zones, and this surely was one.

Side by side, they climbed the steep stone stairs that led directly up the small hill that supported the tower. The grass on the hill was dry and white with sun. Freya felt her temperature rise with the exertion.

A guard at the entrance to the tower informed them that tickets were required, and closing time was a mere half hour away.

"We don't have to go in," said Freya, shrugging off disappointment. Even this high, the breeze was whipping hot air away from her face.

"No, we are here and we have the time. Let us make the most of the evening." Stefan insisted on paying for the tickets, to Freya's discomfort.

Inside the hollow edifice, they climbed the steep stone spiral stairs to the top of the tower in single file. Freya ran a hand over the stones to help keep her balance, and found a long, smooth patch where countless other people had done the same before her. The stones were hot to touch, retaining the days heat. She was glad to reach the top and open air again. The staircase was small enough to be claustrophobia-inducing, especially with the echoes of its history running through her head. She imagined soldiers running up and down these stairs before the internal structure was destroyed by fire, and shivered despite the heat. Somehow, she suspected her own ancestors hadn't been soldiers.

Freya was pleased that the climb didn't rob her unduly of breath; her solo before-work runs were obviously helping to keep up her fitness. Despite the warmth emanating from the stones, it was actually cooler at the top of the tower, thanks to a slight, chocolate-scented breeze.

"Thank goodness people are still managing to grow cocoa beans. I don't know how the world would survive without chocolate," said Freya.

"*I* do not know how the world will survive without coffee. But because of that, I am sure a method will be found to keep our favourite plants alive."

After duly admiring the stonework of what remained of the inner tower - half of it currently covered by scaffolding, ancient stones didn't hold themselves together without help, apparently - they looked out over the city, the red brick and grey slate roofs blending together into the distance. The occasional church or cathedral spire stood out, and the tops of a few trees rose above the rooftops here and there. A small park nearby provided one such clump. Although York had a green belt, it wasn't particularly obvious from here. Freya wished there were more trees.

"I always feel so unpleasantly surrounded by people, in cities," she said.

"The culmination of civilisation does not appeal to you, then?"

"Not especially! No doubt I'm backwards, but I grew up in small towns. There's always so *many* people in a city. It's hard not to feel like just another number." *That sounded silly.*

Freya felt Stefan's eyes on her, appraising.

"Be assured that you are certainly not just another number."

"Er. Thanks. So, about this plan?" Although she wanted Stefan's attention, it was hard for Freya to accept compliments. She never knew what to say in response to them.

"Yes. I have already noted that the attacks form a ring around one area. If you look out over that way, towards the group of trees - see, there are more just by the river - that is one site. And over by the cathedral is another. There are more sites towards the lab, and even as far as the moors. We can investigate the closest of those sites this evening, if we have time. But I am not sure how to remove sufficient variables to make my next move straight forward. This is where I hope that you can help me." He smiled suddenly.

Freya marvelled inwardly at the way the expression transformed his face from a little severe to downright engaging. It made her realise that he didn't smile much.

"Removing variables, now that sounds properly scientific," she said.

"And you are first and foremost a scientist, I take it?" Stefan asked, a ripple of laughter in his voice.

"That's what all my training has been for, after all," Freya retorted. "So, tell me about these attack sites. Have you been to all of them yourself?"

"I believe I have, yes."

"So, what sort of commonalities do they have? Trees? No trees? Lots of people around or just a few? How about public transport routes?"

Stefan looked a little taken aback at her string of questions.

"I must say that I hope these are questions that you can help me to answer. I am more likely to notice the rocks scattered around an area than the people or the trees. Or indeed the buses."

"Oh. That makes it harder." Freya was disappointed. She had had the sense of being about to open a puzzle that might have fast solution, only to find half the pieces were missing.

"No matter, we will be better able to achieve an answer together. But first let us find you some more chocolate. You should not have to make do with the scent alone. And there must be somewhere with better coffee also."

They circled the tower before descending. Stefan pointed out the attack sites in as much as they were visible from the tower. There did seem to be at least one in most directions.

"Is it co-incidence that the attacks are near trees?" Freya asked.

"Perhaps not. If you have more observations like that, we may work well together."

To Freya's disappointment, she couldn't come up with any other intelligent-seeming comments about the sites Stefan highlighted. But it *had* been nice to feel above the hustle of the city. Her thoughts returned to chocolate.

"We could go back the way we came," suggested Freya. "I know there's a cocoa shop, but it'll probably be closed by now."

"I see that you located the important things in your previous tour of the city."

Was he laughing at her? *Oh well, better to have my major weakness known, I guess.*

"I only saw a few things, but that one stuck."

"In any case, I suggest that we go somewhere by the river. It should be cooler there for you, and it is also closer to one of the attack sites."

"Good idea. Do you not mind the heat?"

"I find it most enjoyable."

Freya shuddered. It was hard to imagine not finding the heat of the day oppressive. But she was quietly glad he'd noticed her preference.

***

They ended up in a bar overlooking the river, the late evening sun now swiftly disappearing behind the brick and stone buildings. Freya was fairly sure the archway over the door was supposed to read 'Merchant's Hall', but the olde-style writing made it look closer to 'Merchent's Hell'. She chuckled to herself as they walked in. Was this a place where salespeople were tormented? Maybe bars weren't all bad after all. Unless you were a merchant, of course.

Disappointingly, the interior didn't resemble any sort of hell, not even the one with a single 'l' in Poland that Freya had seen pictures of at school. Freya asked Stefan about the Merchant's place.

"Ah, you must have seen the back entrance to the Merchant Adventurer's Hall, another ancient establishment," he replied, to Freya's disappointment. She'd rather liked the idea of a merchant's hell. Instead, the bar had rather nice white curved ceilings and fairly standard British pub decor, with small tables randomly placed, most with more people than they were designed for trying to fit around them on dark wooden chairs, and an eye-crossing pattern on the carpet.

I wonder if there are any descendants of Loki around here? It never occurred to me to look for them. But making a pub into hell seems like the right attitude for one of them.

When she started perusing the drinks menu, Freya decided that perhaps Loki had already been involved. This place was surely a hell because of the price of the drinks. The noise of the bar was annoying, too. A constant drone of talking, clattering cutlery, the ring of voices all reflected off the hard surfaces. The carpet didn't do much to dampen the effect. Loud pop music played throughout, muffling attempts at shouted conversation.

"...so I told him he was dreaming, and he said it was potion induced..."

"Did you say two more packets of fae?"

"...chip butte, not a super brownie..."

She wondered if any of the conversationalists actually understood each other. Freya could feel the bass beat of the music reverberating in her stomach. She hoped they weren't staying long, or she'd lose her dessert.

Stefan led her past the worst of the noise to a table by the river. The open windows let the noise pour past them instead of bouncing back.

I wonder how river deities cope with cities? There's such a lot that comes out of them - people, noise, effluent. She resolved never to try summoning the resident deity here. If it was anything like her, it would have a permanent headache from the sheer volume.

I shouldn't be such a bumpkin. Everyone around me seems to be enjoying the atmosphere, they're laughing and smiling. Some even dancing. I suppose I could dance to that beat, maybe that would make it more bearable. She was too shy to dance in front of Stefan, though.

Freya sipped uncertainly at the chocolate liqueur that Stefan had ordered for her. There were certainly many layers of chocolate in it, but she suspected it contained more alcohol than she usually consumed in a month - even factoring in Angie's frequent wine offerings. Stefan took a gulp of his own drink - which the waiter had set alight before presenting it to him.

"Ah, this is good. Much better than that pathetic excuse for coffee."

"Is it a coffee-flavoured drink you have?"

"Naturally."

Freya made a face and took another sip of her own drink. She could hardly tell it was alcoholic. Maybe she shouldn't be so worried about drinking it. Really, it was fine. She took another sip.

"Thanks for getting me this. I'll treat you the next round." Freya took a long pull of her drink, savouring its creamy layers. Another swallow, and she was startled to realise she'd finished her cocktail already. The waiter appeared miraculously at her elbow.

Now that waiter is almost certainly a demi, she thought muzzily. *Or maybe related to a house hob - so fast and helpful.*

"Another, ma'am?"

"Sure. Yes. Did you want one, Stefan?"

"Certainly. Another of what I had before. My thanks."

A few minutes later, another set of cocktails made their appearance. Stefan turned to Freya and raised his flaming glass.

"To planning."

Freya raised her own glass and chinked it against his. The flame leapt onto Freya's cocktail, setting it alight. She hastily blew at it until it went out.

"I didn't think these things were flammable!"

Stefan answered with a smile in his voice.

"Perhaps it is just the heat of the night."

"Ha! I'm sure that doesn't make a difference. I wasn't *that* bad at chemistry, you know!" Perhaps the alcohol was affecting her; Freya felt much more inclined to share things about herself than usual.

"I am pleased to hear it. But not all things can be explained by the mundane," Stefan said. There was something proud in his tone.

Not sure what to make of this, Freya returned to the ostensible reason for their night out.

"So, about those attacks. Why should biology come into it? Isn't it more a psychology problem?"

He tilted his head to one side as though in thought, then shook it.

"Usually, you would be correct. However, this is not strictly a human issue. Supernatural biology is required. And a certain awareness of the greater possibilities of the world. This is why you are perfectly positioned to help me." He smiled broadly. "Come, finish your drink. I will show you where the first attack occurred."

"Now? I need to catch the bus soon." Freya looked fruitlessly around for a clock before remembering that she had her own phone these days. She fumbled for it.

"Never fear. There is always a taxi if we run over time. Or I have a place we can stay in town." Stefan swigged the last of his drink.

"We'd better hurry up if we're going to do this, taxis are too expensive." Freya downed the rest of her second drink in a hurry. She didn't remember paying for it...

Yuck. That tasted a lot better a sip at a time. She stood up and wobbled. Surely, she hadn't drunk that much? Oh well, the evening was nearly done, she just had to hold it together a little longer.

"Come, we are not far now. Just a short walk along the river."

He offered his arm in an old-fashioned way. Freya considered ignoring the proffered arm, but two steps away from her bar stool convinced her to do otherwise. Embarrassingly, she needed the support.

This is why I usually stick to ginger beer or a half pint of cider. Loss of control is not fun.

Stefan led the way out of the bar, assisting Freya to dodge an assortment of chairs and customers. At least one table got in the way too.

"If anyone attacks, I'll lurch threateningly at them," she said.

"I am sure they would be terrified."

CHAPTER FIFTEEN

A HOT NIGHT

Outside, the air still held the memory of the day's heat, and walking through the dark streets was like being embraced by molasses.

"Honestly, what happened to old-fashioned English summers where you have to wear an anorak half the time?" Freya grumbled aloud.

"I prefer this temperature, myself," Stefan said. "I am not overly fond of the cold."

Freya waved ineffectively at her face, trying to generate a breeze.

"I'd take the anorak for preference. I hate being too hot."

"This way," said Stefan, ignoring her complaints about the heat this time. He led the way down some concrete stairs near the bridge, to a path that followed the river at a lower level, before twisting sideways into an underpass leading under the road. Freya tried to hold her breath as they made their way through the underpass. It had clearly been used as more than a simple pathway. Towards the end of the underpass, a pair of hooded figures loomed suddenly, blocking their way. Their silhouettes were huge, hulking and long-armed.

"Oh Frigg, trolls," said Freya. She'd forgotten how that trolls often roamed cities, and an underpass was a typical hangout for them.

"Trolls are nothing I cannot deal with," said Stefan confidently.

Freya looked at him in surprise. While he was reasonably tall, muscular and sturdy, he certainly did not appear to be a match for the average troll, even a half-troll. But Stefan did not seem to share her concern at the appearance of the trolls. He strode forward with eager steps. Freya hung back, not wishing to use her self-defence skills unless she truly needed to. Also, those chocolate cocktails were sloshing around inside her in surprising ways. She was not in peak troll-fighting form, even if she had been the sort of person inclined to fight. Which she wasn't. At all.

Stop overthinking this, Freya.

As Stefan reached the trolls, one of them raised a fist threateningly. Typical trolls, they usually relied on brute strength to win arguments. However, this confrontation did not go as Freya expected. Stefan reached for the raised fist and gripped it in his own. He said something to the troll that Freya could not hear, glancing at the other as though seeking confirmation. The troll whose fist was being held pulled it hastily away, shaking it as though in pain. The pair turned on their heels and ran off the way they'd come.

"That wasn't what I expected," said Freya, coming forward to meet Stefan.

"Wasn't it? I don't usually have any trouble convincing trolls to leave me alone."

Freya wondered what he'd said or done to the trolls to make them act so out of character. Her earlier unease made its presence known again. The chocolate cocktails told the unease to mind its own business and go away, wasn't it nice not to have to worry about trolls? Freya shook her head. It was so hard to think.

They took the stairs up to street level again. Freya was glad to be away from the stench of the underpass, and even more happy that they'd apparently avoided trouble so easily.

"I assume that's not the place you meant, where the attacks happened."

"No, that's a little further on. This way." Stefan led her through a series of alleys which frankly smelled nearly as bad as the underpass, and then they turned on to a slightly broader street with cobbled footpaths rising and falling in unexpected ways despite the general flatness of the area. It would have been truly hazardous if she'd been the sort of girl to wear heels. They passed a succession of closed shops, bicycles chained to bike stands, a music centre with a range of guitars on display.

"I thought you said it wasn't far?" she said.

"We're nearly there now." They crossed a more major road and Stefan came to a halt at some tall wrought iron gates flanked by stone pillars. A stone gatehouse stood to one side.

"The castle museum garden? But it's closed!"

"Not to me," said Stefan. "In any case, we only need to get into the gardens."

He raised a hand to the iron padlock, which abruptly glowed a deep red, then dropped to the ground, apparently melted off the gate. Freya looked at Stefan's hand. It was barely visible in the darkness, but didn't look any different.

Volcano demi, remember? Freya reminded herself. The thought didn't shake her unease. Stefan pushed the gate open. It creaked loudly. Freya looked around at the gatehouse, expecting someone to charge out demanding what they were doing. No-one appeared. Perhaps they'd already retired for the night. Or they had learnt to avoid loud noises in the night.

She followed Stefan into the gardens. The ancient trees loomed dark on either side. A soft, rich scent wafted from the direction of the floral border. If she hadn't been worried by Stefan's evident volcanic powers, it would have been tremendously romantic. Stefan clearly thought so too. He dropped back to walk beside Freya and took her arm. She felt the heat of his skin warm hers further. They walked on through the gardens, passing close by the ancient ruined arches that defined the garden, and down towards the river's edge. The scent of night-opening blooms drifted gently through the warm air. Finally, Stefan stopped in an area shrouded by trees and short, flowering shrubs. Their flowers glowed pale in the moonlight. Stefan turned towards Freya, picking up her other hand. Her breath caught.

CHAPTER SIXTEEN

STEFAN MAKES A MOVE

"**I**t is a pleasant spot, is it not? Especially at night, without the daily crowds," Stefan said, holding her fingers firmly.

"Yes." It was; the flowering plants all around reminded her of her mother's back yard, full to bursting of green things. Even the depredations of frequently-visiting were-fox kits hadn't managed to make a dent in that greenery. She spoke the thought aloud. "It reminds me of my Mum."

Stefan laughed, a low churring sound.

"Such a homely feeling. Perhaps I can make it remind you of something else."

He leaned forward, a stray shaft of moonlight catching his cheekbones and straight nose. His lips met hers. The kiss caught Freya by surprise with its intensity. Stefan released her hands and cupped the back of her head as he deepened his kiss. Freya let him do so, exploring the sensation. His hands left a faint tingling on her skin. Was it his volcano demigod powers she felt, or simply the magic of touch? She ran a hand down his spine, and was gratified when he shivered under her fingers. A twig cracked nearby and Freya stiffened, pulling away from Stefan.

"Weren't we supposed to be looking at some attack site?" she said.

"Yes, yes. Of course. But who could resist such a beautiful spot with a beautiful woman?"

Freya was still partly under Stefan's spell - and that of the chocolate cocktails - so she didn't protest his flattery. She didn't give up on her goal, however.

"Well, thanks. It was nice. But where is the site you wanted to show me?" She stepped back, out of Stefan's embrace.

"Only nice? I had hoped for a more enthusiastic response. Perhaps we should try again."

"Maybe after we've seen what we came for."

"You are as wise as you are fair. Very well, this way." Stefan led the way back up the gentle hill.

"You mean we already passed it?" Freya was indignant.

"Only by a little. I wanted you to see my favourite part of this garden first. And you did like it, did you not?"

"Yes, but-"

"And here we are," said Stefan, smoothly interrupting her.

They were very close to the ruined arches again. The arches were lit up by coloured lights. A realistic wolf statue was also gently lit, prominent on a pedestal. Freya looked past the statue with an eye for the ecology of the area - as much as she could see in the dim lighting.

"It's a complete mix! There's no rhyme or reason to this collection of plants, except perhaps that they can all survive outdoors here. I'm sorry, but I don't know what you expected me to see. Unless it's that freaky wolf statue." Her eye was drawn back to it.

"The wolf may be part of this. You know perhaps that we have had an unwise release of wolves nearby?"

"Yes. You said. The rewilding movement, right? But statues don't attack anyone."

"Indeed, and wolves should be too afraid of people to attack, also. So, I am concerned that perhaps we have unreal wolves. Or rather, were-wolves."

Freya shivered.

"Ugh. What a nasty prospect."

"Ah, perhaps we agree on the subject of were-wolves then. And maybe other weres too, given the way we first encountered one another."

"You've got that right. I haven't had a great history with weres," said Freya. *Being attacked by weres twice in one lifetime is definitely two too many times.*

"But that is excellent. I am glad we are of one mind in this. Perhaps we will find more points of similarity too. If we visit each known attack site, then we should form a better idea of the attacker's methodology. And thanks to your expertise in biology, you have already helped me understand this attacker. An outsider, perhaps. One who is not connected to his locale, but who thrives no less for it. We will have to investigate the other sites also. But not tonight; it grows late. Shall we see if you have a bus remaining?"

Freya tore her eyes from the wolf statue.

"Yes, I have to work in the morning, and I'm sure you do too."

"Indeed, but I am used to late hours."

Freya looked at her phone again.

"I've only got two minutes to get to the bus stop!" Hastily adjusting her unnecessary layers of clothing, she looked wildly around for the exit.

"It is several minutes' walk from here. It must be an evening suitable for a taxi."

"But taxis are too expensive," Freya countered. She had planned to send money home to her Mum this week, not splurge on taxis.

"There is an alternative, if you wish. My own place is nearby. It is only a short walk. You are most welcome to stay the night, without strings."

Freya hesitated. What was the right thing to do?

"I have work tomorrow," she said again.

Stefan smiled.

"As do I. We can go together! Or if you prefer, you can catch a bus alone. There is an abundance of buses in the morning."

Freya looked at her phone again. One minute to get to the bus stop. Standing around debating wasn't doing any good. And staying the night with Stefan seemed incautious on a first date, however attractive he might be.

"Let's try for the bus now. It might be running late."

Leaving the gardens seemed to take even longer than entering them. The warm night air swirled around her legs as she ran, like a miasma. There was something wrong - more than just the effects of two cocktails. Feeling as though she were missing something obvious, Freya glanced back. The ruined stone arches and the wolf statue glowed in their spotlights. Something dark and soft-edged flickered and disappeared behind them as she looked.

"There's something -" she began, but stopped speaking as a roar and a squeal of brakes announced the bus passing near the front gate and taking the corner too fast.

"Oh no! I've missed my bus!"

Stefan shrugged elegantly.

How does he make a shrug look elegant?

"This is a shame. But it is not Ragnarök, after all."

"It may as well be, if I get fired for being late to work tomorrow," Freya said.

"You may come home with me. There is room. Also, it is cheaper than a taxi."

Freya hesitated a long minute. She barely knew Stefan. But she wanted to know him better... possibly. His dinner choices hadn't matched hers at all. They probably had nothing in common. But at the same time, it was flattering to have so attractive a man interested in her. And he had that aura about him... The chocolate cocktails decided for her.

"Oh. All right. Lead the way."

They walked the rest of the way to the gated entrance, which still stood ajar. As they neared the gate, the hair on Freya's neck stood on end. There was a large, hairy four-legged shape guarding it. The streetlights glinted off long fur and sharp teeth.

"Stefan. Do you see that?" Freya tried and failed to keep the fear from her voice.

Stefan nodded and, oddly, sniffed. "It appears the beast has come to meet us. How convenient."

The figure let out a spine-chilling growl.

"How do we get past?"

"We attack it first, of course. Before it decides to attack us."

Stefan didn't wait for Freya to reply. He strode forward, arms defensively. The beast growled again, and leaped as Stefan neared it. He twisted as it leapt, out of its path. It landed lightly and leapt again, heading for Freya. She started back, but realised that there was nowhere to run to. This thing was on four legs, and could almost certainly run faster than her. At the last minute, she curled herself into a ball. The wolf-like beast soared over her, growling its displeasure at missing. As soon as it landed, it doubled back. Freya hastily uncurled herself and scuttled back towards Stefan, trying not to feel like a beetle. The beast raced towards her, only to be intercepted by Stefan, who threw himself towards it, bowling it over. It scrambled out from under him as he laid a hand on its ruff. There was a sudden stench of burning fur. The beast yelped, but twisted back to bite at Stefan's hand. Stefan cursed, and clenched his hand into a fist, delivering a blow to the beast's neck where it had been burnt. This time, it ran through the gate and away, whimpering.

Freya took a deep, shuddering breath.

I am really not cut out to be a fighter. The first hint of violence and I freeze. So much for my self-defence classes.

"Are you alright?" she asked Stefan. *No way to ask if that beast is alright.*

Stefan was cradling his bitten hand with the other. He grimaced, but nodded.

"I will be fine when I have dressed my hand. Come, let us get off the streets before the beast returns."

"Don't you need a rabies shot or something if a dog bites you?"

"I will take care of that in the morning. At this time, I am more concerned about getting you away from further attacks."

Freya hesitated.

"You don't think it will attack again?"

Stefan grinned. Somehow it wasn't a pleasant expression this time.

"Not until he has healed."

"But what is it - he?"

"He is a were-wolf, of course. A beast. He is a predator, certainly, but not one deserving of praise. I have been trying to remove him from the area for some time without success. This is why I have asked for your help. Come, this way." He moved off, taking Freya's arm as he did so. Perforce, she went with him.

"But if he's here in the city, then we don't need to go check those other sites. He must be local. Shouldn't we go after him now, before he heals?"

"I would very much like to do so. But I must have reinforcements to prevent him from running away. This is something I am working on. If you have appropriate powers, perhaps you can help. But come, I would not wish to expose you to further danger tonight."

Freya shook her head in confusion. Why all the secrecy and plans to survey attack sites if Stefan knew the perpetrator already? She didn't understand Stefan's reasoning. Maybe she'd just had too much to drink.

It wasn't far to walk - shorter than the walk to the bus stop would have been. Freya was on hyper-alert the whole way, worried that the beast would return.

"Does that were-wolf attack you often?" she asked as they walked, trying to make conversation while listening for attacks. She didn't trust Stefan's blithe assertion that the beast would not attack again.

"No, most often he avoids me. He prefers to attack defenceless women." Stefan's voice was cold.

"Unpleasant behaviour," Freya said with a shiver.

"Indeed. Here we are." Stefan led the way to a gated alley, and unlocked the metal gate. "This way." Down the narrow alley, he turned into an opening in the brick wall, and unlocked a door. Up some uncovered wooden stairs, and yet another door appeared. Opening this final door, Stefan stood to one side to let Freya pass inside.

CHAPTER SEVENTEEN

STEFAN'S PLACE

A warm, soft glow filled the high-ceiling room. The floor was covered with a thick red rug, and a dark leather armchair was drawn up by the empty fireplace. Or no, it was not quite empty, Freya saw. An ancient lava lamp was bubbling gently in the grate, adding its red glow to the room. She took a few steps inside, and looked down at her feet. Her shoes weren't muddy, it was too dry for that, but she felt uncomfortable carrying street dirt into this immaculate place. She slipped her shoes off, pushing them to the side of the door. A step further in, and her feet sank luxuriously into the deep pile of the rug.

Stefan closed the door gently behind him, and fiddled with a dial on the wall. The light level in the room rose a notch as a chandelier came gently to life.

"Welcome to my humble abode," he said, spreading his arms out grandly.

"This is humble, is it?" Freya retreated into sarcasm, feeling intimidated by the grandeur.

"Do you not like it?"

"It looks very warm."

"Yes, perfectly in keeping with our current weather, is it not?"

Freya was surprised into laughing aloud.

"You're not wrong."

"Please, sit down. Can I get you a drink?"

"I think I've had enough..."

"Some coffee, perhaps?"

"Er, no, thanks. I'd take tea, if you have any?"

"For you, of course. I will dress my hand, then prepare tea."

He disappeared into an adjoining room, and Freya heard busy sounds emerging from what must be the kitchen. She walked over and leant against the doorway. Stefan had already applied plasters to his injured hand, and was working with a complicated looking red enamelled machine. Steam hissed loudly, and a tiny trickle of dark liquid descended into a waiting cup. Stefan glanced up and smiled, the sudden change of expression lighting up his face.

"I make coffee for myself. I do not know what I will do if the coffee plants fail."

"Chicory coffee?"

"Poison. Please do not mention it again."

Freya laughed. "I'm told it's very nice. When you're used to it."

"I do *not* wish to have to get used to it. I hope that your colleagues can find a way to save the species. A way that does not involve growing it in Australia."

"They're trying, I'm sure."

"While they try, will you select a tea? I have chamomile or Yorkshire."

"Chamomile, please. I'm surprised a coffee drinker like you has tea in the house."

Stefan raised an eyebrow. "Living in this country, one is expected to have tea."

"True enough."

Tea and coffee cups in hand, Stefan sauntered back into the main room. He placed the cups on a small brass table that Freya hadn't noticed earlier, and again invited Freya to take a seat. He leaned against the mantelpiece, himself. She sat on the edge of the armchair, wriggling her toes in the velvety red carpet. It felt sinfully luxurious. She had a sudden flashback to the stinky old carpet she'd torn out of her room back on the coast. There was no comparison, really.

"I just want to sink into this carpet," she said. "It's so soft."

"Then by all means do so. I would love to see you on my rug."

Freya was revisited by her earlier concern that Stefan was just a bit creepy. She dismissed the idea, however - Stefan had defended her from the were-wolf without hesitation, and that was definitely an admirable attribute.

"Thanks. I think. So, tell me about that creature. Why are you the only one stalking him, who is *he* stalking, and where do I come in?" She took a sip of her tea. *That's more like it. I hope I'm not going to be one of those little old ladies who drink nothing but tea, though.*

Stefan sipped at his coffee. From the way the lines on his face smoothed out, it looked like he had a similar reaction to his own hot drink.

"Hmm. Well, the were-wolf is not really a newcomer to this area. He calls himself Van after the great beast of Norse mythology, Vanagard, but that simply an affectation. He has been here at least as long as I have. Perhaps longer. It is only in the last year that he has become... a nuisance, however."

Freya shifted uncomfortably, although the chair in which she sat was perfectly soft.

"A bit more than a nuisance, if the attacks I've been hearing about are all him."

"Most likely they are. Although it is possible he has acquaintances who help him. I lack the nose to detect them, if so. However, I believe the attacks may all in be areas like tonight, where there are many exotic plants. But I am not a plant expert, so you can perhaps help me with this."

"Maybe he just likes flowers," suggested Freya. "Seriously though, what can be done? Are the police after him?"

"The police believe that a dog, or several dogs, are responsible. The police are a human force in this area, with limited imagination."

"Typical. Last time I needed a police force they were all weres, now when being weres would be helpful, they're all human."

Stefan inclined his head.

"Indeed. That must be most irritating for you. However, it means that if Van is to be stopped, it is up to we non-mundanes to take care of him."

"I don't know that I'll be very useful for stopping a were-wolf," said Freya. "I might just about be able to defend myself from one, but only if I've improved since I last encountered a seriously aggravated bunch of weres."

"Come, I have more confidence in your abilities than that. Surely you can use some of that water affinity you spoke of, or your self-defence training?"

"I don't know if I can. I'm just not that strong - or that practised. I'm not a fighter. You saw that tonight." She took refuge in her tea, holding the warm cup in front of her face.

Stefan was instantly apologetic.

"Please forgive me, I did not mean to push you beyond your abilities. It has been a long night. Perhaps we should retire."

Freya's head *was* whirling from the events of the evening. "I do need to sleep," she said. "I didn't realise how tired I was till just now." She took a sip of her tea, hoping it would combat some of the whirling.

"There is a spacious bed. Come, I will show you."

"I could just stay here, if you have a spare blanket or something. I don't mean to intrude," said Freya. She was losing the battle of propping up her eyelids.

"No intrusion, I assure you. And the armchair is most certainly not designed to accommodate a sleeping body. It would be most uncomfortable."

"I'd hate to make the armchair uncomfortable," Freya smiled, feeling witty. Maybe she should have cocktails more often, she usually struggled to make jokes.

Stefan stood in front of the chair and offered her his uninjured hand.

"Come. I will assist you in ensuring the comfort of the armchair."

She took his hand and let herself be pulled up. Her eyes snagged on something poking out from under the chair. Was that an ID card from work? Stefan must have dropped his. She could feel her own ID card still stowed in her pocket. She struggled to focus. That was a woman's face on it, not Stefan's. She bent towards it, but once again, her head whirled, and she did not object when Stefan put an arm around her waist to steady her as he led her to the bedroom.

CHAPTER EIGHTEEN

AN EARLY BUS

Freya sat on the early morning bus to get to work, trying to forget that she was wearing the same clothes as yesterday. She had awoken in the early hours of the morning with a terrible sinking feeling telling her that she'd missed something important. Mr Fluffbum! She hadn't thought to let Angie know that she was staying out instead of going home last night. Her cat would be missing her. Freya had slipped out of bed to find her phone, but it was down to its last two percent of battery. She'd need that to get on to the bus. She salvaged her conscience by getting ready for the day as fast as she could. She could send a message to Angie from work, ask her to at least feed the cat. She slipped out to catch the bus as soon as it grew light, leaving Stefan still asleep - in his armchair, she noticed with relief. She'd showered and borrowed a comb so at least her hair wasn't a mess. But she felt as though anyone looking at her would see that she hadn't been in her own home last night.

You're a grown-up now, she told herself. *You're allowed a night out if you want to.* It didn't help the guilt she obscurely felt. *Come on, you're even getting to work on time. And it's not like anything happened, really. Don't beat yourself up.*

She ran her tongue over her teeth. Finding a toothbrush was high on her list of priorities. How did people manage who did this sort of thing all the time? Maybe they were better prepared, with travel brushes in their handbags or something. Freya decided that that was not the sort of person she wanted to be. She looked out the window to distract herself. It was harder than usual to concentrate on the slightly dusty summer greenery. The squeal of the bus's brakes announced her arrival. She scrubbed her face with her hands before rising to exit the bus. Combed hair or not, she felt dreadful.

I'm never drinking chocolate cocktails again, no matter how good they taste. She staggered to the front of the bus, thanking the driver despite the headache that was driving a spike through her left temple.

No-one commented on her appearance in the lab. Lab coats were compulsory wear, so only her trousers showed anyway. Her creased cotton trousers. Freya scowled at her incriminating clothes. But... she had mostly enjoyed herself last night. Apart from the troll and were-wolf attacks, of course. It was just the morning after that was not working out.

She collected the day's research material from the pigeon holes where the lab manager, Tony, had organised it. There was a new package, a collection of bark and leaves sent in by a suspicious olive grower who'd noticed her best producing trees looking unwell.

"You're looking a bit peaky this morning, Freya. TGI Friday, eh?" The lab manager was always observant. She'd heard he bred prize guppies at home. No doubt they were closely observed and well looked after, too.

"Yeah, I've got a bit of a headache. I might skip the pub this evening."

"By the look of you that's a good idea. There's still a few reactions to run on yesterday's samples. I'll get Tom to keep those going, if you can just focus on this new package?"

Freya smiled her thanks at the lab manager, and took the package into the clean room to unpack. No sense in spreading whatever plant disease was in it all over the lab. And working in the clean room had the added benefit that no-one would be commenting on her apparent health or otherwise, since only one person was allowed in at a time.

Lunchtime arrived too soon. Her head and stomach were still protesting the night's excesses. Freya stretched in place on her stool. She'd run the standard tests on the new package: looked at the samples under the microscope, photographed them both macroscopically and microscopically, crushed and processed a sample to run with a standard set of diagnostic markers. It would take a few hours for that to complete, so she had no reason to avoid going to the canteen with her fellow workers. Usually, she'd have no qualms about doing so, but she was nervous about running into Stefan after the night before.

Look on the bright side, Freya told herself. *There's nothing supernatural about the job you do, and* almost *all your workmates think you're just human.* It was something she'd worked towards for years, trying to avoid the demi-world with its hidden terrors, and at the same time working with plants in a way that wasn't growing them - growing plants being a feat she'd been unable to master. Of course, she'd just had a night out with a descendant of volcano gods, enlivened by a troll and a were-wolf attack. Her plan wasn't quite on track.

The canteen was busy as usual, the noise of feeding humanity enough to silence all but the most dedicated of conversationalists. Freya avoided the overcooked greens today, opting for a fresh fruit selection that might settle her uneasy stomach. Looking around, Freya saw Phillip the chilli sauce enthusiast seated in a corner with a ring of similarly dressed people, in animated conversation. Her lab-mate Kylie gestured for her to take a seat at the next table over. She moved gratefully in that direction. Freya was about to place her tray on the utilitarian square table when she felt a presence beside her. She smelled Stefan's distinctive cologne through the odour of cooked food.

"No hello for me this morning, Freya of my delight?" Stefan's voice was low, pitched for her ears only.

"Oh. Er, sorry. I had to get to work on time." Freya hoped Kylie couldn't hear them, but Stefan's actions would be hard to miss. He slung an arm around her waist and addressed her lab-mate.

"I hope you do not mind me joining you and your beautiful friend here."

"No dramas, take a seat," said Kylie.

Freya felt the blood rushing to her face, and she avoided Kylie's sharp gaze. She pulled away from Stefan and took the seat she'd planned on, setting her tray down. Stefan pulled a chair across from another table and sat down too. No light lunch for him, Freya noticed. His tray was laden. Clearly, he did not feel the effects of overindulgence as much as she did. Kylie eyed them both in an amused way. She didn't seem so antagonistic to Stefan today for some reason.

"Good night out on the town then?" she asked.

"Er, yes. We went to the Red Dragon, you know."

"Oh yeah, I like that place. It's a classic," said Kylie. "Did you try the bronze dragon ale there?"

"I'm not really an ale drinker," said Freya.

"I sampled it," said Stefan. "It does not live up to its reputation. The copper dragon was better. But Freya tells me that I should report the Australian coffee beans I had to your group."

"That's not exactly what I said," protested Freya.

But Kylie's professional and personal interest was clearly piqued.

"Go on, I didn't know we were growing coffee! Where in Oz did they come from? And more to the point, where can *I* get them?"

"Sorry, I didn't actually go into the coffee shop selling them. Maybe you should head in this weekend and check them out?" said Freya. "It's the one on Coppergate, you can't miss the advertising."

"I'll be there, you can count on it. Coffee from Oz, unbelievable. Was it good?"

"Alas, no," said Stefan.

"Damn. In that case, I'm practically obliged to investigate, right? Get them to up their game."

Freya laughed. Her friend's defence of the benefits of anything Australian was legendary in the lab. And Kylie was now focused on a challenge, rather than on the potential relationship between herself and Stefan. Much better.

Stefan consumed his meal quickly, but still managed to contribute to the conversation; quick, witty observations on the topic of coffee and its variants. Freya wished her brain could keep up. She wasn't in the mood for witty conversation. When Freya had finished her fruit, he offered to take both her tray and Kylie's to the washing-up trolleys. He kissed Freya's hand before he left, in a mock-old-fashioned way that made her wince with embarrassment, even as the touch of his lips on her skin made her tingle.

As soon as he was gone, Kylie turned to Freya.

"So, busy night, was it?"

For once, Freya wished Kylie wasn't so blunt. She nodded.

"I guess you could say that. I am never going to drink chocolate cocktails again, though. You wouldn't believe the headache I have this morning."

"Need a tylenol?"

"Definitely."

"Awesome, you can tell me about your night while you wait for it to take effect."

"Kylie!"

"Kidding. Sorta. Here, I've got some in my bag. Grab some water and you can have it."

"Thanks."

"No worries. First night out with Stefan, was it?"

"Yes. He drinks a lot more than I can."

"Yeah, he drinks like a fish. I reckon that's why he only sometimes comes to the pub. He'd spend a fortune otherwise. Not that he'd be alone in that. You Poms are almost as bad as Aussies with your drink."

Freya ignored this dig at the British. At least, that's what she assumed Kylie meant when she said 'Poms'.

"Do you like him after all, then?" she asked Kylie.

"Oh, he's pretty enough to look at. But if I were you I wouldn't get in too deep."

"What do you mean?" Freya wondered if Kylie was jealous.

"Nothing. Just watch yourself, yeah?"

"I don't understand."

"Hopefully you won't have to. I'm getting back to work, now. Good luck with the headache."

Freya let her head sink onto the table briefly, before realising that there was nothing more likely than that to make people inquire after her health. What was

Kylie hinting at? Could she know that Stefan was some sort of demi? If so, what was Kylie? Freya had had her pegged as a simple human.

CHAPTER NINETEEN

ANGIE MISSES PEOPLE

After work, Freya slouched in the big, faded leather armchair in the living room, trying to get comfortable despite the lingering evening heat. She had a room of her own, but Angie liked to have company in the living room in the evenings. Also, Freya's room was a loft conversion, and Freya had found the heat up there unbearable for the last couple of weeks. Mr Fluffbum rolled on the floor by her feet, belly up to better radiate heat.

Freya had sat in the living room stiffly the first night, wishing she was rude enough to just go to her room and bypass this social occasion. However, Angie was always chatty and welcoming, and Freya had come to enjoy the simple evening ritual. Tonight, however, Freya was longing for her bed, while Angie was full of questions about her night out.

"It's been a hard day, you know," Freya muttered.

"Well, you know my antidote for that!"

Freya laughed, but shook her head as Angie proffered her cask of wine.

"No thanks. I had a bit much last night. That's probably why things feel pear-shaped, I guess. It seemed a good idea at the time."

Angie was sympathetic as she poured herself another glass.

"Oh, it always does. Just look at me, living out here instead of in a proper city surrounded by people."

Freya tipped her head inquiringly.

"Are you telling me you never wondered what a people person like me was doing in a remote spot like this?" said Angie.

"I guess I just assumed you liked it."

"You assumed wrong then. I positively crave the sound of vehicular traffic. The sound of people arguing over their morning coffee is music to my ears. And yet here I am, bunged down in the flippin' countryside." She waved a hand dismissively around, indicating the farm outside with its rolling pastures and bird-infested hedgerows.

"Why do you stay then?"

"Fell in love, didn't I? Picked the wrong man in the pub one evening, and here I am." Her voice held the bitterness of grapefruit pith. "And then he goes and gets a travelling job, leaving me out here. Some days after work, I want to stay at the hospital just for the sound of voices. That's why I get people living in of course, but no-one likes the space these days. It were four months empty before you took the place. Anyway, don't mind me. You're the one who's had a hard day. I spend a bit too much time on my own, some days, and it gets to me. It's always worse after being on the night shift though."

Freya didn't know what to say. Angie had always seemed so cheerful in the past, and now it seemed that underneath the cheer was a festering pit of despair. It was true that Angie's husband rarely made an appearance, turning up for occasional weekends on no particular schedule.

"Um. Do you want some chocolate?"

"That's the best suggestion I've heard all day. Bring on the good stuff."

Freya sighed with relief. Chocolate craving was something she could deal with. She rummaged in her bag and brought out a bar of 75% single-origin Ghana.

"Ooh, you don't do things by halves, do you?"

"If I'm going to spend money on imported chocolate, I want to enjoy it." Chocolate was a weakness that Freya was prepared to fund. Besides, this was fairtrade, organic chocolate. Surely there was something wholesome about supporting that sort of ethic that offset the actual indulgence of buying it? Of course, the cocoa trees that supported her habit were endangered as much as coffee trees were these days. She suppressed the depressing thought, and broke off a square of the dark chocolate, offering it to Angie. Spices might not make it here often, but somehow chocolate still made it across the perilous shipping lanes. So far, anyway. Freya wasn't sure how she'd get through some days if cocoa went the way of cinnamon.

"Thanks, love."

The two women sat absorbing chocolate in silence for a few minutes.

Angie was the first to stir.

"Well then, let's not sit here like stuffed penguins. I picked my problems; I shouldn't sit around complaining about them. Tell me about your evening."

"I don't know that I should…"

"Of course you should, who else will you unburden to out here? Haven't we just been talking about the problems of being in the country?"

Freya had to laugh. It was true; unless she fancied phoning someone, Angie was the logical recipient of her complaints.

"Well, it started with that dinner with Stefan."

"How could that go wrong?"

"It was his dinner choices, I guess." The kitchen clock ticked authoritatively into a brief silence.

"You didn't get onto your vegetarian high horse, did you?"

Freya looked away, pretending an interest in the crocheted doll on the mantelpiece. It was an easy source of distraction. *What an ugly thing to dominate the room. Why does Angie keep it there?*

"You did, didn't you." Angie was reproachful.

"Not exactly. But he chose a steak and I suppose my face showed what I thought. Honestly, I thought I was better at hiding my thoughts. And anyway, it's not like eating steak is helping with climate change."

"I hate to break it to you, love, but your face is, as they say, an open book. You know, the steak could have been lab-grown. A lot of meat is these days." Angie's voice was kind.

Freya cringed inside, but forced a laugh.

"I didn't think of lab meat. I may as well just say what I'm thinking, then, if everyone can tell anyway."

"Let me know when you start, I'd love to be there for the ride."

"I was going to tell you about my evening," said Freya, ignoring this comment. "So, dinner was a bit strained. Though actually I had a pretty nice desert. But it didn't end there. In fact, that was barely the beginning."

"It must have been interesting, since you didn't get home last night."

Freya blushed. "Yes, well. That's part of it. Sorry I didn't message you earlier." Freya paused, unsure if she wanted to continue.

"At least you messaged me today, I'd have exploded with worry if I had to wait till this evening to find out if you were alive or dead. Lucky I was on night shift and didn't notice your absence till this morning. And that cat of yours came in with half a rat, so I don't think he suffered overly. Anyway, go on, you can't just leave me hanging like that. Tell all." Angie was leaning forward, clearly intrigued.

Freya paused, the thought of half a rat in her room threatening to overwhelm her already overburdened senses.

"What happened to the rest of the rat?" she asked faintly.

"Not to worry, I chucked it out back right smart," Angie reassured her.

Note to self, don't walk out the back door without shoes.

"Er. Good. So, after dinner we climbed Clifford's Tower, and then went to a bar. I may have had more cocktails there than was wise."

"An easy mistake to make, love. I've done it myself on occasion, can you believe it?"

Freya's lips twitched up. She certainly *could* believe it. She sat back in her chair, wishing she had another cushion to stop the leather from sticking unpleasantly to her legs. She unpeeled them carefully, but felt them stick again immediately as she adjusted her position.

"Alright, maybe I shouldn't feel so bad about that. But then, we went to the museum gardens."

"Ooh, very romantic."

"Yes, well Stefan clearly thought so. And, um. I guess I did too. But I missed my bus. I *never* miss my bus!" Freya's voice rose a little hysterically. She knew she shouldn't get so upset by a little thing like that, but not missing buses was such a reliable part of herself, the act of missing one was unbalancing. Actually, it was probably the other events of the night that were unbalancing, but Freya didn't want to focus on that yet, and certainly not with Angie, who was surely as human as they came.

"Ah well, not the end of the world. So that's why you didn't make it back then?" Angie's voice suggested she knew there must be more to the tale than Freya had yet told. "Need a refill? Or actually, a first glass?"

"Just water, thanks." Freya helped herself from the jug of water on the ancient smoked-glass coffee table that stood in the centre of the room. "So, yeah. There was more. Stefan wanted to show me the place where, um, something had happened that he'd been telling me about. That was in the museum gardens too. There's a new wolf sculpture there, among the trees. It looks real. Pretty scary, actually. So, after he'd shown me that, and a couple of other things happened, we were just walking along talking about it, and then he turned a corner and said that he had a place just along that road, and did I want to stay?"

"I'm guessing you did want to stay."

"Well, no, but a taxi back here would blow my budget for a year. And it was just a first date. Not even a date, really. Or I didn't think it was supposed to be."

"Fair enough. He didn't force you to do anything you didn't want to, did he?"

"No, nothing like that, I mean, I just went to sleep." She grimaced. "Passed out, more like, as soon as my head hit the pillow. But I don't want to be like my sister." Freya was horrified to find herself descending into sobs. It had been years since she'd said anything about her sister to anyone.

"Now that sounds like it might be the crux of the problem. Do you want to tell me about your sister? You haven't mentioned her before." Angie stood up and walked across the room to pick up a box of tissues. She offered it to Freya.

"Here you go, give it a good snort."

Freya laughed despite herself, and followed the suggestion to blow her nose. She took another tissue to wipe her eyes.

"My sister's not ...around... anymore." Her voice caught. She took a deep, steadying breath. "But when she was, she was always bouncing around from boy to boy. Even when I was a kid. I guess you'd call her precocious. And then - well, something happened to her, and she got pregnant. My Mum looks after her kits - I mean kids - now."

Angie was sitting with her chin in her hand, watching Freya.

"That's quite a back story. Have you ever just let yourself go before?"

"Well, yes. Just after Tammy... left. But nothing came of that."

"No wonder you're in a bit of a tizzy now. It sounds like you're all wound up about your sister's actions. You need to think more about your own. Did you do the right thing by yourself?"

"I didn't do much other than eat, drink and walk around the city."

Don't mention the 'got attacked by a were' part, that would be too hard to explain.

"Well then, did you enjoy yourself, and are you ashamed?"

"Should I be?"

"Heavens, that's not a question for me to answer. All I mean is that you shouldn't judge yourself by your sister's standards. I'm sure you are very different people. Be yourself, that's all."

Freya took a deep, shuddering breath and let it out slowly. She wasn't Tammy. She hadn't got too carried away, not really. And she was far from the sea here too, she was probably safe from the North Sea goddess.

"Angie, you're a lifesaver. Thanks for helping me get some perspective."

"You're welcome, Freya. Now, I'm sure I need more chocolate in payment for my counselling services." Angie leaned forward and snapped another two pieces of chocolate off the bar. She put them both in her mouth and sat back. "That's better."

CHAPTER TWENTY

BACK IN THE LAB

Freya spent the weekend pretending the previous Thursday hadn't occurred, while simultaneously thinking about it constantly. She went for a run, visited a farmers' market to restore her food supplies, and buried herself in novels set in other worlds with no demis or shifters to mar the scenery. Mr Fluffbum clearly approved of this activity, curling up beside her on the bed. By Monday morning she'd more or less regained her equanimity. That lasted all the way to the front gate of her work, where Stefan turned out to be waiting.

"What a glorious morning," he said, swooping in to kiss her, "to meet Freya the beautiful."

Freya enjoyed the kiss, but then she groaned.

"You can't call me that in public! Or kiss me at work, either."

"But it is certainly true that you are beautiful, so why would you protest? Why should I not kiss you?"

"I *do* protest. I can't show my face if you call me things like that where other people can hear. I'm trying to be a professional here."

Stefan gestured around the mostly-deserted driveway.

"There is no-one to hear but the birds, and they do not mind."

"Even so."

Freya resumed walking towards the giant series of buildings that housed her lab, and Stefan's. The walk was lined with tall bushes which teemed with fluttering birds. While Freya hadn't noticed any nature-based demis in her time here, it was clear that some had been here in the past. Unlike most of the shrubs in the surrounding countryside, those beside the drive were flourishing and green despite the heat. Freya wondered if the demi responsible was one of the scientists, or a gardener on the staff. That might explain why she hadn't met them yet.

"Who looks after all these plants, anyway?" Freya asked Stefan, who had swung into step beside her with his usual easy grace.

"Does it matter? I am sorry not to be a fount of wisdom on the subject, but as you know I am a geologist, not a botanist."

"I'm just curious. Oh, look!" Freya sprang into the bushes, ducking low to avoid them catching her hair. "Wild strawberries. I love this time of year." She looked at Stefan's stiff, disapproving face. "What?"

"I am not accustomed to walking with people who suddenly duck under hedges." He reached out and plucked a leaf from her hair, dropping it with distaste.

"Oh. Er. Sorry?" Freya wasn't sure how to react. She shrugged, and offered him a strawberry, biting into her own with pleasure. It was just the way she liked it, juicy and warm with sunshine.

"No, thank you. I will let you enjoy them, since they are clearly a favourite."

Freya felt rebuffed. She'd only wanted to share a delicious treat, after all. She quickened her step, away from the scene. Stefan similarly sped up.

"Do not be angry with me, Freya of the morning. Come, I will take you to pick strawberries tonight. Large ones, that you do not have to scrounge from the ground."

"They don't taste the same. And anyway, all strawberries grow in the ground. Er. Except the ones in those raised beds. And hydroponics, although I think they're still working on that. And..." Freya realised that Stefan was laughing at her.

"What?"

"I am merely appreciating your expertise. So, it is settled, strawberries after work. I will meet you by the gates."

Freya was still wondering about Stefan's hot and cold behaviour when he farewelled her with a kiss just outside the reception area. She hurried to scan in to work, her cheeks warm. Stefan gave her a cheerful pat on the shoulder as he departed for his own area. Freya caught the receptionist smirking at her, but the woman dropped her eyes as Freya silently dared her to say something. Freya wasn't sure if that was a win or not.

CHAPTER TWENTY-ONE

AN UNEXPECTED TRIP

"You know those samples you processed on Friday, Freya?" Tony was waiting for her when she entered the lab, rubbing the back of his close-shaved head in a worried manner.

"Yes?" Freya felt herself switch to alert mode, worries about her foraging habits and what Stefan thought of them falling away. She'd left those samples tidily filed, and sent the results to Tony, as instructed. What could be wrong?

"I took a look at the results first thing this morning. It looks like Xylella." He named a major killer of olive trees from the Mediterranean. "But we're going to need another sample or ten to confirm. There's no stuffing about with that disease."

"So, we email the orchardist and ask them to send more?" Freya wasn't sure why he was bringing this up with her - she was pretty low in the hierarchy of the lab, as its most junior member.

"Not with Xylella. That nasty could totally kill the South's olive industry, and you know it's only just started to make profits."

"At the rate this summer is going, we could pretty much grow olives up here." The morning had been another atypically hot one.

"Yeah, it's been hotter than a baboon's armpit the last few weeks. But this is serious, Freya. I want to send you down to collect the samples. Today, if possible. We can't trust the landowner not to miss some, and you know what to look for, right? You can take appropriate samples from trees that look healthy as well as sick ones."

"Er, yes. But why me?"

The manager grinned at her suddenly, a glint in his usually straightforward gaze. "Do you have kids waking you at four-bloody-am every morning?"

"No..."

"That's why. I would love to go meself, but I'll never hear the end of it if I leave the missus to deal with the kids by herself for a few days."

"Oh. Well, I suppose I can ask someone to feed my cat…"

"Besides, work pays for trains and accommodation. It's a bonus, really. Visit the warm south - oh wait, we've got plenty of warm here too. Visit the South, anyway. See the vineyards and olive groves of Devon."

Freya was suddenly assailed by memories of her wine-loving father talking wistfully of those vineyards. Her eyes misted, and she blinked hastily, not wanting to cry in front of her manager.

"Gods, it's not that bad!" he exclaimed.

"Oh. No, I mean, it will be fine, I guess, I was just thinking about my Dad."

"Well, go think about your Dad while you get on the computer and book some tickets. I want those samples yesterday. This is just the sort of thing those twits in biosecurity are supposed to keep out, but when they fail, it's our job to stop it in its tracks. Right?"

"I suppose so."

"It certainly is. On to it, now."

Freya moved off towards the offices where her work computer was located, then paused.

"Er - where exactly am I booking tickets to?"

Her boss opened his mouth, then hesitated, his mouth hanging open. "I'll get you the address. You'll need to get accommodation for a night or two. And don't forget to take a full sampling kit with you. You'll want a steriliser for your clothes, overshoes, gloves, the works. And remember the samples need to be kept chilled once you've got them. That's essential. It's the main reason to send you rather than waiting on the next mail packet."

Slightly dazed by the sudden change in her anticipated day and the extensive list, Freya sat down to plan a sample-collecting trip to Devonshire. Booking a train was straightforward when she didn't have to cover the cost herself. Sitting at the next computer, Kylie peered across at her screen enviously.

"Got a trip planned, I see?"

"Yes, work trip. I have to go collect samples," said Freya. "But I need to make sure my cat gets fed. I can't just assume my landlady will do it. And I am pretty sure I can't take him with me."

Kylie looked serious for a moment, as though thinking something over.

"I can do it, if you'd like. I'm interested in meeting your landlady anyway. D'you think she'd be OK with me dropping over? My place isn't really cat friendly."

Freya felt a rush of relief as tension she hadn't realised she was holding left her shoulders.

"That would be amazing, Kylie. I'll give you Angie's number. She's pretty friendly, but she does work shifts. All the more reason for someone else to check in on Mr Fluffbum."

"No worries. You can look after my bull mastiff pack next time."

Freya turned to Kylie, mouth open in horror.

"Kidding, I don't own any pets." Kylie laughed at Freya's expression. "I'm just jealous. I haven't had a work trip for ages. Mind you, I bet with the weather so hot, you'll get delays on the train."

"Why's that?" Freya hadn't had the chance to catch many trains - certainly not such a long-distance one.

"Oh, the rails warp in the heat. The trains have to slow down so they don't come off."

"I guess slow is better than the alternative then," Freya agreed.

Kylie waggled her hand in the air. "It depends if the air-con stays on. It's a rough ride if it doesn't. Best to take your own food and drink, too, the rail companies charge a fortune for a packet of crisps."

Freya accepted the information gratefully, and went on to look for suitable accommodation.

"Do you know what sort of thing I should be looking for?" she asked Kylie.

"Oh, you know, just the cheapest B & B in the area. Work'll make you cover the difference otherwise. You'll probably find yourself over the station or next to someone's 24-hour laundry. That's what always happened to me."

"I hope it doesn't come to that, but I guess if work's paying I can't complain too much." Freya's fingers rattled on the keyboard as she initiated her search.

"Y' can complain as much as you like. I've noticed people like to moan, here. Not do anything about it, mind - just moan."

Freya felt a little defensive of her fellow countryfolk, but she had to admit - if only to herself - that it was true. The next moment, she laughed aloud, as the first bed and breakfast that came up in her search was indeed over a station.

"This trip is going to be an experience; I can tell already."

CHAPTER TWENTY-TWO

STEFAN IS DISGRUNTLED

Freya booked herself a ticket for an afternoon train that she should just be able to catch, if she left work at lunchtime to pick up some overnight gear. That left her with a quandary, though. What should she tell Stefan? She didn't have his contact details yet, so she couldn't just message him. An email seemed too impersonal. In the end she resolved to go looking for him.

She started out at the front desk, a place she hadn't stopped at since she got her staff card printed. Hopefully, if she began here, she'd be able to keep the directions straight in her mind. East for the length of a building, turn left, through a set of double doors - no. Freya was brought to a halt by a single door that she didn't have clearance to access. She tried to retrace her steps, only to find herself overlooking the central courtyard, well-populated today by staff enjoying morning tea in the sunshine. Back to the front of the building, to try again. This time she encountered a locked door at the end of a corridor. Starting again from the front desk, she headed west for one corridor, turned a corner and came up against a locked door once again. This time however, someone in a white lab-coat politely opened it for her, letting her through without asking what she was doing.

Probably terrible security, but all the better for me.

She headed down the new corridor, which looked identical to the last one, but with a crossroads halfway down it. She shrugged and turned left. She passed a silver engraved sign on the wall with the title 'geology lab' on it.

Now I'm getting somewhere.

However, try though she might, she couldn't find an entrance to the geology lab. She backed up, and tried turning right, only to arrive at the rear end of the geology lab, where a sign proclaimed 'No entry, authorised persons only'. This sign was backed up with an imposing radioactivity symbol, the triangular black and yellow sign striking more fear into Freya than the curved, clawlike biohazard symbols that typically emblazoned her own lab. She wondered what sort of authorised person would casually enter a radioactive room. As she pondered her next move, the door opened and Stefan himself emerged from it.

"Stefan! Do you work in there?"

Stefan, in the act of striding down the corridor, started slightly before recovering. He turned and smiled glintingly at her.

"What a pleasant surprise to see you, Freya. I thought you would never find this end of the building."

"That's what I thought too, I've been trying half the morning."

"And why is now the time to put in that effort? I have been hoping to see you here for weeks."

Freya shifted uncomfortably.

"It's just, I'm being sent on a sampling trip. Today. So, I won't be able to go strawberry-picking with you after all."

Stefan's face clouded. He looked almost... angry. But his words were smooth.

"That is indeed a tragedy. I had hoped to enlist your help in assessing another attack site tonight, also. But if it is work that sends you far from me, then it cannot be helped. You are not taking a long trip, I hope?"

"Just one night, I think. Maybe two. But I've got to get going, I still have to get all my sampling gear. I just wanted to let you know, so you weren't waiting for me tonight."

"That is most thoughtful, kind Freya. I hope we can renew the search for strawberries and beasts later this week."

"Well, strawberries would be nice," Freya smiled. "See you soon."

Stefan caught her arm as she turned to go, and once again she noticed the warm tingling of her skin as he touched her. He stroked her hair before raising her chin with a finger.

"Don't forget me while you are on your trip," he murmured.

I'm only away for a day or two, how could I forget him in that time?

She couldn't decide if the tingling was a pleasant feeling or not. Memorable, certainly. The thought was subsumed as Stefan kissed her. She enjoyed the sensation for a moment before more prudent thoughts intruded.

"Not at work, Stefan!" Freya patted his arm apologetically as she stepped back. "What will people think?"

"That you are beautiful and irresistible, naturally."

"That's not really the professional image I'm trying for." She tucked her hair back into its braid.

"But it is indubitably the case."

"Er. Thanks." Freya smoothed her clothes nervously. "I'd better get going. See you in a couple of days." She hastily retraced her steps. Hopefully, it would be easier to escape the building than to track down a particular lab within it.

CHAPTER TWENTY-THREE

ENCOUNTERING NIK

Freya spent the first part of her train journey reading a book on her phone or staring out the window. There was evidence of the heat wave everywhere, normally-green fields faded to yellow already, though it was not yet harvest time. Even the hardy buddleia were wilting where they lined the tracks with purple flowers.

As she grew closer to the sprawling metropolis of London, buildings and roads took the place of parched fields. Freya watched the intensifying city with interest. All roads led to London, but she'd never been there herself.

It's a shame I'll only be there long enough to change trains. It would be interesting to visit - though I can see already why Mum didn't want to live there. It looks like it would be hard to find much to eat that isn't already walked on, spat on or has had an encounter with a dog. Of course, that last was a hazard anywhere when foraging for food. Freya reminded herself, again, that she wasn't obliged to forage for food anymore.

The train pulled into the station before she was ready - a much bigger, more up to date station than the one she'd left behind in York. This one was swarming with people. Peering out the window, Freya could see at a glance that the people weren't just humans. Raven-bedecked demi-gods, green-haired goblins, hairy weres and more mingled freely on the concourse, the humans among them not seeming to notice or care. *So, this is the big smoke. Looks... challenging.*

An official-sounding voice brought her back to reality.

"Excuse me, miss, you need to disembark the train. Last stop, miss." The train conductor waited until she began to collect her possessions before moving on to the next lagging passenger. Freya clutched her phone with the ticket displayed on it, shouldered the heavy bag with her sampling gear, picked up the chiller box and hung the smaller bag with her overnight things off one arm.

Thoroughly encumbered, she felt like she bumped against every seat on her way to the exit.

Lucky I'm the last off, I'd probably take someone's head off, otherwise.

Just as Freya thought this, an enraged voice exclaimed.

"Ow. Watch where you're going." The speaker was an older woman with short, greying hair and thick glasses which enhanced the cast she had in one eye. With a sinking heart, Freya recognised the biochemistry lecturer from her final year at uni. She'd only just scraped through that class, the lectures boring her to sleep three times out of four. Associate Professor Beare was the last person she wanted to bump into on the train.

"Sorry!" she exclaimed.

To Freya's surprise, the professor smiled at her, revealing uneven teeth.

"No harm done. You were in one of my classes, weren't you?"

"Ye-es?"

"Get a good job, did you?"

"Er, yes, actually." Freya mentioned the university lab where she now worked.

"Well done, well done. A good step for you. Well, I mustn't keep you, they'll bring out the cattle prods if we stay on the train too long."

Freya looked nervously around, half expecting to see the conductor with an electrified stick. However, there was no-one left in the train compartment. She hurried out anyway, lurching down the steps to the platform. Further away from that odd yet unsatisfying encounter was definitely the right way to go. Now, which way did she need to go to reach her next train? She consulted her phone. Out of the station, into the underground, out at another station. She swiped her ticket to get out, walking past a magic-themed shop on her way. No wonder no-one looked at all the demis and other supernaturals in their midst, Freya thought. If they believed in that, they probably didn't think anything they were seeing was real. Had her Mum spent her life making them hide their nature for no reason? It was a galling thought. Still, perhaps this wasn't normal behaviour for pure humans. It could be special London behaviour.

She looked up to admire the glass dome covering the front of the station. Wait, were those harpies, hanging upside down from the beams, their birdlike wings half invisible against the sky? She was half-sure she recognised the blue-haired, wingless one. Freya hurried on before she could be recognised in return. She was never sure what to make of her wind-demi friend Lio's cousin Nik. Since their previous encounters had ended in violence inflicted on someone, it was probably best that Freya move on without renewing the acquaintance. She'd miss her train for sure if Nik decided someone needed teaching a lesson.

Deep underground in the Kings Cross tube station, Freya discovered that while she had the correct station, she was on the wrong platform. She had about a minute to reverse her mistake in order to catch her next train. She pounded back up the dusty stairs, battling against a surge of humanity and probable demi-gods trying to go in the opposite direction. Across an overbridge, she had a glimpse of her tube-train pulling into the station in a cacophony of squealing brakes. Freya tried to speed up, but it was like trying to run upstream in a flooded river. She dodged bodies, ducked sideways, and abruptly found herself on an empty stairwell. Freya took advantage of the emptiness to fling herself down the stairs two at a time, nearly missing the final step. She lurched and recovered, gasping at the near miss, dashed across the platform and leaped through the doors just as beeps sounded for them to close. Panting, Freya leaned against the wall of the train, clutching at a disturbingly warm enamelled metal bar to keep upright.

Made it. I hope this is the right train after all that.

The next station announcement sounded, reminding Freya that she had to change trains again - that meant up an escalator and down another, never once seeing the light of day. She emerged from the tube train at last without further incident.

Just one more train... I wish there was a way to avoid this mess on the way back.

Shouldering her luggage once again, she tagged out of the tube system and gratefully approached the covered, but at least naturally lit concourse of the Waterloo train station.

CHAPTER TWENTY-FOUR

AVOIDING OLD FRIENDS

"Trying to avoid old friends, are you?"

Freya stopped in her tracks. The blue-haired Nik, the harpie she'd been trying to avoid at the previous train station, had sauntered up beside her. Freya was careful to sound confident as she replied. Nik would surely pounce on weakness.

"Not at all. I haven't seen you for a long time," Freya said.

"Apart from at Kings Cross station a few minutes ago."

Fenrir's teeth, she did see me.

"Sorry, I wasn't sure if that was you. You were rather high up."

"Only way to get away from the crowds. Plus, most people can't believe what they're seeing, which is always a bonus. But don't be a stranger. There are few enough demis who know what they are in this town. Not that you're staying, I see."

"No, I'm just on my way through for work. Do you live here now?"

Nik gave a short, bitter laugh.

"When do I get to *live* anywhere? I'm always just passing through. But I've been here a while. Long enough to want to escape."

"That doesn't sound so good." Freya shifted her sampling bag from one hand to the other. The straps were biting through her fingers.

"It sounds like what it is. Plenty of opportunities for all comers, but that means you have to put up with all comers too. And all stayers. I've had enough of it."

"What about Lio, have you seen him lately?" Freya stopped juggling her luggage long enough to look hopefully at Nik. She'd give a lot to hear something of her childhood friend.

"Not I. I thought he was hanging around you like always." Nik's voice was scathing.

Freya looked away. She rather wished Lio was hanging around like he used to, as well. Although maybe things would work out with Stefan. He didn't seem the type to come and go. It was a shame she wasn't out picking strawberries with him now in some country idyll.

Though the way the heat wave is going, the strawberries would be dry and shrivelled.

"No. I haven't seen Lio since I moved inland."

"Lio always did like the coast. Despite the weres and trolls."

"Does that mean there are less weres and trolls here? I thought I saw a bunch of them at Kings Cross."

"There's always a bunch at the stations. More than you see elsewhere. Liminal zones, you know. Transitional spaces. People pay less attention there."

Freya herself was splitting her attention between Nik and the platform numbers.

"This is my platform. I have to catch a train."

Nik surprised Freya by turning to her and giving her a hug, bags and all.

"Look for me when you come back. You are coming back, right?"

Freya nodded.

"Yes, I should come back through the day after tomorrow."

"Good. It's been too long since I saw a familiar face. I might even go north with you."

Freya wasn't sure if that was a threat or a promise. Lio had always called Nik dangerous, but today she just seemed lost, like one of the homeless people who crowded the stations.

"Maybe see you later, then." Freya walked out onto the platform, checking the carriage numbers until she found her allocated one, and boarded the train. She took her seat and sighed deeply. Seeing Nik had revived a host of emotions she thought she'd outgrown.

She'd spent a lot of time with Lio in the year after her sister disappeared. More time with Karim, at first, but then he'd left for university. After that, Lio had seemed like a good person to talk to, when her friend Aisha wasn't available. He'd seen her go through so many losses, after all - her house, her cat, then her sister. He'd helped her overcome weres, found her cat, and been a friend when she most needed one. He'd even enlisted Nik's help when Freya's troubles with were-foxes seemed insurmountable. But then she had finished high school and got a scholarship to go to an inland university - not the same one that Karim had gone to. She hadn't seen Lio since. Freya hadn't realised how much she missed him until seeing Nik had rekindled the memory of their time together. She smiled a little even now, remembering his exploits. She hadn't missed Nik, though. The blue-haired demi had always been an unknown quantity to Freya, aggressive without obvious cause.

The train gave a lurch, and Freya realised she was staring blindly out the window at the backs of graffiti-covered buildings.

Guess I didn't miss much scenery. Maybe I should go out and see Aisha after this trip. Mum too, I suppose. This travel business is fraught with more dangers than I realised, if it's making me want to go home.

The rhythmic swaying of the train settled in to a steady pattern as they pulled out of London again, and Freya sat back. This was the longer part of the journey. She should probably review the sampling procedures her boss had written down for her before Freya hurried out to reach the first connection of her journey. It would be embarrassing to make a mistake on her first unsupervised outing. But she found herself thinking of Lio rather than her job as the train travelled on through the lengthening day.

CHAPTER TWENTY-FIVE

GOBLINS ON THE TRACKS

It was probably an hour later when the train gave another lurch. This time, Freya was thrown forward against the small table in front of her.

What was *that?*

Freya took quick gasping breaths, shocked by the suddenness of their stop. Her ribs felt bruised. There were exclamations and mutters from the other passengers as everyone else recovered. Out the window there was nothing but fields and hedgerows. They hadn't reached their destination yet. Why had they stopped?

The train jolted forward again, provoking further cries from the passengers. Freya felt her ribs gingerly. Probably not broken, luckily. She wondered if it would be safer to stand up and hold on to something. She didn't want another table-inflicted bruising. The train's speakers crackled to life.

"All customers please stay seated as the train passes through a section of warped track. I repeat, all customers please stay seated."

So much for her standing plan. She resumed looking out the window. There were several other tracks visible now, a few curving off to some other destination. There seemed to be figures working beside the rails, all adorned with high visibility vests. She squinted at them. Were those goblins? They seemed to be removing track, rather than straightening it. There was a large lorry parked near the railroad, and several of the short, green-tinged haired were loading sections of track into the lorry.

Oh well, so long as the track I'm on doesn't get removed, I suppose it's alright. But surely it's dangerous to have missing tracks? She gave a mental shrug. *What do I know about track repair anyway?*

She watched curiously as the goblins levered up the next section of track. It took three of them to carry it. How come no railway security types were challenging them? Unless they *were* the railway security types. It wouldn't be the first time an institution was taken over by supernaturals.

The conductor entered Freya's carriage and began checking tickets and asking if anyone had been hurt in the abrupt stop. A couple in front of Freya were demanding a refund. The conductor waved off their demands with a suggestion that they contact head office, and continued on to Freya's seat.

"Ticket, please," he said.

Freya pulled out her phone to show him.

"Thank you, miss. Any injuries to report?"

"Nothing worth mentioning. But could you tell me what's going on over there?" She pointed at the lorry, now being loaded with yet another piece of track.

The conductor's eyes flicked over the scene without interest.

"Routine maintenance, miss."

"So, nothing to do with our train just about coming off the rails, a moment ago?"

The conductor looked briefly uneasy, but he brushed it off.

"No, no. That's just normal track warping given the extreme temperatures today."

"Oh, good."

The conductor looked as though he didn't know what to say to this piece of sarcasm, but he moved on to the next row of seats without further comment. A few jolting movements later, and the scene was out of sight.

Why are goblins taking railway tracks? It would definitely cause an accident if a train tried to follow that route.

Her own train rounded a corner, and Freya spotted what seemed to be the same lorry the goblins had been loading, waiting at a crossroads for the train to pass. She read the writing on the side.

Vulcan construction. Metalworks.

Yet another demi who wasn't being shy about his heritage. Freya wondered why her Mum had bothered spending so much time on hiding what they were. It looked like no-one else worried about it.

Oh well, if the goblins with their demi-associated construction firm were working in broad daylight, someone must know what they were doing, and the missing tracks wouldn't be a problem. She hoped.

CHAPTER TWENTY-SIX

SMALL TOWN DEVON

As Kylie had predicted, the cheapest bed and breakfast at Freya's destination had been so near the station that if a train went by, the whole house vibrated. Luckily, not many trains did pass this particular station, so Freya thought she'd probably get a reasonable night's sleep. Thanks to the long dry spell, there was no chance of the room being damp or mouldy. In fact, it was rather nice, she thought, looking around the airy, pale yellow room. There were giant bird silhouettes on the walls, and a vase with a dried-flower arrangement on the bedside table. Perhaps the owner was a descendant of Hestia, the Roman household goddess, or of Fand, the Irish bird shapeshifter goddess. Or then again - Freya smiled to herself - perhaps the owner just liked birds. She shouldn't fall into the habit her mother always did, of assuming that people were of demi-origins until proved otherwise. No matter how many demis she spotted in the streets.

Thanks to the long sunlight hours of summer, Freya was able to go out and find a meal in daylight. The whole feeling of the town was different to the north, with paler stone, less brick and a lot more wood. The houses tended to be white with grey roofs, and the town undulated gently over the hills. Those hills continued, more brown than green, past the houses, as far as the eye could see.

She found a cafe and bought a drink, keeping the receipt as Kylie had suggested so she could claim back the expense. *Luxury.* She sat drinking her iced chocolate and looking out the window, wishing that there was more than an overworked fan to keep the heat at bay. It was even hotter here in the south. She should get something more substantial for dinner, but what, and where? Tomorrow she'd have to take a taxi to the olive grove where her first sample had come from, and take more samples from the surrounding orchard. She was much more comfortable with that prospect than with walking around strange places when she didn't know where the rough areas were to avoid them.

"Excuse me, miss, we close in five minutes," said the cafe owner beside her. Freya hadn't heard her approaching.

"Oh, sorry. Er - could you tell me a good place to get food around here?"

"There's a greasy spoon just a couple of doors down. But they'll be closing too. You're probably best off with a kebab shop. There's quite a few of those, open all hours. Just keep walking either direction and you'll find one."

Freya thanked the owner and rose, taking a final swallow of her drink. Sounded like kebab was tonight's menu. She'd certainly eaten worse as a child. She smiled reminiscently. She'd never forget the first time she and Tammy had tried to cook dinner for the family, with just foraged greens and unripe cobnuts to work with? That meal would probably have worked with a splash of olive oil and some pasta, but as a stew it had not been a success.

As always when she thought of Tammy, Freya was hit with a tide of what-if thoughts. What if her sister had not chosen a were-fox as a life-partner? What if Freya had been able to do a better summoning, so that Tammy could have been saved without the dubious help of the sea-goddess Nehalennia? What if they'd got on better in the first place? She shook her head as though to shake loose the thoughts. If only that worked. Keeping moving was about the only thing that did. Time to find that kebab.

CHAPTER TWENTY-SEVEN

THE DOOR WAS LOCKED

The guest house door was locked when Freya returned, half a falafel kebab wrapped up in foil in her bag. She had to knock to gain entry - unusually, she hadn't received a key to the front door, only to her room. No-one answered the door at first. Had the occupants all gone to bed? Would they let her in? It wasn't that late - light still touched the edges of the sky that showed between rooftops. She put her hands in her pockets and looked around as she waited. The outside of the guest house was painted a matt cream, a contrast to the stone houses that lined the rest of the street. Train tracks were hidden behind the building. Large bay windows jutted out of the front of the building.

One of those windows is mine. I hope I get back into it tonight.

She knocked again. The door jerked open without warning.

"Yes?" a gruff voice demanded.

Freya barely stopped herself from leaping back like a startled deer. The stranger standing in the doorway was quite clearly annoyed at the interruption to his night. He was wrapped in an ancient plaid dressing gown despite the lingering heat of the day. He frowned up at her - a long way up. Although evidently over middle age, he was not much taller than four feet.

Is he a household deity? Or a kobold, maybe?

Freya wasn't sure, but he was definitely not pure human.

"Sorry, I'm staying here. I don't have a key though."

"Hurry up and come in, then. Don't keep me waiting all night," said the short man.

"Sorry," Freya said again. She didn't think it was worth getting defensive based on his tone. He'd let her in, after all. She'd met a different person when she checked in earlier, a slender, willowy woman who had immediately made Freya feel large and ungainly by her mere presence. That woman had been polite and friendly, though. And almost certainly the creator of the ambiance in the guest house. Everything was carefully thought out, even the soap in the bathroom perfectly positioned, reclining on a carved wooden soap-dish.

"Mind you wipe your feet," the man groused.

Resisting the temptation to roll her eyes, Freya did as she was asked. This must be the night shift guard, or something. He certainly didn't have the customer service skills of the Hestian demi-goddess. Freya hastened inside and up to her carefully curated room. In the morning she'd have to get straight out into the field in order to get her sampling done. But right now, she just had time for a bit of reading in bed...

It was after midnight when Freya reluctantly switched off her phone. It was down to its last few percentages of battery and needed to recharge. She wished that she'd kept in touch with some of those handy Hephaestus-demis she'd met at uni. They were mostly engineers, and at least one had figured out how to extend a phone's battery life. He'd made a small fortune from his fellow students. Alas, Freya's own extended-battery phone had had to be replaced last year after she'd dropped it while reading in the bath. The new mundane one wasn't nearly as good.

She lay in the dark, listening to the strange noises of a house not her own. She could hear a stranger snoring in the room next to hers. A shame the household demi-goddess hadn't thought to fix *that* problem. Crickets chirruped outside, the sound floating in on the breeze from the window Freya had left a crack open. She was just drifting off to sleep when she was awakened by the dull sound of flesh thumping flesh, quickly followed by a scream. She sat up with a start, heart pounding. Was it out on the street? A woman's voice rose hysterically. There was another thump, and the voice cut off, replaced by sobbing. The lower tones of a man's voice rumbled; the words unclear but the unpleasant sneer in his tone reaching Freya's ears. Someone must be having an argument. Should she call the police? What was going on out there? She padded over to the window and peered out. There was no-one visible. She shivered, not from any chill but from the fear of unseen violence. The man's voice abused the unseen crier, telling the woman to be quiet. Freya couldn't stand by and listen. She'd been attacked by were-foxes herself as a teenager - she'd often wished someone had intervened then. Helping the stranger outside felt like paying it forward. She pulled on a pair of trousers so as to appear at least semi-dressed, and hastened downstairs to the front door. She turned the door handle without result. It was locked. She shook it, uselessly.

A figure in flowing white appeared next to Freya. Freya swore inadvertently. Another silent mover; this town seemed to be full of them.

"Why are you trying to go out into the night?"

It was the woman who had checked Freya in, elegant despite the hour.

"It sounds like someone's being beaten up out there. Someone needs to stop it!" Freya was urgent, upset.

"It's not safe out at night."

"Well, obviously not. But someone has to do something."

"I will call the police. But usually in these cases, no-one is found when the police arrive."

"You mean it happens often?"

"I am afraid so. The world is a dangerous place." The woman drifted down the hall and picked up a telephone. Freya could just see it gleaming in the nightlights that decorated the stairs. It was an old-fashioned rarity, a land-line phone.

"Hurry, please," said Freya.

Someone evidently answered the phone then, for the woman introduced herself and described the situation. She put down the phone with a click after a few minutes.

"They will investigate. Hopefully within the next hour, they said."

"But that woman could be badly hurt. And she'll probably be gone in an hour."

The woman shrugged. "I've done what I can. Please, go back to bed before the other guests are disturbed."

Freya glared in frustration, unable to put words to her feelings. With no alternatives, she climbed back up the stairs - quietly. In her room she investigated the window. It was rather a high jump, but perhaps she could make it. She couldn't stand by while someone was being hurt, and the police clearly hadn't yet arrived. Freya opened the window as wide as it would go - and discovered that it wouldn't open wide enough to let her out. She was trapped inside. Her breath started to come quickly in her throat, her heart rate quickening. This was intolerable. Fingernails bit into her palms. She threw her head back to scream her frustration to the night. There was a flash of lightning, thunder boomed loud - and then there was a face at the window. A familiar face.

Freya shut her mouth with a snap. "Lio! What are you doing here? There? I mean, outside my window?"

Lio seemed to be clinging to the edge of the window frame.

"Give me a minute, this is harder than it looks," he said.

Freya could believe it - after all, he seemed to be hanging on by his fingertips, the tendons of his hands standing out as he clung on. Her rage of a moment before was forgotten in the astonishment of seeing Lio again.

"I'd help, but I can't get the window open," she blurted out.

"Can't you try something with the dried flower arrangement?"

Freya looked at Lio suspiciously.

"Are you making fun of me?"

"Not at all. It's got fennel and ivy. You've used those before. Bring them over and get singing!" Lio's voice was ragged, his fingertips, pressed on the sill were white. It didn't look like he'd be clinging on much longer. Did that matter, for a wind demi? He seemed to think so, at any rate. Freya hurried over to the bedside table, which was indeed adorned with a vase of dried flowers. She picked up the whole thing and raced back to the window, nearly tripping over her discarded clothes as she did so.

I wish I was better at being tidy, I bet other demigoddesses don't trip over their own belongings.

"OK, I have them. Now what?"

"Summon! Now, if you don't mind."

Freya wasn't sure what she'd be summoning on this hot, dry summer night, but she opened her mouth and sang anyway, holding out the dried flowers like a sacrifice.

A mist began to form in the room with her. It thickened quickly into a human-shaped blob. A husky, breathy voice whispered into the room.

"Who calls me and why?"

That's exactly what I imagined mist would sound like if it could talk. Freya supposed she had better respond to this unexpected presence.

"Me. I mean, I called you. I need you to help my friend outside the window."

"Now, please," urged Lio. "I'm slipping."

The mist flowed through the window. Freya peered down, and saw it slow and reform underneath Lio. It seemed to be solid, for his dangling feet were suddenly pressed against it.

"That's better, thank you," he said. "Now, how about opening the window while you're at it?"

Freya examined the window fittings. A security latch held the window so that it opened just a few centimetres.

"How do I get a mist goddess to open latches?" she asked, not expecting an answer from anyone.

"Ask her to rust them away," Lio replied promptly.

"Oh. I guess that makes sense."

She brandished the dried flowers again.

"Please rust the window latches," she commanded the mist.

"As you wish," the mist goddess whispered. The pillowlike cloud disappeared from beneath Lio's feet. He clutched the window frame again with an astonished cry.

"Hey! My hands really aren't made for this sort of thing," he gasped.

The mist paid Lio no attention – *how would a mist look if it was paying attention?* - but concentrated on the bolts securing the latches. Under Freya's impressed gaze, they became orange and started flaking away within seconds.

"Looks like I can try the window now," Freya advised Lio. "Hold on a bit longer." She rattled the window, and this time, the security latches gave way. Freya opened the window wide. The mist oozed back into the room. "Thank you," she said politely to it. She leaned out the window. "Are you coming in, then?" she asked Lio. He made a face at her.

"Yes. But I'd appreciate a bit of help."

"I thought I already got you help," she said, as she extended her hand to the struggling demi, who was trying to swing first one leg, then the next, onto the thin sill. He took her hand gratefully and heaved himself up, almost pulling Freya out before clambering the rest of the way into the room.

"Would you mind not summoning me to the outside of a locked window, next time?"

"I didn't realise I *did* summon you. Don't you usually just turn up?"

"Not in weather like this. It's much too calm. You definitely called me."

"That's odd. I was frustrated and I yelled - actually, I'm amazed no-one responded - but I didn't try to call you. I'd have used a phone for that. If I had your number. Er. Assuming you even have a phone. That reminds me. Did you notice a couple outside? I thought I heard someone being beaten up out there."

"And your altruistic instincts kicked in?"

"Something like that, yes. But it turns out this guest house is locked up at night, and I couldn't get out, and I kept hearing these awful sounds," Freya's voice rose and she talked faster, her voice ragged.

"Hey now, it's OK. We have a way out, now. And if it helps, I saw a police car arrive just now while I was hanging about outside your window."

"You didn't think to mention that?"

"I was otherwise concerned," said Lio. "I was afraid they'd try to pick me up as a burglar. Or more importantly, that I might fall."

"Oh yeah. Sorry."

Freya looked past Lio to the street. Opposite the guest house and a little further up the road, a uniformed officer and a large male figure were intermittently highlighted by red and blue lights, the man standing at a belligerent angle, fists clenched and chest jutting forward. There was no sign of anyone else.

"Well, that's something, I guess." Freya hoped the unknown woman had had a chance to get away from her attacker. "We should make sure the woman he was attacking is okay, though." She turned to the mist, which was beginning to dissipate. "Are you capable of checking on someone?"

There was nothing but silence and dampness from the mist.

"I guess that's a no, then. Any ideas, Lio?"

Lio shrugged.

"Not without a helpful storm to blow me around, sorry. But since you've managed to summon the old Brythonic goddess there, you could get her to let us out the front door. That way we can check on your possibly-attacked woman, and get back in here again too without further need for heroics on my part."

"Clinging on to a window while I summoned some mist was heroic, was it?"

"You better believe it. And like I said, that mist is probably all that remains of one of the ancient goddesses of these parts. Show some respect for the mist."

There was a twinkle in his eye as he said this, but Freya thought he was serious all the same. She looked at the mist.

"Is that what happens to old gods and goddesses? Really? Most of the ones I've seen have been quite intact."

"My guess is that no-one really knows about that one anymore."

"That's sad. At least she could help tonight." Freya turned to the wisps of mist that curled around her bed. "Alright, mist. Goddess. Whatevs. Thanks for your help tonight. Can you unlock a door downstairs?" Freya waved a hand in the general direction of the door. The mist obediently flowed towards that door. As mist went, it was the most helpful manifestation Freya had ever encountered. She looked at Lio. "Come on, then. You can tell me where you've been for the last three years once we're outside and won't disturb the other guests. Though given no-one came running - other than you - when I screamed, I guess they're not easily bothered."

That's rather concerning, really. Maybe this town is more dangerous than I realised.

Downstairs, the mist coagulated once again, this time in the region of the door handle. Freya was reminded of dry ice in school science experiments. This mist seemed much more versatile, however. After a few moments, the door handle dropped off with a thunk. Freya winced at the sound, but no-one appeared this time.

"That'll be hard to explain. I hate to damage this place, it's so well-looked after."

"Give me a few minutes with a screwdriver and I can probably fix it," suggested Lio.

"That'd be great if I had a screwdriver with me, but it's not a standard part of my sampling kit."

"You have a sampling kit?"

Freya wasn't sure if Lio was teasing her or not.

"Well, yes. I'm here for work. This" - she gestured around at the mist and the open door - "this is just a distraction. Thank you, Brythonic goddess. You may go," said Freya. She didn't have salt to hand to aid her in ending the summoning, so she had to hope that words alone would work. Then she remembered the dried flowers she still held. She waved them in what she hoped were suitably mystic patterns. The mist dissipated more slowly than it had arrived, but Freya was reluctant to step through it before it had gone. For one thing, anything that could dissolve metal so fast probably wasn't safe to walk through. For another, it seemed disrespectful. It took an unconscionably long time to disperse, though. Freya contained her impatience while she waited by shifting from foot to foot. This evolved into a few dance moves she'd learnt at a club while she was at university. *Five-six-seven-eight...* She stopped when she noticed Lio watching her with a slight smile on his face.

"What?"

"Nothing."

A few minutes later, the mist was gone. Freya put the vase of dried flowers down on the hall table. With the slight thunk as she set it down, the whole arrangement disintegrated into dust.

"Oops. I guess I won't be using that for summoning again. I hope the owner doesn't mind too much. Maybe I can collect some more flowers while we look around out there. Anything growing is probably dried already, it's been so hot."

She pushed the door, which swung open silently. *Thank goodness for houseproud guest-house owners. No creaky doors. She's really going to notice that dusty vase, though. Better move it when I get back. And find a screwdriver for the door.*

CHAPTER TWENTY-EIGHT

NIGHT SEARCH

Outside on the footpath, the evening was still; only the miniature suns of overhead streetlights lit the night now. The police car had gone.

"Just like old times, eh Freya?" suggested Lio.

Freya started walking in the direction she thought the fight had been in.

"Not quite. No-one's chasing *me*. And the weather's better."

Lio caught up with her after a step or two.

"Only if you like a drought. Just wait till the storms come, that'll be more my style."

"So long as I don't lose any more houses I can put up with it. But how come you're here now? There's no storm other than that lightning I saw just before you arrived."

Lio looked embarrassed, glancing away. In the low light, Freya couldn't tell if his skin was darkened by a blush, but she rather thought it was.

"Yeah. Sorry about that. I can't seem to get about without fanfare, these days."

"And I haven't seen you for years because...?" Freya let her voice trail off.

"You didn't call." They walked into a dark patch between the street lights.

"You never gave me a number."

"Not like that. I felt you call, tonight." Lio's face was visible again as they walked into the influence of the next streetlight. He was definitely flushed.

"That's odd. All I did was get really, really annoyed."

"Maybe nothing else has annoyed you that much in three years then," said Lio. "Although I guess I'd prefer it if you called me because you wanted to see me."

Freya was silent. She was sure she had had serious frustrations in all the last few years. After all, those had been the years that she was at university, sitting exams and the like. Frustration had been a big part of that. She'd never thought to call Lio, though.

"Tell you what, how about you get a phone, it's a much easier way to call people," she suggested at last.

"My living circumstances aren't favourable to phones. But I suppose I can try," Lio said.

They left the light and entered another dark patch. There was a small scuffling noise from behind a tall fence.

"What was that?"

A rustle of leaves, and a grey cat appeared out of the darkness. It looked at Freya with glowing yellow-green eyes, and started to purr.

"Oh, puss. You startled me," she said to it. She crouched down and held out her hand, and the cat delicately sniffed it before rubbing its cheek against her. "I miss my cat already."

"Why isn't he here with you?"

"He's getting old. He doesn't travel as well as he used to. So, I asked a friend to feed him while I'm away. Besides, it's hard to find a bed and breakfast that takes cats."

"It would be good to see him again. We were close, you know."

Was that a wink Lio gave her? They'd only ever been friends. Was he hinting for something more?

"Perhaps you should come visit then. Let's concentrate on looking for the woman I heard." Freya gave the cat a final pat and rose to her feet again. "Let's go."

A long, fruitless search through empty darkened streets followed. From time to time Freya plucked flowers from weeds standing tall in abandoned lots.

Weeds seem to be the only thing that's enjoying this heat.

Eventually, Freya had to admit that there didn't seem much chance of finding the woman.

"Perhaps she's found somewhere safe," said Lio.

"I hope so. I just didn't want to leave someone else in the same situation as me."

Lio took her hand and squeezed it. "You know if that ever happens again, you can call me. But I hope it doesn't for your sake."

Freya could only nod, mutely. Hearing someone else being hurt had roused terrifying memories that she'd rather forget. She squeezed his hand in return, and changed the subject.

"I better get some sleep. I have to go collect samples in the morning."

"You mentioned a sampling kit. Is that what you're doing here? Sampling what?"

"Yes, I'm looking for a disease. A plant disease that could wipe out agriculture in this area."

"I guess I'd better let you go sleep then. If that's what you really want." He gave her a wicked grin.

Yes, definitely he's suggesting something. But tonight is not the night to follow up on that, even if I want to. I have Stefan, now. It wouldn't be right to accept Lio's advances, would it? Strange how attractive the idea was, though. She realised suddenly that she'd left her hand in Lio's. But she was distracted by a noise in the bushes again. She looked around, and realised that they were back in the area where they'd met the grey cat. Was it the cat again, or had that rustle indicated something larger? She hardly had time to wonder when the bushes parted, and a woman stepped out. Her face bore an enigmatic expression as she looked from Freya, to Lio and back again.

"I hear you were looking for someone," she said. Her voice was pitched low, as though she were afraid of being overheard.

Peering at the woman in the dim streetlight, Freya thought she could see bruises on the woman's face.

"Yes. I heard someone being attacked, earlier. I wanted to see if they were alright."

The woman blinked slowly, reminding Freya of a cat. "Are any of us alright, really?" she asked reflectively.

What do I say to that?

"Well, some of us feel OK from time to time, so I've heard," Freya ventured. "But are *you* alright? I mean, are you safe? There's no-one else about."

"When you live in the shadows, you know better than to assume that empty streets mean no-one is near."

Freya shivered, the woman's words taking her back to her first encounter with were-foxes. But that was years ago, and miles away too. This town should be safe enough, surely. She noticed the woman had her hands held to her stomach. A well-rounded stomach. That wasn't fat, either, Freya realised. The woman was pregnant.

"Is there anything we can do for you? I'm a stranger here, but I'm sure I could help if you need a doctor or something."

"No doctor." The woman laughed hollowly. "But I heard you talking to him." She pointed her chin at Lio, not moving her hands. "Have you got somewhere I can stay the night?"

Freya thought of her rented room, the broken front door and window hinges rusted away.

"Er, sort of?"

"Don't worry, I don't take up much space." The woman glanced at Lio again, and seemed to come to a decision. "No-one will even notice me." The streetlight seemed to dim for a moment, and the woman's features blurred. A minute later, Freya was looking down at a small grey cat with a very rounded belly.

"Not another were," groaned Freya.

The cat turned her back and sat down, twitching her tail irritably.

"Oh, sorry. I didn't mean to offend you. It's just - well. History, I guess. Water under the bridge." Freya told herself she had to move on from her fear of weres. After all, this cat appeared to be no threat, and she certainly wasn't a were-fox. Hadn't she just been saying how much she wanted to help whoever had been hurt?

It's easy to think I shouldn't be scared. Harder to action. "I guess it will be easier to sneak you in like that, anyway. I'm only here for a night though. So, you see I haven't got anywhere permanent to offer you," Freya over-explained.

The cat turned around and rubbed against Freya's leg.

"I guess that means you're OK with just a night's rest then."

The cat started to purr.

"Just as well I'm used to cats," muttered Freya. She raised her voice a little. "Lio, looks like we found who we were looking for after all. Time to head back to my place, I guess."

It was probably just Freya's imagination that Lio looked disappointed to have more company.

Freya pushed open the damaged door to her guest house, and the grey cat trotted in without looking back. *I guess she knows where she's going, then. Or maybe it's just cat confidence.*

"Have *you* got somewhere to sleep?" Freya asked Lio.

"I always find somewhere. Life's full of adventures."

Freya thought he sounded a little wistful. It seemed a shame to turn out Lio after she'd just met him again.

"So long as you like adventures." She paused with her hand on the door and turned to Lio, who was standing patiently on the step. "Oh, I forgot to say! I met Nik on my way down here. Did you know she's been living in London?"

"*Now* you decide to fill me in on the news?"

"Well, we've been busy..."

"True enough. For your information, I haven't been in touch with Nik for a long time. She left the coast about the same time you did. Was she well?"

"Hard to say. She was in a train station. It didn't seem to be her natural setting."

"No, I can imagine her being pretty fed up having so many people around her."

"She was."

"Well, give her my regards if you see her again. I always prefer to keep on Nik's good side."

Freya smiled. She could imagine that it was wisest to do that - before the train station, the last time she'd seen Nik, the blue-haired girl had been hunting down were-foxes as though they were cockroaches.

"Is she really a harpie, then?"

"She made me swear never to say one way or another." Lio smiled ruefully. "I keep my promises to her. It's more than my life is worth, not to."

"Oh well. No mysteries solved tonight, it seems." Freya hesitated. "Would you like to join the pyjama party in my room, tonight? I think there's enough blankets to share out, though there won't be much space."

"I would be honoured. And perhaps that will give me time to locate a screwdriver."

"That's the best thing I've heard all night. I've been feeling bad about all the damage we've caused."

Freya pushed the door closed and tried to fit the door handle back on. The handle itself appeared undamaged, but she couldn't make it stay. Eventually she bolted the door closed with the chainlock and bolt combination at the top of the door, leaving the handle on the floor. Frigg knew what her landlady would think. Maybe Lio would be able to find that screwdriver.

Upstairs, Freya found the grey were-cat sitting in the hall, waiting for them. She led the way to her room. It was going to be cramped with three people in it, but she could hardly turn out either of her guests. She took the top blanket off her bed and offered it to Lio.

"Lucky it's a warm night," he commented as he spread it out on the dark grey carpeted floor.

"Lucky you're being a gentleman." She smiled.

"Always."

The cat ignored their exchange and leapt up onto the bed. She turned in a tight circle, treadled the remaining covers for a moment, then curled up into a tight ball. Looking at the little remaining space, Freya wondered where she was supposed to sleep now. Oh well, she'd paid for the bed. Or at least, she had paid and work would be paying her back. She should try to sleep in it. She turned back to Lio.

"Don't be a stranger. It's been too long."

"Since you have called me, I hope to see you more often," said Lio, standing close.

Funny, Lio standing so near doesn't feel like an invasion of my space. Maybe it's just that I've known him so long.

"That would be nice. Goodnight, Lio."

Lio lifted a hand and stroked her hair, a curiously intimate, yet nonthreatening gesture. Freya caught his hand, but released it without comment. She wasn't yet sure what she wanted from Lio. Nothing she wanted to share in front of an unknown were-cat, anyway.

"Goodnight, Freya."

CHAPTER TWENTY-NINE

BREAKFAST KEBAB

It was hard for Freya to wake up next morning. She'd tossed and turned for what felt like hours, aware of Lio's presence nearby but not sure what to do about it. The grey cat taking up the centre of her bed didn't help. She finally awoke when her phone alarm reached such a high level of warning that it buzzed itself off the bedside table and thumped onto the floor. Freya sat up with a start. She checked the time.

"Frigg. I've missed breakfast." She'd been looking forward to that breakfast.

Remembering the events of the previous night, she looked around. Her heart sank a little as she realised that there was no sign of Lio. His blanket was neatly folded on the antique-looking chair in the corner of the room. Freya stumbled over to the window. New bolts gleamed at its side. Over on the table, the flowers she and Lio had collected as they walked the night-time streets were arranged in the original vase. Several petals were left on the table. Freya peered at them. They were arranged into words: *See you soon.* Lio had clearly awoken earlier and been busy.

I wonder if he managed to fix the front door, too? She wished he'd woken her up before leaving, though. She'd only just begin to think about the possibilities of his return, and who knew when she'd get to see him again? Freya threw herself into the shower trying to wash away uncomfortable thoughts. Four minutes later, she was awake enough to get into some clothes. She got changed in the bathroom, feeling uncomfortable about changing in front of an unknown were.

Thank goodness for ensuite bathrooms.

She picked up her sampling bag, and debated the rest of her gear. Maybe it was better to leave it here. It was hard enough carrying the sampling kit and her bag. She packed everything up and put it by the door. The cat was still asleep on the bed, a paw over her face. What should she do about that? She stroked the cat's head, then pulled her hand back.

This is a bit weird. If it was a normal cat I wouldn't think twice, but I'm stroking the head of a stranger. Who slept on my bed. There's something wrong with this picture.

"Excuse me. Puss. Whatever your name is. Do you want to leave now?"

The cat opened one eye, and stretched luxuriously. Her teeth showed as she yawned. Then she crawled under the still-rumpled bedclothes. The small lump seemed to expand, until a human-sized shape filled the bed. The woman's smudged face poked out from under the covers. She yawned, almost as widely as she had done as a cat, then, clutching the bedclothes to her.

"Is there breakfast?"

"What? No. Breakfast is over, and I missed it and I'm already late for work. I can't help with breakfast." The bruises on the woman's face were making her feel bad about not offering more help. "Er. Sorry. I can give you a flapjack."

The woman's face fell. She was clearly not a flapjack fan. Freya hurried on.

"Look, I have to go to work, and it would look bad if you're found in here. Have you got anywhere to go?"

"Not really. I haven't quite figured out what to do yet."

"Well, where would you usually go? Have you got somewhere safe?

The woman's lower lip began to tremble.

I have no idea what I would do with a crying stranger. Though she looks like she's got reason enough to cry if she wants.

To Freya's relief, the emotions the woman was expressing didn't proceed as far as actual crying. Perhaps that was part of being a were-cat. Most cats didn't like to admit emotion.

"I moved here with my boyfriend. I don't know anyone else."

"Well, I know exactly no-one here. So, I suppose you're one up on me there." Freya hesitated. *How do I ask this?* "Er. Did your boyfriend -" she waved a hand at the bruises decorating the woman's face.

The response was so quiet that Freya barely heard it.

"Yes. But he loves me, I know he does. He just had a bit much to drink. After I turned cat and he saw me turn."

Unexpectedly, Freya felt an enormous swelling of outrage that she didn't know how to deal with. It exploded into words.

"It doesn't matter if he was drunk, no-one should treat you like that. It sure doesn't look like a sign of love. And there's nothing wrong with being a cat. Is he a pure human? Was it his first inkling that you are, well, a cat, too?"

Funny, I never thought I'd be defending any sort of were from a pure human's actions.

The woman cringed away from Freya. Freya immediately felt terrible.

"I didn't mean for him to see me. And I don't think he's pure human, but he's never shown any signs of anything else," said the were-cat.

"Oh, don't cringe like that. I'm not angry at you, just at the way you've been treated. Look. I have to get to work. Er. How about a safe house? If I found one, would you go to one? At least until, afterwards?" Freya nodded at the woman's swollen belly.

The were-cat looked away and down.

"This baby is why he's so angry with me. He didn't want a family. I couldn't help getting pregnant, either. You know what happens with cats and sex, right?"

"What? Oh." A memory from one of her rare non-plant-based university classes popped into her head. Cats had almost guaranteed pregnancy. She hadn't known it applied to were-cats as well to actual cats. Of course, this was the first time she'd met a were-cat. *Let's face it, it's not something I wanted to know.* "In that case, you should definitely stay away. Hold on. I'll just do a quick search." Freya found her phone, still plugged in by the wall despite its abrupt relocation to the floor. A search showed that there was a safe house in the area, but its location was a closely guarded secret. She supposed that was reasonable - a safe house might not be very safe if it was easily found by Internet search.

"Here. Use my phone, call this number. Then I'll get you a taxi to wherever it is, okay?"

"I guess I can do that."

"You can. Here."

Freya handed over her phone, and took a discreet trip to the bathroom to give the woman more privacy to make the call. When she emerged a few minutes later, the woman seemed to be regaining her confidence.

"They said there's a place for me. I'd like to go, I think."

"Great. I'll call a taxi. You can give them the address."

She placed the call and ushered the woman downstairs. Fortunately, no-one else seemed to be about. Freya noticed in passing that the door was unlocked, and it seemed to be fully functional. *Thank you, Lio.*

Freya waved as the woman climbed into the taxi.

"Good luck Puss!" she called. *I never even asked her name. Oops.*

Freya hastened back upstairs to get her sampling kit. She clattered down the stairs again and out the door and was outside only a few minutes later than she'd originally planned to leave. Just before her own taxi arrived, she remembered her half-eaten falafel kebab, digging it out from underneath the wallet, jacket, secateurs and other useful things she'd unthinkingly piled on top of it. She felt a pang of guilt that she hadn't found it earlier, to offer to the cat-woman. Still, who would want to share a half-eaten old kebab? She took a large bite, and hoped the taxi driver wouldn't mind her chewing. *Better a stale kebab than nothing. I just hope I don't get food poisoning.*

CHAPTER THIRTY

THE OLIVE GROVE

After a longish drive, the taxi she'd taken dropped her off at the gate to the olive grove she'd come to sample. It was just the sort of place Freya had always imagined her Dad would like. The trees laid out in rows down a gentle hillside; a formal stone gate marking the start of a metalled drive which curved off into the middle distance; grapevines grew in tidy lines on the more distant hills. Their leaves were lush and green; clearly some irrigation had been going on here. The olives Freya could see looked healthy, too. Of course, coping with hot, dry conditions was what olives were good at. She walked down the drive, sampling kit banging against her, wishing she'd thought to ask the taxi to drive her further in. Lavender bushes grew along the edges, purple flowers releasing their soporific scent into the warming air. Bees covered every bush.

The honey from here must taste good.

One last turn of the drive brought her in sight of an unassuming stone house with a large barn beside it. A middle aged woman in overalls came out of the barn as Freya arrived. The tail of a grey cat disappeared around the corner of the barn.

That cat is the same colour as last nights were-cat. How odd.

The overalled woman called out to Freya.

"Hello. Are you the disease expert?"

That brought Freya up short for a moment. She hadn't really thought of herself as an expert in anything. She abruptly felt like an impostor.

"I guess so," she said. "I've come from the plant health lab."

"Oh, good. I'll take you to the affected block right off. You can't think how worried we are. I'm Min, by the way." The woman belatedly offered her hand to Freya, who shook it uncertainly. She wasn't used to being treated like a business person - the only type of person Freya usually associated with hand-shakes. Most people stuck to nods.

"As in Minnie mouse, or as in Minerva the olive goddess of wisdom?" Freya couldn't help but ask.

The woman looked sideways at Freya, dimples appearing in one cheek as she smiled. Freya noticed she had smile lines around her eyes, too. A cheerful person, then. Freya liked the look of her.

"I think you're the first person ever to ask me about the mouse. What with the olive grove and suchlike, most people go straight for the goddess." Min led the way down a farm lane surrounded by mature trees.

Freya blushed.

"Sorry. Usually I would, too. But I watched a lot of free retro TV growing up," she said. "And I'm a bit short on sleep."

"I saw a few of those shows too. But I prefer the goddess as a namesake."

"Who wouldn't?" Freya wondered if this woman was an eponymous demi, like herself. It wouldn't do to ask outright though. She'd have to watch for clues.

"In any case, here we are," said Min, sweeping her hand in front of her to indicate the section of trees Freya had come to see.

Several trees on the edge of the grove were brown and desiccated, very unlike the glossy leaves and large bunches of fruit that had adorned the many trees they had already passed. Someone had put yellow plastic tape around the area, making it look like a crime scene. Perhaps it was, in a way. The disease had to have got here somehow. Freya set down her sampling kit, grateful not to have to lug it any further. She donned the protective shoe covers and lab coat she'd brought with her. She wouldn't have to be too much of an expert, it appeared. Anyone could see something was wrong with the trees here. The area felt like something malignant had appeared in paradise.

"This doesn't look good. How long have the trees been like this?"

"It started perhaps a month ago. At first we thought it was simply some storm damage. But then it got worse, and started to spread." Min shrugged. "We thought we should report it, because nothing we've tried has worked so far."

"Alright. Tell me what you've tried, and I'll take some samples."

The conversation quickly became technical as Min detailed what treatments she'd attempted on the trees. Freya snipped samples from the obviously affected trees, using a ladder to reach the higher branches. She bagged and labelled each sample, shaking each one to remove any insects before stowing it away in her chilled sampling box. At last, she'd finished. It had taken hours, and the sun was westering. Freya wished she could take off some of her protective gear. She was getting a headache.

"Alright, now I've done those trees, I'll need to sample the surrounding area, to see if it's gone any further."

"But surely we'd notice if it had spread out of the olives," protested Min.

"Perhaps, but my job is to make sure. Besides, I'd hate to have to travel back all this way because I'd missed something simple. Not that it isn't nice here, of course." Freya's lack of sleep was taking its toll. A more substantial breakfast would probably have helped, too. So would lunch. She wasn't sure she'd manage basic human politeness much longer. "Besides, you've got these lavender hedges. They're a potential host too, you know."

Min paled.

"Not the lavender. My grandmother planted that. It's - it's *heritage*."

"I'm sorry. Hopefully it will be OK, but I have to check." Freya did so, sampling lavender and apparently healthy olives in a wide ring around the diseased trees, cleaning her secateurs between each sample. The malignancy felt like a throbbing miasma on the edge of her senses. There were threads of it extending beyond the clearly diseased trees in all directions, but one direction tugged at Freya.

"Right, we're done. Although - do you have any plums trees, or cherries, on the property?"

"Yes, we have several in the home orchard. Why?"

"Regulations say I should sample them, too. Just in case." *Regulations sounds much more official than 'I have this bad feeling'.*

Min sighed, apparently not thinking much of regulations.

"Come on, then. This way."

Freya followed the olive lady past the barn and into a small fruit orchard close to the house. She sampled the fruit trees as she had the olives. The bad feeling she'd had earlier didn't have any directionality now. How had this plant disease got here? And was it more than just a mundane disease?

Min was hanging back by the door to the house.

"Is that all you need to do?"

"For now, yes. I'll take the lot back to the lab, and spend the next week working on it. My boss will be in touch if there's any urgent action to be taken." Freya's manager had been very clear that she wasn't to deliver any bad news about the disease identity in person. Apparently that was always done by email, 'to avoid unfortunate consequences', whatever that meant. Freya was glad she didn't have to deliver bad news in any case. She rather liked Min, who clearly loved her trees. Freya didn't want to be the one to tell her she'd likely have to burn them, and apply toxic chemicals to the plants that remained.

Will that work, though? This feels like more than just a disease.

"Would you like a cuppa before you go?" asked Min, unaware of Freya's gloomy thoughts.

"Would I ever. Thanks." Freya couldn't resist the offer, despite her bad feeling.

They sat in the orchard, on a set of white painted wrought iron chairs that had seen better days but offered irresistible comfort to Freya's weary feet. She sipped her tea with relief, feeling her headache ease.

"It's a lovely place, here," she offered conventionally.

"Yes. It's been in my family for generations, but the olives were planted just before I was born. I think that's why they gave me the name, actually. Though my mother always talked about it being a family name. She came from Italy, so I suppose it could have been. She was the one who actually planted most of these olives. People said she was crazy to plant olives in England, but now look at them!"

Freya smiled.

"She obviously knew what was coming."

"She did. I just wish she'd lived to see it thriving. Because it has, until now."

"So, what do you do with the olives from your farm?"

Min sat forward, enthusiasm informing every line of her body.

"Well, the leccino and frantoio varietals we press for oil. We've got manzanilla growing well now, I pickle those and take them to farmers markets. And we've a few maurino which I think are going to be great growers in the next couple of years."

Freya blinked in the face of this outwelling of information and tried to look knowledgeable. Olives were nice enough trees, but she didn't have the in-depth knowledge of them that Min clearly enjoyed.

"You really like your job, then?"

"It's perfect for me. Apart from having to worry about the weather. And..." her face clouded again, "diseases. Which of course is what brings you here."

Freya didn't want to get into details of diseases, either, even though it was her job.

"Weather's always a problem," she agreed. "At least you're inland enough that you shouldn't have problems with the rising sea levels."

"There's that," said Min, "but the storms do still blow in every year, and the less well-rooted trees come down. I've started pruning our trees shorter, so they're not such big wind-traps."

"That seems a shame, they're magnificent trees when they're big."

"Yes, but shorter is better for harvest, too. It's not all bad."

They sat in silence for a while. Freya was wondering if Lio ever visited this out-of-the-way olive grove when storms came through. Her thoughts moved on to Stefan; it seemed a natural segue. Both men were attractive, but each one had a very different energy. She wondered idly what Stephan would think of her impromptu mist-summoning. She suspected it wasn't his style. What would he have done, if he'd heard worrying sounds in the night? *I wonder if Min was alone on this farm.* She'd said 'we', though.

"Are you-"

Both women had started to speak at once.

"You first," Freya smiled.

"Sorry. I was just going to ask. Er. Well, there's no easy way to say this. Are you a demi, by any chance?"

Freya's tongue seemed to stick to the roof of her mouth. How had Min known? Why was she asking?

"Is it so obvious?" she asked, unsticking her tongue at last.

"I am sorry, I didn't mean to scare you - you're as white as a sheet. It's simply - well. I don't see many around, and something told me you might be one. As am I, of course."

The admission reassured Freya a little.

"I don't believe this. Do you know, I spent my entire childhood being told not to show that I was a demi in any way. And you're the second person in a month to out me. What am I doing wrong?"

Freya's voice expressed her frustration.

"Sorry, I didn't mean to upset you. I just thought it was nice to meet another one. You've a sort of glow to you, that's all. A quality of being? I don't really know how to describe it."

"Do you know how many hours of after school training my Mum put me through so I could identify demis? And you just look and can see."

"Well, yes. Sorry."

"There is no doubt about it, I got short-shrifted in the demi power stakes."

"At least you *are* a demi. I've got cousins on my father's side who are pure humans, and they don't even know what they're missing. No gods, no goddesses, no putting your hand on a plant and feeling its life force. It must be a much more dreary way to live. Here, have another cup of tea, you look like you need it," said Min.

"Thanks. But I don't feel that life-force of the plants thing, either. That's why I got into plant diseases, because I can't grow them myself. My heritage as a fertility goddess is worthless."

"Are you sure? You seem to know exactly which plants are ailing."

Freya considered for a while.

"I guess I hadn't thought of it like that. Perhaps you're right. I'll have to put the idea to the test."

"Spoken like a true scientist,' laughed Min.

Freya grinned back.

"Well, I have had years of training, after all." Freya was beginning to relax into the idea of being known as a demi, at least to this other, friendly-seeming demi. "I guess you are a plant-growth specialist, then, working with olives and the like?"

"Yes. That's partly why I love this lifestyle so much. It lets me do what I do best without questions. And being here gives me the opportunity to help others out from time to time, also."

"My Mum would have loved it here. She's a plant demi too. She can grow a summer's worth of produce in a month, so long as she's settled. But we never were settled, growing up, so I didn't really realise that at first. Maybe she didn't either. We might have been better fed otherwise." Freya frowned. "I wonder why we never did head this way? My Dad was a wine-seller, I always thought the South would be more his style. Maybe that's why he left." She looked up at Min. "Sorry, I don't mean to burden you with my family history."

"That's no trouble. Families can be tough, I hear."

"Do you have one, or is it just you on this farm?"

"Oh, it's me and my husband. The plan was to have children to pass the farm on to, but that hasn't worked out. We take in a few extras from time to time, to make up for that." Min was gazing out over the orchard, her eyes focused on something unseen. The corners of her mouth were turned down.

"I'm sorry." Freya didn't want to intrude on this private grief, but once again she felt like her heritage was worthless - surely a decent fertility demigoddess should be able to help with what was probably a fertility problem?

Min shook her head.

"Not your problem. I should have known better than to marry a half-elf. There were bound to be issues, I just hadn't thought of species incompatibility."

Freya's mouth opened in astonishment. She hadn't realised half-elves existed. She looked around, half-expecting to see an elf crouching in one of the trees. Min's eye's twinkled as Freya tried to look around for the half-elf without seeming obvious.

"He's off getting seedlings just now," Min explained. "He has a better eye for them than me."

Freya looked at her empty cup in embarrassment. But she couldn't help asking.

"What's the other half, then?"

"Dryad. So, he's not human at all, really. But I love him, so I just have to work with all that goes with that. And he's great with trees, of course," Min added.

"Well, in that case, I truly hope that the disease that has struck your trees can be successfully contained. As a plant demi and a half-dryad, you must both be very attached to this place." Freya had never met a dryad. Since Min's husband was not in sight, it didn't look like she was going to meet one today, either. And although replanting large areas of land to mitigate climate change was beginning to happen, she hadn't seen any of the new forests, which were probably the only other places likely to contain a dryad these days.

"Yes," said Min. "This place holds our hearts." She rose. "Thank you for your visit today. Tell your mother she's welcome to come visiting, if she wants to meet another demi in the same field. And I hope we find out what disease we've got soon."

Freya drank the last of her tea, and stood up.

"I'll pass on your invitation. Thanks. And... maybe you could consider some insect control. Just while you're waiting for the results. My boss will get back to you with our findings." There, she hadn't given away the problem, so she was following her boss's orders, but she had given Min information that might help her keep at least some of this magnificent grove alive. If only she didn't feel that more than just science was needed here. She didn't want to see a fellow demi lose everything. Freya picked up her sampling kit, now heavy with samples. It was time to head north and see exactly what she had. And also, to test what she had learnt from Min. Perhaps she did have some other demi power to develop after all. Freya was on her way out of the farmhouse when she noticed the small, round-stomached grey cat watching her from on top of a chair. *"Puss?* I guess you did find a safe house. Well done. Though it seems we could have shared a taxi."* The cat didn't move, but broke into purrs. Freya waved at her as she left. *I still don't know her name. But at least she's fallen on her feet. Typical cat.*

CHAPTER THIRTY-ONE

TESTING MAGICAL THEORIES

Walking back up the long, tree-lined gravel driveway, Freya hesitated as she spotted one of the diseased trees. *Maybe I should try out Min's ideas about power now. Just in case.* She wasn't quite sure how to go about such a thing, though - the only way she'd accessed power in the past was by summoning water-deities with song. *I guess I try that again. Without reaching out for a naiad.*

Staring fixedly at the brittle, browning leaves of the afflicted olive tree, Freya hummed under her breath, an old song about the tree of life with roots that anchored the world. It seemed appropriate, somehow. Something teased at the edge of her senses. She found herself focusing less on the tree itself, and more on her general surroundings. There was something about the heat that was more than simply an unfortunate weather pattern. She shook her head impatiently. She wasn't trying to sort out the drought problem - that was almost certainly due to the continued effects of climate change, though she supposed it was possible that a major god or goddess had got involved too. Either way, she was looking for a more localised problem. She didn't have the knowledge or power to solve the world's biggest problem.

She forced her attention back to the tree. There *was* something there. A blockage, the tree seeming healthy enough below it, but dry and dying above. It felt somehow malignant, not simply a disease but a wilful application of evil.

I'm being melodramatic. But it does look like someone's applied something nasty and non-mundane. If she squinted hard enough, it looked like a grey smudge travelling along the trunk and up the branches. Almost like a braided stream...

It looks like water. Can I control it like water? Freya looked around for something to fashion into a thyrsis - a Dionysian wand, to help her harness the heritage she had from her father. The grass around the olives was grazed short, but there were some longer patches around the lavender bushes that dotted the driveway.

Rustling along the verges of the drive, she found an assortment of plants to suit her purpose - some trailing ivy, a stalk of fennel, some very late cowslips. *I bet this isn't what Mum thought I'd do with all that botanical knowledge she stuffed into us as kids. It's not what I thought I'd do, either.*

Freya wove her finds together, and turned back to the afflicted tree, humming her song again. She tried waving her thyrsis at the tree, but nothing seemed to happen. Hmm. Maybe she needed a different song? No, surely the world-tree song was the best one for an ailing tree. Thinking back to the early summoning lessons she'd received from her sister, Freya realised she had neglected to draw a circle before starting. Picking a stick from the lavender - no point in stressing the olive tree further by selecting a stick from there - she paced out a circle around the tree, trailing the stick through the short, daisy-studded grass. Raising her thyrsis, she tried singing again. This time, she saw a green glow arising from the base of the tree. *That's right, keep the water flowing. It's just like a river that's been blocked.* Freya mentally encouraged the tree's internal waterworks to break through the twinned bacterial and supernatural barrier. For a moment, she thought the sap would simply ooze out of the trunk, so great was the pressure built up below the closed vessels that should carry the tree's lifeblood. But with a sudden spurt, the sap broke through in her mind's eye, flooding the dry riverbeds of the tree's arterial vessels. *That's it, keep going. Get rid of that grey gunk.* She paced around the tree, chanting at it. *I must look a right plonker doing this. But I'm sure it's working.* A few repetitions of song later, she was as certain as she could be that the tree was free of disease. Already, the drooping leaves seemed to be standing straighter, their access to water restored. It seemed there was something to Min's idea that Freya could apply her power to plants. She couldn't make them grow, but perhaps she could stop them from dying. Freya punched the sky, standing by the olive tree all by herself. *I can do something useful with the non-mundane, after all.* Then she took a sample from the tree she'd just treated. Just in case.

The malignant feeling had dropped away from the tree she had treated. Maybe there was hope for this olive orchard after all.

So long as I can figure out where the disease came from, of course. Otherwise, someone's just going to bring it in again. But who would do that to someone as nice as Min?

Freya looked around. There were more drooping trees in this grove. Perhaps she should practise her newfound skill some more.

She did a small circuit of the grove, trailing her stick in the grass. Then grasping her thyrsis, she raised it high and began to repeat her song. Just as before she pictured the riverlike structures within the trees, dammed here and there by the disease. She paused under one particularly bushy olive and closed her eyes, the better to picture dams breaking. In her mind, the rivers of sap grew stronger and stronger, until with a gush that she could almost hear, they broke through the diseased barriers. There was a drip on her head. Then several more. She opened her eyes and looked up. The olive tree she stood under was weeping sap from every leaf.

Oh. Perhaps I overdid it. It seemed there was more control required to master this new skill than she had thought.

A movement in the tree caught her eye. To her astonishment, large green eyes were glaring down at her. The owner of the eyes detached himself from the upper branches, where he had been lying, and climbed stiffly down. His skin was golden-brown and slightly wrinkled about the corners of the eyes, his hair silver-gold like the back of an olive leaf. His fingers were long, thin, and brown. They were also dripping clear fluid that could be sap.

This must be Min's half-elf, half Dryad husband! Freya found herself backing up. "Oh. Er. Sorry. Is this your grove?" she babbled.

The half elf nodded regally. "It is. And I thank you for your efforts. Though you could perhaps restrain yourself to disease control next time."

Freya's face was drenched with sudden, embarrassed heat. "I didn't realise there was anyone else here. Sorry. Er. I hope you're alright?"

The half-elf looked ruefully at his dripping hands. "Fortunately, I am not all dryad, so yes, I will be alright. And so will these trees, which admittedly is a better state than they would otherwise have been in." He looked up at her, sharply. "Which is not to say I wish to experience that again. Please, practise elsewhere." He sighed. "Unless of course we have more visits from those accursed were-wolves. In that case I will invite you back to clear our groves again."

Freya's head was reeling, but she latched on to this point. "So, you know who brought the disease in?"

"I suspect, that is all. There is an unholy alliance of sorts between some demis and were-wolves." He looked sideways at her suddenly. "You don't seem the type to be associated with them. But perhaps I should keep my suppositions to myself."

Freya looked wide-eyed at him. "I'm not part of any alliance," she protested. "Especially not one that spreads disease. That's criminal!"

He shrugged. "No doubt. In any case, thank you again. You'd best be on your way. There's no need to get further involved."

Feeling thoroughly dismissed, but burdened with more mysteries than ever, Freya picked up her sampling kit and bag. As she left the grove, she plucked a single twig from one of the trees she'd cured.

I wonder what it looks like inside?

CHAPTER THIRTY-TWO

FREYA GOES BACK TO YORK

"Please accept our apologies for the continued delay to this service to London, Waterloo," repeated the saccharine voice of the train's announcer. It was at least the third such announcement. This time, however, the announcer added more information. "We are currently experiencing delays due to warping of the rails. The train is operating at a reduced speed for safety."

Not again. Freya groaned. There was no chance she would make her connecting train north now. She turned to look outside and banged her forehead against the glass.

Ow.

When she'd recovered from her self-inflicted injury, Freya resumed gazing at the scenery out the window, which was passing by considerably slower than usual. Unfortunately, there wasn't much to see other than dry fields, devoid of interesting vegetation, unless the viewer was exceptionally keen on oilseed rape. Her eyes soon glazed over with boredom despite the bright yellow expanses the flowering plants created.

She found herself dwelling on Min's husband's words. What had he meant about an alliance of demi-gods and were-wolves? She found herself thinking uneasily of Stefan. But he didn't seem to like were-wolves at all. Surely he couldn't be involved with any such grouping. And she couldn't imagine why anyone would want to kill off trees that were a source of food. She shook her head in confusion and resumed staring out the window.

The interior of the train wasn't air-conditioned and the temperature inside was getting unpleasantly hot. Freya once again considered whether it was worth visiting the train's small shop for a cool drink. Earlier, she'd decided against it, not wanting to leave her samples unattended.

Yes, this time I will, she decided. *It's not like there's a stop anytime soon. And no-one's likely to want withered bits of plants, anyway.*

She stood up and lurched unsteadily for a few steps before gaining her train legs, grabbing randomly spaced poles and the backs of seats to steady herself. The shop, when she reached it, was a disappointment. A few flapjacks of the sort that she'd subsisted on as a child adorned the clear plastic shelves. A solitary can of fizzy drink stood above them.

"Can I have that one, please?" Freya asked the shop attendant politely.

"No. That's display only, see." The woman behind the small counter turned the can so that Freya could see the small handwritten label on it. *Sample only.*

"Oh. But are there any more?"

"That's the last one, sorry." The woman's tone was anything but sorry. Freya found herself wondering if this woman was part troll. Or maybe goblin, like those maintenance workers she had seen on her last train trip. Something grumpy, certainly.

I hope those rails have been replaced.

"How about a bottle of water?" she asked. Freya's own water bottle was already empty.

"The last one sold half an hour ago, sorry." The smirk on the woman's face suggested she was not sorry at all.

"Tea?"

"We're all out."

"Anything liquid at all?"

"Not till we restock in London."

"Oh."

Freya wandered disconsolately back to her seat. London was a long way away. She felt even thirstier now she knew she couldn't get a drink.

No wonder we can't get imported spices anymore, if I can't even take a train journey across the country without encountering delays in both directions and running out of water.

She looked out the window again. As she did so, the scenery stopped moving entirely, juddering enough to make Freya grab wildly for her seat. The train had stopped.

What now?

The train driver's voice helpfully crackled to life at that moment, but he sounded stressed.

"Please accept our apologies for the further delay to this train. We are awaiting the replacement of a section of track between here and Swindon. Please remain in your seats as we may restart our journey at any time."

Freya groaned aloud. Those goblins *had* removed vital track, after all. At least her train had been going slow enough to stop before reaching the missing section. But how much time would this further delay add to her journey?

After they'd remained stationary for a good hour, during which time Freya's tongue began to stick to the roof of her mouth with thirst, a worrying thought struck her.

I hope the samples don't overheat. They're supposed to be kept chilled. I wasn't counting on this much delay en route.

Half the experiments she was supposed to run on those samples wouldn't work if they warmed up.

She felt the outside of the sample bag. It was covered with condensation and her hand came away wet. The samples inside would be heating up. She considered the moisture droplets on her hand.

I suppose I could lick my sample bag if I get really thirsty. And don't mind picking up half a dozen bacterial infections.

Probably not an option, she decided with regret. She wasn't *that* thirsty. Yet. But meanwhile, she had a problem. If the samples she'd gone all the way to Devon to collect arrived in less than prime condition, she'd lose the respect of the lab manager, at best. At worst, she could lose her job. After all, sample collection was in the must-do section of her job description. She wanted to ace her job, not lose it. And she wanted to explore the magical possibilities for curing plant diseases, too. She felt like she was on the brink of discovering a whole new world of prospects with that. Losing her job would seriously hinder that.

After her encounter with the proprietor of the train's shop, Freya didn't entertain any illusions of being able to store samples in the shop fridge, or even buy ice. Freya looked around the carriage. Nothing inspiring there. Just a few teenagers daring each other to greater feats on some online game, each teen talking loudly whilst gazing at their phone. Some even shouted as though in pain, while not moving at all.

Must be a good game. Probably one of those ones I missed out on by not having a phone early enough in life.

A scattering of older men and woman were immersed in laptops or old-fashioned paper books. The window was warm, heat seeping through the glass from the blazing hot day outside. She'd have to do something innovative to keep her samples from deteriorating. But what?

Nothing scientific occurred to her. And they were on a moving train - barely moving, but still - so no handy rivers she could use to cool her samples. What she really needed was an ice god. Unfortunately, she couldn't think of any way to access one. There was the Holly King, or Frau Holle, but given the warming of the world over the last few decades, it seemed likely that neither of them would be particularly strong, even if some of their descendants happened to be on the train. Or there was that Scottish one… Freya racked her memory, trying to pin down the name. Caill- something. The queen of winter. One of those Gaelic names that she could never remember how to spell. No, that sounded like a path to disaster. A winter queen would probably want to do more than just chill a few samples. Still. A memory of a song sprang into her mind, and she hummed a few bars.

Maybe she should just get off the train at the next stop and simply buy some ice. But then she'd miss her train home, and the samples had to be fresh, that was the whole problem. She leant her head back against her chair and covered her eyes, trying to think of options. The rhythmic swaying of the train got into her head and turned itself into a song. What were the words? She hummed the tune to herself, trying to remember. Was it the dogs of winter? Hounds, maybe. Like Lio's hounds. But she was a long way from winter here. During the storms of her childhood, Freya had never thought she would miss winter. Yet here she was, wishing for snow. She pressed her lips together, the corners of her mouth tipping down.

"Is everything all right?"

Freya opened her eyes with a start. Holding onto the back of Freya's seat with bony fingers was her old biochemistry professor, looking at her with a worried expression.

"Oh. Yes. I'm fine, really. I was just trying to figure out how to keep my samples cool. We're running a lot slower than I expected, and if they overheat the whole trip will be a pointless waste of time and I'll lose my job. Sorry, that was probably a bit much information, but I'm worried. Er. How come you're on this train, too?"

"Is there a reason I shouldn't be?" The professor's voice was suddenly icy, and her worried expression was replaced with a suspicious glare.

"No, of course not. It was just a surprise to see you again, that's all."

"Yes. Well, you have clearly forgotten what you knew of chemistry."

"I have?"

"Yes. Otherwise, you would have made yourself some instant ice-packs to cool your samples."

"Oh, I started out with those." They had been part of the sampling kit she'd brought. A heavy part, too. "But they've warmed up now."

"Then make more." The professor's voice was irritated.

If she'd sounded like this during lectures, I wouldn't have dared to fall asleep.

"Um. How?" Freya asked humbly.

"By combining the relevant chemicals, naturally. You can reuse the packs; you just need some fresh ingredients."

"Could you remind me what those ingredients are?" If she had a professor on hand, she may as well make use of that professor's expertise. Especially since she'd slept through her lectures.

"Water and fertiliser."

"Neither of which I have."

"Oh, for heaven's sake, child, there's water in the taps in the lavatories. You aren't drinking it, so it doesn't matter how recycled it is. And as for fertiliser - or ammonium nitrate, which is what you really need - I happen to have some samples on me."

In response to Freya's astonished look, Professor Beare snapped;

"I've been to an agricultural conference, no need to look at me like that."

Freya wasn't sure what expression had been on her face. Maybe a horrified one, since the most well-known use for ammonium nitrate was as an explosive. She decided she'd better be polite - this was too useful an opportunity to mess up. She manufactured a smile that felt as processed as that chemical probably was.

"In that case, it would be wonderful to have your expertise to help me preserve my samples. Thanks."

That was some serious sucking up. I hope it works.

The professor still looked at her askance, but softened sufficiently to bark out some instructions.

Following the professor's directions, Freya retrieved the now-warm instant ice-packs from her sampling kit, emptied them into the overflowing rubbish bin in the lavatory, and refilled them with luke-warm water. She swayed with the train's motion as she did so, and managed to splash some of the liquid onto her shoes.

Ugh, experiments like this were the other reason I didn't enjoy biochemistry.

Still, she had to get her samples back in good shape, so she lurched and staggered her way back down the carriage. Professor Beare was waiting with a small tube of something white and crystalline.

"Here you go. Just a little in each bag, seal them up, and shake."

Freya did as directed, and was gratified to feel the bags grow chill beneath her fingers. She smiled at the old woman.

"That's amazing, thank you so much. I really appreciate it." She tucked the refreshed ice packs into the sampling kit.

"You're welcome. With any luck those will last till you get back to your lab. Perhaps you'll look in, next time you're visiting the university." The professor smiled, displaying crooked teeth.

"Sure." It seemed a safe enough promise. Freya had no plans to return to her university town anytime soon.

Freya watched the old woman walk back along the train, presumably to find her own seat again. Freya was struck by how much older she looked now, her hair grey and wispy, only a year after she'd taught Freya. Quite haglike, if you thought about it in the right way. Professor Beare... an odd name, really. It reminded her of something. She couldn't quite remember what, though. She typed the name into her phone. And there it was. Under the biographical entry for the professor, another entry. An encyclopaedia description of Cailleach, queen of winter - also sometimes known as Cailleach Beare.

How about that. I needed an ice deity - and I got one. Or more likely the descendant of one. Stefan shouldn't worry so much about frost-folk, they're helpful.

There was a sudden lurch, and the train started moving at last. As her carriage rattled over the replaced rails, Freya saw that lorry again, the one with Vulcan Construction printed on the side. It was pulling away from the railway, wheels skidding as it took off at speed.

I hope that's the last I see of those crazy rail-thieves.

CHAPTER THIRTY-THREE

NIK AGAIN

The rest of Freya's trip back to York should have been dull, after the unexpected encounter with Professor Beare, the demi queen of winter. She found a northbound train with a spare seat about to leave from London's Kings Cross/St Pancras station, boarded and deposited her precious samples at her feet. It was time to relax.

Her reverie was interrupted by a thump on the roof of her carriage. The unmistakeable sound of footsteps on the roof followed. Freya looked up at it warily. When the door to her carriage burst open, she was ready to take on whoever opened it with a thrown chiller pad if need be.

However, the blue-haired head that poked around it was entirely familiar.

"Nik!"

"Have you any idea how many dark blond women have boarded trains heading North today?" Nik asked, thumping herself down in the seat opposite Freya.

"Er... lots?"

"More than you would believe. Why can't you dye your hair some useful colour? Pink would suit your style, I think."

Freya touched her hair self-consciously. She'd thought of dying it plenty of times, but never been brave enough. Pink hadn't been on her colour palette of choice.

"Sorry to make your life so difficult, but I think I'll skip the pink."

"Spoilsport. Anyway, I was about to give up when I saw you get on this train. Where are you heading?"

"Er, York. Or a bit outside it."

"Not to the coast? That's a shame, I could do with some water that isn't brown."

"You could take a train to the coast from York." suggested Freya, half-hopeful.

"Except then I'd end up in Scarborough. Nah, I'll give the old city a look-see before I decide what to do next. Though I'm a bit over cities," Nik said.

"Yes. Me too, and I didn't even stay in London."

A smile broke out on Nik's face, making Freya stare in surprise. She'd never seen such an expression on Nik before.

"Who'd have picked it, we have something in common," Nik chortled.

"I guess. And I assume you like Lio, since you always used to turn up with him."

"Well, Lio's the only tolerable one of his brothers. Zeph's a wimp and the rest are only too happy to pick a fight. So yeah, I guess Lio's OK."

Freya rolled her eyes at this lack of enthusiasm. Still, Nik had never been the effusive type. She noticed that Nik only had a small bag, nothing like the gear that Freya herself was toting.

"Is that all you have?" she asked, then wished she hadn't. It seemed unkind to point out Nik's lack of possessions. But Nik tossed her head carelessly.

"All I need. Unless I have a personality change. I'd have thought someone like you would be used to travelling light. You used to move nearly as often as Lio and me, from what he told me."

Freya fidgeted with the zip on her backpack. It looked likely to break soon - she'd tried to fit too much in it for too long, and the fabric around the zip was showing the strain.

"I'd like to stay in one place. A person can get sick of moving."

"Don't I know it. But the place has got to be the right one. Sure you've found that, yet?"

Uncomfortably, Freya thought that Nik had hit the nail on the head. She *wasn't* sure she was in the right place. She hated being told what to do all the time at work. And being at the bottom of a hierarchy. But surely that would get better as she worked her way through the ranks. She hadn't been there for long.

"You're not sure, are you? Got someone?"

"Well, maybe. Though it's not really your business, is it?"

"Why shouldn't it be? We're old acquaintances. And Aeolus knows, Lio talks about you enough. He not good enough for you?"

There was a jerk as the train started moving at last, throwing Freya back in her seat, and Nik forward. She caught herself before she fell into Freya's lap.

"Thor's balls, I wish they wouldn't do that. But what about you and Lio?"

The train lurched a second time, then drew out of the station more smoothly. Freya spared a final glance for the crowded concourse as they slid away from it.

Weird place.

"What about me and Lio? I saw him for the first time in years when I was in Devon, but he up and left again while I was asleep. There's never been *time* for 'me and Lio'." She looked back at Nik, hoping for understanding from this close associate of Lio's.

"Yeah, I guess him being drawn back to his island all the time isn't the best for relationships." Nik was leaning her head on the headrest of the seat. Freya thought she looked tired, as though maybe she hadn't slept well in days.

"Is that what happens? He's never said." She leaned forward in interest, hoping for more information.

"Oh, he hasn't told you, has he? I'd better not then. He can wash his own laundry in public if he wants to."

"Um. Do you see him much?"

"Not since I decided to give London a try. The problem there is that so many other types are giving it a try, too."

"Many weres?"

"You got weres on the brain? Nah, no more than trolls, kobolds, goblins. Heap of demis. Hobs are a dime a dozen too. Waitressing usually. Crazy place."

"Wait, goblins? I saw some of those working on the rails on my way."

"Doesn't surprise me, they're always into engineering and mechanics."

"Even if it's removing stuff?"

Nik shrugged.

"Sure, if they're using it elsewhere."

There was a clatter at the far end of the carriage.

"Tickets out, please." A train conductor had entered and was making his way slowly up the carriage, inspecting online tickets as he did so.

"Thor's armpit, I'd better make myself scarce." Nik winked at Freya. "Roof entry doesn't usually go with a valid ticket." She sauntered towards the other end of the carriage, slipping through the door just as the conductor reached Freya.

"Your friend there have a ticket, does she?" he asked in a stern voice.

What do I say?

"I guess. She was just, er, visiting the facilities," Freya temporised.

"Good, I'll be able to catch her when she comes out, then."

It didn't sound like he believed in Nik's ticket. To be fair, Freya didn't, either. She didn't think she could give that away, though.

"Sure. Here's mine." She showed her ticket, and hoped that Nik had some way of avoiding the conductor. It would be uncomfortable, to say the least, to have her removed from the train. There was a bang at the far end of the carriage, and Freya heard a faint thunk on the roof again.

It sounds like Nik is skilled in avoiding conductors. Why am I not surprised?

Nik didn't reappear until after the next station, well after the conductor had tired of waiting for the toilet door to be unlocked. She sat down again in the seat opposing Freya. There was a fresh smear of what looked like soot on her face, and her short, blue, curly hair was wind-ruffled.

"Wouldn't it be easier to buy a ticket?" Freya asked curiously. She couldn't imagine how hard it must have been for Nik to squeeze out the window and cling on to the roof of the speeding train.

"Sure, if I had money, that'd be grand," Nik said.

"Oh. No wonder you're heading out of London."

"Got in in one. Speaking of which, d'you have anything to eat?"

Freya looked at her assorted bundles with some dismay.

"Er. Flapjack?" After that leftover kebab for breakfast in Devon, she'd restocked her bag with non-perishables at one of the convenience stores she'd passed on the train platform. Not having enough to eat was a private nightmare.

"I'll take it, thanks."

Freya bent down and unzipped her long-suffering rucksack.

"Here." She pulled out one for herself, too. It had been a long day without many food breaks. Or water breaks, for that matter. She slurped thirstily from the water she'd also bought as she hastened through the train station. "You were talking about goblins before you went for some fresh air," she prompted Nik. Nik paused mid-chew, but thankfully swallowed before answering Freya.

"I don't think I was, but if you want to know about goblins, I can spill."

"Go on. I haven't really come across them much, but I suspect I should know more about them."

Nik nodded, taking another enormous bite of flapjack.

"This is the worst flavour, you know."

"You want to be fed; you'll have to take what you can get."

"Yeah, yeah. But goblins - they're more common in cities. Metalwork, light industry, that sort of thing. Since you spend most of your time mooning about in the countryside you probably don't see them. There are plenty in London. They get more jobs than I ever did. Good guys on the whole though."

"I have to admit I can't see you in a job," remarked Freya, hoping that wasn't a deadly insult. Luckily, Nik threw her head back and laughed.

"Nah, me either. But I have to live, same as everyone else. My best jobs so far have been in security. Wander around, look tough, and beat up people if they don't follow the rules. Plenty of cash jobs in security, too."

"I see what you mean, but rather you than me," Freya said, trying and failing to envision herself even wanting to be involved in that sort of job. Nik shrugged again.

"Suits me. What with one storm or another, I never got much education. Might have been different in London otherwise."

"Did you want to? Get educated, I mean?"

"Sure, I had dreams. Doesn't seem much point now, though." Nik transferred her gaze to the scenery, ending the discussion. Outside, the sun was setting. The dry fields almost glowed in the evening light, red-gold. It was all too easy to ignore the lost harvest that such beauty represented. But perhaps Nik saw something different, mused Freya. A world which hadn't let her pursue her dreams. Did Lio have the same problems? She was suddenly aware of how much she had gained. Despite the poverty in which she'd grown up, she had got to go to university, to find a career which didn't rely on unreliable demi-abilities. She bit her lip. Who was she to judge someone's hard-won security jobs?

Nik looked back at Freya with a twinkle in her eye, and the moment passed.

"Want to see something funny?" Nik asked. "See how fast this train can really go?"

"Er, no. I'm happy so long as it gets to York safely."

"But you'd like to get there soon, right?"

"Well, yes, I have to drop off my samples before they warm up again."

"Right. Back soon."

Nik popped out of her seat and strode down the carriage, leaving her bag behind this time. Freya eyed it curiously. Would it be snooping too much to see what was in it?

No, not worth the risk. Who knows what Nik would do if she caught me in the act?

Once again there were clunkings from the end of the carriage, this time followed by rapid footfalls on the roof that quickly faded. The train, which had been gently rocking from side to side, began to clank in earnest, lurching frighteningly around the curves in the tracks. Glancing out the window, Freya realised that the hedgerows between fields were flashing by much faster than before. Soon, they were a blur.

I hope we don't crash into something. Like another train. She clung on to the sides of her seat and closed her eyes. What was Nik *doing*?

Freya wasn't sure how long the high speed part of the trip lasted, but she noticed when it stopped. As the train began to pass the outlying suburbs of York, it abruptly slowed, the sudden change in acceleration pressing Freya back into her seat. She recovered herself, prying her stiff fingers from the sides of her seat at last. As she was shaking her hands to try to regain their flexibility, Nik reappeared. Her hair was swept back and her cheeks glowed with excitement, exertion or both.

"Have a nice ride?" she asked.

"Um, no!" Freya said. "I thought we were going to go off the rails!"

"I wouldn't do that. Far too much hassle dealing with the aftermath. But we're nearly to York now, I thought you'd be pleased."

"Yes. Well. Thanks for that. Since I'm still alive and in one piece, I guess that's okay."

"Suit yourself. I had fun. It's been ages since I used storm winds. I don't know that the train driver liked it though, he looked a bit shaken when I left the engine."

"Tell me what you did, exactly?" asked Freya.

"Just gave the train a bit of a push. The trip was taking too long, you were about to get deep and meaningful."

"Sorry, next time I'll try for jokes instead. Or I would if I could ever remember any."

"Nah, it's ok. You're not the joking sort anyway."

Freya rolled her eyes. She might not be good at jokes, but she didn't need Nik pointing it out.

The train was slowing in a much more controlled manner now, chugging gently into the station.

"Come on," Freya said. "Let's get off this train before you get anymore 'fun' ideas."

Freya wasn't sure whether to be glad or sorry when Nik muttered something about looking up old friends, and disappeared off into the dark streets before Freya could invite her home, swap numbers, or any other such thing. Thanks to the early arrival of the train, she was able to get a bus to work and deposit her samples in the lab cold store just before the gates were locked for the night. It was something of an anti-climax after the revelations and worry, but Freya was just as glad of that. She wanted to go home and think about what her newfound ability could mean. She just wished she'd seen Lio again before returning inland.

CHAPTER THIRTY-FOUR

LABWORK

The next few weeks passed in a flurry of labwork, organising and processing the samples she'd collected. Kylie was drafted in to help, somewhat to Freya's discomfort. Although she liked Kylie, Freya didn't really want to discuss Stefan with her. But sure enough, as the two of them sat at a lab bench and macerated pieces of olive tree ready for testing to try and detect the unwanted disease, Kylie started talking about him.

"You still spending time with Stefan, then? After your dinner out?"

"Yes... some."

"You need to be careful what you promise him." Kylie held her sample in the mixer for an unnecessary few seconds, pressing her tube down to activate the mixer.

"I thought he was Mr Good Guy. You know, covering you when you were short of cash, protecting defenceless women, that sort of thing."

Kylie snorted.

"He *is* good at that sort of thing. It's just that having done that, he feels entitled to everything else in your life, too. And he's got a bee in his bonnet about a few odd things."

"He hasn't seemed like that so far. Not to me, at least."

Kylie picked up another sample and inspected it under a microscope before snipping off a piece to process.

"Wait and see," she said darkly. She changed the topic abruptly.

"You've got a lot of diseased sections, here. But some look different. Like they're recovering, maybe."

Freya checked the sample. Sure enough, it was from the tree she'd attempted to cure with her demi abilities.

"That would be good, right? There's no cure known for that disease."

"That would be bloody brilliant. If we found a cure, we'd be on the money train, that disease is killing plantations all over Europe," Kylie said, distracted from Stefan for now.

"Except we don't get extra money for anything we do while we're here, do we?"

"Nah, that would be the time to go freelance. Before announcing the discovery, mind, otherwise the university would own the cure."

"Is that what you would do?" Freya asked curiously.

"Oh, yeah. There's way more cash to be made as an independent. Better lifestyle too - other people pay for you to travel. I'd jump at that if I could."

Freya nodded slowly. Clearly there was more to think about than just making a magical disease cure work. Maybe there was a way to do the job she wanted to do, without being bossed around all the time. Her thoughts were interrupted as Kylie returned to the topic of Stefan once again.

"But seriously, Freya. You want to watch yourself with Stefan. He was great for a while with me, but then he went weird. That's why we split. I just don't want to see you experience the same thing."

"Well, thanks for the warning, I guess." Privately, however, Freya thought that maybe Kylie was just jealous. Her own interactions with Stefan since their first night out had been almost entirely positive. Almost enough to make her forget about missing Lio. If only Stefan wasn't so keen on public displays of affection. And didn't have those occasional outbursts about frost giants. Not to mention the frequent encounters with supernaturals as they investigated sites where Van or his cohort had staged an attack.

If the heat wave would just ease off, Freya thought, *things would be going quite well.*

CHAPTER THIRTY-FIVE

HOME TO THE COAST

The train ride to her mother's home on the coast was dull but at least it didn't take long. Freya had received a call from her friend Aisha, who also still lived on the coast there, asking her to come visit, urgently, please. She hadn't elaborated on the phone. Taking the cheaper bus instead would have added several hours to the journey.

Freya alighted from the train and made her way through the arched station. The cafe owned by Aisha's family was just outside the station doors. Freya poked her head in the door.

"Aisha, are you in there?"

"Freya, about time!"

Freya laughed.

"You're supposed to say something polite about how much you've missed me, aren't you?"

"Nah, you know me too well for that. Of course, I've missed you, but honestly how long since you've been back? It must have been years." Aisha gestured for Freya to follow her to the back table of the cafe, which was nearly empty. A large grey cat sat on a counter nearby. It started purring when it saw Freya. She gave it a quick pat.

"Um, yeah. It has been. Sorry. I guess I've been avoiding The Family. At least Isis here hasn't changed her mind about me." She patted Isis the cat again before letting her backpack fall off her shoulder to the floor. The were-fox clan that made this town home was known colloquially as The Family.

"What about Mr Fluffbum?"

"Here he is," Freya said, hefting the cat cage containing her pet. He doesn't enjoy travel much these days."

"Poor cat, he must be getting old." Aisha bent down to greet Mr Fluffbum, who lifted his nose to return the greeting. "Oh good, he remembers me. Have a seat, Freya. We're between trains just now so I shouldn't be rushed off my feet. I know you always wanted to get away from The Family. But things have changed, you know. It's not like it used to be, us versus them. You'll see." Aisha hustled back to the coffee machine - newly installed since Freya had been here last - and took out some cups. She waved one at Freya invitingly.

"That sounds more worrying than things staying the same. Just tea, please, I still don't drink coffee." Freya watched with interest as Isis the grey cat sauntered over to exchange glares with Mr Fluffbum.

"Wait till you see your nieces and nephews. You won't recognise them, I bet." Aisha poured hot water onto some tea for Freya, and created an unpleasant hissing as she prepared a drink for herself with the shiny machine at the counter. Freya waited for the sound to subside before trying to speak again.

"Are they still furry?"

"Just wait and see. I'm not going to say." Aisha finished making her drink, swirling frothy milk into it, then picked up Freya's cup and took them both to the table. "I can't believe you haven't been back in all this time, you know. You're supposed to be my bestie."

"I've been pretty busy, you know. Getting my degree, finding a job. Traveling, even. Work sent me to Devonshire last week." Freya knew she was avoiding the real issue, but she didn't want to dwell on the reasons she'd stayed away. She gave Aisha a placating pat on the arm. "It wasn't you."

"Well, I wish you had come back sooner. You've missed a lot." Aisha looked away for a moment, fighting some strong emotion.

Freya noticed tears welling up in the corners of her eyes.

"What's wrong, Aisha?"

"Nena's gone. The heat was too much for her heart. That's why I'm here. In the cafe. Full time, now. And that's why I asked you to come. I know you liked her."

"Oh, Aisha, I'm sorry. Why didn't you let me know sooner?"

Aisha's face puckered.

"I didn't know if you'd come."

Freya rose and offered a hug, wiping tears away from her own eyes. She *had liked* Aisha's grandmother Nena. The old woman had let her and Aisha hang out in her cafe many a time when they needed somewhere safe and warm, but outside their houses. That seemed ironic, given that too much warmth had hastened her end. She felt a growing resentment of the year's abnormal heat. Until now it had just been uncomfortable. She hadn't realised that heat could kill.

Isis leapt off her counter and padded over to Aisha, rubbing her head against Aisha's consolingly.

"Thanks, Freya. Thanks, Isis." Aisha addressed the woman and the cat equally. She slid back into her seat opposite Freya. "It's just been a hard time, you know. I'd been working here part time, of course, but I was saving up to do an online business course. I've got big plans for Karim's lightweight shelters. I was all set to start next term. But now, I'll have to run the cafe. I just don't see how I can study *and* work full time. And the heat has been awful - you know we don't have cooling in the cafe, it's no wonder Nena couldn't take it." She half-sobbed again, suppressed it, and took a shaky, consoling sip of her coffee, as though a drink could fix anything.

"Aisha, that's awful. I'm sorry." Freya cast around for something positive to take from the situation. "But there's got to be some way. Can't your Mum take over?" Freya was impressed - she didn't think she'd have managed to study as well as running a cafe.

"Mum's never wanted to work here. That's why I was helping out, when Nena started to get sick."

"A cousin, then?" Freya had a vague recollection that Aisha had a clutch of cousins around. Freya had never really got to know them, though.

"They all have their own jobs. I do have one idea though."

"Go on, then, what is it?" Freya leaned forward; tea forgotten.

"You're not going to like it."

"Let me guess, you've met a daylight vampire who lives on espresso. Or you discovered one of your cousins is part hob and wants nothing more than to keep a cafe in order. Or, no, Isis can actually transform into a human and is ready to do more than act as cafe mascot." After her encounter with a were-cat, that didn't seem like such an unlikely idea. But as Freya's guesses grew wilder, Aisha started to smile. When Freya named the Isis, Aisha broke into a laugh. The cat in question looked up with a small 'mmrrrp'. Aisha patted her reassuringly.

"No, none of those crazy things. Especially not Isis! Though I'm sure she knows the most out of any of us about how the cafe works. No, it's crazier than you can guess." Aisha looked searchingly at Freya. "Promise you won't be mad, OK? Remember how glad you are to see me and how much you want things to work out well for me."

"You sound like you're preparing me for more bad news. What are you going to do, Aisha?" She narrowed her eyes suspiciously at her friend. "You've got something planned that I really won't like, don't you? I guess that's what I deserve for not coming back to see you for so long."

Aisha took a deep breath, letting it out slowly.

"Gareth came by a day or two ago. I was telling him about my problems," Aisha paused, looking at Freya then glancing away before their eyes could meet.

"Gareth the were-fox?"

"Yes, him."

"Gareth the bully?"

"I guess that's how you knew him, yes," said Aisha.

"I didn't realise you passed the time of day with were-foxes," said Freya in a tight voice.

"Well, things change, you know. Anyway, he was here, and I told him my troubles. And he - well, he's offered to do half time for me. So, I could do my course, and keep the cafe too."

Freya could only stare. She became aware that her mouth was open, and shut it hastily.

"That's quite a turnaround," she said at last. "How long have you been on speaking terms with Gareth?"

Gareth had been the bane of Freya's life in her last year at school. It was hard to believe that Aisha was now not only talking to him, but was planning to job share with him in her family's cafe.

"Don't look at me like that. He's changed since we all were at school."

"He'd have to. Someone would knock him over the head, otherwise."

"Yeah, well apparently someone just about did, when he was running with those obnoxious cousins of his. Made him think about his life choices." Aisha glanced up at Freya. "Some blue-haired girl, is what he told me."

"Oh. Nik." *Who knew Nik could do some good? Though I'm sure violence isn't a good way to turn around someone's life.*

"Yes, oh. Anyway, he's been much more like a decent human being for a couple of years at least. As you'd know, if you came home more often."

"You're better at guilt-tripping me than Mum."

"Maybe I should have guilt-tripped you sooner, then. You know you're missing out on the best years of your nieces and nephews. They'll be teenagers if you wait too long to visit next time, and then they won't want to see you anyway."

"I thought we were talking about you and your degree and business plans?" Freya tried to derail Aisha's accusation, but she felt the razor slice of guilt anyway. She *should* have come back more often, not left her Mum to deal with her sister's offspring alone. Except that she wasn't doing so alone - she was bringing them up along with the local were-fox pack. A pack who Freya didn't get on with.

"Look, Freya," said Aisha. "I know why you haven't come back sooner. I get that you had a traumatic time here. But the world is changing, and things are different here now. You should know that before you arrive at your Mum's place, anyway. Just... just try to remember that not everyone is the monster you might have thought them, not anymore."

"Are you still my friend, then, in this not-monsters-anymore world?"

"Always. And don't you forget it."

"Good. It sounds like I'd better go see what else's changed around here."

"You got that right. But be kind, Freya."

"Am I not usually?"

"Apart from not visiting, sure."

Freya winced.

No doubt about it, I should have come home sooner.

"No need to rub it in. Look, I'll go see Mum and then maybe we can do dinner?"

"You may find yourself needed at dinner. Come over for a drink with me later. Or dessert, we can do dessert."

"Sounds good." Wondering what dark hints Aisha was trying to give her, Freya drained her tea and stood up. "See you for dessert. And I'm really sorry about Nena."

CHAPTER THIRTY-SIX

WERE-KITS

Freya approached her old home with trepidation. She'd had some superficial contact with her Mum in the years since she'd left for uni, talking on the phone, but she hadn't been back. The end-of-row house looked the same as ever, a two-story red brick home next to the road. The space behind the house wasn't as lush with vegetation as Freya had expected - from the little she could see over the tall wall. She knocked on the door, feeling like a stranger. Her mother's voice sounded from somewhere inside.

"Who is it?"

She sounds stressed.

"It's me," Freya called.

"Oh, Freya. Let yourself in, please," her mother, Danae, called back.

Feeling a little miffed at this lukewarm welcome after several years away, Freya opened the door all the way - and immediately regretted it. A pack of hairy canines very nearly bowled her over. Mr Fluffbum - still in his cat carrier - gave a terrified yowl.

"Fenrir's teeth, get them off me, Mum! They're scaring Mr Fluffbum!"

"They just want to say hello. As do I."

Freya fended off the russet-hued, bushy-tailed bodies that surrounded her in order to give her mother a hug.

"You've taken your time to return," Danae said.

"Yeah. I've been busy. As have you, by the looks of these hairy mutts." She patted the head of the foxy canine currently leaning against her leg. Were-foxes or not, they were relatives. It was hard to be fearful of beings she'd played with as kits.

"Don't call them that. They're not stupid, you know. As they'll tell you themselves shortly. So, what brings you home at long last?"

Freya sighed. She'd hoped to exchange a few pleasantries or something before the expected offensive began.

"Aisha called me to tell me about her Nena. She asked me to come."

"And you came for a friend when you wouldn't come for family?" The hurt in Danae's voice was clear.

"You didn't ask me to come, Mum."

"You should have known to do so."

Well, this conversation isn't getting anywhere fast.

"So, tell me about these smart nephews and nieces I have. Are they staying with you full-time now?" The furry nieces and nephews in question leaped playfully at her, apparently delighted to meet their aunt again. Freya looked at them sternly until they dropped to four paws again, eyes still hopefully fixed on her.

"Don't try to change the subject, Freya. They're still just here for weekends. You know I have to work."

"Look, I've only got the weekend too, can we not ruin it with arguments already?"

Danae's shoulders slumped, and she suddenly looked twice her age; a beaten, worn-out old woman.

"I thought I'd lost you, too," she muttered.

Freya's guilt threatened to swallow her alive. She beat it down, telling it that she was with her mother now. It wasn't Freya's fault that her Dad and her sister had both left the family. Really, it wasn't.

"Oh, Mum, I'm sorry. Of course, you haven't lost me. I've just been busy. But I'm here now. Can I help make some dinner?"

"Come on, then." Danae turned towards the kitchen, but looked back at the enthusiastic canine welcoming committee. "You lot come too, but change before you come back into the kitchen. I don't want hair in the food like last time."

Freya flattened herself to the wall as the horde poured past her in a flurry of fur. *OK, five is probably not a horde, but it sure feels like it in this house.*

She took the opportunity to release Mr Fluffbum, opening the carrier. He sniffed the air, looked wildly around and fled upstairs. Freya sighed.

In the kitchen, Danae opened the side door that led to the back yard, and indicated to the pack of canines that they should go outside. They tumbled out happily.

"Don't forget to change," Danae warned again. She turned back to Freya. "So. I'll re-introduce you to them later. Here's an onion, get chopping."

Freya left her suitcase at the foot of the stairs and did as she was told, privately marvelling that it was a bought onion pulled from a string bag, rather than a handful of home grown spring onions. It was late in the year for spring onions, of course. Meanwhile, her mother set a pot of water to boil on the cooker, and started chopping tomatoes. Those did look homegrown, a variety of colours and shapes that were quite beautiful to behold.

"Nice tomatoes, Mum," she said, hoping to defuse her mother's irritation. The large knife in her mother's hand was hitting the board with short, sharp thuds. There was more force than seemed safe behind those thuds.

"*They're* doing well in this heat, at least. But I have to keep reminding the littles not to eat them green. They're right scavengers," said Danae, referring to her furry grandchildren.

"At least they're eating vegetables now."

"There's that. I still have to get some meat in their diet. I cook it outside when I can. Or buy it pre-cooked."

"And are they changing, now, too?" Freya let her voice drift upward in an invitation for her mother to elaborate. She finished chopping the onions and hunted around for a suitable pan to put them in. There seemed to be more pans than she remembered filling the cramped cupboard space under the bench.

"Yes. I thought it wouldn't be for a year or two yet, but they started changing at the beginning of summer. Most inconvenient since I was taking them for a walk on the beach at the time." Danae intercepted Freya's pan search, stepping in to pull a large pot from the cupboard in front of her. She set it on the cooker next to the pot of water. "In there, please." She gestured with her own knife. Freya gave the knife a wide berth as she brushed chopped onions into the pot.

"So, they changed out in public? What did they change into?"

"Nothing I have a name for. Fur and flippers, anyway. But that's to be expected, I suppose. Given their parentage." Danae's lips twisted down.

"I miss Tammy too." There wasn't anything else Freya could think of to say. Her sister's abduction by the sea-goddess Nehalennia had hit the family hard. The return of her offspring had just made the situation more challenging - part of the reason that Freya had stayed away. It was easier to be her own person away from family ties and sorrows. She didn't want to dwell on the past.

Will we ever move past this?

"Did anyone see? What did you do?" asked Freya aloud.

Danae's voice was ragged when she spoke again, emotions rippling her vocal cords in unexpected tremors, but her tone soon strengthened.

"As it happened, the only ones on the beach were were-foxes. There's always some about in this town, as I'm sure you remember. So, I didn't have to explain anything. Fortunately. I have no idea what I could have said to explain *that* to a pure human." She shook her head silently as though the memory of her lack of words became the present, then turned to the cupboards and pulled out a pack of dried pasta. The water had yet to come to the boil, so she set it down on the bench again.

"Wow. That was lucky. And do they control their change now?" Freya searched for and found the expected jar of dried green herbs from a rack on the bench. She offered it to her mother.

"Pretty well, for kids. I suppose it's possible that their were-fox heritage means they grow up faster. You have no idea how difficult it's been, Freya." Danae stirred the onions in their pot, a few minutes too late. They were slightly charred on the edges. It looked like the evening meal would be charcoal flavoured as well as herb flavoured. "I only have them at weekends but I have to work all week. I never get a break. They wake up at dawn. I am just run ragged!" Danae's voice had been rising, and she appeared to catch herself.

There was no escaping the guilt wave now. It crashed around Freya's ears. She gasped involuntarily.

"Oh Mum, you should have let me know. I have a phone these days, I *am* only a text away."

"Did you burn yourself?" asked Danae.

Even now, she never understands me. The thought gave Freya enough annoyance to break free of the all-consuming guilt long enough to realise that she was getting spattered with tomato juice. Danae had added the chopped tomatoes to the onions, and they had begun to spit red juice all over the kitchen.

Freya hastily found the lid and placed it over the soon-to-be sauce. It would need the herbs added soon, but there was no need to let the mess get worse. Finally, she answered the question.

"No, I'm fine. I just wish you had some extra help. Can't you negotiate with The Family? I mean, they all earn heaps, and there's more of them. Can't one of them babysit now and then?"

"I don't want to lose the littles entirely, and I'm afraid that's what would happen if I show weakness. It's not like we have a legally binding agreement."

"Tricky," agreed Freya.

Were-foxes were the other reason, perhaps even the main reason that Freya had stayed away.

"You have no idea. Well, perhaps you do. You *were* here the first year. And the littles are much better behaved now than they were then. Honestly, they were worse than kittens that first year."

The water in the larger pot was boiling now. Danae put the pasta into the water, swirling the long strands with a spoon until they softened enough to stay under water.

"Yeah, I do remember, Mum. I just about had to go barefoot the winter I was here with them - they kept chewing up all my shoes!"

"Mine, too."

"Pests."

Mother and daughter grinned at the shared memory, a momentary harmony between them.

The moment was shattered by a scuffle at the door. Teeth were bared, someone growled, another yipped - a typical fox-like sound.

"Stop that right now or you're not getting any dinner," commanded Danae.

To Freya's surprise, the unruly participants fell apart immediately. They ducked out of sight for a moment, and the empty doorway was filled with naked children.

"Oh, kids, go get some clothes on," said Danae. This was clearly a frequent request, judging by the ragged chorus of 'Yes, Gran,' that issued from the gaggle. The children looked curiously at Freya as they passed her. They seemed much more subdued as human children than they had as fox kits. When they had gone, Freya commented;

"They look just like humans now. Are they foxes most of the time, or humans?"

"I'm trying to get them to be humans more often. They look too much like foxes to take them out for dog walks anymore. And if I take them to the beach they're that other thing. With gills. The trouble is they have about as much self-control as the average four year old."

"So, Tammy was right about the gills! I'm guessing four-year-old control isn't great."

"Exactly."

"So do they go to school?"

"Not yet. The were-foxes have them during the week. That's their problem. I pick them up after work on Fridays. Honestly, I don't think school could hold them yet. And they seem to prefer fur to clothes. That's cheaper, mind." Danae sighed deeply, and drained the pot of pasta. "Can you finish that sauce, please?"

Freya stirred in the herbs and added a sprinkle of salt. As she did so, she was surprised to see Danae bringing out a tin of fish.

"Don't look at me like that. Fish is the cheapest way to keep those kids in taurine, which apparently they need thanks to their carnivorous heritage. Believe me, if I could raise vegan foxes I would. But the supplements are too expensive. I figure Nehalennia can't begrudge a small can of fish a day for her future followers." Danae named the sea-goddess who had taken Freya's sister and returned her sister's offspring.

"It's just, we spent our whole childhood with you telling us how bad it was to kill animals for food, how we'd offend every god or goddess in existence if we did."

"Well, things change. And I don't eat it myself. *I'm* not changing my ways. *I* still have gods and goddesses to placate." Danae dumped the cooked pasta unceremoniously back into its pot, and tipped a portion of fish into five out of seven bowls. "Right. Let's get everyone fed."

CHAPTER THIRTY-SEVEN

MOTHER-DAUGHTER TIME

Dinner was a messy affair. The kitchen ended up spattered with orange grease thanks to the youngest members of the family sucking up spaghetti too fast. Freya was glad she hadn't had to deal with younger brothers or sisters herself. Looking at these children, she could appreciate why Tammy used to get irritated with her. When she said as much to Danae, as they sat at the table watching the kits play outside after dinner, Danae shook her head.

"Just wait till it's your turn and you have to deal with it every day. And you're lucky your Dad moved out when he did, or you might have had younger brothers or sisters to deal with."

"Would you have liked that, Mum?" Freya was feeling unusually bold - she'd never usually ask her mother such a question. She supposed it was the presence of the were-fox kits that made her think of such possibilities.

"Gaia wept, no. I had enough to do keeping the two of you fed. Although..." her eyes lost their focus as she looked into the mists of memory; "Dion did say something once about having another child. Probably with that harlot he took up with after the house went down the cliff. I didn't ask for more details; I was too angry at the time. But you may have a brother out in the world somewhere." Danae's eyes snapped back into the present as Freya jerked back in her chair, making it shriek against the kitchen floor.

"Seriously, Mum? And you never said anything to us? What if we'd met him and not known he was a brother? Ugh, there are all sorts of nasty possibilities." *I can't believe Mum kept a brother from us. Even if she* was *mad with Dad.*

"I'm sure you would have recognised someone that closely related to you. And anyway, I didn't want to even think about Dion being with someone else. It wasn't necessary for you to know."

"I can't believe you, Mum. You have such - such *warped* priorities!"

"I made the right decision for me at the time, thank you," said Danae. "As you have made your own decisions; I'll thank you not to question mine."

Freya stood up. She no longer felt like enjoying the warm evening with her mother.

"I'll come back and help with the dishes later. I'm going to see Aisha. She needs my help."

Danae looked up at her daughter steadily. The dying light caught the lines around her eyes and intensified the shadows under them. Once again, she looked old to Freya.

"I'm glad you haven't forgotten your friend," Danae said, "but don't forget your mother either. I may not be the best mother in the world, but you're mine and I do love you. I'll see you later?"

The uncertainty in her mother's voice stabbed at Freya. Was she unkind, to have left her mother alone for so long? And to be leaving now, when an unexpected revelation had thrown her world into turmoil? She made her lips smile, hoping it wasn't too much of a rictus grin. Anger made the expression stiff.

"Sure, Mum. I just need to think a few things through, OK?"

She took her plate to the sink on her way out. It really was the least she could do.

CHAPTER THIRTY-EIGHT

AISHA & DESSERT

Freya found Aisha at her home, as she'd expected. She'd left Mr Fluffbum perched on top of a wardrobe with his own bowl of fish, well out of fox reach. The usual troupe of cats attended Freya's arrival at Aisha's house. She patted heads and scratched chins until the cats considered that they had had enough attention from this newcomer.

"Are we staying in for dessert, or going out?" she asked Aisha.

"Going out. I want to be able to talk." Aisha glanced behind her to indicate the presence of the rest of her family in the house.

Freya nodded understandingly.

"Anywhere good to go these days?"

Aisha flashed a grin, momentarily seeming more like her usual confident self.

"There is nowhere as good as my cafe, but I don't want to have to do the dishes or open up. So, I guess we can go to the Lonely Cat." She named a cafe which was down near the waterfront. Freya had never actually been inside, since the only cafe she had frequented as a high school student was Aisha's family's station cafe.

"So long as the tide's not in tonight," cautioned Freya. "I know there are no storms forecast, but I try to avoid the shore these days, you know."

"Yeah, I know."

A moment of silence passed as memories from four years ago sat between them. Freya's experiences on the waterfront hadn't been the worst of what happened that year, but they hadn't endeared her to the area either.

"Come on, then, or the cafe will be closed."

It was a long walk to the cafe from Aisha's house near the station. Freya felt out of place despite the familiarity of the streets. Small things had changed; a stretch of road had been re-sealed, some shop names were altered. Passing the pub on the corner, Freya saw that the usual hanging baskets of flowers had withered and died.

Aisha followed Freya's gaze.

"We've had water restrictions since late spring. No watering of non-essentials allowed. Turns out that includes street flowers."

"How about the allotments? And the greenhouse?"

"Your Mum's the one to ask that. And I haven't been out to the allotments for years. You're the only one who managed to drag me out that way, you know."

"It just seems a shame to let the plants die." Freya looked back towards the desiccated baskets as they passed out of sight.

"Better them than us, though, right?"

"But we need plants to survive, too."

"Not pub flowers. Nice to have, not essential for life."

"Life is more cheerful with street flowers."

"True enough. I don't know why they don't take them down; no-one needs to see the dead baskets."

They continued down the hill.

"So, tell me what else has changed around here," Freya said.

"Well, the big wheel is still off limits, since the foundations got damaged in that storm a couple of years back. The mall got flooded again last winter, without any supernatural help as far as I could tell. Otherwise, I think most things are the same. Actually, the floods are just more of the same, too, we get them every storm, now. I've already told you about Nena." Aisha's voice broke for a moment. She was obviously more emotional about her grandmother's loss than she was prepared to let on. Freya reached across the distance between them to pat her friend's arm in sympathy.

"How about Karim, any word from him?" Freya had had a brief fling with Aisha's brother Karim. He had been her first serious boyfriend, in fact. All things considered, she was glad that her friendship with Aisha had survived the breakup.

"He's not great at letting us know what he's up to. Last heard of as a helper on a dig excavating near Luxor. So, living his dream, I guess. Actually, he makes me material for storm shelters every time he comes back. That's a big part of why I need that business degree."

"Well, that's good." It was a weak sentiment, and Freya knew it, but she couldn't find it in herself to be more positive.

"It's great, if you ask me. Who knew a school project could be so useful?"

"Not me! But I'm feeling a bit off balance, being back here again," Freya said.

"Yeah, I guess it must be a bit weird since you've been away so long," Aisha agreed.

"You're not wrong. Now I've been home, I guess I know what you meant about how things are going, here. I... I had a bit of an argument with Mum. It turns out she's been holding out on information all these years. Apparently I have a half-brother out there somewhere!" She gestured dramatically at the surrounding countryside.

"No way!" Aisha was suitably startled.

"That's what I said, too. I just can't wrap my head around the idea. And I can't *believe* she never even told us. I mean, I know she's never forgiven Dad for leaving us, but I didn't know he was even in contact with her. All those times I was missing him, and we could have been talking to him! *And* I have an unknown sibling somewhere out there. Honestly, the thought just makes me incandescent."

"Those are pretty big revelations. Probably deserving of chocolate." Aisha pulled Freya across the road just behind a lorry heading down to the port.

"Chocolate is definitely required. I don't suppose you still have those contacts to get the good stuff?"

"Afraid not, apparently their supplier's trees succumbed to some blight or rather. Something up your alley, really."

"Now I'm depressed as well as angry," Freya said. She stopped mid-step, seeing a large lorry with 'Vulcan construction' emblazoned on the side, pulling up to a building further along towards the pier.

"How come you're looking at that lorry, then? We're here."

Freya belatedly realised that they were standing at the door to a cafe. The silhouette of a black cat adorned the lintel of the door, and loopy writing proclaimed that this was the Lonely Cat cafe.

"Sorry, it's just I thought I'd seen that same lorry when I was on the train to Devon. Weird. Maybe it's a big firm." She shook off the thought. "Is this cafe run by one of your family connections, then?" she asked Aisha.

"Naturally, or we wouldn't be here."

"It's a long way into were-fox territory, isn't it?" When she'd last lived here, the were-foxes had been investing in the port operations, and this cafe was very near to that.

"That's the point, actually. We've been negotiating territory with them since you were last here. Partly because of your sister, and her kits. They gave us an opening. It's not just us versus them anymore."

"It's hard to imagine that."

"You don't have to. Have some dessert with me, and I'll initiate you into the secrets of our negotiations."

"So mysterious!" Freya teased.

"Hey, how many chances do I get to be mysterious? I'll take what I can get," Aisha grinned over her shoulder at Freya as she opened the door to the cafe. "Now please enter into this dark and shadowy lair."

The cafe was in fact brightly lit. Cushions padded the chairs and cat towers adorned the corners, complete with purring cats. It was about as far from a dark lair as Freya could imagine.

CHAPTER THIRTY-NINE

THE LONELY CAT CAFE

Aisha and Freya were quickly settled into a table by the window. A tabby cat - clearly not lonely despite the name of the cafe - approached them as soon as they were seated. It rubbed against their ankles for a few minutes, providing a pleasant distraction until their desserts and drinks arrived.

"You didn't really tell me about your job yet," said Aisha. "How is big science working out for you? Is it all you'd ever dreamed of?"

Freya wrinkled her nose at Aisha.

"It's not like that," she said. "It's just that I can do things with science that I can't with demi powers. Well, different things, anyway. And as for the work - well, I'm still getting used to it, really. There's lots of time in the lab. Lots of people telling me what to do. And it's weird having lunch in a canteen with so many others. There's this chilli guy, he's super odd. I thought he was your classic geek - he's the policy analyst, dry as anything - but then it turns out he is a chilli fanatic. He invited me to go see his chillis, which sounds like a weird pickup line. But I asked my lab mate Kylie, she's going to come with me. So, I guess I'll see what that's like." Freya stopped, realising that Aisha was gaping at her.

"Wait, you know the *chilli king*? He is like, legendary. Can you get me an invite? Or at least access to his chilli sauce?"

"You're kidding, right?" Freya looked at Aisha's face carefully - had she missed any obvious cues?

"I am really not. Honestly, Mum has been telling me about the chilli king of the north my whole life. She thinks chillis are even more important than tomatoes. Maybe we need to get the chilli king and your mum together, they could take over the north with that combo."

"Woah, slow down. I can't believe you know about that guy. Let alone his sauce. You've never mentioned him before," Freya said.

"Well, the way you reacted when Mum gave you spicy food that first time, I figured you wouldn't be interested."

"That's true enough." It had taken Freya what felt like hours to drown the taste of chilli from her first meal at her friend's house. "But honestly, I didn't think chillis were so important."

Not to mention they burn like lava. Who needs that in their food?

"You need to pay more attention, girl. But seriously, I would give real money for some of that guy's sauce. Let me know if you can get some, alright?" Aisha sounded hopeful.

"Alright. But I thought we were here to talk about your family and the weres? Or Gareth?"

"I told you things have moved on. It started with you and your mum having part-time care of your sister's kits."

"Just Mum, really."

"Yeah, sure. I get that. But it provided an opening. I mean, you're my friend, so you and your mum were seen as cat-allies. And then the kits were looked after by you *and* by the were-foxes. I don't know, it just made it seem like things were possible. My Mum has even been meeting with Lisichka." Aisha named the were-fox matriarch who had sought to make Freya's sister Tammy a part of the local were-fox clan.

"That sly b-" Freya caught herself before cursing the most powerful supernatural in the area, barring the local sea-goddess. She took a deep breath and let it out slowly. "Sorry. You were telling me things are different now."

Aisha, who'd been watching Freya with a worried expression, nodded slowly.

"Yes. I know it's a big change, but it's actually improved things around here. Because we're not out-and-out rivals, I think there's less bullying. Or maybe it's just that things are different outside of school. Anyway. You remember how the were-foxes were bidding for the port?"

It was Freya's turn to nod, though she hadn't thought about the status of the port in years. She supposed that just showed how out of touch she was with the state of affairs here.

"Well, they were only granted a temporary lease. It's up for renewal now. So, we're negotiating with them to run it jointly. The port needs to be raised, anyway, to deal with the new sea levels. It would mean lots more business, and of course we want things freighted out by rail, not lorry. Anything that goes through the station increases our revenue. That's the other reason I'm studying business."

"I had wondered. It wouldn't be my first choice of study!" Freya tried to lighten the mood. "Can you still keep the weres in line during meetings by setting fleas on them, or is that not good business practise?"

Aisha's lips twitched as she tried to suppress a smile.

"Don't think I haven't considered it!" She snorted laughter. "Imagine Lisichka trying to scratch an itch when she's wearing those long elegant dresses."

Freya snickered, too.

"I bet that would speed up negotiations."

Harmony restored between the friends at least for the moment, they concentrated on eating for a few minutes.

A thought struck Freya and she paused mid-bite. She set down her forkful of chestnut mousse.

"You said your family wants to get more freight going through the station, right?"

"Yeah, that's right. Because one of my cousins runs it, just like my family runs the station cafe."

"Well, It's probably nothing, but that lorry I saw earlier, it was the same one that I saw down south. There were goblins loading railway tracks into it. Which was weird enough, I mean, no-one but railways use railway tracks, right?"

"Right. The metal's not worth much for itself, that I do know. But did you say goblins? I thought they were only on the continent these days."

"Apparently not. I'm sure these were goblins. But I only saw them for a few minutes while my train was on a go-slow because of the heat." Freya grimaced. That had been an excruciatingly long trip. "The point is, what was that lorry doing up here? And do the were-foxes have anything to do with it?"

Aisha was looking puzzled, her head on one side. After a few moments, she shook her head, and took a bite of her apple crumble before continuing.

"No, I can't see a link. It sounds like just one of those odd coincidences. Unless... Maybe they were just getting the rails for cheap iron, not for tracks. Or perhaps they... Hmm. Who doesn't like iron?"

Aisha and Freya looked at one another for a moment.

"Fairies!" they chorused together, then laughed. No-one believed in fairies. Well, almost no-one.

"What about elves, though?" asked Freya after a minute or two. "Lio once told me that the sort of elves we read about as kids don't exist, but that there's some other sort associated with thunderstorms. Different from sprites. And he'd know, he's good with weather. Also, I met someone recently who claimed to be married to a half elf." Freya shrugged to indicate that she had no evidence for the elfhood or otherwise. "So, I was thinking - what if all that iron is a sort of lightning rod?"

"Why would goblins be carting around railway tracks to possibly make lightning rods for elves, and what does it have to do with the port here?" Aisha said in a doubtful tone.

"It sounds crazy when you put it like that. But I want to find out."

"Curiosity killed the cat, they say! But you know I'm descended from the cat goddess. I want to know too."

"Let's work on it together then."

They raised their cups in a toast. Clunk! Freya's chocolate spilled over the side of her cup.

"Fenrir's teeth! I was enjoying that!"

CHAPTER FORTY

SATURDAY NIGHT IN

The rest of the weekend passed uneventfully enough. Aisha was working Saturday, so Freya spent time with Mr Fluffbum and with her young nieces and nephews. They seemed to spend at least as much time in fur as they did in human form. She could see why they weren't being sent to school yet. Their fur forms made her nervous, as did their snappish teeth. It was still hard to accept that she was related to weres. She'd known about them for years, of course, but she hadn't been around for most of those years. In fact, she'd *avoided* being around. Now she had to make up for that by getting to know them from scratch.

Literal scratch, Freya thought ruefully as she bandaged a cut on her hand from one of the were-fox's claws.

Freya attempted to make peace with her mother by cooking the meals, and doing a bit of tidying up around the place. The antics of the were-kits made this essential if she didn't want to trip over sticks in the hall and skirt around discarded clothes everywhere else.

Aisha visited for dinner on Saturday night.

"Look at us go, what wild young things we are," she joked.

"Yes, Saturday night has never been more pumping," laughed Freya. They were sitting in the back yard with glasses of iced tea, were-fox kits rolling around in a mock-fight nearby. Danae had pleaded a headache and gone inside early, taking advantage of having someone else to look after the kits.

"Seriously, though, you should come visit me. Have a break away. Maybe we could go look at the moors. It would be good to have a friend to explore them with," suggested Freya.

"A break would be nice. I'd have to make sure Gareth is trained, though." Aisha's tone was challenging.

Freya ignored the challenge. Gareth wasn't her problem anymore.

"Make a bunch of food and put it in the freezer. Then all he has to do is serve the customers and make drinks."

"He's a good cook, I think he'll cope. But I hope you can get me an in with the chilli king."

"I can't believe he's such hot property," Freya said.

Aisha groaned. "That had better be an accidental pun."

"You'll never know." Actually, it had been. But there was no need to tell Aisha that. "All right. I'll see if I can get you invited to one of his soirees," she agreed. "Depending on how it goes for me, of course."

"Ooh, fancy!"

Freya threw a dandelion at Aisha.

"I can at least ask him about buying his sauce. I'm told he's keen on selling it. OK?"

"Thanks, Freya. My Mum will be over the moon."

"And in return, you will keep an eye out for Vulcan Construction lorries at the port and anything else rail-way related. Or otherwise weird. Alright?"

"No problem. Though actually, I'll probably get my cousin at the Lonely Cat to do the eyes-on at the port. She'll have a better view than I will up at the station."

"So long as you let me know. I don't know why I'm so interested, but it feels like it might be important somehow." Freya laughed uncertainly. "Maybe it's just a distraction from all these changes."

"Don't worry, they're changes for good," Aisha assured her.

"I hope so. Anyway, the sun's just about down. Let's get rid of our charges."

Freya rose to her feet, Aisha following suit.

"OK, bedtime, all. Time to change," Freya announced.

Freya and Aisha herded the fox-kits inside to the bathroom, where they changed one by one into human-shaped children, and were cajoled into brushing their teeth. Freya shook her head at them as she waved them upstairs.

"I can't believe how big you've all gotten."

"Tell us a story, Aunty Frey-frey!"

Freya felt tears pricking at her eyes. No-one had called her that nickname since Tammy had stopped doing so. How many years ago had that been? The thought was dislodged by the clamour of the young weres.

"Alright, you lot. Settle down and get into bed, and I'll tell you all a story."

She followed the hoard - or should that be the pack? - into her old bedroom. As the were-foxes entered, Mr Fluffbum leaped from a bed to the dresser, tail lashing furiously. When it became apparent the kits were staying, Mr Fluffbum leaped out the door and dashed downstairs. Freya sighed. Her cat had not enjoyed this visit home. She looked around her old room. It had been converted into a dormitory, small beds filling up all the available space. Aisha mimed walking down stairs with her fingers and pointed at herself, before leaving Freya alone with her relatives.

"So. A story. Well. Would you like one from a book, or one that I make up?"

"One that you make up, please!"

"Alright, since you ask so nicely."

She took a breath, wondering what story to tell these modern-day hybrid weres. Stick with the classics, why not?

"Once upon a time, there was a little girl who liked to wear a red hood..."

Some time later, she quietly slipped out of the room. Her fairy tale had had a mixed reception. The were-kits had rooted for the wolf in the tale, and been disappointed by its ending. She'd spent some minutes after the kits went to sleep looking at their faces, trying to trace the lines of her sister's features in these young ones. She wondered if Danae did that, too, trying to recapture some of Tammy's lost vitality.

Just across the hall was Tammy's old bedroom, now Danae's. The door was closed. *Well, that's symbolic of my whole life. Mum's door is pretty much always closed.* Once, she'd gone into that room for comfort, to smell the essence that her sister had left behind. Now, it was just another room, her mother's refuge these days. Nothing of her sister remained there - at least Freya assumed not.

So many changes. It was hard to take it all in. She supposed it was her fault for not coming home for so long. But somehow, she'd always imagined that nothing would change at home while she was away, that she'd return and find everything the same. *I should have known better. Only change is constant. Thanks, Herodotus.* She had avoided most philosophy at uni, but a few things from first year had stuck. Not the most reassuring things, it seemed.

CHAPTER FORTY-ONE

AN EVENING CHAT

Downstairs, Aisha was waiting for her on the couch that would later be Freya's bed, patting Mr Fluffbum. The cat had done everything he could to avoid the were-foxes. Aisha's black hair was loose for a change, flowing over her shoulders. Freya had always been envious of Aisha's dramatic colouring. Her own hair was much lighter, but not really light enough to be called blond. The uncharitable might throw around the term 'mouse'.

Some demigoddess I am.

Freya sat down beside Aisha and leaned back. Looking after kids was a lot more hard work than she remembered. Of course, those kids had been kits when she was here last. It seemed almost miraculous that they could speak to her now, as well as yip.

"So, what else has been happening with you?" Aisha asked. "You must have been pretty focused on work lately. I've hardly gotten a text in weeks."

"Sorry. I guess - well. I met someone at work. Stefan. He's taken a lot of thought. And time."

"Well, is he nice? What does he look like?"

"Er, he's got red hair. He's pretty tall too. He's got muscles, which is pretty rare in an academic. I'm actually not sure if he's nice. I mean, I can't decide. Sometimes he is, sometimes he's odd."

Aisha rolled her eyes.

"If the answer's not a straight yes, then don't stick with him. Simple."

"But he's really attractive, too."

"Still needs to be nice. Don't go all ooh, yummy bad-boy, Freya. You're too old for that." Aisha tossed her black hair back, and stared pointedly at Freya.

"It's not like that!" protested Freya.

"What is it like, then?"

"Well - I guess part of the problem is that he ordered a steak on our first night out."

"He's not a vamp, is he?" Aisha screwed up her face, indicating her opinion of vampires.

"Yuck, no. You know that's never going to be my style, I have more self-worth than to want to be food." Freya shuddered at that idea. She picked up a cup someone had left beside the couch earlier, and considered it. It wasn't a cup she had used, but there was a ring of dried tea in the bottom. She imagined that's all that would be left of someone who went wilding with vamps. She put it down again. Time enough for dishes later.

"Well, thank goodness for that. That's one point in his favour, then. Anything else?"

"Well... He's got some vigilante thing going. He talks about defending his territory, but he's not a were. There have been some pretty nasty attacks on lone women around York lately. He wants me to help him find out who's doing it. Using my apparently unique biology skills. Actually, we were attacked the first night I went out with him, by a were-wolf."

"Bastet wept, you got attacked? Are you OK?" Aisha demanded.

"Yeah, I'm fine," Freya reassured her friend. She pulled at strand of hair from beside her temple and started twisting it. She'd always found braiding relaxing in times of tension. "Stefan sent the were-wolf packing. He knew the were-wolf who attacked us. He thinks it's the same one who has done all the attacks, but he doesn't have proof."

"I'd have thought you could provide eye-witness, if he attacked you?"

"He was wolf-shaped at the time. And the local police are humans. The most I could do would be report a dog attack," Freya said.

"Why would a were-wolf attack a bunch of women, though?" pondered Aisha.

"Maybe if he had the same attitude as Lachy and the rest. You know, entitled. Misogynists."

"Ick. That sounds pretty suspicious, Freya. I mean, not to knock your biology skills, but you work with a bunch of PhDs, don't you? Surely some of them are more into detective work than you - you majored in plant disease, not forensics, right?"

"You know I did. And there's bound to be more qualified people around. But he asked *me*."

Aisha looked at her enquiringly.

"Isn't finding an attacker more of a police job?"

"Well, yes. I guess. But it's a were-wolf. And you know that the police aren't always good at keeping on top of that sort of thing."

"It depends on who is running the local police, yes. But tracking an attacker sounds dangerous. I hope you're not going out on your own."

"Honestly Aisha, you sound like my Mum. Have you any idea how many self-defence classes I have taken in the last three years?"

"Not really, but you don't want to have to use those classes, do you?"

Freya knew Aisha had a point, but she didn't want to admit as much.

"What about you, then? Is your bully-turned-bestie more than just a friend?"

"Freya! Of course he isn't. He may have improved his personality traits, but he hasn't improved his looks any. And I'm the wrong gender for him anyway."

"Oh," Freya said. *That explains a lot, I guess.*

Aisha was still talking.

"I wouldn't get involved so close to home, either. Sometimes, I want to go away for a bit just so I can meet someone a bit exotic - or at least someone who hasn't known me my whole life, so *I* can be the exotic one."

"Well, why don't you, then?"

"It's hard when you end up running a business 24/7. But I'd like to meet this Stefan. Maybe you can work in a meeting when I visit. What do you think?"

"I can try, I guess. Come visit soon so we can go up to the moors. I'm not sure they're a good place to go in winter. It's probably better to go when it's not full of mud and mist. Or snow."

"I'll come as soon as I'm sure Gareth's able to do my job at least half as well as I can."

Freya laughed. "Will you ever make it, then?"

"Gareth's a fox. He's smart. I'm sure he'll be able to manage the basics."

Reassured that her friend hadn't completely gone over to the dark side of the were-foxes, even if she was counting one as a friend these days, she followed up on another thought that had been teasing her.

"What happened to the older were-foxes? The nasty ones? You know, Lachy, Tobes, that lot. Are you negotiating with terrorists?"

"Bastet, no. They all left a couple of years back. Improved the tone no end by taking themselves off. I'm not sure where they went, actually. But they're not here."

"That's one good change, then."

"It certainly is."

"Well then. I don't suppose this town has changed enough that there's somewhere to go out dancing, is there?"

Aisha goggled at Freya.

"You, dancing? Since when?"

"Since uni. I took some classes, for fun. Once I'd taken all the available self-defence classes. There was no-one I knew there at first, so it didn't matter if I looked stupid. I had this idea that if I learnt how to dance I'd be less clumsy, but that hasn't worked out. It's fun to try, though," Freya said.

"And does *Stefan* dance?"

"I don't know. It hasn't come up. Stefan's been more focussed on checking out outdoor spots where attacks have occurred."

Aisha looked disappointed.

"Oh well, to answer your question, the only place to dance is at the pub, like always. Is that something you fancy?"

"Probably not." Freya sighed. "Too many people who *do* know me. And too loud, and likely no decent music. Maybe we can just dance here. Without waking Mum. Or the kits."

"Good luck with that. The kits are all light sleepers, at least when I've been babysitting them. Maybe that should be fox-sitting. Anyway."

"Anyway, it sounds like I'm out of luck. Maybe another time."

"Maybe when I visit you."

"Yes, after you've taken me shopping in York. But I'd like those attacks you told me about to be a thing of the past. I hope you and this Stefan do sort them out before I get there. Even better, Stefan without you. Be careful, Freya."

"I'm always careful."

It was strange to be farewelling her mother on reasonably good terms the next day. Stranger still to hug were-foxes goodbye, promising to return soon. One thing hadn't changed, though. Freya was glad to turn her back on the sea - once she was a safe distance away.

CHAPTER FORTY-TWO

AN OUTING WITH STEFAN

Freya heaved her bucket of strawberries another foot along the row of plants and set it down again. A large berry rolled from the top of the pile in the bucket and plunked gently to the ground. She had managed to reschedule her planned strawberry-picking trip with Stefan and the day had turned out sunny and warm - again.

"I suppose I should stop picking," she said. "I'll just lose them if I try for more. How about you?" she asked Stefan.

Stefan glanced at his half-full bucket.

"I have sufficient for my needs, thank you." He retrieved a large, plump strawberry from his bucket and offered it to her. "Here, why don't you try one?"

She took the strawberry and ate it, feeling self-conscious as he watched her do so. Freya couldn't help but think that Stefan looked out of place in his well-tailored outfit in the middle of the straw-lined strawberry field. His plastic tub dangled from one hand, certainly not overflowing the way Freya's was.

"I'm too hot after all this time in the sun, anyway. Didn't you want to show me an attack site somewhere near here? If we put the strawberries in the shade, they should last alright." Stefan's agreement to picking strawberries had been dependent on visiting the nearby site.

Stefan stepped closer. "Do you not enjoy the sun? Most people appreciate the heat of summer."

The heat of summer is beating on my back and my head is pounding. I've had enough of the sun.

"I appreciate cool drinks too," she said out loud, once again feeling that Stefan's nearness seemed to intensify the summer heat.

Stefan laughed. "I would have summer all year round if I could. With or without cool drinks. It is wonderful to be free from frost-folk."

I wonder exactly what he's got against frost giants and such, Freya wondered. *He's never said.*

"We need the cold times as well as the summer, or we wouldn't have half the things we eat. Like cherries. And I like winter too," Freya objected. "At least I do when I'm living in a warm house."

"Ah, you do like warmth then," Stefan said, triumph in his tone.

Freya avoided the argument. It seemed a shame to quarrel in a strawberry field anyway.

"About that drink," she suggested.

Stefan shrugged.

"Very well. Pass me your excessively full strawberry receptacle and we will purchase a drink when we've reviewed the attack site."

Handing over her bucket, Freya followed Stefan through the field to the shed where their pickings were weighed and paid for.

Five minutes later they were in the shade, Stefan's car making the distance between the strawberry farm and the site he wanted Freya to inspect a mere inconvenience. Tall trees shadowed a road that began in countryside and ended in the city. At this point, it was well-to-do suburbs with iron railing fences.

"This is nice," Freya began, appreciating the cool greenery. She stopped, spotting wilted leaves on several of the trees. "That's strange. Those trees are showing the same signs of disease as those olives down South." A chill ran through her at the thought that the crop-killing disease had made it this far up the country.

"Tree diseases are unlikely to impact on an attack. Although I understand that that is the first thing that would draw your attention, I have heard that a European disease is spreading widely. Is there anything else of note?"

Freya looked around, trying to be forensic in her gaze.

"There's plenty of places to hide, I suppose. No sign of an attack that I can see, though you'd really need to be trained for that, I think." She had already visited several attack sites with Stefan over the last couple of weeks, and had failed to find much of note, apart from the odd diseased plant, which did not appear to interest Stefan. She had enjoyed the time with him however, as he was always attentive and flattering. This time, she spotted something new. "But look - there must be a fox living around here." She pointed to a narrow gap under a gate that had a few strands of reddish fur adhering to the bottom rail.

Unexpectedly, Stefan's face clouded with anger. He bent over and plucked off the fur, bringing it to his nose, before dropping it on the ground.

Now that's odd. I thought he said he didn't have a great sense of smell?

"Excuse me. I must make a phone call." He stalked back to the car to collect his phone, and was shortly making annoyed-sounding noises to someone on the other end. Freya stayed near the gate where she'd seen the fox fur, trying not to eavesdrop. Out of curiosity, she picked up the fur and sniffed it herself - very briefly.

Ugh, that's fox alright. Maybe Stefan isn't hiding anything about his nature. But why would smelling fox fur make Stefan angry? A disturbing thought struck her. *Maybe it's not fox fur. Maybe it's were-fox fur.*

She edged closer to Stefan.

"I told you to be careful," he growled into his phone. "There's not supposed to be evid-". Seeing Freya approaching, Stefan broke off. "I'll speak to you about this later," he said before ending the call.

"Is something wrong?" Freya asked.

Stefan seemed to calm himself with an effort, unclenching his bunched fists one finger at a time.

"It is nothing for you to concern yourself with," he said. "Come, have you seen anything else of interest? Anything that matches the other sites?"

Freya hesitated. She wanted to ask if Stefan knew any were-foxes, but couldn't think how to approach the subject.

"When I think about it," she said haltingly, "all the sites would be good for foxes to live. But the attacks were by were-wolves, weren't they?" She lifted her eyes to meet Stefan's hazel ones.

He blinked slowly.

"Yes, indeed," he said slowly. "Were-wolves are most untrustworthy."

"It must have been such a surprise for the woman who was attacked here," she said. "I hope she's OK now."

Stefan's mood seemed inexplicably to lighten.

"Oh yes. I am quite sure that she is fine. Come, we should find you a drink."

Freya was sitting with Stefan in the garden bar of a pub not far from the supposed attack site, sipping on an iced soda and lime, when her phone pinged. She set down her drink.

"Oh, it's Aisha," she exclaimed, before busying herself reading the message.

Stefan was occupied on his own phone, sending messages at speed. His half-drunk pint of ale sat on the table between them, gleaming red in a shaft of sunlight. He glanced up briefly as she spoke, but quickly returned to whatever was so engrossing on his phone. Before receiving Aisha's message, Freya had been seriously considering calling a taxi to get home, though she wasn't sure what to do about her strawberries in that case. Now, she had other things to think of.

Aisha's coming for a holiday visit. I'd better book some time off work. The thought of seeing her friend enlivened Freya, who had been feeling somewhat abandoned - which was not at all the way Stefan usually treated her. She turned towards Stefan to tell him her news, but bumped her glass. It promptly fell off the table, soaking her skirt.

"Ugh, look at this," she said, putting her phone on the table and holding the edge of her dripping skirt away from herself. "At least I wasn't drinking red wine. Would you mind keeping an eye on my things while I go clean up?"

Stefan transferred his gaze to Freya, who blushed with sudden embarrassment.

"I don't know why this sort of thing always happens to me," she said.

Stefan seemed to come out of his angry reverie.

"Your things will come to no harm. Please, do take the time to dry yourself. That must be uncomfortable."

Relieved that Stefan had started paying attention to her again, and seemed to have lost his anger, Freya went inside to dry off. Perhaps the outing hadn't been a complete loss after all.

CHAPTER FORTY-THREE

THE CHILLI GUY'S PARTY

Freya got a ride with Kylie to the chilli guy's party. It was deep in the countryside, ill-serviced by buses. They'd driven down a long hedge-bordered driveway, jolting over numerous pot-holes, before arriving at an old two-storey red brick house. Freya looked around with interest.

"It looks like quite a large place for a bachelor," said Freya as they walked up the path to the front door.

"Sure does. Ten to one he rents out rooms or something."

"Hard to imagine many people renting way out here. Even you live in the city, don't you?"

"Nah, I'm out in the wops too. That's why I have a car."

"Funny, I always think of you as a city girl," said Freya, "but it's convenient for me that you have a car."

"It's a bit of a pain sometimes, but it's better for me to be away from dense populations."

"You don't like crowds?" asked Freya, feeling sympathetic.

"Nah, it's safer, is all."

Funny way to put it. Why 'safer'?

The policy analyst, or as Freya now thought of him, the chilli guy, met them at the door when they knocked. He had evidently dressed up for the occasion, his shirt unrumpled for a change, shoes polished black instead of nondescript trainers. He fussily directed them to hang their bags on a coat rack in the hall, before inviting them further inside. Freya tugged at the short skirt of her dress, uncomfortable in party finery when she was used to casual clothes in the lab.

"Please come through this way. You're the last ones to arrive, bar one or two people who are unlikely to attend, although I live in hope, of course," Phillip said in a lugubrious tone.

There were framed photographs of chillis on the walls, alongside certificates proclaiming first places and commendations from some chilli society that she'd never heard of. The floors were covered with ancient black and white checkered lino. The chilli guy led them through a long hallway to the back of the house and into a large conservatory.

"Welcome to the first home of my chilli empire," he proclaimed. "This room is where I started out. It's far too small now, of course, but it has served me in good stead. You can see some of my newer specimens on display in here." He gestured expansively. A variety of potted plants were dotted around the room, each one bearing distinctive pepper-shaped fruits. "I like to think of my operation as an ark. Future generations of Britons will have access to the best possible chilli varieties, thanks in part to my humble efforts."

"Um. Great. Well done," said Freya. She hoped her face wasn't contorting the way it wanted to, as she tried not to laugh. She caught a glimpse of Kylie's face, mouth decidedly straight but eyes twinkling merrily. A smile tugged at her own lips and she hastily smothered it.

"Come through, please. There will be an announcement before the dinner, but make yourself at home in the meantime."

Several small groups of people already occupied the conservatory. Freya recognised about half of them from the institute, but the rest were unfamiliar. Freya instantly regretted accepting the invitation.

This is going to be dire. I hate meeting new people.

The chilli guy led Freya and Kylie up to the nearest group.

"I think you know everyone here," he said. A distant chime sounded. "Ah, please excuse me, I must see who else has arrived." He abandoned Freya and Kylie, shoes squeaking on the black and white floor as he departed.

Freya looked at the sea of strange faces in some confusion. She homed in on the half-familiar ones in desperation.

"Haven't I seen you in the canteen at lunchtime?" she asked a short, plump blond woman.

"Yes, probably. I'm in the pest animal control lab." The woman nodded in the absent chilli guy's direction. "Phillip always likes to invite a few new people along, so you won't find yourself alone in wondering who is who. It's usually worth it for the food, though." She licked her lips, revealing slightly longer-than-average eye teeth. "I'm Diana."

How appropriate, that a woman named for the huntress should be in animal control. She doesn't look much like a huntress, though. More like a schoolteacher. Apart from those teeth.

"I'm Freya. I'm part of the plant disease lab. Er. Does Phillip do this sort of thing often? "She felt uncomfortable using the chilli guy's name, but she could hardly call him 'the chilli guy' in his own house, no matter how many chillies were on display.

"Once every couple of weeks in summer. I think it depends on how many new varieties he has to release."

"Varieties?"

Diana pointed towards the pepper-bearing plants. Light from the westering sun glinted off the short blond hairs on her face.

"Of chilli. He's one of the major breeders, you know."

"I didn't, but I guess that makes sense."

"It's a bit of a conflict of interest, I suppose, since he's in policy, but no-one minds too much. Come on, I'll introduce you. Phillip never remembers to do that."

Diana looked at Kylie with raised eyebrows. Kylie stepped forward with a hand outstretched to shake.

"I'm Kylie. We met at work."

Diana ignored the hand.

"Who could forget that accent. You were in my focus group last week, weren't you?"

"Yeah, that was me."

"You certainly contributed many of your opinions," Diana said.

"You betcha. I'm always glad to give my two cents worth." Kylie glanced at Freya, and lowered her voice - though not much. "You haven't had to go to one of those yet, have you?"

"Not yet."

"Be glad."

Diana cleared her throat, glaring at Kylie.

"Freya, let me introduce you to the others in my team - those who are here," she said.

Freya cocked her head questioningly at Kylie. Did she mind being left out of the introductions?

"Go on, knock yourself out," Kylie said. "I'll just stand around and admire the chillis." She smoothed her wavy mid-brown hair away from her face and nodded at Freya.

Freya trailed after Diana, wondering if there was any hope of enjoying the evening.

Diana led Freya to a series of people who were standing around the conservatory in small groups, drinking glasses of wine or beer. Freya was getting irritated at being introduced as 'Freya, the new girl' before she'd met three people. She soon lost track of the names she was told. She wished someone would offer *her* a drink. Freya was beginning to be reminded of the huddles of kids at her last school. Who was the bully around here? It seemed like there was bound to be one. Maybe Diana was the one - she certainly hadn't been kind to Kylie. But before she could figure out if that was the case, a thin ting-ting sound caused the assembled guests to fall silent. Phillip strode into the room, tapping a spoon against his glass. He hit the glass twice more in a jaunty pattern. He seemed to stand straighter here than he did at work.

"Thank you all for coming this evening. As you all know, I like to have these little get-togethers when I have a new variety to introduce to the world. Tonight is no exception. And I'd especially like to thank Kylie and Freya for attending this evening, as it's the first time either of them have been here. Welcome, both."

Freya's face was engulfed by a wave of heat. She hadn't realised this event would be so formal, or that she would be singled out. She looked around, trying to avoid the assembled gaze of the multitude, and spotted Kylie beside a door to the outside. *She* didn't appear embarrassed at being personally identified. The chilli guy continued with his speech.

"In a few moments I will show you tonight's real star, but first, please charge your glasses."

A hubbub of voices broke out as everyone shuffled to fill their glasses. Freya took the opportunity to break away from Diana, heading for Kylie. Halfway there, she encountered the drinks table.

At last.

She found a glass of what looked like orange juice and snagged it. Then she played dodgems with people's elbows, trying to keep her glass un-spilt. When she finally reached the doorway where she'd seen Kylie, she was nowhere to be seen. Freya peered out the door. It led to a back garden far larger than the house had led her to expect, and beyond that, a series of polytunnels rose white and gleaming towards the horizon.

"Kylie?" she called.

CHAPTER FORTY-FOUR

KYLIE IS A WERE-DEMI

Kylie materialised silently at her elbow, startling Freya. She jumped, and her orange juice splashed out of her glass. She gulped at it hastily, anxious not to lose all of it - she didn't want to have to battle the crowd inside for another one. But the juice had an unexpected aftertaste. Not orange juice, after all - or at least not just orange juice.

"Odin's eye, Kylie, this juice is spiked with chilli!" She opened her mouth and panted, trying to dislodge the burning sensation. Kylie had the effrontery to laugh.

"You should see your face, Freya! It's red enough to light up the garden, no need for a torch. I guess you're not a big fan of the hot stuff, then?"

Freya decided that panting wasn't helping and closed her mouth. It still felt like she was breathing fire.

"You could say that, yes. But I wasn't expecting to find it in juice!"

"It's probably sangrita. Mexican orange juice. After all, everything Phillip does outside of work is Mexican, or so I've heard. I reckon if you scull it, it won't be so bad."

"Not taking that option, thanks. Sounds awful. I wish I'd known. I'd have stuck with water."

"Never mind, you escaped the spiteful Diana, at least."

"No thanks to you. I had to come find you. You must have really annoyed her on that focus group she mentioned."

Kylie snorted with laughter.

"Yeah. I told her what I thought of her mouse traps. She didn't want to hear it."

"What are you doing out here, anyway?

"Just cooling off and admiring the chillis."

"I thought you'd be a party person."

"Nah, only when I'm in the mood. And that Diana put me right off. Besides, if I wanted heat I would have stayed home in Oz."

"Shame about this summer, then."

"It sure is. I thought rain and mist were a dead cert when I came here. That's why I even came. And what do I get? Bloody climate-change induced drought. Unbelievable."

They were silent a moment, watching the last wisps of light leave the sky.

"Looks like a beaut cloud bank building up out there," said Kylie. "Maybe we'll see an end to the drought soon after all."

There was a distant flicker of lightning against the dark clouds on the horizon. Freya shivered despite the oppressive heat. It looked like sprite weather. She hated sprites.

"Perhaps we should go in now," she said. As far as she knew, Kylie was mundane. But that wouldn't put off sprites.

"You go if you want," said Kylie. "I need to cool off a bit more before it's safe for me to go inside. If I encounter that Diana again just now, sparks will fly."

There she goes, talking about safety again. What's going on with her?

"You really don't like her, do you?" asked Freya.

"What was your first clue? Seriously, though. Someone will get hurt if I go back inside before I'm totally calm. It's the same reason I avoid cities now. And since it's been so stupidly hot and dry here, a spark would be all it takes to set a fire. Just like back home."

Why does she keep talking about sparks?

"What was it like, back in Australia? Do you miss it? You don't talk about it much."

"Hell, yeah, I miss it. Don't miss the bushfires, though. They're a total nightmare, these days. Even the cities aren't safe, not with me around. And afterwards, the scavengers feast. It's bloody tragic. That's what made me come here. No bushfires here. Not unless..." Kylie trailed off.

"Unless what?"

"Never mind. I just need to make sure I stay away from people who make me mad. Like that Diana creature."

"Creature seems a bit harsh."

"I like to call a spade a spade. And she is absolutely a creature. Honestly, I get steamed up just thinking about people like her. Smelling them, too."

"I didn't notice her wearing perfume," protested Freya.

"Not what I meant. Though I'm sure she finds perfume just as nasty to the nostrils as I do, so I doubt she was wearing any. Doesn't mean I have to like her or what she stands for."

Thunder rumbled in the distance, and Freya glanced back towards the conservatory. They really should be going back inside. Just as soon as she'd figured out the reason for Kylie's dislike of Diana.

"What does she stand for, then? Apart from mousetraps."

"I just don't like her ethics. I know, I know," said Kylie, as Freya raised an eyebrow at her. "It sounds hoity-toity to talk about someone's ethics - but it's true. I don't like her reasons for doing stuff. And the stuff she does is dodgy as."

"I see. Well, I don't, really, you haven't said what she does. But what do you mean about perfume - are you allergic or something?" Freya asked uneasily.

Kylie turned to face Freya.

"You really don't know, do you?" she said.

"Know what?"

Kylie shook her head slowly.

"Diana is a nasty piece of work whose pack should be ashamed of her, assuming she even has one. She represents everything that weres shouldn't be. She's manipulative, she applies her natural talents in ways that frankly I am appalled by, and she doesn't even have the decency to be honest about what she is."

"Wait, she's a were?" said Freya in shock. "I've been following a *were* around a chilli party?" She hastily replayed the last few minutes in her mind. Diana's hungry look. Her lack of perfume, was that a hint? Those teeth... Yes. "I've been following a were around a chilli party!" Freya couldn't believe she'd been so close to danger without realising it. She must be out of practise, not to have noticed earlier. Or maybe she'd just been trying so hard to be normal, she'd forgotten to take note of the signs of the non-mundane.

"You have. And you-"

"What about me? I'm just a regular person," said Freya. Uncertainty gave her voice a slight waver. She'd tried so hard to blend in here, hoping to avoid the pitfalls and dangers of the demi-world.

"This nose does not lie," said Kylie, tapping her own longish nose with a finger. "If you're a regular person, I'm the friggin' Queen of Sheba. Come on, don't be such a bloody galah. I *know* you're not a mundane."

Freya took a step away from her friend, eyes fixed on Kylie's nose.

"Do you mean you're some sort of were too?" she asked.

"Nah, I've just got a great sense of smell." Kylie rolled her eyes. "Of *course* I'm 'some sort of were'." Kylie's air quotes were easy to hear. "I thought you knew that."

Freya found her breath coming fast as she began to panic. Not only had she been following a were around a party, her best friend at work was one too. There was a sudden cheer from inside the conservatory, and she jumped, before realising the source of the noise. Perhaps the chilli guy had revealed his latest chilli triumph. Whatever that looked like. The sound prevented her from edging back inside, though. Besides, there was a were inside, too. She was trapped out here, her friend suddenly a foe.

I can't believe I'm having were-trouble again. Though - I guess she's not attacking me.

"Frigg's sake, Freya. I'd never have brought it up if I'd known you would turn out to be a snowflake. What are ya, some sort of racist? I thought we were friends," said Kylie. Her eyes started to glow softly, green in the dim light. Freya could hear her own heartbeat pounding in her ears as she broke out in a sweat.

"Er, yes. We were. Are. Friends, I mean. It's just - I don't have a good history with weres. Childhood trauma you know, that sort of thing." Freya felt like she was babbling. Kylie's eyes were making her nervous.

"You say 'weres' like we're all the same. Do you even know what sort of were I am?" Kylie said.

Freya flinched from the scorn in her voice.

"Um... no. Not yet."

"Right then. How about you have a bit of a think and see if you can figure that out, and I'll just take myself for a walk before I burn this whole chilli empire down by mistake." She turned away and started stalking towards the rows of polytunnels, which were presumably filled with chillis. The air seemed to sizzle with her anger. Some of the plastic on the nearest tunnel began to blister and melt. *That's odd. I'm sure* weres *don't usually have that effect on their surroundings...*

"Wait, Kylie! What do you mean? I thought you said you were a were, not some sort of fire demi," said Freya, disturbed by the unexpected threat.

Kylie half-turned towards her, non-committal. She was clearly still angry.

"Yes, I'm a were. But my great, great, great Grandad was a lightning deity, which means I have to be super careful not to get angry. Like I said, sparks can fly. Literally."

"Wow. That sounds... scary. I didn't know. I'm sorry, Kylie. Is there anything I can do to help?" Freya felt that she was on firmer ground with deity-based problems. But Kylie just stared at her with those glowing green eyes.

Freya tried again to mollify her. The last thing she needed was another angry were or demi around.

"It's not you, exactly. It's just - I've had some bad experiences with weres, in the past. It's probably prejudiced me. But you've been a good friend. I guess I should try to look beyond my prejudice."

"Excellent idea. How about you work on that. Now if you'll excuse me-"

"But I can help!" *Never mind pretending to be a mundane, it sounds like she has a problem that a water summoner could actually help with.*

"I don't want your help. Not now. Just give me some space, y'know?"

Freya hovered reluctantly near the conservatory door. She'd been out here a while, and Kylie clearly didn't want her company now. Not that she wanted Kylie's company, either. Or did she?

What do I do now? Kylie's my ride home. Do I want a ride home with a were? Even a were who has been my friend?

Of course, there was a were inside at the party, too. Freya shivered. There had been altogether too many weres in the last few minutes. But what sort of were could Kylie be? For that matter, what about Diana? Diana didn't remind Freya of the were-foxes back home. She was much twistier.

More ferret-like than anything else. Are there were-ferrets?

It was hard to imagine a ferret-god - and that's what would be required for were-ferrets to exist, if Freya's friend Aisha had it right. Then again, Freya's Mum could have the correct theory - *she* had always maintained that weres were the descendants of other non-mundane beings, just like trolls, elves and sprites. Freya wasn't sure if either of them was correct. But she was sure she didn't want to spend time around weres, whatever their origin. Except maybe her nieces and nephews. It was all too confusing.

So what about Kylie? She's been nothing but friendly till now.

Kylie claimed to be a were and those glowing eyes surely backed up her claim. But Freya had no idea what sort of a were she could be. Something Australian, presumably. Kylie wasn't bouncy enough to be a were-kangaroo. Snorting in amusement at the thought, Freya quickly ran through the possibilities.

Friendly, big brown eyes, brown hair, not too furry... honestly, I have no idea. Maybe I should look up Australian weres online. Or even just Australian animals.

Freya's musings were interrupted by another grumble of thunder. Casting a worried glance over her shoulder in the direction that Kylie had disappeared, she stepped back into the conservatory. Kylie might be descended from a lightning god, but *she* certainly wasn't. The last thing she wanted was for the evening to be interrupted by sprites. That would really destroy any semblance of normality she'd managed to maintain.

Kylie stalked off into the darkness. Feeling rejected, but not sure if she wanted to repair the rift - *How could I be friends with a were?* - Freya let her go.

CHAPTER FORTY-FIVE

A PARTY AND A FIRE

Inside, a susurration immediately filled her ears. Apparently the party was in full swing. A range of snacks were laid out on small tables now, and people stood around nibbling, laughing and chatting. After her experience with the chilli orange juice, Freya eyed the snacks with trepidation. It seemed likely that the chilli king of the North's favourite foods also contained chilli. She shuddered at the thought. She was getting hungry, though. Was there anything safe to eat here? After poking around for a few moments, she decided to try a small bowl of what appeared to be black beans, accompanied by rounds of corn chips. There was a red sauce in another bowl, too, but Freya wasn't trusting that. To her relief, the beans were unadorned by chilli in any form - though the food *was* rather bland. Maybe there was something in the chilli guy's fondness for spices after all. Just not chilli. Freya spotted some wedges of lemon and squeezed that onto her beans.

A voice at her shoulder made her jump. Was there no end to people startling her while she dealt with citrus tonight?

"I'm so glad you've rejoined us. For a while there I thought you must not be enjoying my little get-together," Phillip said from just behind her. "Have you admired my latest collection yet? I have just revealed a lemon-scented chilli. I should think it will be very popular."

Swallowing her mouthful of bland beans, Freya wished she had something to wash it down with.

"I didn't see that one yet, no. I thought you said you only had a few plants at home?"

"Only a few inside, these days, yes. My polytunnels are more of a business than a home."

"They're extensive," Freya said.

"Moderately so, moderately so," agreed Phillip. "But they're predominantly unheated, so alas, many species are as yet beyond my reach."

Despite her general dislike of chillis, Freya was professionally interested.

"You haven't talked to any of the geologists about getting heating then?"

Like Stefan, Freya thought.

"I'm afraid I don't get along with the geology team. Professional differences," said Phillip, tight-lipped.

I really struck a nerve there, Freya thought. *No wonder Stefan didn't want to come without an invitation.*

"So how do you get hold of the seeds?" she asked aloud.

"Oh, I have an extensive network. We exchange seeds with each other, and I breed a lot myself. Just my little hobby, you know."

Freya thought of the rows and rows of polytunnels she'd seen outside.

Some hobby. He must employ tens of people to run those things.

"Oh yes?" she said politely. "Do you have many people working for you then?"

"Just a few happy souls to give me a hand now and then," he said evasively.

Freya nodded in what she hoped was an understanding manner. Why would he deny the personnel needed to keep his operation going?

Is the chilli guy hiding something? Or is Stefan?

Diana oozed over to join Freya and Phillip. Freya glanced at her warily, much more on edge now that she knew the woman was a were.

"Such wonderful food you always provide, Phillip," she gushed, pouncing on what appeared to be a whole finger-sized chili stuffed with some sort of meat. She ate it with evident relish, reaching for another as she swallowed the first. "But excuse my manners, Freya, you must try this!"

Freya took a step away.

"No, I'm fine, thanks."

"Perhaps you'd prefer one of my special char grilled corn cobs, instead?" offered Phillip.

"Er, sure." That sounded unoffensive. And Phillip was clearly proud of his offerings; she'd have to take something. Freya abandoned her bland beans and picked up the suggested corn. It was sprinkled with something suspiciously red. She took the smallest possible bite. At first, it was quite good - Phillip had clearly found the limes he longed for, and applied them to the cobs. A moment later, the fire of a thousand suns hit her mouth. She gasped, then croaked.

"I just need... a glass of water... please."

Diana smiled, a small, gloating smile. Freya decided that whatever sort of were she was, Kylie was right to dislike Diana. The woman was just mean. Phillip hustled away to a drinks table, and returned with a full glass of iced water. He had a second glass of milky liquid in the other hand.

"The burn usually dies down after a few moments, to be replaced by the most enjoyable taste sensation," he assured her.

"Great," Freya said after a huge gulp, her mouth still on fire. "I'll look forward to that.

"Take this one. It's more effective than water," he suggested, proffering the milky liquid.

Freya took the second glass and swilled the yoghurty-tasting contents. The burn eased to a more manageable smoulder.

Apparently Phillip wasn't vindictive, just obsessive in his passions. Freya suspected Diana wasn't so pure of heart.

"But Kylie. Where has she gone? I had hoped to introduce her to some of my specialities too," Phillip said.

Freya wondered briefly if that was the real reason Kylie had gone outside - to escape offers of specialities that she wouldn't enjoy. But no, she had seemed genuinely upset.

"I expect she's gone to explore your unrevealed chillis," Diana interjected.

Phillip gave a worried glance towards the garden and the polytunnels beyond. Following his glance, Freya saw that it was completely dark out there now. There was no sign of Kylie.

"Oh, I do hope not. Some of my experimental plots are at quite a delicate stage just now," Phillip said with a gentle moan.

"Perhaps you should head her off, Freya," Diana suggested.

"No, no, that wouldn't do at all," Phillip said. "Freya wouldn't know what tunnels to avoid. No, I'll have to go myself. Although I hate to leave my guests." He hovered, indecisive. This was more like the behaviour Freya expected from the policy analyst she was familiar with from work. How was it that he could go so quickly from a megalomaniacal chilli king to an uncertain, rumpled clerk?

"Your guests will be safe with me, Phillip. I'm sure you won't be long, in any case," Diana said, patting Phillip on the shoulder.

As she did so there was a bright flash and a phenomenally loud growl of thunder - the house seemed to shake with it. In the wake of the thunder the guests all paused for a moment, stunned. Then a babble of voices filled the silence.

"That must have been right overhead."

"There was a lightning strike!"

"It hit something. I think it hit something!"

"Look, there's a flame!"

Through the glass walls of the conservatory, Freya could see a thin flame wavering to life between the garden and the polytunnels. It flared and spread faster than she had thought was possible through the dry landscape. An orange glow lit up the night.

"My chillis! Help, please!" cried Phillip.

There was a concerted rush to the outside door from some of the guests. Others dashed for the corridor and the exit - evidently not everyone present was prepared to fight fire. Freya was part of the former crowd. After a brief tussle as too many people tried to get through the door at once, Freya came out ahead.

Kylie went that way. And she was angry. Did she accidentally call down a lightning god?

Hastening towards the fire seemed foolhardy, but Freya thought she might just have a way to deal with this problem. She'd been thinking about it earlier, before Kylie stalked off, but she hadn't managed to tell Kylie. Who was a were. Freya still couldn't quite grasp that. How could she have made friends with a were? No time to deal with that problem now, though. Freya rounded the back of the nearest polytunnel, the earthy odours emanating from it a reminder of childhood visits to her Mum at work. Weeds grew around the edges of the tunnel walls, and Freya snatched at them as she ran, gathering a handful of them, heedless of the sting of nettles. Ignoring the tunnel's entrance, she ran on and found herself on one side of the fire. It had spread further while she ran, and was now leaping around the edges of four tunnels, and racing through the grass towards the house. Through the smoke, Freya could just make out human figures whacking at the fire with jackets and brooms. There was another couple on the side closer to her. They didn't seem to be paying much attention to the fire - from their body language they were too busy arguing. There was something about them that seemed familiar. However, before Freya could identify either figure, a waft of smoke billowed from the fire, hiding them from view. When the smoke dissipated, only the fire-fighters were in sight.

All right, I'm probably hidden enough. No-one should know I'm a demi if I do a summoning from here.

Thanks to the ongoing heat wave, only a thin scattering of grass broke the surface of the dirt, so it was easy for Freya to use her sandalled foot to draw a circle in the dirt around her. She started to hum, thinking about what words to put to her song. She should have spent more time looking at maps of this area; the only water sources she could think of were the great rivers that flowed through the city - the Foss and the Ouse. With a mental shrug, she decided to go with them. The fire was endangering people and houses now, it had to be stopped somehow. Before she could start her song, however, a small grey shape came hopping - hopping?! - out of the firefront towards her. She looked at the thing in surprise. It had short arms, big dark eyes, long feet, brown fur and a pouch. Definitely Australian. She hazarded a guess.

"Kylie? Is that you?"

The thing blurred - although that could have been the smoke haze, which was getting worse by the second - and a moment later Kylie stepped towards her, dark smudges marring her made-up face.

"Who else would it be," croaked Kylie. "I told you I can't afford to get angry."

"So I see," said Freya, assuming that Kylie was the source of the lightning. "Hopefully I'll be able to help with that in a moment. With this fire, anyway. But what in Frigg's name are you? I mean, even though I've seen your were-form now, I still have no idea."

Kylie looked askance at Freya.

"I'm a were-quokka, of course," she said. "But don't you dare say I'm cute."

"Alright, I won't. Tell you what, maybe you can tell me all about it some other time. Right now, could you give me some space? I'm going to summon a river god or two."

"Hell, really? In that case, I'm off. The last thing I need is to meet more gods." Kylie shimmered back into her grey-brown wallaby-like shape, details blurry in the smokey darkness, and hopped off into the distance.

Well, that was weird. I wonder what a quokka is? Maybe if I survive this summoning I can find out. She doesn't look *dangerous.*

A gust of wind blew sparks in her face, and Freya was recalled to the seriousness of the current situation. The fire was providing so much light now that she could see ivy growing in the hedgerows that edged the field of polytunnels. She left her circle long enough to break off a twig from the hedge, and wound the ivy around it, capturing her bundle of weeds with the same motion.

"Right."

A deep breath of smoke made her cough, but when she recovered, she sang out as loudly as she could, calling the distant river gods with promises of riverbeds and renown. After a few rounds of song, she had to break off because of the smoke.

What can I use as a mask? Short top, short skirt... I should dress with more options in future.

With a shrug, Freya crouched and buried her face in her cotton skirt. The soft fabric eased her overheated face. But her eyes were still watering from the smoke. But below the crackle and roar of the spreading flames, she could hear a far-off rushing of water. The first trickle arrived in seconds, diverted perhaps from some tributary. The muddy brown water carried grass and sticks from its journey, but it trickled directly to Freya's circle.

"Over there, please," she said to it hoarsely, pointing. "There's a fire to quench."

Obediently, the water ran past her towards the fire. It seemed to grow in size and depth as it approached the fire. The river water must be arriving. There was a sizzling sound as water met fire, and steam billowed forth. Freya worried that she hadn't managed to call the main bodies of water after all, and her small trickle would be overcome by the flames.

She rose from her crouch in order to sing some more, but quickly realised her mistake. Crouching, she'd been able to breath. Standing, the smoke was acrid and thick, and impossible to see through - or to breath. She hastily crouched again, and clutching her home-made thyrsis, she sang again.

If only Tammy could see me now, she thought. *She'd laugh if she knew how often I've found myself using the summoning skills she taught me. Before saying she told me so.*

Tears misted her eyes. Given how much the smoke was already making her eyes weep, for a change she could tell herself it wasn't happening.

Focus, Freya.

The rushing water sound was louder now, and closer. Suddenly, Freya found herself knee-deep in water, the gushing liquid completely ruining her supposedly protective circle.

So much for that...

Freya was forced to stand or be washed into the fire area as the combined floodwaters rose and swallowed the fire. In a surprisingly short time, the orange glow from the fire was gone, along with every last spark. There was still a haze of smoke in the air, and everything smelled - either of burning, or of mud. In the dim light remaining, a huge hump of water formed in front of Freya, shaping itself into an old man, complete with flowing brown beard.

I'm sure that's not what they usually mean when they describe hair as flowing, Freya thought, looking at the watery beard shape that continually remade itself. She forced her mind away from such trivialities.

"Thank you for extinguishing the fire. Please return to your usual course now." She bowed, hoping that would do. Usually, she'd dismiss a summoned deity with salt, but she hadn't thought to search the catering tables for seasonings before rushing out. Hopefully politeness would work instead, as it had with the mist deity in Devon.

The river deity sloshed uncertainly from side to side.

"Is there something you want?" Freya asked it.

"Freedom." It spoke in a voice reminiscent of the flood that had brought it here, but slower. There were undercurrents in this voice, a sense of age.

"I can't remove the locks. I haven't that power. I'm sorry." She was - she'd felt the frustration of this river back in the city, with Stefan.

The watery being spoke again.

"Power. Rain."

"You're not much for words, are you?" commented Freya. "Look, I don't have power. Not to give away. And I don't know how to call rain. Though I guess I sort of did it once by accident. But I'll do my best if you go back to your course now."

The deity didn't move. "Power. Rain. Freedom," it said again.

Standoff. Great. What do I do now?

There was a sloshing sound, and Phillip strode through the water to stand beside her.

"I think you'll find a sprinkle of this does the trick," he said, holding out a small bottle of red flakes. He took off the lid, and sprinkled liberally.

Chilli flakes?

"Chilli spreads in water, you see. So, the burn gets worse. This is only a small dose, but I think we'll find that it's more than enough to move a recalcitrant deity. I have spent many years breeding this particular type; I find it much more effective than the original cultivar." He spoke in the same dry, matter-of-fact tone that he used to discuss plant import policies. As he spoke, the deity recoiled from the small flakes dotting its surface, and the floodwaters began to recede. Freya could only stare. How had she never known that chilli was so effective against water deities? For that matter, how did this dull, dry, human know? Perhaps it was a special one type of chilli.

I wish I'd had some of that when I was trying to save Tammy.

Phillip screwed the lid back onto his jar, and slipped it into a trouser pocket. Freya followed it with her eyes, wondering how she could get some - then jerked her eyes away as she realised it must look like she was staring at his crotch.

"Now then, I suppose I'd better see to my guests before I assess the damage here." He squinted at Freya. "Thank you for your assistance, I should have hated to lose my chilli library. You may be sure that I won't let anyone else know who called in the river." He turned and sloshed away, the water around his ankles rather than his knees now.

Wet though it was, Freya sank to her knees in the darkness. Standing seemed just a bit too hard right then. So much for blending in with mundane human life.

CHAPTER FORTY-SIX

FINDING KYLIE

The threatened storm held off while the guests were leaving the party, smoke-stained and bedraggled. Freya had loitered outside as long as she could, unsure what to do about her soggy dress and her missing ride home.

"Come inside, now, do. I have brought in some towels for my guests to dry off with. I can't do much for smoke inhalation, alas, but there is plenty to drink at least." It was Phillip, apparently intent on rounding up his straying guests.

Freya stood up, squelching rather.

"Thanks. I could use a drink. And a towel."

And a complete change of clothes, but I'm not asking for that, his wardrobe wouldn't help me much!

The mental image of herself dressed in Phillip's rumpled clothes did much to cheer her up. She followed Phillip back into the conservatory, where a number of smoke-smudged people were quaffing sangrita, adorned with a surprising range of towels, from Hawaiian-flowered beach towels to small, khaki coloured hand-towels that seemed more in keeping with the chilli guy's demeanour. Freya turned down a proffered glass of sangrita in favour of plain water.

If I ever come here again, I'll bring my own drinks.

Casting an eye over the assembled crowd, Freya could not see Kylie anywhere. However, Diana was much in evidence, bustling around officiously and fiddling with the music system.

"Phillip, why don't you have any dance music? Everything here is at least a decade old." Diana's strident tones were easy to hear over the murmurs of the other guests.

"I prefer to talk to people at my get-togethers. You must know that by now, Diana."

"Surely, after we've extinguished a fire like that one we all need to let our hair down a little," Diana said.

Freya wondered why Diana bothered. She might not be the best at navigating social situations, but if the host said no, there was no point in arguing. Turning her back on Diana, Freya looked around for anyone else she knew. She didn't want to have to walk home, it was too far. But the ring of faces blurred around her. The night was becoming too much. She approached Phillip, skirting carefully around Diana who was now attempting to set up her phone as a music source for the speakers.

"Excuse me, but have you seen Kylie?" Freya asked. Right now, she'd take a known, non-carnivorous were over an unknown, probably dangerous one. Phillip raised his eyebrows at her.

"Your friend? No. I haven't seen her since she slipped out earlier. To be completely honest, I am concerned that the fire started shortly after that. I have had no problems with her previously, but I simply cannot risk damage to my chilli library. If you can find her, I would appreciate it if you would take her away at this juncture."

Freya's shoulders slumped.

"I don't think she meant to do anything," she muttered. "She was trying to calm down, she said. I guess I didn't help with that."

"I am sorry to hear that. Still, if you could find her, I think that would be for the best. But before you go, I must show you this." Phillip held out a small potted plant, pale-yellow chillis adorning its branching twigs.

"Er… it's very nice," Freya said.

"This is my newest variety. I didn't want you to miss out on seeing it, and you were outside when I revealed it earlier."

"Oh. Thanks." Freya tried to make appropriately appreciative noises despite her distaste for chillis. "Lovely."

"Thank you. It has many uses, above and beyond its obvious value as a delicious culinary ingredient."

Freya considered Phillip's earlier use of chilli to dismiss the river-deity. Perhaps she shouldn't underestimate his chilli obsession.

"I'm glad to hear it. Anything I might need when dealing with," Freya glanced around to make sure she wasn't too close to anyone who might hear - no, Diana was gyrating to her own beat on the other side of the room - "um, supernatural beings?"

"Not beings such as the one you called earlier. But I find this one useful with other non-mundanes. Please, pick one fruit and take it with you. It may prove useful. And it does have a delightful lemon aftertaste." The last sentence seemed a little louder. Freya looked over her shoulder and found that Diana was approaching. She plucked the proffered chilli and closed her hand around it.

"Thank you for inviting me," she said formally. "I'll just go see if I can find Kylie now."

She tried to tell herself that she didn't scurry away, but she didn't think she was fooling anyone. She left through the black and white hallway, letting herself quietly out the front door after collecting her bag. Kylie's bag was still there, so Freya unhooked that and took it, too.

Outside, the lingering smell of smoke was overwhelming, though a stiff breeze had risen. A light over the front door illuminated the garden, casting strong shadows behind the shrubs that punctuated the lawn. The shadows moved oddly in the wind, and Freya peered at them. There was something wrong about the shape of one of those shadows. Freya stepped onto the lawn to take a closer look. The shadow moved.

Freya started back towards the door, but stopped as the shadow unfolded itself into a familiar shape.

"Kylie? What are you doing out here?"

Kylie looked hunched and miserable.

"Hiding from Phillip. He'll never forgive me if he thinks I caused that fire in his tunnels."

"Did you? I wasn't sure."

"Sort-of. That is, I didn't mean to, but that's the sort of thing that always happens with me when I get mad. Is that my bag? Thanks. I didn't want to go back inside to get it."

Freya held out Kylie's bag silently. Kylie looked sideways at Freya.

"You don't mind, then? Me being a were? I thought you might go home with someone else."

"To be honest, I thought about doing that. I wasn't kidding about having had bad luck with weres. But then - I don't know anyone else well. And I've never seen a were like you. You know, without sharp teeth."

"Just wait till you see my claws," interrupted Kylie.

"Yeah, scary. You looked like an herbivore."

"Have I ever told you about drop-bears?"

"No, but you're not that, are you? You said a quokka, whatever that is. Plus, we work together, so I thought maybe I should try to fix things up. Maybe?" Freya actually wasn't sure if such a thing was possible. But given the way the night had gone, it was worth a try to get a friend back.

"I guess. How about you tell me why you're so scared of weres, and I'll see if I can find my keys. Then we'll see if I'm in the mood to drive you home."

"Deal, I suppose. I'll give you the short version."

CHAPTER FORTY-SEVEN

DRIVEN CONFIDENCES

At first Freya sat silent and uncomfortable, unsure where to start. She soon found that Kylie wasn't the sort to wait out discomfort.

"Well then, if you tell me about your were-issues, you can stop sitting around like a stoned pigeon," she said.

Freya was startled into a laugh.

"I'm sure I'm nothing like a pigeon," she protested. She related her teenage experience to Kylie in halting bursts of speech while Kylie negotiated the narrow road.

Her car's headlights reflected from gleaming puddles in the ruts on both sides of the road. Fresh mud from the visiting river adorned the first foot or so of the hedgerows. Wrapped up in her story, Freya didn't notice at first. But as she came to the part where her sister was torn from her and her Mum by the sea-goddess, she focussed on a particularly deep puddle, just before Kylie splashed unheeding through it. Water splashed dramatically over the windscreen and she was brought abruptly back to the present.

"That river was a bit much, wasn't it?" she said guiltily.

Kylie glanced at her a moment before switching her windscreen wipers up to their fastest speed.

"You think? It did the job. Good enough, I reckon. So, now you've got that off your chest, can you see that I'm nothing like a bunch of bully-boy foxes? They're bad news even in Oz, y'know."

Freya sighed. "You're right, of course. I need to stop judging by supernatural type, I guess."

"That'd be a start."

Kylie's tone was tart, which stung, but Freya couldn't really blame her.

"Speaking of starting, do you know how that fire started? Phillip was suspicious that you did it," Freya said.

Kylie groaned and banged her head on the steering wheel theatrically. "So much for my introduction to the chilli king," she muttered. "No, if I'd started it, the fire would have been in the house instead. The problem was that I encountered my ex-boyfriend while I was out there trying to cool off. We... had words."

Freya stared at Kylie. "Having words leads to fires? Your temper is that bad?"

"Don't push me, know what I'm saying?" Kylie said, her tone half-joking.

"You're pretty fierce for a herbivore," Freya said.

"Don't give me that, I know you're a vegetarian too."

"I'm not really fierce," Freya argued. "There's not much call for it when hunting the vicious tofu-beast."

"No? Perhaps you should be. In any case, having words can lead to fires. Especially when the words are had with a volcano demi who is snooping around a party when he's not invited."

Freya felt her fire-warmed cheeks grow cold.

"You're talking about Stefan." It wasn't a question.

Kylie drummed her fingers on the steering wheel. She turned abruptly to Freya.

I wish she'd pay attention to the road.

"Yep. My ex. He was out there. Has he told you much about himself?" Kylie asked.

"A bit. Not nearly as much as he should have, it seems." Freya forced the words out through lips that didn't want to move.

"Yeah, right. He and I were a bit of an item not long before you arrived. I guess I should have told you when he started sniffing around you, but I didn't know, then."

"Know what?" Freya felt a sinking feeling in her middle. Whatever Kylie was going to tell her couldn't be good. Not if she was hedging around it so much.

"I'm pregnant. And Stefan's the father."

Freya felt the air leave her lungs with a whoosh. She couldn't think what to say. *No wonder she's so easily upset.* She took a deep breath.

"Does he know?"

"Not yet."

"Er. When are you due?"

"January."

Freya counted the months backwards in her head. *At least that means the baby was conceived before I arrived on the scene.*

"I don't know what to say, Kylie. Congratulations? Um... what do you want Stefan to do?"

"If I knew that, I'd have said something to him already. But there didn't seem much point when he was chasing you so hard."

Freya shifted uncomfortably in her seat. She hadn't thought about what relationships Stefan might already have had. *He didn't tell you he had any.*

"What do you want *me* to do?"

"Back me up when I tell him. It's like you said, I have quite a temper for a herbivore. You seem to be able to keep calm. I could do with someone calm around so I don't blow his head off with a lightning bolt. Otherwise, you understand, I'd be pretty furious with you. But since you didn't know, I guess I shouldn't hold it against you."

Nausea roiled in Freya's stomach as she thought about just how close she and Stefan had been of late.

Kylie brought the car to a stop, somewhat to Freya's relief. She still couldn't see any more than the thin beam of the headlights, and she was certain Kylie couldn't either.

"Don't get me wrong. I don't want Stefan back. He's a power-hungry bastard, and he was mostly attracted to me because of the lightning-demi thing. But I can't afford to lose this job - I'm not a citizen, I don't get any benefits if I get fired. I'd have to take the slow boat home to Oz, and that would about kill me. So, I need him to give me some support. You're a good friend, Freya - or you usually are, when you're not being weird about weres. Can you back me up? You're welcome to keep Stefan if that's what you want, but I need that support."

"I don't know that I'm the right person to give backup against Stefan. I mean, we've been doing a bit of investigating together and gone out a few times, but I don't know him *that* well."

As is terribly clear, since he didn't tell me about Kylie.

"Say you'll do it, c'mon, Freya."

"I guess."

"Such enthusiasm, I'm overwhelmed. Seriously, though, this means a lot to me. I don't have a lot of friends to rely on over here."

"I'll do what I can." Freya sighed. "I guess this means I have to get over being scared of weres."

"Sure does. Although, if they've got big sharp teeth, I'll be scared too."

Freya laughed, feeling like she'd gotten over a huge hurdle.

"We'll be scared together, then. Shall we go on before we start floating home?"

"Yeah. Good-oh."

CHAPTER FORTY-EIGHT

STEFAN APPEARS

"I never thought I'd say this, but I wish it would rain. I'd even welcome a storm right now," said Freya.

It wasn't quite as hot out here on the moorland as it had been while Aisha and Freya were shopping in the city the day before, but the effects of the long dry spell were far clearer out in the countryside. The storm that had passed through after the chilli guy's party hadn't done more than briefly dampen the ground. The grass was brittle and pale. Trees were wilting or already dead, far earlier than their annual autumn ending. The unaccustomed heat beat down on the pair as they meandered up the valley towards the high moorland.

"Yeah, it's crazy seeing the brambles dying off, I thought they could survive an apocalypse," Aisha said.

The berries which should be plump and juicy at this time of year were instead desiccated, skeletal husks. Freya sadly crumbled one in her hand before tossing it away.

"Not this apocalypse, apparently." She turned away from the withered bush.

So much for a fun day out getting free food. While she no longer had to rely on foraging to keep herself fed, blackberrying was one of the most enjoyable - and shareable - forms of foraging, and she looked forward to it every year.

"You're the expert, Freya, is there anything else we could find around here? It seems a shame to come away with nothing," commented Aisha.

"I guess we could go up on the tops and see if there are any bilberries."

"If they're anything like blueberries, that's a plan."

"Well, sort-of. There might be a breeze up there, anyway."

The track led them up a steep hill, away from the marginally more lush valley and into windswept moorland. The earth was cracked where it was exposed between patches of heather.

"Look, that'd be a bog if we were here in winter. We'd have to watch our step or risk going into a deep pool of mud," said Freya, pointing to one such area off to the side of the track.

"I knew there was a reason I don't usually visit this sort of place with you," laughed Aisha.

"Come on, it's a nice change from retail, isn't it?" Freya an internal shudder. She'd put up with the shops for her friend's sake, but they weren't her natural habitat.

"Sure, for a day or so. But I like the city, too. I don't want to be out in the wilds my whole time off. Bring on the shopping centres!"

Freya smiled at her friend's vehemence.

"I'll go in with you again, but don't expect me to spend all day in a mall. You know I'd go insane if we did that."

"I know," said Aisha. "You're too wholesome for malls."

Freya made a face at her friend's teasing.

"It's not that," she protested. *Wholesome or not, it's too hot to talk.*

Silence fell for the next few minutes, the steepness of the hill robbing them of the breath to chat. They crested the hill at last, and Aisha flopped dramatically onto a patch of dry grass.

"Phew. Do you really do this sort of thing for fun?"

"Sure. I like being out and about, seeing what Gaia's growing, since I'm no good at growing anything myself. Although there aren't any hills like this near where I live now, so this exercise is tough on me too. And we're not having much luck with finding growing things, either," Freya said mournfully.

She gazed out over the rising moor, the lack of trees giving her a view of at least as much sky as earth. The sky was unusually blue, with no clouds to relieve the beating sun. There wasn't even a cool breeze. If they went far enough west they'd reach the windy coast, but Freya had no intention of going that far; she hadn't moved inland only to walk back to the sea. The moor was dotted with heather as usual, but up close she could see it was crispy and dry.

"I don't know if we'll find bilberries either. It's so hot."

"Good weather for sunbathing, at any rate," said Aisha.

"Fine for you. I just burn." Freya's mousy hair and fair skin matched her Norse name.

"Wear sunblock, then. Or a hat."

"I've got both, I just don't like wearing hats. And sunblock feels disgusting. Anyway, let's get a move on or we'll only see heather today. Don't you want to get to the Abbey too?" Rievaulx Abbey was a famous local landmark - though it was a long trek on foot from their current location.

"If it's going to stay this hot, I'm happy to find a breeze and call it quits," Aisha said, fanning herself.

"All right then. We can head down the hill again if you want. It just seems a shame to spend all that time getting here on the train and then not see anything apart from some dried-up blackberries."

Aisha rolled to her feet with a loud groan. "You win. Lead on."

Freya consulted her map before she did so. "Straight on across the moor. There's a cafe near the Danby beacon, that should be more your sort of thing."

"Now you've given me the hope I needed to carry on. They'd better sell cool drinks."

"I'm certain of it," said Freya. "If they don't, they're mad as hatters and want to run their business into the ground."

"Well, you never know. Want to bet they only do nice hot tea?"

Freya grinned. "I'm not taking that bet."

They trudged on. There were still hints of purple on the heather from time to time, enlivening the brown expanse.

"I'm sure something moved over there," said Aisha, pointing to the left of the pebbled track.

"Probably a hare. Or a grouse, maybe?" Freya looked at Aisha questioningly. Aisha knew her birds.

"It was bigger than that. Maybe someone let their dog off leash."

"Let's hope it's well-behaved, then, or *I'll* be grousing." But Freya was too hot to care much about someone else's stray dog, even if it was a danger to other wildlife on the moor. At least it was past the nesting season for pretty much all the birds she could think of.

For once Aisha and I are in complete agreement. I can't wait to get to a chilled drink at that cafe. We should have left this walk for a cooler day.

Ahead of them, dry branches rattled and a large dog-like form stalked onto the path. Its coat was grey and brown, ungroomed, hanks of fur dangling off in clumps. It advanced towards them; light eyes focused on their faces. Its lack of vocalisation - no barks, no growls - was as ominous as its steady approach.

"Er, Aisha. I don't think that's a stray dog. Or if it is, it's one with a lot of wolf in it. Look at that long muzzle."

"I'm looking. But I'm more concerned by its teeth than its muzzle." Aisha stopped short.

"I'm more concerned that we're a couple of hours walk from anywhere, and both dogs and wolves are faster than humans on foot."

This is not a good time to remember that comment of Stefan's about beasts on the moors.

"Time for bribery then?" said Aisha.

"I'd say yes if I had anything a dog might enjoy. Got anything yourself?"

"As if. You know I'm not a dog fan."

"Any chance of summoning fleas or locusts today, then?" That was Aisha's special talent.

"I'll give it a go," Aisha said. "Fleas should do the trick." Aisha raised her arms and aimed them at the dog. "Bastet, take this sacrifice!" she cried.

The dog shivered, an odd thing to see in the heat, then paused to scratch at an ear with its hind-paw. Then it shook its head and advanced again.

Aisha shook her own head ruefully. "That thing looks as though it's already had its share of fleas. It's not bothered by more, even divine ones. I should have tried locusts, but with it this hot, there's a good chance they'd turn up in plague proportions."

"If that dog attacks, I'd risk your plague of locusts. Meanwhile... Maybe we should just back up. Perhaps it's just defending its territory," said Freya.

They walked slowly backwards the way they had come. It was awkward trying to keep facing the advancing canine, without tripping on the uneven path. It wasn't long before an unseen root tripped Aisha, and she fell heavily.

"Why is it always me who falls over?" she complained, getting to her feet hastily.

"It's usually me, I'm sure of it," Freya reassured her. Though her tone was light, her breath was coming faster. The wolf-like dog had leaped forward when Aisha fell, closing the distance between them to only a handful of metres. When Aisha arose, it resumed its slow padding.

"This is getting too freaky for me, Freya. Can't you try summoning a water-deity?" They had reached the edge of the flat land; the path descended steeply behind them.

"I can try, I guess. Though water seems in short supply up here. Anything I call probably won't have much power." Freya raised her hands. The wolf-dog's eyes flicked towards her hands, and it growled at last, displaying a mouthful of long, surprisingly white teeth. It abruptly transferred its gaze past Freya, then to her surprise, it cringed and loped back in the direction it had come, vanishing into the heather. Freya looked around.

"Stefan! What are you doing here?" she exclaimed.

Stefan, breathing only a little heavily after his ascent of the hill, lazily lifted an eyebrow.

"Walking, of course," he said. He indicated his clothes, typical of the attire worn by walkers on the moor - unlike Aisha and Freya's casual trainers and clothes, Stefan was wearing hi-tech fabrics and branded boots. He stepped close to Freya, laying a hand on her waist and bending his head for a quick kiss. Freya stepped back, feeling uncomfortable with public displays of affection from Stefan after Kylie's revelations two weeks earlier.

"But - here? I mean, this is a big place. I guess I'm just surprised to meet someone I know. Er. This is Aisha, my friend. Did you do something to chase that dog away, just now?"

"Not on this occasion."

"That makes it sound like you have in the past."

"Oh, you know what they say, the past is a mystery. Here we are, it is a wonderful day, and to my joy we have encountered one another. All else is beside the point. Although did I not suggest to you that you avoid wide open spaces?" Stefan took a step closer again. Freya shivered. Stefan was suddenly a little threatening, somehow, although he didn't make any dramatic gestures.

"You said to avoid them alone. I'm not alone, Aisha and I were walking together. We just now encountered that dog-thing, but before that we were fine. We would still have been fine." Freya was indignant, and a little scared. She didn't appreciate being told what to do, especially not by Stefan, after Kylie's revelations.

"Of course you would," Stefan agreed smoothly.

Aisha chose that moment to interject. She thrust out a hand in a business-like way.

"Hi. I'm Aisha, Freya's friend. And your name is?"

Freya could have hugged her. Trust Aisha to pick up on Freya's discomfort. Stefan stepped past Freya to shake Aisha's hand formally, despite the casual setting.

"Stefan. I am most honoured to meet you, Aisha. It is a delight to meet a friend of Freya's. No doubt she has told you much about me."

"Not really," said Aisha lightly.

Freya interrupted before Aisha could make a rude remark. "So, since our canine friend has run off, perhaps we should continue our walk. Stefan, which direction were you going?" said Freya.

"Oh, onwards to Danby, naturally. I believe there are some most interesting archaeological finds in the area, of which I would like to know more," said Stefan.

Freya looked at Aisha, who shrugged.

"We may as well carry on," she said. "As you said, dogs are faster than humans. We could be at risk whichever direction we go. But if I see a handy stick, I'm taking it with me."

"A shame about the lack of trees up here, then," Freya said.

Aisha gave the low scrub around them a dark look. "Yes."

CHAPTER FORTY-NINE

WOLF ATTACK

The three of them walked on in an uneasy silence at first. However, Aisha, never one to tolerate uneasy silences for long, was soon chatting freely again.

"So, Stefan, I take it you know Freya from work?"

Stefan nodded regally.

"Yes, we are both employed by the local university."

"Ooh, fancy. And are you in the same area of research, or what?"

"No, I am in geology and power management. But our paths cross from time to time all the same." He directed a dazzling smile at Freya, who blushed.

"Freya was telling me about the chilli sauce guy at her work. Are you for or against?" Aisha asked.

"I am not sure that I understand the question." Stefan looked puzzled.

"For or against chilli, I mean. Me, I love it. But I've yet to convince Freya here that it's worth the earth it grows in." Aisha glanced at Freya.

Freya wished she was better at reading faces. Stefan didn't seem to notice, striding lightly along behind them.

"Ah, I comprehend. I am decidedly *for* the chilli. Phillip makes a wonderful hot condiment, so long as it is applied sparingly."

Freya was as puzzled by this conversation as Stefan appeared to be. Who cared about Phillip-the-analyst's chilli sauce? She turned her gaze to the moor again. There was a flicker of movement.

"Look! A grouse!"

"One would hope so, given the large investment in managing this area for ideal grouse habitat." Stefan was dismissive.

Freya felt hurt by his indifference to something that excited her.

"Yes, but it's still nice to see them. So often they're camouflaged."

The grouse flew off a short distance and was swallowed by the heather. Freya continued to scan the skies, hoping for more wildlife sightings, though the day was really too hot for anything much to be out and about.

"I wish we'd been able to get here earlier, when it was still cool," she said, looking at the heat shimmer over the moors with distaste.

"Yeah, that's the problem with not staying out here. We have to spend half the day on a smelly old train," said Aisha. "Though I did see a buzzard on the way."

Stefan seemed puzzled by their conversation.

"But why do you not stay nearby? There is an abundance of accommodation in the area. I walked here from my own bed and breakfast this morning."

"That's fine, if you can afford to pay tourist prices," Freya said.

"If it is merely money that is an issue, then I invite you both to stay this evening at my own accommodation. I am sure the proprietor will be happy to have more bookings. The place was nearly empty this morning."

Freya looked uncertainly at Aisha, who shrugged.

"That's a very generous offer, but we couldn't possibly -" Freya began.

"No, no, I insist - assuming it does not disrupt your plans too much, of course."

Freya was uneasy at this excessive generosity, but wasn't sure how to avoid it.

"We'll think about it, and decide at the end of the walk."

"Excellent."

They walked on, the heated air seeming to muffle even the skylarks who sang unseen in the blue sky. Bees buzzed slowly between flowers, the heat seeming to slow even their rapid wing beats. Freya wiped sweat from her forehead, wishing she could do so in a more attractive manner. With Stefan here, she was more aware of her dishevelled state.

Stop it, Freya, it doesn't matter how messy you look.

In the distance, a series of mounds came into view. Freya spoke with more effort than seemed reasonable, given the flatness of the current path.

"Those must be the burial mounds."

"Sounds macabre," Aisha said.

"At least they're not recent. Those mounds must be thousands of years old. Plenty of time for ghosts to settle and ancient gods to be forgotten."

"Do you know of any gods here?" Aisha asked. "My parents never brought me up here, or mentioned local gods. Bastet and the weres tended to overwhelm everything else." She glanced back at Stefan, who was humming to himself as he walked, appearing to pay no attention to their conversation. Freya followed her gaze, and muttered to Aisha;

"He's a demi too. Volcano god. I told you, didn't I?"

Aisha looked suitably startled.

"Not that part, no. Is he safe?"

"As far as I know. I mean, he works in academia, that's not exactly volatile, is it?"

Aisha widened her eyes to convey some emotion that Freya missed, but raised her voice to include Stefan.

"So, you're staying around here, do you know about those old mounds?"

Stefan gave no indication of having heard their earlier, whispered conversation.

"But of course, I read the guide book before I came. They are simply the remnants of the ancient Bronze Age, burial places of the people who stripped the last of the forests from these moors."

Freya and Aisha looked around at the barren expanse of moorland.

"Forest, really? Hard to imagine," Aisha said.

"I suppose three thousand years will change a place. At least with so few people living around here, we shouldn't have any problems with stray gods," Freya said.

Maybe up here was a place where she could let down her guard and simply exist, like a mundane human. Though it would be more enjoyable to do that if it was a bit cooler. "A tree or so wouldn't go amiss though. We're too big to hide in the shade of the heather like that grouse did."

"Yeah. I don't know how Karim copes in Egypt," Aisha said.

"Rather him than me," Freya said. "Although I'd like to travel and see it for myself - just without the heat. I heard it got over 50 degrees out there last year."

"I'm not even tempted," Aisha.

"And who might this Karim be?" Stefan's question was whipped out so suddenly that Freya jumped.

"My brother. Why do you care?" Aisha asked, her tone hard.

"I am merely curious." Whatever emotion had caused Stefan's antagonism was controlled when he next spoke. "In any case, you were speaking of gods. I believe there were once many followers of Woden here. And later, when the Romans lived in Eboracum - York, as we know it - their soldiers worshipped Mars, Hercules and the like." He shrugged. "Typical soldierly gods."

Freya shivered despite the heat. She was not fond of soldierly gods or their followers. Or Wodenites, for that matter.

"Well, let's hope they're all moved on," she said.

"An interesting fact that I came upon in my reading was that many of those gods were symbolised by the wolf. And of course, thanks to the so-called rewilders, we now have wolves here again," said Stefan.

"Not right here, surely. It's not good wolf habitat, anyway. They like trees," Freya protested.

"Oh, but assuredly so. You were retreating from one when I came upon you earlier."

Freya shook her head. "It may have been part-wolf, but I'm pretty sure it had some dog in it, too. After all, wolves don't usually attack people, especially not on their own like that. I think it was a mistreated stray. It certainly looked like it needed a vet, or some ringworm tablets or something."

"Have you seen many wolves in your life?"

"Not exactly." She could hardly count the were-wolves that had inhabited one town she'd lived in during her childhood - they'd mostly kept human forms.

"Whereas I have seen them in several countries. I believe the one we saw *was* a wolf. Happily, it recognised me as a superior being, and retreated." Stefan seemed pleased with himself.

"That's a fair sized ego you've got there," Aisha said. Her tone was not complimentary.

Freya sighed. She didn't want her friends quarrelling, even if Aisha was right. Stefan was acting very strangely today, even leaving aside his unexpected appearance on the moor with them.

"How about we report the sighting. If they've actually got wolves in an unfenced area, someone must be collecting that sort of data," she said.

"Spoken like a true scientist. By all means, let us report it." Stefan's tone was back to his usual style.

Aisha interrupted. "Well then, if you're all in agreement, let's speed up. I'm hanging out for that cool drink, and I think if we're out here much longer you two are going to be lobsters." Aisha was laughing as she spoke, but Freya could tell she was serious.

She's probably right about us turning into lobsters, too. I should have worn more sunblock.

"Whereas you will be some other form of crustacean?" she teased. "What's your preferred type?"

"No lobsters or crabs for me, thanks. I'll stick with tanned and svelte like a seal." Aisha and Freya both laughed. It was a long-running joke between them.

They strode along more swiftly, the speed of their passage creating a welcome breeze on their faces. Freya would still have preferred a slower pace - it was much harder to spot anything, plant or wildlife, at this speed.

"Wait a moment. It looks like bilberry bushes over there." Freya pointed to some low, nondescript bushes to one side of the track. There were clusters of small, dark berries still clinging to the twigs. "Just a quick stop, alright?"

"Oh, all right, but only to make this walk worthwhile. One grouse and one threatening dog is not what I was hoping for when I agreed to come out here!" Aisha complained.

Stefan did not join them in harvesting bilberries. He stood watching them as they picked, their hands staining when the fruits accidentally squished. Aisha tried eating one.

"Ugh, I thought you said they were like blueberries!"

"I said a *bit* like blueberries. Bilberries are better cooked," Freya assured her.

"And there was me looking for a fresh snack. Oh well, they'd better be worth it."

"They will be, in a pie."

Aisha made a face. Before long, the small bag they'd been using to hold the bilberries was full.

"There, plenty for us and still some left for the birds," said Freya with satisfaction.

Aisha rolled her eyes.

"If you're done, then let's move on. It's not getting any cooler."

**

They were nearing a standing stone when it happened. Silently, the wolf-dog they'd seen earlier rose up from the side of the track and hurled itself upon Stefan, its teeth snapping at his neck. He reacted faster than Freya thought possible, grabbing its forelegs and spinning it away from him. Unfortunately, away turned out to be straight into Aisha. Too startled to summon her usual fleas or locusts, she struggled with it as it snapped its teeth near her face, its front paws scrabbling as it fought to stay upright.

"Come off it, I never did anything to you," she snarled back.

Freya reached for the wolf-dog to try and pull it off her friend, and found herself pulling off handfuls of fur.

I was right, it really does need a vet, whatever it is.

She cast around for inspiration. It was so dry up here, and not a cloud in sight. Her water-summoning ability wasn't going to be much use. But to save her friend, she was prepared to try. She started to hum. It was time to call in a water spirit.

She didn't get a chance to complete her summoning, because Stefan pushed past her and reached for the wolf-dog again. He grasped it around the chest, and this time when his hands touched it, it yelped and struggled away from both him and Aisha.

"Off you go, doggy," said Stefan, tossing the squirming beast into the bushes beside the path, where it lay whimpering in pain.

Freya saw in horror that it had two hand-shaped burns etched right through its fur down to the skin.

"What did you do to it?"

"Nothing it did not deserve. It could have killed me, or your friend. Now it should have learnt its lesson." Stefan scowled at the whining animal, which certainly showed no sign of wishing to attack now. It was trying to lick its wounds, with some difficulty. Freya didn't know what to say. It *had* tried to attack them, and Aisha had been in serious danger, but she hated seeing any animal in pain.

"We can't just leave it there. It might not survive, like that."

Stefan, about to stride off again, hesitated.

"Nature's not very kind when it comes to living and dying. We can surely do better," said Freya.

Unexpectedly, Aisha chimed in. "Yes, we should make sure it's looked after. It wasn't really trying to attack *me;* it was just startled. You did *throw* it at me."

"Oh, very well. I will carry it to safety, since you do not wish to leave it to live or die as nature decrees. My apologies for the direction of my throw." Stefan approached the wounded wolf-dog again, which immediately jerked to its feet to flee. Stefan caught it by a hind leg and bundled it up somehow. It ended up slung over his shoulder like a sack of potatoes, its mouth held firmly closed by Stefan's hand. His touch did not seem to burn it now, though it certainly cringed away from him. "I sincerely hope that it is not far to a village with a vet," he said through clenched teeth.

Curiously, the wolf-dog stopped struggling at the mention of a vet.

"If there's a vet in Danby, it should be just off the edge of the moor near here," said Freya.

"Then let us hasten there with all speed," said Stefan grimly. Apparently the wolf-dog was heavy. Freya couldn't help but feel grateful that he was carrying it, however.

They made an awkward party walking into the old-fashioned stone village. One scratched girl, one dog (or wolf) encumbered man, and Freya, all dripping with sweat. To Freya's surprise, there was a vet, and the surgery was even attended. The consultation took a while, as they had to explain how they came to be carrying a dog with some very strange wounds. Stefan cut through Aisha and Freya's muddled explanations with a curt phrase.

"We found it on the moor."

The vet did not suggest that the animal was a wolf, though she did mutter something about *stupid celebrity trends getting out of hand.* She also did not ask about the curious shape of the burns, since Stefan glared at her when she began to comment. Instead, she talked directly to the wolf-dog.

"You'll have to stay somewhere nice and cool. You're very dehydrated, and you need time for the medications I've given you to take effect. Are you staying nearby?"

"No," said Freya, assuming the question was directed at them, not the dog.

"Yes," said Stefan at the same time.

The vet looked up at them, a weary expression crossing her face.

"Well, whichever of you *is* staying nearby should be taking care of this dog. He's obviously had a hard time lately, and he's not up to more travel. He doesn't have a microchip. A few days in a quiet environment with lots of tender loving care, that's what he needs. Are you able to provide that?"

Freya nodded vigorously. She felt responsible, even though it was Stefan who'd caused the wounds on the wolf-dog, and it had been in poor shape when it attacked them. She winced, thinking of how hot Stefan's hands must have been to have such an effect. Those hands had caused a pleasurable tingling on her skin, not burns. Why the difference? And could that change? She shuddered inwardly. Stefan was turning out to be quite a different man to what she'd thought.

CHAPTER FIFTY

CATS AND DOGS

In the end, Aisha called Stefan's bed and breakfast and booked rooms for them both, despite Freya's misgivings. It was the only place with rooms available, which took pets, and taking a wolf-dog on a train for hours seemed unfeasible. Fortunately, the owner allowed pets, and its position on the edge of the moor even meant that Freya might get some of the cool early morning wildlife-watching she'd hoped for. Gravel crunched underfoot as the three of them entered the stony carpark of the bed and breakfast. The building was ramshackle, with add-ons evident from the wooden sections protruding from the older stone of the main house. Ivy covered the stony walls and made concerted efforts to attach itself to the newer additions. The middle-aged owner opened the front door when they rang the door-bell, and fussed over the wolf-dog with the assurance of a born dog-person.

"I'll put you in the ground floor ensuites, that way you'll be able to take him outside when he needs it. He looks like he's been in the wars, poor fellow. You've just come from the vet's you say? That's good to hear. Just let me know if there's anything I can do. I've a spare bowl you can use for his water. Do you have some food?" The stream of amiable chatter only ceased when the bedroom door closed behind them, a good fifteen minutes after they'd arrived. Aisha and Freya's eyes met, and they both exploded with laughter. Freya felt better after that. She told herself it had nothing to do with Stefan retreating to his own room next door as soon as they arrived.

They'd bought cold drinks and dog food in the village - which did have trees. Clearly there had been enough time since the Bronze Age for some more to grow here. Freya found a glass in the bathroom and poured out some lemonade.

"Here you go Aisha. I'll use the bottle."

"Cheers, then."

Freya set her bottle on the bedside table nearer the door. The cool drink had been worth the wait.

There were two ground floor ensuites, one double, which Stefan was already ensconced in, and one billed as a 'family room', with a double and a single bed in the one room. Freya was briefly reminded of the week her family had spent in such a room after their house was washed away. This place was quite a different prospect, however, well-kept and welcoming despite its low ceiling.

"Well, this is not how I expected the day to go," said Aisha.

"Me neither. I thought we'd be just about getting on the train home by now. And then the bus. And then trying to work out dinner. I guess things could be worse. Although we still have to figure out dinner."

I'll have to ask Angie or Kylie to feed Mr Fluffbum. Again.

"I'm sure we can do that easily enough. But first we have to argue over who gets the double bed."

"You always starfish, you can have it."

"Done!"

Bed decisions made, Aisha's attitude surprised Freya. She took charge of the care of the wolf-dog as soon as they had had their drinks, installing it in their room with a bowl of water and the food they'd purchased in the village. She wheedled a dog comb from the bed and breakfast owner. Once the half-starved wolf-dog had sated itself with food and drink, Aisha sat down on the floor beside it to comb its fur. Freya sat on her bed to make cat-feeding requests by text while Aisha struggled with the tangles.

Unexpectedly away overnight.

Can u feed cat?

On night shift. Ask friend?

Key under front mat.

Fortunately, although Angie was working, Kylie was amenable to driving over Angie's place to feed Mr Fluffbum - after Freya offered to fill tip boxes at work for a week. Cat problem fixed; Freya lay back on the bed. She was glad of the opportunity to get away from Stefan for a while and consider what had happened. It was certainly not how she'd imagined introducing Aisha to Stefan. And his behaviour had been very strange.

"He's usually really nice, you know," she found herself defending Stefan to Aisha, though her mind stole back to Kylie's complaints of his hunger for power.

"That's not the way he's come across to me today." Aisha was combing the wolf-dog's mane, removing a lot of extra fur in the process. Its transformation from stalking beast to biddable companion animal was startling.

"I know. I'm sorry. He did bring the dog though." She rolled onto her stomach, watching Aisha's reaction.

"Don't be sorry, Freya, it's not your fault how Stefan behaves!" Aisha stopped combing and looked fiercely at Freya. "Don't you ever blame yourself for the way someone else acts. He's a grown man, he should be able to control himself, volcano demi or no."

Freya looked away.

"It's just he was so nice to me. Before. I mean, he's still being nice, inviting us to stay at the same place as him."

"That's just money, that's not being nice. No, it's the way he's treated this guy that's got me really mad. Sure, he - you know, the dog - attacked him, but Stefan didn't have to burn him!"

Freya found herself nodding.

"I know. It's worrying me. But then, so is that wolf. I mean, dog. Whatevs. Its behaviour is just really odd."

"Don't talk about him as though he wasn't there," Aisha objected.

"Sorry. You're not usually so into canines. I mean, what with Bastet being a cat goddess and all." Freya had never seen Aisha spend any time with dogs before. Perhaps spending time with Gareth the were-fox had changed her attitude.

"Bastet may forgive me being nice. But have you thought about why a wolf might be out on the moor alone, and acting so oddly?" said Aisha.

"Rabies?"

"Freya!"

"It's OK, the vet said he doesn't have that, thank Frigg," Freya said.

"No, I was thinking about the fact that it's full moon tonight. You know what that means," Aisha said.

"Oh, no, not weres again." Freya flopped back onto her bed and flung an arm over her face. She wasn't sure she could cope with weres on top of Stefan's odd behaviour.

Aisha nodded. "That's what I'm thinking."

Freya rolled over so she could still see Aisha brushing the wolf-dog's fur. It was a soothing thing to watch, and she felt like she needed soothing. The wolf-dog itself had pricked up its ears, but was still lying full length on the floor, appearing to enjoy Aisha's ministrations. It was as long as she was.

"How can you stand to be so near it, when it attacked you?" asked Freya curiously.

Aisha shrugged.

"I think it was just an accident that he hurt me. I mean, if he had been seriously trying for my throat now," she shuddered dramatically, "he could have done so easily. And he didn't. I guess after babysitting your nieces and nephews, I've got a fairly good idea of when a canine means to harm me or not. Bastet knows I've had plenty of inadvertent scratches from them."

Freya grimaced, feeling guilty that Aisha knew her relatives so much better than she did. And also, guilty that her relatives scratched her friend.

"That reminds me, I'm supposed to ask you to go see your nieces and nephews again sometime soon. So, they don't forget your scent," Aisha said.

"Oh, Fafnir's breath. I know I should, it's just so nice not to have complications. That's the best thing about living away from home, you know. That, and getting to decide what you do and when you do it."

"I am sure it is, but don't rub it in. This holiday is the first time I've got away from home in longer than I can remember," Aisha said.

"At least you did get away. And look, we get to stay in a moorland farmhouse after all."

"With a large furry thing that's not a cat. Bastet may never forgive me."

"I guess that depends on what large and furry here turns out to be." Freya glared at the wolf-dog, which looked up at her and wagged its tail.

"Should be interesting. At least his mood has improved since we first met," Aisha said.

"True."

There was a ding as a message arrived on Freya's phone.

"Stefan wants to talk," she announced, after checking the message. She rolled to her feet. "I guess I'd better check in with him. Are you OK here for a bit?"

Aisha nodded, but still looked concerned.

"The question is, are *you* OK with Stefan for a bit?" she said.

"Well, before today, we were getting on rather well..."

"Better than you and Karim last time you met?" Aisha asked.

Freya stuck out her tongue at Aisha.

"Much better. Last time Karim and I met he was hanging off the arm of some rich kid whose Daddy was an archaeology professor."

"Oh, yeah. Sorry, I sort of put that incident out of my mind. It's a shame you guys didn't work out."

"Yeah, it is. But at least you and I are still friends."

"Always. Go see Stefan, then, but mind you don't bump your head on his ego."

Freya laughed. "I'm sure it's not *that* big."

"Could have fooled me."

CHAPTER FIFTY-ONE

MOORLAND B & B

Freya opened the door to the outside air and was hit by a wall of heat.

"It's like an oven out here!" She fanned her face. The only effect was to make her feel hotter.

I can't believe this heat. Is it climate change or something more?

The whole summer had been like this, a panting heat that sapped at her strength. She was beginning to think it must be supernaturally enhanced. She wondered how she could find out who was behind such a thing - and who could possibly think it was a good idea. Freya gave a mental shrug and walked the short distance to Stefan's door, tapping politely.

"Come in."

Freya opened the door and stepped inside, her eyes adjusting slowly to the relative gloom. Stefan was lying on top of the coverlet of the double bed, his hands clasped behind his head, staring at the ceiling.

"What brought you to the moor, today?" Freya asked, startling herself. She hadn't meant to lead with that thorny issue. Of course, pretty much everything she felt needed talking about was a thorny issue. Apart from Stefan's treatment of the wolf-dog, she and Kylie hadn't managed to talk to Stefan about Kylie's pregnancy.

Stefan spoke to the ceiling.

"Why, you, of course."

Freya felt a stab of irritation. Couldn't he look at her at least?

"But how did you know where I'd be? I organised this trip with Aisha, not with you."

"As to that, if you leave your emails open on your phone, and your phone on the table, then of course I will see them. There is no mystery to solve."

"So, you just read *my* emails on *my* phone and invited yourself along? That's not done, you know." Freya's nails bit into her skin as she clenched her fists in anger.

"I wished to spend more time with you. And as you know, I am still hunting the were-wolves. I suspected that you would not be safe - and indeed, you were not, were you?"

Freya found herself at a loss for words. Stefan didn't seem to understand that he'd transgressed. And while they had been attacked, it was Stefan who'd borne the brunt of that attack. The wolf-dog had seemed content with merely eyeballing her and Aisha - and had miraculously become tame when they'd suggested getting it aid. The whole thing was suspicious, now she came to think about it.

"Look at me, Stefan."

Stefan sat up at last, and directed his gaze at her. His eyes were glowing golden-red.

Now that's disturbing.

"Er. Not like that."

"How else should I look at you? I travelled to spend time with you and keep you safe, and you shut yourself away with your friend and the thing that attacked me. Do you not think I have feelings too?" His fists were balled on his thighs, and he leaned forward urgently.

"Um. Sorry. But you did hurt that dog, we had to do something for it. And that's another thing I wanted to talk to you about. I've never seen anything burnt like that before." But her thoughts jumped back to their first night out together, and she realised that Stefan must have burnt the were-wolf that attacked that night, too. She shuddered.

Stefan's shoulders slumped, though his fists remained clenched.

"My apologies. I was startled by the attack, as I am sure you can understand. It will not occur again. In any case, given the condition of the dog - or wolf, as I believe it to be - it was in dire need of a change of surroundings."

"I suppose so."

"Please, close the door and come in properly. There is no need for fear."

Not sure if she was being supremely stupid or just reasonable, Freya did as she was asked.

"Come. We have been good friends and more. Put the afternoon behind you and welcome the evening." Stefan stood up as he talked, and opened his arms wide. His eyes seemed to be back to their normal hazel now.

Freya hesitated a moment longer before stepping towards Stefan. His hands touched her bare shoulders and she flinched.

"Be not afraid. I will never hurt you." Disappointment or hurt deepened Stefan's voice.

But his hands felt pleasantly warm as always, no more than that.

Am I misjudging him? Is he safe? For that matter, is a volcano demi-god ever safe?

Freya's misgivings were muffled by sensation as Stefan's lips touched hers, and she felt the familiar thrill of response as his hands stroked her body.

"Sorry." Wait, how come she was apologising to him? She wasn't the one burning dogs with her bare hands. Or reading other people's emails. Or seeking power that wasn't theirs. Or leaving their pregnant girlfriends - but no, Kylie hadn't yet told Stefan about her pregnancy. Finding the right time at work was not easy. But Freya had heard the pain of her rejection in his voice, and hated that she was the cause of that pain. There didn't seem to be any easy answers this afternoon. Freya put her arms around Stefan, trying to hug away her confusion. She wished she thought it would work.

CHAPTER FIFTY-TWO

DOG GROOMING

Aisha was still grooming the wolf-dog when Freya re-entered their shared room some time later. To cover her embarrassment at how long she'd spent with Stefan, she started talking at random, throwing words like darts.

"That thing has got to be groomed by now. I thought you liked cats, not dogs."

Aisha shrugged.

"I do like cats. I could hardly do otherwise, given my family tree." Aisha's family were descended from the Egyptian cat-goddess, Bastet.

Freya nodded understandingly.

"But I've had to get used to canines in order to fox-sit for your Mum. And this guy needed the attention. You wouldn't believe the number of burrs he had stuck in that fur. But he must have had a nice owner once - I mean, look how good he's being now, even though it must hurt to have some of these tangles brushed out."

The canine in question was lying with his head on Aisha's lap, stretched out full-length across the floor. He lifted his head to look back at Freya, and opened his jaws in a doggy smile, tongue lolling.

Freya couldn't help but laugh.

"Aisha, I think it knows which side its bread is buttered on. Look at that grin."

Aisha grinned herself.

"You may be right. I guess he's not in pain from those burns now. The painkillers must have kicked in, he's so much more relaxed."

Freya could only agree that that had to be a good thing. Her stomach roiled at the thought of those burns. She and Aisha *had* seemed to be in danger, but did Stefan have to use his demi-given powers in such a way? She couldn't help but think that there must have been a better solution.

"So, now that you've made him look handsome again, how about we leave him to sleep off his injuries for a bit, and get some dinner?" she suggested.

"I suppose so." Aisha addressed the wolf-dog directly. "Will you be alright if we leave you in here for a bit?"

The wolf-dog looked steadily back at Aisha, and dipped his head as though in understanding.

Meanwhile, Freya was having second thoughts.

"Do you think we should leave him inside? Don't dogs tear up furnishings and things if they get bored indoors?"

Aisha considered for a moment.

"Nah, I think he'll behave. Besides, the vet said he'd probably sleep for several hours. And look, he's already looking sleepy, now I've stopped brushing him."

This was true, Freya had to admit. The wolf-dog's eyes were closed, and his sides heaved gently.

"Let's go now, then, so we're back when he wakes up," she said.

"Lead on." Aisha stood up, easing the wolf-dog's head off her lap, and Freya giggled.

"You might want to change, first. Otherwise, you could be mistaken for a dog yourself. I mean that in the nicest possible way."

Aisha aimed a mock-slap at her friend - making sure it didn't connect - and then looked down at herself.

"Oh. I see what you mean." Aisha's shorts and t-shirt were covered with dog hair. "But I didn't bring a change of clothes, other than a jacket in case of bad weather. Hmm. Maybe we can order in?"

"I doubt there's anywhere that does delivery around here. We're pretty isolated. Maybe the owner will have a suggestion."

Aisha brushed futilely at her hairy clothes for a few seconds before giving up.

"Oh well, hairy it is. Watch out, if there's a full moon I may feel inclined to howl."

Laughing, the two exited the room in search of dinner.

CHAPTER FIFTY-THREE

A WERE-WOLF IN THE ROOM

They achieved dinner with more ease than expected. Stefan had emerged while they were talking to the owner. He looked freshly showered, dark red hair gleaming wetly in the evening sun.

"Dinner? It is no problem. I will drive us to the village. We can dine in the pub."

"They do very good food there," put in the owner approvingly.

Is she a friend of the pub owner? We'll be lucky if we can find more than a plate of fries, I bet, Freya thought cynically. But she went along with the plan. It was an unaccustomed convenience to have a car and driver.

Freya was pleasantly surprised when she was able to find a salad despite the drought-induced shortage of vegetables. She chose not to notice what Stefan selected. The old stone building was stuffy in the heat, but it had a garden bar, so they ate outside, admiring the view over the valley. The gathering dusk brought out biting insects, which drove them inside again before Freya was quite ready to move.

I need to get back into exercising more, if a day of walking makes me this exhausted.

She hadn't been keeping up with her usual exercise regime since starting work at the lab, her runs being interrupted by travel. She stood at the window, glass in hand, looking out at the moon rising over the moors. The sky was a deep blue with streaks of pink, and just a couple of clouds.

"Look at that. It's beautiful, isn't it?"

She turned to share the sight with Aisha and Stefan. They were glaring daggers at each other across a wooden table.

"Oh, don't fight, please." *OK, maybe that was a bit weak. I'll have to work on my friend-placating skills.* "Aisha, come look at the moon rising."

Whatever the two had been saying to each other, Freya hadn't heard, but it didn't look like it had been pleasant. Aisha drained her own glass and set it down with a plunk that was audible. She marched, rather than walked, over to the window.

"Full moon. We'd better get back to the bed and breakfast," she said.

"Why the hurry?" asked Freya.

"Full moon? Wolf-like dog? Do these things say anything to you?"

Freya raised her eyebrows. "I know, you suggested that before," she said.

She looked over at Stefan, who was staring morosely at his empty glass. As the driver he'd stuck with water. "Anyway, let's get Stefan to take us back now."

Aisha hesitated. "I think you can do better, Freya."

"I don't want to talk about Stefan right now. I don't want any arguments. Let's just go."

It was only a few minutes later that they rattled up the hill and into the bed and breakfast carpark again.

Aisha scrambled out of the car immediately, and started making her way around the main building to their bedroom's entrance. Freya took the time to thank Stefan for his help getting them to dinner and back. It seemed only polite - and it might diffuse some of the tension she felt snapping around them.

She was finding it difficult to balance her emotions; Aisha's dislike of Stefan, her own horror at the burns Stefan had inflicted on the wolf-dog, her knowledge of Kylie's undeclared child and her annoyance at Stefan having read her emails conflicting with the desire that Stefan usually aroused in her.

When she arrived outside their room, Stefan following behind, Aisha stood at the door, listening.

"I can't hear any howling, at any rate," she reported.

"That's a good start, I guess," Freya replied, a few seconds later than seemed natural. *She must be worried if she hasn't gone in without me.*

"Pay attention, Freya. If we really have a were-wolf in here, we need to be on our guard."

"A were-wolf, you say?" Stefan's quiet, measured voice behind them had a dark undertone. He sounded like some evil overlord, for a moment, in Freya's overheated imagination.

"Well, maybe not," Freya said reassuringly.

"The beast we hunt is a were-wolf," he said, still in that soft, menacing tone.

"We're much too far away for him to be the same one, even if it was," Freya protested somewhat incoherently. "And he could just be a big dog."

Even though I thought the dog that attacked us today was a wolf, earlier. And so did Stefan.

"Quit arguing about what our stray might be, you two. I'm going in," said Aisha.

"Are you sure you don't want me to go first?" Freya asked.

"Sure, I'll just wait here with your boyfriend," Aisha said sarcastically. She paused. "Stefan? Freya, where did he go?"

"He was here a moment ago. Surely we would have heard him walk away on this gravel?" Freya said.

"I'd have thought so too."

"Maybe he left something in the car. Never mind, let's see what we have inside. We have to sleep in there, after all."

Aisha opened the door and stepped in. Freya imagined her peering around, waiting for her eyes to adjust.

"Aisha? Is it safe? Are you OK?" called Freya.

"Come in and see for yourself!" Aisha reached out and flipped the lamp on, its light flooding out into courtyard. Her shadow stretched out in the middle of the rectangle of light. Beside it was a second shadow.

CHAPTER FIFTY-FOUR

AISHA TEASES A WERE-WOLF

Aisha stood in the open doorway as Freya crunched up beside her. There seemed no doubt about it, their erstwhile dog guest was a were. Either that, or some strange man had let the dog out and stayed in himself while they were out eating. He stood tensely in front of them, hands covering his privates, his lack of clothing revealing large welts on his skin that must be the burns incurred when he was in dog form. *Or wolf form*, thought Freya. There was no doubt in her mind that this was a were-wolf. He was gaunt, ill-fed, and surprisingly un-hairy for a wolf. Dark eyes stared back at them over high cheekbones. *If he's a wolf, he's not a good hunter. Or maybe the drought has affected game as well.*

"Hi, I'm Aisha," said Aisha, putting out a hand in invitation for a handshake. The man glanced down at himself, removed one hand while spreading the other wider, and shook Aisha's hand politely.

"Roman."

His voice was gravelly and hoarse. His remaining hand was also not quite well-placed enough to cover all it needed to. Freya covered her eyes.

"Seriously, Aisha, did you have to do that? The poor guy's naked, you could have waited to shake." Freya noticed the barest quiver of a wink as Aisha lowered an eyelid ever so slightly.

She did that on purpose. Why did she do that?

"Oh, sorry, where are my manners. This is my friend Freya. Somewhere out in the dark is her boyfriend Stefan, who by the way is the one with the seriously overheated hands. I'd avoid him if I were you."

Aisha, what are you playing at?

Freya tried to get her friend's attention with a head tilt, but Aisha angled her body away from Freya's, deliberately ignoring the hint.

"You seem to be a bit under-prepared for the moors though, so I suggest you slide on into the double bed there. Fortunately, Freya and I already agreed that I'd get the bigger bed, so she can't object me offering it to you instead."

"Aisha!" Freya only got out the one word of protest before Aisha turned to her. Aisha was clearly suppressing a grin, the corners of her mouth trying to twitch up.

"Surely you're not suggesting we put him outside for the night?" she said.

"I wasn't going to say that and you know it," said Freya.

"So, I'm offering our poor naked guest a chance to sleep in a comfortable bed, and incidentally the chance to cover himself, which I know is forefront in your mind since you're looking anywhere but at him."

"Big of you to think of me."

"Isn't it? And any moment now, I'm going to suggest that you take Stefan's bed and put *him* out into the cold. Since we're a bed short, now." Aisha waved a hand at the two beds in the room.

"I'm not sure I'm comfortable with that. And I thought you didn't like Stefan, anyway?"

"I don't, which is why I think you should boot him out, rather than sharing his bed."

While they argued, the naked man backed away from them - he'd been standing on the rug where they'd left the wolf-dog sleeping - until he bumped into the bigger of the two beds. He turned and scrambled into it, covering himself with the old-fashioned floral coverlet.

"Excuse me, ladies," he said.

They turned towards him.

"Sorry to interrupt, but I'd like to know more about that man who attacked me."

Freya and Aisha looked at each other.

"You first," they said together.

"Go on, Freya, you know more about him than I do," said Aisha.

"Oh, all right." Freya turned reluctantly to face Roman, who was now decently covered, if the floral coverlet could be considered decent. He looked uncomfortable still, bare hunched shoulders and crossed arms clearly putting him in a defensive position.

"Well, Stefan is a demi. You know about them right? I mean, you're clearly not just a human yourself."

"Very observant," said Roman dryly. "What was your first clue?"

"There's no need to be rude. We're the ones helping you, remember? You didn't look like you were in great shape when you were threatening us on the moor," said Freya.

"I wasn't threatening you; I was trying to get you to go away."

"It looked like threatening. Big teeth, growls... what do *you* call that?" Freya obliterated her own question as she rushed on. "And what were you trying to get us to go away from, anyway?"

Roman looked hunted.

"I can't say."

"And yet you expect us to tell you everything about ourselves? That's hardly fair."

"Not about you. Just the demi."

"I don't know that his secrets are mine to tell," Freya protested.

"She - Aisha, was it? - just said he was your boyfriend. You must know something."

"It's a recent relationship. Probably up for debate now, anyway."

"Please. I need to know. Not just for myself," said Roman.

Aisha looked intrigued.

"Are there others with you around here?" she asked.

"Not my secret."

Freya gave a huff of annoyance. Why was he echoing her?

"Look, you know plenty about Stefan. You know he's a demi, and yes, he was the one who burnt you. With his hands." Freya shivered. She didn't want to think about that. "It was probably in self-defence, since you were leaping for his throat at the time. Maybe you should tell us about that?"

But Roman was shaking his head.

"Thank you for taking me to the vet. And I suppose I should be glad that your hot-handed demi carried me there. But I was defending... more than myself. And he smelt like a threat."

"I think you're going to have to tell us a bit more. After all, you're in my bed." Aisha smiled demurely at Roman, who blushed to the roots of his hair.

Freya shook her head at Aisha. Why was she flirting with this were-wolf? Her tastes had never run that way before. Perhaps her growing association with the were-foxes had dulled her distaste for weres.

How come my life is always beset by weres? Surely there are other non-mundanes out there who could bother me instead? Ones that don't burn strangers?

"At any rate, please don't attack Stefan again. I don't know that we could take you to the vet as you are now," Freya said.

"I wouldn't go, like this. And the need is no longer so great," said Roman.

"Aha, so was it something specific about where we were on the moor? Are there others like you up there?" Aisha pounced on the idea as swiftly as a cat on a mouse.

Roman snorted, softly.

"You're as bad as a cat, toying with its prey," he muttered.

Aisha smiled.

"Glad you noticed."

"It wasn't supposed to be a compliment."

"And yet, I'm pleased."

The two verbal combatants stared at each other, each one clearly daring the other to blink first. Freya grew uncomfortable.

"Aisha, how about you debrief hairy, here. I'm going to find out where Stefan went. Somehow." She backed out of the room, wondering when exactly she'd been dispossessed of it.

"Sounds good, Freya. I'll keep you updated." Aisha glanced at Freya just long enough to give her a cheeky grin.

Freya rolled her eyes. Aisha must have been working far too hard, if she was letting her hair out to play with a were-wolf.

"Please do. And be careful."

"I'm always careful."

The door shut softly between then.

CHAPTER FIFTY-FIVE

OUTSIDE IN THE DARK

Freya stood outside the door in the dark, wondering what she should do now. Look for Stefan, yes. But how? She had no idea where he would have gone, at night outside this isolated farmhouse. Was he fixated on the idea that the mysterious attacker, Van, was out here, somewhere? It seemed an unlikely proposition. Even with a car, this area was over an hour from the places that the previous attacks had taken place. Somehow, Freya thought that such attacks would be more spontaneous, not something that a person - or being - would drive hours to do. Then again, she'd never felt the need to attack strangers in dark places, so perhaps what *she* thought was reasonable didn't apply. Freya gritted her teeth. She needed to do something, now that Aisha was thoroughly occupying their supposedly shared room. She hoped Aisha would be safe - and then snorted. Aisha had been happily shut up in that room with the were-wolf - Roman - for several hours already. Nothing had happened then. Did moonrise change anything other than the were-wolf's body shape? And what *was* he protecting, out on the moor?

She mentally shook herself. There was no point in standing around here speculating in the absence of information. Time to look for Stefan, and apply logic and science to the problem of the were-wolf later. Even if science didn't acknowledge the existence of were-wolves. She grinned at the irony, then went to the first, logical place to look for Stefan - his room.

It was only a few steps to Stefan's door. Freya tapped gently but heard no response. She gave a louder tap. Still no-one answered. She opened the door and looked in. The room was dark. She felt around for the light switch. Light blinded her for a moment, but when her eyes recovered from the dazzle, she saw that the room was empty. Stefan's bag was on the suitcase stand in the corner, and the floral cover on the bed was still rumpled. Where could Stefan have gone?

Time for the next logical step. Outside. She switched off the light and closing the door again, looked around. The rising moon made it easier to see outside than she had expected. The lumpy shape of barrows high on the moor were silhouetted against the starry sky. Something moved beside one barrow. Freya's blood froze, her imagination providing her with a host of chilling scenarios involving barrow-wights, ghosts and walking dead.

Stop imagining impossibilities, she told herself firmly. *There are plenty of real things it could be. Maybe it's just Stefan.*

Hesitantly, she stepped off the gravelled driveway, climbed over the nearest drystone wall - scraping her hand on the rough stone as she did so - and onto the moor.

It was harder than she'd expected to get to the barrows. Once they were no longer silhouetted on the horizon, they didn't really show up against the background moorland. After several minutes of slow uphill progress, Freya stumbled on a patch of grass that stuck up unexpectedly tall, then tripped as her next step took her into a rabbit hole. She lay for a moment on the hard ground, feeling the prickle of short grass on her bare legs. A strong smell of sheep dung filled her nostrils.

Fenris' teeth, what am I doing out here?

She levered herself upright again, brushing herself off as she did so. Where were the barrows now? She thought the darker smudge to her left might be the nearest one. She adjusted her course and headed that way, pleased to find that her encounter with the rabbit hole hadn't done her any major damage. She'd hate to have a twisted ankle out here.

A growl was all the warning she got. A flicker of movement caught her eye to her right, claws bit into her shoulders, and her hastily raised arms were being grazed by teeth. The beast attacking her was too close to see properly, but it was nearly as large as she was. Much too large to be a real wolf. She wasn't sure, but she thought it was the were-wolf, Van. Stefan had been right after all. At least that meant that Roman wasn't the enemy - just as well, since she'd left Aisha alone with him.

Wrenching her arm away from the teeth, she kept an elbow between her throat and the were-wolf's jaws as she staggered backwards. Luckily she didn't find that rabbit hole with her foot again. The were-wolf dropped to its feet, but leaped for her throat once more as her arm sagged in relief. Remembering Stefan's successful defence against Roman, Freya managed to grab the beast's forelegs, one in each hand. She could see its disturbingly human eyes glaring at her, this close up. That left its snapping teeth all too close to her throat, but she straightened her arms and pushed it back slowly. Would forcing its legs apart work as her defence instructor had claimed would work against a dog attack? She didn't want to kill the were-wolf, though he seemed to be doing his best to take out her jugular. She wished she knew why - she was surely not a threat to him. Of course, that woman from accounts hadn't been a threat either. Perhaps it was time for a less conventional approach. There must be something she could call around here that might help. But she had no hands to spare to search for appropriate greenery to help her summons.

I'll just have to chance it.

Hastily smudging a circle around herself with first one foot, then the other, Freya opened her mouth and sang - breathy, forced and out of tune at first. She was too busy fending off the attacking were-wolf to think of words, so she sang notes alone.

I must look pretty stupid, wrestling with a savage beast and trying to sing a capella. *Still, I can't think of anything else to do. And I don't fancy being eaten.*

Van made another lunge for her jugular and she faltered for a moment, then redoubled her summoning efforts.

Please, something come. Anything.

At first, Freya didn't notice the mist rising. But when it began to blot out the moonlight, it was impossible to miss. Van noticed it, all right. As a thick fog coalesced around him and Freya, he stopped growling and began to whimper, instead. He wrenched himself out of Freya's grasp - had he been able to do that all along, she wondered? - and ran off, away from the patch of mist and more importantly, away from Freya.

I guess it's too hot and dry for a proper water deity up here. A shame, a river sweeping the were-wolf away would work well right now.

"I can't begin to thank you-" Freya began, addressing the mist. Warm hands grasped her waist from behind. She shrieked.

"It is only I, Stefan."

Freya couldn't speak from shock for a moment. Then she twisted to face Stefan.

"What were you thinking! I could have killed you just now. Or I might have died of fright, I'm not sure which would come first!"

"Come now, fair warrior maiden. I knew you must display aspects of the Valkyries of your heritage, despite your dirt-grubbing past."

"My *what* past?" Freya asked warningly.

Stefan didn't seem to take the hint, for he went on.

"Yes, surely you know that the original Freya was more than just some fertility goddess. She chose half the fallen for Valhalla. This is common knowledge, yes?"

"It's hardly relevant right now. Didn't you see what was happening? I was fighting for my life here. And then you turn up without warning just as I drive off my attacker. It's really, really not the time for casting aspersions on my upbringing. And I have zero desire to be likened to a Valkyrie," snapped Freya.

Stefan only chuckled, and transferring his hands to her shoulders, turned her gently to face the full moon.

"It is a compliment to your abilities. I did not intend any aspersion, only to indicate that you have not had formal training. And look. The moon is showing us our enemy."

Freya blinked at the sudden change of subject. Her eyes followed Stefan's pointing arm. Along the horizon a wolf shape loped. As they watched, it stopped near a barrow, put its muzzle to the sky, and howled. From distant corners of the moor, other howls answered it. Fox-like yips joined in from somewhere nearby. It seemed the were-wolves had allies. Freya shivered, but she said;

"If formal training means killing things, then I'm not interested."

"Even if they're trying to kill you?" Stefan asked.

"So far, I've managed to get away without killing anything in return. I'd quite like to keep it that way." Behind Freya and Stefan, another howl joined the song. "If they let me."

CHAPTER FIFTY-SIX

WERE-WOLF GATHERING

Feeling unprotected out on the moor with no solid walls to put between her and the were-wolves, Freya shivered again as she heard the howling wolf repeat its cry.

"There are so many of them," she muttered to Stefan.

"Not so many that we could not take them, you and I," said Stefan.

"I don't *want* to 'take them', as you put it. I want to go back to my room and hide under the covers until morning. Possibly later."

Stefan laughed softly.

"I know you are braver than you pretend, my Valkyrie maiden. Come, let us find these arrogant weres who dare to proclaim my territory as their own."

"I'm not brave at all. I'm realistic. Last time we were attacked I froze. I have some self-defence training and that's about it. None of that was geared towards were-wolves. For some reason, my defence teachers thought humans would be more of a problem."

"Very short-sighted of them. I take it they were also humans?"

"Mostly. A few were demis who didn't know it, though," Freya admitted.

"That seems an immense sadness. To be the product of greatness and never realise it."

"I don't know. It seemed relaxing, to me. Not having the expectation of power just because of who your ancestors were. I envy them that," Freya said.

"I do not. And you should not either. You have power in abundance, I am certain of it."

"I am certain that I don't want to pick a fight with a bunch of were-wolves. We don't even know what they're doing out here. Why not leave them be?" Freya pulled away from Stefan, who merely chuckled infuriatingly.

"Because, dear maiden, they seem disinclined to let *me* be. Or indeed to let *you* be, which should be of more concern to you."

"Look, I admit that that's concerning, but we have no evidence that these are the same beasts that have been attacking people. Apart from the one I just drove off, which looked suspiciously like Van. Um. Well. You can't just blame some were-wolves - no matter how much I'm inclined to do that - because they happen to be creeping around a moor at the same time as-"

"'ware the beast!" shouted Stefan.

Freya whirled around. A new were-wolf was leaping towards her, teeth bared, eyes still eerily human despite the wolf-shape of the rest of it. She raised her sore arms defensively, desperately wishing for a wall at her back. A moment later, she realised that Stefan was at her back, defending himself from a second were-wolf. Yet another leapt at him, then Freya had to give all her attention to fending off a were-fox. *Foxes and wolves fighting together? That's not normal.* Teeth grazed her thigh and she swung round, trying to dislodge the were that clung to her. She felt a sinking sensation in her stomach as she realised that she knew the were-fox. *Lachy. The first were-fox who ever attacked me.* The were-fox snapped at her ankles, distracting her.

"Fenris's teeth, not another attack on my legs," she growled. "How will I ever wear summer dresses again if I keep getting scars?" Her worries about inflicting violence on others abruptly dropped away as the were-fox's teeth sank into her skin. She kicked, hard and fast the way her self-defence instructors had taught her. A shame they hadn't had wolves or foxes in mind when they discussed technique. Although the were-fox dodged away from her kick, it twisted back on itself ready to leap again.

If things go on like this I will have to wear armour plated trousers. Even in summer.
She parried a high lunge with her elbow.
I need a better solution.
She realised she was panting and fast running out of energy.

"I can't keep this up, Stefan. Can we get out of here? I don't even know why they're attacking us!"

She kicked at Lachy again, catching a tender spot mostly by accident. The were-fox backed off.

Stefan grunted as he heaved away a were-wolf.

"They are attacking because they believe that *my* territory is theirs. They are incorrect, of course." He threw another attacking wolf away from him. Freya noticed the wolf did not immediately get up.

"But why fight about it? Weres are intelligent beings, why not talk instead?" She ducked as a wolf launched itself at her throat, and whirled to kick it away. Stefan reached for the wolf and hurled it further.

"They are not acting like intelligent beings. Why should I dignify them with respect?"

"I admit I don't like the way they're behaving either. But why is it your territory all the way out here? Do you need so much? Couldn't they have some too?" Freya wasn't sure if the growling noise she heard then was one of the were-wolves or Stefan.

"It doesn't matter why I need it. It is mine." He muttered something under his breath. Freya thought it sounded something like 'useless employees'. But that made no sense.

"Fine, it's not a great time to talk. I get that. But can we retreat now?" Freya threw herself sideways to avoid a lunging were-wolf, then followed up with a kick. Stefan performed a similar move at her back.

"I will never retreat from a foe. Especially not one who contests my superior rights. You should not be disputing this."

This is really not looking good. How do I get out of this situation? I've already called on the water deities here and it's just too dry. Stefan doesn't want to leave. What I need is a good storm...

"Lio!"

"That is *not* my name." Stefan's voice was more of a snarl than that of the were-wolves. "Who is this Lio? One of the weres? Is that why you wish to retreat?"

"What? No!" Freya was flustered by Stefan's suddenly aggressive tone. "Lio's an old friend. That's all. He's not any sort of were."

"And you choose the middle of a fight to exclaim his name?" Stefan raised his arms threateningly at a were-fox who was advancing more cautiously than the previous were-wolf.

"I just thought he might help us."

"I need no help," Stefan said, his tone softly menacing, and somehow more frightening for being quiet.

"I didn't mean to imply that you did. But *I'm* struggling, here," Freya explained.

"Let me show you why you need not call on this 'friend'," Stefan said. He raised his voice, apparently to address the were-wolves and were-foxes. "And why people I employ should stick to their contracted duties and not turn on me."

CHAPTER FIFTY-SEVEN

VOLCANO DEMI

Freya shivered. Stefan sounded more murderous than the howling were-wolves. And what did he mean about employees? Surely he hadn't been hiring these weres? Her mind flashed back to Kylie's comment about similar things happening to her when she arrived in York. Was Stefan playing some deep game she had been unaware of? What else was he capable of? She stepped away from his sheltering back, only to be pushed back towards him by two growling were-wolves. Out of the corner of her eye, Freya saw Stefan raise his hands above his head. He cried out in a thunderous voice, a series of words that Freya didn't understand. As he called, the dry ground beneath her feet seemed to grow hotter and began to shake. Rocks tumbled off the distant barrows, and the earth itself seemed to roar as the small shaking grew to into an all-out roll. Were-wolves whimpered and broke off their attack in order to flee, tails firmly tucked between their legs, stumbling as the earth failed to be in the expected place beneath their feet.

Freya fell to her knees, feeling unsafe on two legs. But the ground was hot to the touch; she hastily stood again, facing Stefan this time, swaying and trying to keep her balance.

"What are you doing, Stefan?" Freya asked warily, though she thought she could tell what he was doing. He was calling the magma from deep underground. "Please stop. You don't need to prove anything."

Stefan didn't seem to hear her. His fists were clenched and a vein in his temple pulsed. He was clearly putting forth a great deal of effort.

"Stefan! At this rate I'll have to call Lio just to get things cooled down. Stop now!"

A short distance away, steam started rising from the earth. The low heather started to shrivel. With the vegetation already dry from the prolonged heat wave, a scrub fire seemed inevitable, at the very least.

"Do not threaten me with your paramours. Can you not see how powerful I am?" Stefan said melodramatically.

"Yes, very powerful, great. But I'm not sure what you mean by paramours. Can you stop now, please?"

"You mock me."

"I don't! I just don't want to have to deal with a fire, alright? And earthquakes really truly scare me."

Stefan's only answer was to raise his hands a little higher. The rumbling of the earth increased. Freya dropped to a crouch, hands on the warm ground to steady herself.

"Lio!" she yelled, trying to imagine a call going out to him wherever he was, in case that made a difference. He'd said she had the power to call him. Now would be a great time for that to be true. Unfortunately, Stefan did not appear to appreciate this evidence that Freya was thinking of someone other than him. He gave a wordless cry of rage. The ground in front of him buckled and cracked. Shrubs were tipped sideways, roots exposed. Freya scuttled away on all fours, trying not to feel like a bug about to be squashed. The earth was too dry for boiling mud, but small crumbs of earth fountained out of the cracks and wisps of steam escaped.

"Don't you think you've demonstrated your power now, Stefan?" she called, straining to be heard over the sound of the earth moving. It was getting harder to see. Freya risked glancing up, and saw that fast-moving clouds were covering the full moon. There was no sign of the were-wolves now. Presumably they'd made the most of Stefan's distraction and fled.

Freya wished she could do the same. The rising wind was warm as it flowed over her skin and whipped away the steam. Distant thunder rumbled as though in answer to the earth's moan of complaint. Time to come up with her own distraction.

"So, you're bringing up the magma, right? Very impressive. But I thought this area was ancient sea-bed, not a geothermically active region."

Stefan lowered his hands a little, looking nonplussed.

"It matters not. There is magma under the earth's crust wherever we are in the world."

"But it must be way, way down here, right? I mean, it's not like there are hot springs in the North York moors. They'd be a much more fashionable place if there were."

"I am not interested in hot springs or fashion. Why do you bring them up?" The earth rumbled and shook, backing up his complaint.

"I just thought if you're going to all this effort, you might consider doing it somewhere there's a spring, too. You know, to create some hot pools. I'm sure they'd be very popular," Freya babbled.

Stefan growled wordlessly before he answered.

"I do not need popularity. I need my weres to do their jobs and keep other weres away while I go about my business."

Stefan turned away to kick at a growling were-wolf. "Yes, I know you are here, Van. I have told you before to leave my women alone. Go deal with that rogue pack, or go home."

To Freya's surprise, Van didn't attack again, but backed away, hackles raised but tail down. *What does he mean by telling Van to leave 'his women' alone? How many does he have?* Her ears rang as she realised that she was probably included in that category.

Stefan ran forward and grabbed for the were-wolf, who tried to turn and run at the last minute. Stefan let him go, raising his voice to shout to whoever or whatever was out on the moors. "Most of all, what I want is for the frost-folk to be defeated everywhere. There should never be ice again!" The earth shook again as Stefan raised his fists high to emphasize his point.

I wish I was better at this 'don't get angry people more annoyed' thing. And I really hope that the rising wind means Lio is on his way. It sounds like Stefan might be the one behind this heat wave. Or at least part of it. Surely even a volcano demi can't raise the temperature everywhere, for so long. There must be others he's working with.

Lightning split the sky, lighting up the ravaged moor. In the flash of light, Freya saw that most of the ancient barrow closest to her was now just tumbled rock. The only were-wolf she could see was lying on its side a little way away. It wasn't moving.

Worry about suspicious heat waves later. You've got more pressing issues. Come on, Lio, anytime now. And I hope you've got a better plan than I do. Since my plan is just to get some help, and perhaps a bit of rain.

Freya decided she'd better have another go at calling a water deity. Those clouds looked like they were carrying plenty of water - perhaps she'd manage more than mist, this time. She crouched, grabbing blindly for handfuls of the vegetation around her feet, then started singing - under her breath, so that Stefan wouldn't question her motives again. Unfortunately, the first song that sprang into her head was entirely too ambiguous:

'The earth, the air, the fire, the water, return return return…'

She wondered briefly when she'd come to rely on words as much as tune in her water-spirit summonings. Time to return to wordless tones. A few tense moments of humming later, Freya was sure the clouds were massing faster. The steam rising from the parched earth was hovering just above her, but there didn't seem to be enough of it to form a full-fledged deity this time.

Where are the bogs when you need them? This heat wave is causing more problems than I had realised.

"Hide me please, water spirit," she whispered, waving her handful of plants. Promisingly, the mist descended around her. She switched to singing words again, hoping for something more distracting than a mist. At last, rain spattered from the clouds, huge drops that hissed as they struck the overheated earth, driving through the mist around her. Wind howled through the sky, louder than the were-wolves had been.

This better work.

CHAPTER FIFTY-EIGHT

LIO TO THE RESCUE

Another thunderclap shook the ground, although that could have been more rocks falling as Stefan continued his quest to display his might. Or perhaps he thought he was banishing frost-folk? The chances of frost-folk surviving in a heat wave seemed low. The rain fell harder, plastering Freya to the ground. She could barely see Stefan now. There was a rush of wind that half-blinded her and swirled the remaining mist into crazed patterns, and then Lio was beside her, offering his hand to help her up from her crouch. Freya gladly took his hand - warm, not hot, she noticed - and stood up uncertainly, ceasing her song. The rain eased, though it still seemed to be falling a little way off. The mist swirled around her at waist height, doing little to camouflage her or Lio now that they were standing.

"Thanks for the help. I think you can go now," she told the mist. She wasn't sure about that, though. The ground was still rocking, making it hard to stay upright. It reared up to eye-level, perhaps questioning her decision.

"Yes, really. I'll call again if I need you," Freya assured it.

It sank to the ground, and disappeared bit by bit among the raindrops, merging with the steam from the hot earth.

"Looks like you're in a spot of bother here. Care to fill me in?" Lio said. Something whistled just over his head and he ducked.

Freya turned to the direction the projectile had come from and saw Stefan stooping to pick up another rock.

"Er. Long story. Stefan here was just trying to show me how powerful he is." Freya indicated Stefan who was glowering at the newcomer from a little way away, tossing his rock from hand to hand, perhaps trying to decide how much of a threat Lio was. No were-wolves attacked him now. "Actually, he's succeeding, but I can't say as I'm enjoying the experience."

Stefan scowled, clearly hearing her words.

"You should be appreciating my abilities," Stefan said in a carrying voice. "As my employees should also." Freya got the feeling that he wasn't really talking to her anymore. Were there weres out there in the dark who owed their loyalty to Stefan? If so, it was a shaky loyalty at best, based on their actions.

"And what is Stefan to you?" Lio asked in a low tone.

Was that wistfulness in Lio's voice? Freya wasn't sure.

"Yes. Well. He's my boyfriend, I guess. Or he was. But I don't much like the way he's been behaving lately." Her mouth turned down involuntarily. She'd thought Stefan was special, different. He'd made her feel special too. Until now. "And I don't know how to get out of this situation, then I remembered you said I could call you... so here we are. Any ideas on how to calm an angry volcano demigod?"

As though to highlight the problem, red-tinged lightning crackled above them.

"You certainly like a challenge, don't you?" Lio squeezed Freya's hand and released it. The night air felt colder after that. "Hmm. The best thing I can think of to do is to call my brothers. I don't really like to do that - but perhaps their destructive instincts will match your Stefan's."

Stefan raised his arms as though to welcome the lightning, which flickered around him. Thunder growled and shook the earth nearly as much as Stefan's magma-calling had done. Freya edged away, feeling for stable ground with every step, pulling Lio with her.

"I don't think he's my Stefan anymore," Freya muttered. "Or he won't be, soon. Only I don't think he agrees." Her voice returned to normal strength. "But anything is worth a try. At this rate there'll be lava any minute, and I don't think a bit of mist will quench that. Imagine having to explain lava to reporters!"

The ground under Stefan was beginning to glow too.

Surely he can't withstand standing on molten rocks? Freya thought.

"Since I never get to stay anywhere long enough to meet reporters, that doesn't worry me. But lava - no thanks. I'll call my brothers in. But my brothers don't always have the best behaviour. There's a chance Nik could come too, though I don't know if she's in calling distance."

"I don't mind if Nik comes, I guess. Are your brothers worse than she is?" Freya asked.

"Do you see me hanging out with them?"

"Well, no."

Stefan bent and scooped up something glowing from the ground and threw it towards Lio and Freya.

"Don't make me hurt you," he called to Freya.

"I'm not in charge of your actions, you are!" Freya yelled back.

"There's your answer, then. Have you got somewhere safe to go, if I call in my brothers?" Lio asked.

The ground rocked, and Lio put out a hand for balance, assuming a bent-legged warrior posture that reminded Freya of a yoga stance.

"Back to our bed and breakfast. But Stefan is staying there too." Freya's feet were getting hot through the soles of her shoes. Stefan hadn't let up on the magma thing. She looked back at him. He was staring at her with an unreadable expression on his face, but he hadn't tried to move closer to her and Lio. Maybe he had to stay in one spot in order to call up magma? Volcanoes weren't exactly mobile things.

"Better than nothing, I suppose. Though it would be better to leave the area entirely. Somehow. Tell you what, if the moor catches alight, go down to a river valley and summon a river deity, alright?"

Freya nodded. Down in the valley, there would be enough moisture for the local deities to be powerful still.

"Alright. Get ready to go, on my signal," Lio said.

"OK. But you'd better be careful too, Lio."

"Naturally. I value my skin nearly as much as I value yours," he said, then catching her hand, he raised it briefly to his lips, before releasing it and raising his one arm. "Go now!"

Freya froze for a moment in surprise at his action. She'd known Lio for many years, but it was only recently that she'd begun to think of him as having the potential to be more than just a friend. Stefan's presence in her life had stopped her from acting on that thought. She hadn't realised that Lio might be thinking the same as her. But if there was a worse time and place for this realisation, she couldn't imagine it.

"Go!" repeated Lio. "I'll see you again."

Freya nodded, but glanced guiltily at Stefan. His expression reflected his rage and betrayal. But she remembered him hurling were-wolves from him and raging at her failure to appreciate his power - and turning up uninvited on her trip with Aisha. Not to mention Kylie's unsolved child support issues.

"Sorry, Stefan," she called - then ran. Behind her, she heard Lio shouting out strange words - presumably the names of his mysterious brothers.

"Reas! Skeir! Toss! Russ!"

Those are almost wind god names. Like his.

The wind rose sharply, buffeting Freya as she stumbled through the heather. The temperature dropped rapidly as the wind-speed increased, until Freya was shivering. The raindrops began to swirl and lift on the breeze as they began to freeze. Wind demi rescuers or not, she needed to get away. Some of that wind must come straight from what remained of the Arctic. Behind her, thunder rumbled. The earth bucked again, tossing Freya to her knees.

Ow. Why do grazed knees hurt so much?

Icy rain started to patter down around her. It quickly turned to sleet.

There goes the heat wave. Though I should be glad it's going. I suppose this effect is just local, though.

Freya got to her feet again and risked a glance backwards. There wasn't much to see; the rain disguised much of whatever action was taking place. However, Freya was able to pick out a small group of male figures standing in various aggressive poses around the patch of moor that glowed and trembled. Wind whipped fire from patches of heather that had caught fire. While she watched, the fire roared upwards, fanned by the wind into a mini-tornado that whipped towards Stefan. He dived sideways and into the path of one of the wind demis, who took a swing at Stefan. He ducked and returned the punch, and Freya heard a roar of rage from the unknown aggressor. The fire tornado subsided as quickly as it had arisen. *Maybe that's the sort of bad behaviour I'm supposed to be avoiding. I'm good with that.*

Stefan flung more glowing rocks, and the earth shook again. A different figure leapt from one dark patch to another in an attempt to get closer to Stefan.

Honestly, it's turning into a boxing match. Is boxing better than magma? It wasn't a question she could answer.

A flicker of blue caught her eye and she saw Nik loping across the moor towards the fight, grinning wildly. A pair of goblins followed her, brandishing what appeared to be a carpet cleaner and a window brush. Apparently Nik had brought friends along. Freya rolled her eyes despite herself. It was great to have people come to help her, but these? She wasn't sure how much help *they'd* be. Nik glanced her way and to Freya's surprise, gave a cheery wave. It seemed Nik was in her element in a storm with an angry volcano demigod. Around Stefan, points of red lightning formed as a small host of storm sprites appeared. It looked like Stefan was calling in some help of his own.

Sprites, that's the last thing I need. I really hate storm sprites.

Even as the thought formed, one of the sprites arced her way, the air sizzling as it grounded far too close for comfort.

That's it. I'm out of here.

Freya hurried on, back towards the farmhouse, stumbling and lurching across the moor, and wishing for once that there wasn't quite so much vegetation to trip on.

After the dramatic events of the last few minutes, she'd almost forgotten the injured were-wolf that had brought them to the bed and breakfast.

CHAPTER FIFTY-NINE

WERE-WOLVES RETURN

"**B**ut I don't understand what you're doing here." Aisha's voice carried quite clearly though the door to their room was closed. Freya was about to go back into their shared room when the overheard conversation inside gave her pause. She waited for the answer to Aisha's question. Would the were-wolf give an honest reply? Freya wanted to know what he was doing here, too.

"I am scouting. Primarily." Roman's gravelly voice was hard to hear.

Freya put an eye to the crack around the door, and found she could just see a sliver of the were-wolf inside the softly lit room. She heard the unseen Aisha laugh.

"That's not much of an answer. Come on, give. We've done our best for you, why don't you come clean with me. Mr Hot Hands isn't here to inflict pain now. With any luck, Freya will distract him for the next few hours. She seems to want to, anyway. Bastet knows why - I mean, sure he's got looks, but personality? Not that I've seen."

Freya's face burned.

Eavesdroppers never hear good of themselves, remember.

Roman's voice rumbled a reply. Something about manipulative wiles, Freya thought. Aisha responded, her voice much clearer.

"I just don't want to see her hurt. She's been through a lot with her family, and she's my best friend."

"Then you should help her to dislodge her parasite."

That came through clearly enough. Stefan's not a parasite. Hmm. Maybe he's something worse though.

"But she doesn't want me to. Anyway, I was asking about you. It's not exactly wolf territory up here, or so Freya tells me. And she would know - even though she mostly studies plants now, she's got the best animal and folklore knowledge of anyone I know."

Well, that's something, I guess. Not all bad.

"Very well," said Roman. "I can tell you a little. You know that there are wolves in Britain again?"

"Yeah, but I thought they were down in Bristol or something."

"Some are. Some are near here. But this area - or a little further south, in the wolds - this was the last area that wolves existed in Britain. The last area they were hunted from. Extirpated. And therefore, the last area where were-wolves existed freely in this country, able to hide in plain sight thanks to our wolf cousins."

"Sure, but that's ancient history. Still not telling me what you're doing here," said Aisha.

Freya admired her tenacity. Roman wasn't going to be able to wiggle out of answering Aisha's questions so easily.

She should train as a lawyer, not a business-person.

The sliver of Roman that Freya could see moved. She thought he might be pacing the short distance of the room, as he appeared and disappeared again. He stepped softly, however. She couldn't hear footsteps.

"You are persistent, aren't you?" he said.

"No curiosity like that of a cat, so they say."

"And do you define yourself that way?"

"Sometimes. But you were about to tell me about yourself."

A brief bark of laughter.

"Yes. Diversion accepted. So... the 'ancient history' you dismiss so readily is more relevant than you might think. There is a long history of wolf persecution here, but also a long history of were-wolves. So, when the wolves were returned, there were many here who were free at last to embrace their true selves. Unfortunately, there are as many were-wolves of dubious personal persuasion as there are humans. It was my pack's dream to reclaim our territory without humans noticing, but one or two rogue packs have decided instead to prey upon humans again, forgetting perhaps that this behaviour led to the genocide we saw in past centuries."

"You sound like a historian."

Another deep laugh.

"I sound like what I am. Doctorate in the history of domestication of dogs. Dr Canid, at your service."

"Seriously Dr Canid? Isn't that like, Dr Dog?"

"Seriously Dr. Not seriously Canid, though. I just liked the name." Roman's voice was amused. Freya decided she liked him after all. Should she be liking a were-wolf? He didn't seem much like those attacking her on the moor. Perhaps were-wolves came in different flavours after all. It seemed strange to think that way. But she had a sudden memory of her sister's teenage crush, a were-wolf who had saved Freya from a flood.

Perhaps I shouldn't have been so quick to judge all were-wolves.

"And what are you doing here, Dr Dog?" asked Aisha.

"Trying to find a place for my family to survive. Without lone wolves, or those acting like them, destroying our chances. But it turns out there are some others in the area who don't like were-wolves trying to reclaim territory. Your friend's lover in the next room is one of them."

Freya stiffened. Stefan? Could he really be part of a general persecution of were-wolves? Uneasily she remembered him talking of having territory. And his reaction to the wolves on the moor. Many clues pointed to him being a part of Roman's problem - maybe even the mastermind. Was he involved in whatever was stopping this were-wolf from being well-fed and housed? Stefan had certainly been acting suspiciously, turning up on her moor trip, attacking Roman, and then arriving just after her fight with the rogue were-wolf, Van. *What is it with me and doglike things?*

Freya shifted from foot to foot. She hadn't been exactly keen on weres herself - and she'd said as much to Stefan. Was she just as guilty by association? Lost in self-recrimination, she missed Aisha's next question. When she next focused on the conversation, Roman was still talking.

"...I don't have children or a mate of my own. It's my extended family I'm looking out for. My sister, her children, her husband." Laughter. "No, not your typical were-pack. I don't know if they exist anymore. I know some towns are run by were-packs, but they're more like paramilitary groups. They don't bear much resemblance to the old ways, that is certain."

"I don't much like the sound of paramilitary types running towns," said Aisha with distaste. Freya could sympathise. If it weren't for Aisha's family's moderating influence, their own town could have been a were strong-hold - though were-foxes no doubt ran things differently to were-wolves.

"I am sure they have their place. But I agree, I prefer not to live that way. My sister's husband is a refugee from such a place. That is part of why we are trying to return here. We need a better way to live, not so many boundaries." His voice softened. "Allowance for making mistakes, too."

Aisha's voice again, sharp as a whip after Roman's soft rumble.

"Whose mistakes are you trying to get away from?"

Roman's reply was almost a sigh.

"My own, more than anything. But your friend must be getting cold outside the door. Please, do invite her in to join us."

Fenris's teeth, how could I forget about were-wolf noses?

"What, is Freya out there? How do you know?" asked Aisha. Roman must have made some explanatory gesture, for Aisha responded.

"Oh. I see."

Freya took a hasty step away from the door, so as not to be pressed against it when it was opened. She was glad she did, because Aisha flung the door open with alacrity.

"Freya! How long have you been out there? No, scratch that. What's wrong with you? And where's Stefan?"

Freya looked ruefully down at herself. She was soaked, her clothing was in tatters, and several welts were oozing blood. She must look even worse than she felt.

"It's a long story. Just let me in, alright?" Freya said wearily.

Aisha stepped hastily aside so that Freya could enter the room.

CHAPTER SIXTY

EXPLANATIONS

The first thing Freya did after firmly shutting the door behind her was check the room for obvious quake damage. To her surprise, everything seemed exactly as she had left it - apart from Roman, who was decidedly more chipper than previously.

"Did you two not feel the earthquakes?" she asked. "Or hear them?"

Aisha and Roman looked at one another. Aisha shrugged.

"I guess I thought a car might have driven into a wall a while back. But I was a bit distracted just then, so I didn't do anything about it."

Roman looked a bit sheepish for a moment, but then straightened.

"I am not sure about earthquakes, but I heard howling. Since I recognised those responsible and wished to avoid them, I didn't draw attention to them."

Freya rolled her eyes. She'd been battling for her life out on the moor, and these two hadn't noticed a thing? Well, Roman had, but...

"I'm afraid you'll both have to pay more attention to current events. I know you're injured, Roman, and we'd planned to stay here tonight. But things have gone a bit pear-shaped between me and Stefan. I don't think it's going to be safe here after all. Not that I have an alternative plan just yet. And, er, there are a few violent beings out there at the moment which we should also avoid - and I don't just mean Stefan or those were-wolves. And actually, I saw that brutish were-fox Lachy as well."

Aisha was staring at Freya as though she'd gone mad.

"We can't just up and leave, Freya," she said. "Roman here isn't in any shape to go for some midnight run across the moorland, assuming that's what you have in mind?"

"I was thinking of a taxi, actually. To the train station perhaps. Or to your place, Aisha. That might be best."

"Feeling rich, are we?"

"You know I'm not. But I'm sure we're not safe here - and we wouldn't be safe on foot either."

"There won't be a train until morning, you know that, right? And the chances of getting a taxi out here are slim to none."

Freya sighed. She hadn't thought out the logistics of this plan.

"Well, maybe we can take shelter at the... the pub. Or knock on the door of that vet. Assuming she lives at the clinic, I guess."

Freya felt that she was clutching at straws, but she also thought that they were in danger if they stayed. She felt another pang of guilt-and-annoyance for Stefan. If only he hadn't been so pig-headed about fighting those weres. If only he hadn't wanted to prove his power. Now, she felt like everything she'd been trying to achieve was being undone.

"Do you know, I was trying to live as a mundane, this year?" she told Aisha.

Aisha blinked at this non-sequitur.

"Really? I can't imagine why."

"Because otherwise this sort of thing happens!" Freya waved her arms around, trying to indicate the were-wolf in the room and the raging volcano demigod and assorted other demis outside.

"Freya, I think 'this' happened because you got involved with the wrong guy. Although... maybe I can understand that." Aisha's eyes slid towards Roman for a moment. Then she shook her head. "I don't think mundanes have such violent altercations though. Maybe you should try harder to meet some."

"I thought I was. It didn't work out that way."

"Yeah. Shame."

The friends stood looking at one another for a moment. In the silence, the sound of the wind whistling through the chimneypots was easy to hear.

"Angry beings, you say," Aisha said. "They wouldn't have brought down a storm, would they?"

Freya raised her eyebrows, letting the sudden sound of hail clattering on the window answer for her.

"I see. They have. So now you want us to traipse all the way across the moor, in a demi-driven storm, to avoid an enraged volcano demi. Who also owns the only car in the area. Have I got that right?"

"You left out the were-wolves who were attacking me earlier. Stefan drove them off, but I'm sure there are still some around out there."

"Oh, good. That makes it *so* much better," Aisha said. "You've had quite the night out there, haven't you?"

"One I wish I could forget. Seriously, Aisha, what can we do?"

Roman cleared his throat. He'd been so silent, Freya had all but forgotten his presence.

"I am fairly certain that I could make sure any were-wolves did not attack you. If I travelled with you, that is. I cannot help with demi-gods, however."

Freya nodded slowly.

"If you were to return to your wolf form, Roman, perhaps we could go to that vet. Then take the first train of the morning." She looked at Aisha appealingly. "That way we only have to make it to the village on foot. Stefan was somewhat engaged with the wind demis when I left. He'll probably be distracted a while longer, though I have no idea how much power he or they have."

Aisha looked reluctant. She never did enjoy wet weather, Freya recalled. She wasn't sure if that was due to her cat-goddess heritage, or just a simple human preference for the sun.

"It's either that or wait here for Stefan to return to the room next door, where he might decide that one series of earthquakes is not enough, and he needs to create a geothermal hot spa right here."

"Wait, a spa? What do you mean?" asked Aisha.

Freya blushed.

"I was trying to persuade him that he was in the wrong place for bringing magma to the surface, since there were no nearby springs to warm up. Er. I don't think it helped."

"Freya, you have seriously got to work on your tact!" Aisha said.

"I know it was lame, but it was the best I could come up with at the time. A shame it didn't seem to work. I'd love a good hot pool."

"You're my best friend, Freya, but sometimes I do wonder at you. And your taste in men."

"How was I to know Stefan was a volcano demigod with a temper?"

"You have a knack, that's all. What train did you want to take? I mean, east or west. Maybe we shouldn't be heading back to York just yet if we're trying to avoid Stefan."

"I guess not," Freya said reluctantly. "So, we head for your place?"

Aisha grimaced. "My family's place, you mean. They won't be too happy about me bringing home a were-wolf. A male were-wolf, at that."

Freya nodded understandingly. A family of cat-goddess demis were unlikely to welcome a were-wolf, and Aisha's family, while not completely backwards, were still on the conservative side when it came to their daughter.

"We can head to my place if you prefer," she offered. "It's small, but I'm sure Angie wouldn't mind. She loves company."

The room unexpectedly shook. Dust filtered down from the ceiling and the beams creaked ominously. Freya grasped at the doorframe, Roman sank into a crouch, and Aisha did likewise.

"You know what? I'm prepared to risk my parents' wrath rather than risk going in a direction your boyfriend expects. My place it is," Aisha said.

"You're the best, Aisha. Thanks. And I'm sorry about your missed shopping opportunities," Freya said. "We'll have to plan another trip."

"I am so holding you to that."

"Perhaps I can be of assistance in overcoming parental qualms," interjected Roman. "I find many parents settle once my qualifications are known."

"Many, eh?" Aisha asked with a raised eyebrow.

Roman coloured slightly, though it was hard to tell with his dark skin.

"One or two, certainly."

Freya suppressed a smile. She suspected that there would be more pointed conversation between these two for a while.

"Alright, so if we're going to have to evacuate to avoid Stefan, let's pack up. Roman, can you, er, change? I don't think we want to add stolen sheets to the list of things the landlady is going to be annoyed about," Freya said. "And it's got cold outside."

"I can, but you must know that I cannot speak in my other form," replied Roman.

"I figured, yeah."

I'm glad I'm not a were. I'd hate having to give up speech.

"So be it."

Relieved that they had the beginnings of a plan, and impatient to get started, Freya darted about the room retrieving her own things and stuffing them into her backpack. Mostly charged phone, that was a good change. There wasn't much else to pack, since they'd only been planning a day walk. Sadly, that meant she had nothing suitable to wear in a storm.

I hope the north wind heads back where he came from sooner rather than later. Although maybe I shouldn't hope for that - the winter wind might be more of a match for a volcano demi than anything else.

It was hard to hope for snow on a summer's night.

While Freya debated the relative merits of wind gods, Aisha had also completed her packing. Roman had slid entirely under the sheet, and an assortment of growls and whimpers were emerging from under it.

"I think it hurts to change forms when he's injured," Aisha informed Freya.

Sure enough, a few moments later the wolf-dog that they'd first encountered on the moor crawled out from under the sheet. Apparently Aisha's attentions had done some good - his coat was smooth instead of matted, at least. But the burn wounds were still starkly evident. Freya looked away from them.

"Right, that's us. Let's go, if we're going to," she said.

CHAPTER SIXTY-ONE

MIDNIGHT ON THE MOORS

It took all Freya's resolve to open the door again. Although she'd been the one to insist that they couldn't stay, she had begun to second-guess herself while she packed. Surely Stefan wouldn't hurt her. He'd said as much himself, not so very long ago. But that had been before she called Lio. And before Lio had so very publicly shown an interest in her. She wasn't sure what that would do to Stefan, but it had to have hurt his feelings. Unfortunately, from what she'd seen, a volcano demi with hurt feelings wasn't healthy to be around.

Come on, Freya. Open the door and get it over with.

The blast of icy wind that accompanied the opening of the door almost sent Freya back inside again, clad in shorts as she was.

"This is insane," muttered Aisha, clutching her light summer jacket to herself.

"I know, I know. But it's better than a new volcano in the middle of the moors, isn't it?"

"I don't think there's ever been a volcano in the moors, it's sedimentary rock and glacial valleys," said Aisha.

"Impressive, you must have paid close attention in that last science class we had together in school," teased Freya, trying to lighten the mood before she cried with the stress of it all.

"You bet I did. That was the time we had that good-looking teacher. And look where it's got me. Going out into a supernatural storm on the strength of improbable geological activity."

"What can I say? You always said you wanted adventure."

"Now I know how wrong I was. Just for that, you can be the one who explains to the vet in Danby what we're doing banging on her door in the middle of the night."

"Aisha!"

"What are friends for?"

Freya waited for Aisha and Roman to slip through the door before yanking it closed. The wind tried to keep it open.

At first there was nothing to see but rain and occasional flurries of snow. However, as they moved away from the buildings, the force of the wind varied, gusting violently and then falling away to almost nothing. At those times, Freya could see a glow in the earth of the moor, out where Stefan must be. Lightning cut the sky, and she was almost sure she saw Lio just above the glowing patch. Somewhere hounds bayed, and she shivered, remembering the storm hounds that sometimes accompanied Lio. There was a roiling mass that could be bodies wrestling with each other. There seemed to be more snow falling over there, large white flakes flurrying in the wind. Those violent brothers of Lio's, perhaps. She thought about the cold, and the wind, and the names Lio had called.

I wonder who Lio's father is. Some wind god, I suppose. Though it could be a grandfather, or great-great.

She hurried her small party down the road. The rain had frozen into slick patches of ice in places, and they skidded more than they walked. The bitter cold was so fierce that Freya soon couldn't feel her face or her fingers. She stuck her hands under her arms to warm them up, but was soon forced to put out her arms for balance again. There was nothing to be done for her face but hope that they reached the village soon.

"We're not going to make it at this rate," Aisha shouted in Freya's ear to be heard over the wind. "We're just not dressed for it!"

"I know, but there's nowhere else to go," Freya shouted back.

Roman, who had been limping along in Aisha's wake, suddenly leapt in front of them, growling. He was facing forward, not back. Were some of the missing were-wolves out there?

But Roman was edging sideways, snarling over his shoulder at them. What did he want them to do?

I wish he could talk as a wolf; it'd be much easier to understand than growling.

Freya stumbled on an unseen rock and nearly fell. Aisha clutched at her arm, and Freya was momentarily distracted by the coldness of her hand.

It's much too cold out here. Aisha's right, we won't make it.

A stone wall loomed on one side of the road. Roman stopped growling and leapt onto it, pausing briefly at the top to direct a stare at Aisha before disappearing over the other side.

"We'd better follow him," Aisha said. "I think he's trying to tell us something." Aisha walked over to the wall, and vaulted herself onto the top of it. It was higher than the average three feet of drystone, but with plenty of outcroppings for handholds.

"I hope he's not just deciding he's had enough of us and he's off to make his own way on the moors again. Not that it looked like he was doing well at that." Freya followed Aisha, but paused by the wall. There was a bit of shelter there which was a welcome relief from the wind.

"Oh, come on, Freya. I've been talking to him. He's not the type to abandon people. That's why he's in such bad condition. There's a sort of war going on between his people and some other weres. I'd guess they are the ones you got attacked by - you were very brief in your description there, by the way. Anyway, I'm sure Roman's one of the good guys."

"I hope you're right." *I'm counting on it, really.*

Sheltering from the wind wasn't helping nearly enough. Freya used her half-frozen fingers to find handholds in the rock, and clambered over the wall too.

Once over it and up the hill a few metres, she stopped again, this time in surprise.

"What are you doing?" she hissed at Roman.

The were-wolf looked at her for a moment, as though to say 'isn't it obvious', before resuming digging at a grassy patch of ground between two rocks. That wasn't what had startled Freya. It was the fact that the rocks were positioned on the side of a long, scrub-covered barrow, rising up on the edge of the moor.

"Don't dig up the barrow," Freya said. "They're burial mounds. There's probably bones in there!" A horrible thought struck her. "That's not why you're digging, is it?"

"That's disgusting, Freya, how could you even think it?" Aisha said. "He's trying to show us something in there. Look!"

Even as she spoke, Roman's scrabbling claws broke through the earth to reveal a narrow cave.

"Shelter!" exclaimed Aisha.

Freya was not so sure. Although she was freezing out here, and seriously beginning to wonder if she had frostbite - she couldn't feel her face at all, now - she really, really didn't want to take shelter *inside* a barrow. On the other hand, while she couldn't feel her face, she could still feel her toes, and they were sending her stabbing messages about how cold they were. Roman was using his front paws to widen the opening, and Aisha was trying to help from a perch on the side of the barrow. It seemed that her small team were united in their plan.

"Oh well, I guess Stefan wouldn't think to look for us in there, at least. And it's just for a few hours, right?"

Freya discovered she was talking to herself. Roman and Aisha had slipped through the crack and out of sight. With a sigh, she scrambled in after them.

CHAPTER SIXTY-TWO

Inside the barrow

Freya had braced herself for all sorts of horrors when entering the barrow. In fact, she could see nothing. She was still crouched, having no idea how much space there was inside to spread out in.

"Aisha? Roman? I hope you're in here," she quavered. Something touched Freya's hand and she stifled a shriek.

"It's just me, Freya," Aisha said. "Sorry if I scared you. I thought that if we're trying to avoid your boyfriend, we probably shouldn't be making mysterious lights shine out of a barrow. Although that could make for some great stories for the locals, maybe we should do it after all. I've got a flashlight on my phone."

"I believe it's usually called a howe in these parts. But I doubt the locals would care for lights appearing from it, in any case," Roman said, surprising Freya. She'd thought him still in wolf form, unable to talk. There must be more space in there than she'd thought. Somehow, she'd assumed that the barrow - no, *howe* - would be full of earth. But her questing fingers found rough stone, with little indents in it - chisel-marks, perhaps. She touched Aisha, in front of her, and stopped her hands wandering further in case she found Roman - who was presumably naked again. She wondered that she'd never noticed the were-foxes in her coastal home village lacking in clothing. Perhaps they had stashes of clothes hidden around the place. That seemed like a suitably foxy thing to do.

"Can you hear the wind anymore?" she asked suddenly, realising that part of her unease stemmed from the abrupt cessation of noise.

"No, it cut off right after we climbed in here," Roman said. "I believe there was a wind-demi coming down the road, that is why I turned us off the road and into this barrow, or howe, if you prefer."

"I hope that means that Lio's brothers are gone. We could make it to a proper shelter then. Assuming Stefan isn't still raging out there, of course."

"I suggest that we wait in here a while longer, just in case. I don't know this Lio, but from what you said I doubt his brothers are the type we should be chancing across on a dark night," said Roman. "Also, we would be much safer in here than outside."

"You're extrapolating a lot from one sentence," Freya said, feeling nettled. She might resent being the leader, but she really hated having her leadership usurped in any way.

"It's my job, as a historian, to extrapolate from little."

"I guess. Well, you're more or less right, anyway. Lio's always warned me about his brothers being violent. Tonight's the first time he's even suggested that they might be useful. Stefan must have scared him, too." Freya sighed. It was hard to reconcile the elegant, chivalrous Stefan she was attracted to, with the overly powerful, determined-to-prove-his-worth demigod who'd emerged tonight.

Maybe that's what Kylie meant about Stefan being power-hungry. It just seemed so hard to believe.

Aisha chimed in, bringing Freya back to more current matters.

"Lio's that sprite or wind demi, isn't he? The one who used to turn up occasionally when you were still at home."

"Wind demi. Yes. Why?"

"How come you don't go out with him, instead of the scary volcano demi?"

Good question. Why don't I?

"Because he never sticks around long enough for me to consider it, I guess. And he's never asked."

"Shame. Maybe you should ask him."

"Maybe. But hardly relevant right now. Look, I want to know what's going on out there."

There was a rumble, and Freya felt dirt showering down on her from above as the earth shivered.

"I guess Stefan's still in a mood." She sighed. The wind howled again, and Freya relaxed a little. The wind demis were still around. "I suppose we can wait a bit longer," she said. "It sounds like they're still at it. I'm beginning to feel my fingers again, at least."

"Yeah, I'm getting my toes back. But I hate being in the dark. Roman, can you see in here?" Aisha asked.

"A little. But as far as I can tell, this mound has been excavated and re-covered. There are no relics left that I can see. No bones, either. Also, we would have been unlikely to find this open space, if it was an undisturbed howe," the were-wolf answered.

"Thank you, professor," Aisha said, only a little sarcastically. "Does that mean no barrow-wights either?"

"I have not encountered any historical texts concerning barrow wights, so I am unable to reassure you on that. My nose tells me that only rodents live here."

"I'm not sure that I am reassured by that revelation," Aisha said.

"Your catlike side is not intrigued?" asked Roman, a smile in his voice.

"Strangely, no."

CHAPTER SIXTY-THREE

A DISCOVERY

The wind was still cold at Freya's back, but the heat of the preceding day had not yet dissipated from the enclosed space they had entered.

Could be worse. At least I'm not entirely frozen, now. But given Stefan is busy bringing magma to the surface, I'm not entirely happy about being underground. It seems like a step in the wrong direction, somehow.

The rock walls ended in a bumpy ceiling just above her head, when she cautiously stood, hand held above her to prevent bumping her head first. Underfoot felt like dirt, dry and dusty and smelling of dank earth. Her hand hit the roof. She thought of small scuttling creatures living in the crevices and snatched it back. But the ground shook again, and she put out a hand to steady herself. Her cold fingers encountered something colder and bumpier than the surrounding dirt. It was hard to tell with numb fingers, but she thought it was stone. She pulled at it, wondering what sort of thing would be wedged into the walls here. It came out abruptly. Freya had been pulling with enough force that she fell half out of the narrow slot they'd come in through, scraping her arms in the process as she tried to save herself.

Outside it was not nearly as dark as inside the barrow. A thin layer of snowflakes blanketed the ground, the light colour making it easier than usual to see in the night. Staring up at the sky, half-stunned, Freya wondered what it was she was looking at for a moment.

The barrow was on the edge of the moorland - they'd nearly reached the drop-off into farmland when they'd diverted to it. From where she lay, Freya had an excellent view out over the moor, and also down into the valley. The valley was mostly dark, only a few lights on in the village to mark it. The sky took up most of her view, dark, but with pale clouds bursting and reforming with terrifying speed. It was dizzying to watch.

I guess the wind demis are still around.

She rolled over to look the other way. The moor was covered with snow, clouds roiling above it, except for one spot, showing dark against the white backdrop. Flashes of red appeared and disappeared, and steam hazed the area.

Stefan must be there. I guess the snow can't settle because the earth is so hot.

Freya was glad he was still alive, no matter how misguided that might be. But did that mean that she, Aisha and Roman were safe? They hadn't come nearly as far away from the farmhouse bed and breakfast as she'd thought.

A flash of lightning lit up the area, and she saw a group of men tussling on the ground in the darker spot.

At least if the ground is dark, it's not lava anymore.

One figure was tall and bearded.

Not Lio.

That one seemed to be wrestling with Stefan, although it was hard to tell from this distance. Freya squinted, trying to make out more details. She inadvertently squeezed the stone thing in her hand as she tried to see. As though the sun was coming up, she found she was making out more details with every passing second. She looked down at the figurine in her hand with awe.

What are you? she wondered.

She could now see that the figurine was a crude wolf shape. She shuddered and let it drop to the snow. The darkness immediately returned. Cursing, she felt around for it. Clutching it once again, she experienced the slow return of night-vision. Wriggling around so that she could see the battleground without uncomfortable twisting, Freya saw a couple of men - Lio's brothers, presumably - help each other away from the area. One was limping, the other held an arm tenderly. Lio *was* there, darting across the moor and back apparently at random. Freya was reminded of his youthful propensity for racing. The bearded man still wrestled Stefan, so perhaps Lio was distracting him? As she watched, Lio stumbled on a rock, and fell, directly in front of Stefan. She couldn't help her gasp. Before she could see what happened to Lio, a tug on her feet alerted her that Aisha and Roman were not insensible to her odd position.

"What are you doing out there, Freya?" Aisha hissed. "Aren't we supposed to be to sheltering from the cold, and from those dangerous demis?"

Aisha's words alerted Freya to the fact that she was lying on the snow in her short sleeved t-shirt. The warmth of her body had already melted the uppermost layer, soaking her to the skin. She sat up, realising how chilled she still was. Aisha was right, they should be sheltering.

"Don't interrupt now," she muttered, trying to see what was happening to Lio. But it was too late. She'd lost sight of him. "I found something," she told Aisha. "An artifact, I guess. Maybe your professor friend in there can tell us something more about it."

"Maybe you can tell me why you're lying around in snow - snow in August, I might add - instead of sheltering inside like a sensible person?" Aisha said acerbically.

"I can see in the dark!"

"Well done you, I'm sure, but that's no reason to freeze."

"No, I mean I can see in the dark when I hold this statue-thing I found."

There was a pause. Freya imagined Aisha re-arranging her assumptions.

"Maybe you had better show it to Roman, then."

"I will. But first - oh, Fenris's teeth, I can't see him anymore."

"See who?"

"Lio. He was over by Stefan - and by the way, we're not nearly far enough away yet - and he fell. I can't see him anymore." Worry gnawed at Freya, distracting her from her physical discomfort. She couldn't see any of the fighting figures anymore, not even Stefan. Where had they gone?

CHAPTER SIXTY-FOUR

THE BATTLE CONTINUES

Roman appeared in human form behind Aisha. Freya could see him all too clearly with the artifact in her hand. Luckily, Aisha's body blocked any details Freya wasn't interested in seeing.

"Did you say you have found something of interest?" he rumbled.

"Most definitely. Here, Aisha, show him this." Freya passed Aisha the figurine, accepting the return of darkness with some reluctance.

"Interesting. Wolf-shaped, I see. But not congruent with the era of this howe at all. It's the wrong sort of stone for a start. And quite the wrong style for bronze age. It must be a more recent deposit. Perhaps whenever the excavation took place, someone lost it."

"So, we won't get ghosts or barrow wights following us if we take it?"

"Since those are purely imagination, I'd guess not," Roman said.

"You don't notice anything else? Like a change in your vision?"

Freya imagined Roman glancing sharply at her - she couldn't see such detail anymore.

"Not just now, no. It is possible that it contains some element that affects demis and not were-wolves. But that would require further study," Roman said.

"Okay. Study it, then. But can you see Stefan - or anyone else - from where you're standing?"

"From where I am standing, I can see Aisha's head. No more."

Freya thumped the snow in frustration. "They could be anywhere out there! I don't think we can wait out the storm in here after all. We'd be trapped if Stefan or someone else dangerous found us in here. It's not actually snowing anymore, at least." Freya scrambled to her feet.

"It's still colder out there than in here," argued Aisha.

"Yes, but in here is underground. Now that I can feel my extremities again, I think I'd rather be out in the fresh air. As far away from underground powers as I can get."

"When you put it that way, I suppose a short evening stroll won't hurt. But only as far as the village, alright?" Aisha said.

"We're still going to have to wait for a morning train, so yes."

The second part of the journey was just as painful as the first. Although Freya had been able to feel her fingers again, that didn't last long outside with fresh-fallen snow. The brief thaw meant that her trainers were soaked, which didn't help her toes, either. Despite his injuries, Roman was the best equipped for this trek, once he'd changed back into wolf form.

"For the first time ever, I see some point in being a were," she remarked to Aisha.

"I know, right? I am jealous of that fur too. Especially now it's better groomed," Aisha said. She was just as ill-dressed for the conditions as Freya. "You know, I always thought Karim had bad luck living in such a hot place, but I'm beginning to think that hot is quite attractive right now."

"That's not what you said when we were out in the heat yesterday."

"There's no need to throw my ill-considered words back at me."

They were going downhill at a steady pace.

"We should be there in twenty minutes or so," Freya said encouragingly. Then she noticed a flickering glow in a field off to one side.

Don't get involved, Freya, she warned herself. *Lio will take care of himself. So will Stefan. Ugh, that's not a situation that's going to work out well. You just have to get yourself, your friend, and one wounded were-wolf to safety.*

"What's that?" Aisha asked, pointing.

"I think it's Lio and Stefan. Maybe his brothers, too," she said.

"They're a bit close to the road, aren't they?" asked Aisha.

Frigg, Aisha is right. I'd like to check on Lio, but we shouldn't risk getting so close to Stefan.

Freya sighed. It was hard to adjust her worldview to think of Stefan as evil. *Maybe just misguided?*

She could see the dark sides of the drystone walls and hedges that outlined the road curving around through the snow-covered landscape. If they kept following the road as they'd intended, they'd end up right beside the glowing spot.

"Pass me that artifact, Roman," she said. She'd let him keep it, earlier, not sure what long-term side effects supernatural night vision would have. Freya figured that if it didn't affect his vision, it shouldn't affect anything else. The were-wolf had been padding along with it held in his mouth. Now, he trotted over to her, enabling her to take it.

"Thanks. Ugh, it's got spit all over. Did you have to do that?" She glanced at Roman, fully visible now she had the figurine in hand. He raised an eyebrow at her. Apparently were-wolves retained that trait from their human forms. Freya sighed. "I suppose you couldn't help it."

Looking down towards the spot where she thought the demis were now battling, Freya could no longer see the bearded one who she thought had brought the snows, or the two who had limped away. Nik and her goblins were nowhere in sight either. It was just Stefan and Lio down there. Lio seemed to be running circles around Stefan - he couldn't have been too hurt when he fell, earlier. Stefan was hurling... were those balls of lava? Freya's jaw dropped. Stefan must have located a thinner part of Gaia's crust. Or was he simply heating loose rocks with those hot hands of his? It probably didn't matter, except that molten rocks without a magma channel might be less likely to result in the obliteration of the whole area. Lio dodged the molten missile, and returned a lightning bolt.

So Lio's not defenceless. I always thought it was him who scared away the weres when I was a teenager. Looks like I was right.

Nevertheless, she cringed on Lio's behalf when Stefan hurled another glob of lava, which passed so close to Lio that his hair caught alight. He patted at it frantically, and she was relieved to see that he was able to smother the fire. Lio shouted something at Stefan, who paused in the act of stooping to the ground for another handful of lava. Freya couldn't make out the words - alas, it seemed that the figurine helped her sight but not her hearing. Stefan made some reply, his stance belligerent. Lio held out his hands in a 'what would you have me do' gesture. Stefan turned his back, and started to stalk away, down the hill. He cast a couple of glowing rocks to the ground as he went. Where they landed, small fires began to smoulder, the snow melting vanishingly fast.

"Care to tell us why you're standing still and gasping at intervals, Freya?" Aisha's voice startled Freya out of her trance.

"Oh, sorry. I forgot you couldn't see what's going on down there."

"A fire is what it looks like," Aisha said.

"Well, I guess that's true, now. But only because Stefan and Lio were fighting. Did you see the lava, at least?"

"If that's what the glowing balls were, then yes. You sure do pick your frenemies, Freya."

"How was I to know he was like that? Anyway, it looks like Lio is coming this way now. Here, Roman, can you take this thing again? It's handy seeing in the dark, but I think I've seen enough, now." She held out the figurine until Roman's teeth gently took it from her.

Really, he's nothing like what I imagined were-wolves would be like.

CHAPTER SIXTY-FIVE

AFTERMATH

To Freya's relief, Lio appeared shortly afterwards, jogging up the hill to meet them, going the long way round to climb through a gap in the hedge. Freya was glad she'd given up her night-sight. She was pretty sure she didn't want to see the effects of that burn on Lio's head.

I'm still never going to make it as a nurse.

"Thanks, Lio," she said.

Lio nodded, then grimaced and stooped to the road to gather a handful of snow, which he applied directly to the side of his head.

"Anytime, I guess. Except, not just for a little while, OK? I think it's going to take some time to recover from that fight."

"I'm sorry, I know you try to avoid violence," Freya said.

"I do. I had hoped that my brothers would stay longer. But apparently babysitting my brother Reas's storm hounds for three years is only a small favour, not worthy of an entire battle with a volcano demi. Or so he said as he left."

"That doesn't sound terribly equitable."

"No, I didn't think so, either. It was probably an excuse to get away. At least my brothers came, though. I'd have hated to do that without Reas's snow cooling things off. And the rain you summoned was essential. There's no snow without water." He gave her a warm smile.

"So - is it over? What did Stefan say? At the end, I mean."

Lio looked sad.

"He said he wouldn't forget you. And that I was a fool for interfering. And that nothing was up to me, anyway. At that point, I agreed, and pointed out that scaring a woman probably wasn't the best way to win her over. That's when he walked away. I don't know what's between you, exactly, Freya, but it doesn't seem like he's a healthy personality type to be involved with."

Freya bit her lip.

"I'm sorry I brought you into it, Lio. I thought we were all about to go up in smoke, one way or another. Are you much hurt?"

"I'll live. Though I'm glad Reas's snow has lasted this long, despite being out of season. That's probably the real reason he didn't stay, you know. It's not a good time of year for him. Russ and Toss got themselves into a muddle early on. Skeir's always fickle, so no surprise that he wasn't a stayer. Of course, I didn't bother calling Zeph. He's probably the only one you should meet, though. One day. At least you thought to call me, this time." He quirked one side of his mouth up. "That's probably more than I've ever told you, isn't it? I must be more rattled by the fight than I realised."

"I guess I know your brother's names now. It sounds like you cover most of the wind-gods between you."

"You could say so, yes. Though none of us are full deities, so we don't have full powers, either," Lio said.

"Is there anything you need? I mean, none of us have more than a few plasters, I think, but can we help?" Freya asked.

"Thank you, but no. I have pressing duties at home, I cannot stay. As usual." He sighed.

Lio *was* being unusually talkative, Freya thought.

"We're heading for the village. We'll take Roman to Aisha's place, to recuperate, you know. He had an altercation with Stefan earlier. Yesterday, by now."

Really, Stefan seems to be fighting with everyone I meet.

"You're welcome to come too, "said Aisha. "I've only caught glimpses of you from time to time, but you were there when Freya called in the rainstorm a few years back, weren't you?"

She sounded weary, Freya thought. No wonder - after walking all day, they'd now been walking half the night, too.

"Thank you. I'd stay if I could. But although I can now come when called, I cannot stay as long as I would like. There are unavoidable things to do at home." Lio's voice was sad. "I'll just say goodbye and go."

"Sounds like descending from Bastet is better luck than I used to think," commented Aisha.

Lio nodded.

"Definitely a more peaceful option than some."

Freya impulsively stepped closer to Lio and hugged him.

"I wish you could stay. But thank you so much for coming."

Lio hugged her carefully back, like someone holding something precious.

"Call me again." A shadow of laughter crept into his voice. "Some time when you are without associated volcano gods would be ideal."

"I might just try that." Freya rested her head against Lio's shoulder a moment before stepping away. It felt strangely comfortable.

"Until next time, then." Lio raised a hand, lightning crackled, and he was gone.

Freya and Aisha stood in silence a moment. Freya smoothed down her hair, which was waving wildly in the aftermath of that electrical blast.

"Well, he's a better pick than your volcano demi. A bit flighty, though," said Aisha.

"Yes. Sometimes I feel like I've barely started a conversation with him and he's off again. I don't know, maybe it's a wind demi thing. But you can see why I never got things off the ground with him. No time!"

"Yes, I do see. But even so... well. Let's not dwell on things that can't be mended just now. Roman, are you still here?"

The were-wolf stepped forward and nuzzled Aisha's hand briefly.

"Yes, I see you are. So, it looks like the excitement's over, and we're still stuck on a snowy hillside. Let's get down to the village where we can freeze in peace," she said.

"Very funny, Aisha. I'm prepared to wake up that vet, you know. Now I've been out in the cold a while, I think I know exactly what state we'd be in if we stayed out all night in it. Since I don't think icicles can catch trains, I'll try to get us a better shelter for the night," Freya said.

"Sounds like an excellent plan. Lead on to shelter."

CHAPTER SIXTY-SIX

THE VET'S PLACE

The vet didn't answer her door at first. However, after a second round of pounding, she opened it cautiously, evidently worried about what sort of people might be thumping her door in the middle of the night. Her pepper-and-salt hair was unbound, falling across her round face in short wisps. She seemed much less calm and professional than the previous day, but her acerbic tones were just the same.

"Oh, it's you lot again. Lost someone, did you?" she said.

"Sorry to wake you," said Freya. "We had a difference of opinion with… the man who was with us earlier, which has resulted in us not having anywhere to stay tonight. We'll be off in the morning, but we wondered if you would mind if we borrowed your floor tonight?" She made a face. "We don't know anyone else here, or we wouldn't have bothered you."

The vet was looking sceptical, but her face softened as she looked at Roman, who was doing a good job of looking forlorn and cold, tail tucked between his legs. He seemed to have excellent acting skills as a wolf - or maybe that wasn't acting.

"I've only got a little place here, but since it's for the good of my patient, you can have the sitting room for the night. It really will be the floor, though - there's no space anywhere else." She opened the door a little wider to let them in. "You may as well come in, you're only letting the cold in by standing there." She shivered dramatically. "And when did it get cold, anyway? It was too hot to sleep when I went to bed."

Freya found it politic not to answer that question. No need to start explaining wind demis to a probable mundane. The three of them trooped inside.

"Come through, the sitting room's just behind the clinic." The vet led the way through the tiny reception area, through a short corridor which reeked of disinfectant, and through another door into a much homelier environment, set about with a plump two-seater couch, an overstuffed ottoman covered with khaki corduroy, and an upright piano taking up most of one wall. "You can sleep here. Facilities are through that door, and I'll expect you gone by 9. The clinic opens then. I'm Mary," she added, clearly as an afterthought.

"I'm Freya, that's Aisha. Thanks ever so much," said Freya. "We only had summer clothes, so when the weather turned we were afraid we'd get hypothermia or something."

"I'm only doing it for the dog, so don't thank me too much." She went over to a wooden tallboy squeezed between the door and the sofa. "Here, I don't have extra blankets, but you can use a few towels. It's bitter tonight, but I'm not putting the heating on in August." She tossed them an assortment of ragged towels that had seen better days. "Now, I'm going back to bed and I don't want to be disturbed. At all. Understand?"

"Absolutely."

Freya waited for the vet to trudge back upstairs before turning to Aisha.

"You owe me one, now," she said. "You know I hate asking strangers for things."

Aisha shrugged.

"It's good for you. Character building. But thanks. I feel better being inside an actual building, and this is much more comfortable than a barrow." She shook out her towel - light blue, with darker blue flowers patterning the edges, but so thin it was almost see-through. "I have a feeling I'm really going to miss the mattress at that bed and breakfast, mind you."

"Yeah, me too. Bags the sofa!" Freya turned to claim the small sofa - only to find that Roman was already there, stretched out luxuriously, and fast asleep. "Oh, Frigg."

Aisha snickered.

"Guess you're on the floor too. Come on, there's a rug at least. Get some sleep before we have to get up again."

Sighing at the injustice of the were-wolf getting the only comfortable spot, she laid out her own towel - brown with bleach stains splashed across it - and lay down.

CHAPTER SIXTY-SEVEN

MORNING PICKUP

Aisha woke Freya the next morning.

"Come on, Freya, we have to go. Time to go catch that train."

Roman was standing by the door, looking much perkier than the night before.

Freya groaned and rolled to her feet. Her body protested, telling her all about the many bruises she'd acquired yesterday.

"Is there time to find breakfast first?"

"Only if we go now. Come on, Freya, you've slept in. You didn't wake even when the vet came through."

"Seriously?"

"Seriously. And she popped her head in a couple of minutes ago to remind us that we have to leave before her clinic opens. Which it does in about five minutes."

Freya hastily crammed her wet shoes onto her feet, but took the time to fold the towel which had ended up being used as a blanket. She might be naturally untidy, but that made her hyper-aware of other people's neatness.

"Right, let's go."

She waved to the vet as they passed through the clinic area. The vet's face lit up when she saw Roman pacing beside them, looking much healthier than last night.

"Until next time," the vet called brightly. Clearly, she was a morning person.

The snow had melted overnight, the wind returning to its usual prevailing direction. The sky was a glaring, bright grey, quite a change from the blue of recent weeks.

Freya looked at her phone to check the time. There was a message from Kylie, assuring her that she'd fed Mr Fluffbum, but when would Freya be back?

"I've got a better idea than taking the train," she announced, quickly replying to Kylie's message. "I'll ask for a lift. I think it's time we consulted with someone who knows Stefan at least as well as I do."

They waited at the train station anyway. It was a little out of the wind, and there weren't so many glaring passers-by. A surprising number of emergency service vehicles passed by, heading to the moor. Several news crew cars also passed them. Freya pretended not to be interested.

She purchased something to eat at the small shop nearby, and Aisha treated them all to hot drinks. Roman lapped at an open cup of coffee.

"Are you sure were-wolves can drink coffee?" Freya asked, watching him do so.

"It's probably better than hot chocolate," Aisha said. "Even your were-fox relatives don't drink that."

"That's the best argument I've ever heard against being a were," said Freya with feeling, before sipping her own chocolately drink.

"Lucky you didn't turn when you got bitten that time," Aisha retorted. "You would have, you know, if Nena's and Karim's ointment didn't work."

"But Lisichka said it didn't work that way," Freya protested.

Aisha turned to her and raised an eyebrow. "And you trust everything a fox says?"

Freya slumped. "Good point. I never knew how lucky I was. I guess I can forgive Karim his transgressions, then, since I can still have my chocolate and eat it too." She hesitated, then asked in a falsely cheerful voice, "So, do you still have some of that ointment? I have quite a few were-inflicted scratches."

Aisha bit her lip. "There might be a bit left in Nena's stash. Let's hope so."

Kylie drew up in her small car some time later. She surveyed the ragged group with a look of weary astonishment.

"Y'know, Freya, when I warned you about Stefan, I wasn't expecting to get a call from a disaster zone. There's nothing else on the news this morning. You must have riled him right up," she said. "Are you sure that thing is safe?" she added, looking at Roman.

Aisha slung an arm over him. "I'll vouch for his behaviour," she said.

"Just no teeth, right?" Kylie said firmly. "And Freya, I didn't realise you were seeing Stefan this weekend. We had things to say to him, remember?"

"Yeah. Sorry about that," Freya said. "He wasn't supposed to be here."

"'S'alright. I know what he's like," Kylie said, somewhat reassuringly. "Your cat's in the back, Freya," she added. "I didn't know if you were going away or what, so I talked to your landlady and packed him up. I don't think he'll like your wolf though. I'm not sure I do either."

"He's not *my* wolf," Freya began to explain.

Rather than growling, as Freya half-expected him to do, Roman looked at Kylie beseechingly and tilted his ears forward.

"Oh, all right, you can get in the back," Kylie said to him. "But not behind me. I'm not driving with a wolf breathing down the back of my neck."

Roman leaped gracefully into the back of the car when Aisha held the door open for him. Aisha slid in after him, clearly glad to be out of the icy wind.

Freya leaned over into the boot of the small car and saw Mr Fluffbum blinking back at her from his cat carrier. She let her hand down for him to sniff, then scratched his chin through the bars. "You think of everything. Thanks, Kylie."

"You're welcome. But I expect a full recount of your night on the way."

Freya eased herself into the passenger seat, taking care not to bump her bruises or lacerations.

"I have just had the most difficult weekend of my life," she announced to Kylie.

"What, walking on the moors with your friend? What's hard about that? Not that I'd walk there by choice, mind."

"It was the were versus demigod battles that made it hard. That and the prospect of going to see my Mum."

Kylie laughed at the comparison, as Freya had intended.

"You're lucky I picked you up, then," she said. "It's possible that that is one of the benefits of living this far away from Oz," she said. "I don't need excuses not to visit my family in the weekends. Not that I don't love them of course, but distance can be easier."

Freya considered the time she'd spent away from her own family. She'd been lonely, but also free to find her own self, and make her own choices, however good or bad.

"Yes, I know what you mean," Freya said.

"So, what happened with you and Stefan? Were there seriously battles?"

"Seriously, there were. It was terrifying. I mean, I'd seen a bit of what Stefan can do before, but earthquakes? And lava? That was taking things too far."

"Woah, girl, what did you do to him? I mean, sure, he and I broke up, but it wasn't because the earth was moving. Pretty much the reverse, really."

It was Freya's turn to laugh.

"So, Stefan didn't rock your world?"

Kylie grinned, clearly in a better mood. "Too much information if I tell." She sobered. "Though it's a shame you didn't get to talk to him about me. I guess if he's in that sort of mood there's not much point my asking."

"I'm sorry," Freya said. "I don't know what to suggest. Maybe talk to Tony, he has children. He might have some suggestions."

Kylie nodded.

"Yeah, that's not a bad idea. I might just call my Mum anyway. Despite our differences, she might actually have a clue about what I can do. Not that I'll ever put it that way to her, she'd never let me live it down if I told her I was asking her for advice."

"You must have a very different relationship with her, compared to me and my Mum."

Kylie looked wistful for a moment, then returned to her usual down-to-earth style.

"Ten to one we'll be hurling insults a minute into the call. No need to envy that."

But I do envy that. At least it's evidence that she cares.

Her thoughts shortly returned to Stefan, however.

"I can't help but wonder what he meant by shouting about his employees, though," she mused aloud.

"You didn't mention *that* before," Aisha said.

Freya looked over her shoulder at Aisha. "Sorry," she said. "I guess a few things distracted me from it."

"It sounds important," Aisha said. "Does it link in with those attacks you told me about, do you think?"

Her hands gripping the steering wheel tight enough to show white knuckles, Kylie chimed in.

"Yes. It does."

Freya stared at Kylie.

"You know about it?"

Carefully steering the laden car around an icy corner, Kylie took a moment to answer.

"I've heard things," she said. "After I split with Stefan, before you turned up, Freya. Stefan's a consultant on top of his regular job, that's how come he's always got money. But you know how I said he's power-hungry?"

Freya nodded, holding tightly to the door-handle as the car skidded around a particularly tight corner.

"Yeah, well it turns out he's got a bee in his bonnet about collecting powerful people to help him with his frost-folk fetish. He tests them using weres. Seeing if they'll join him, maybe? I don't know, it seems weird to me. But yeah, once I told him I wouldn't use my lightning-demi heritage in his cause, he wasn't interested in me anymore."

"That is beyond weird," said Aisha.

"Yes," Freya agreed. "It doesn't make much sense. But I guess it agrees with the facts - if Stefan's employing were-wolves and were-foxes, I mean. But why was he dragging me around all those attack sites then?"

Kylie looked at Freya long enough that Freya urged her to look at the road.

"Maybe he wanted to see if you could be swayed to join his cause?" Kylie suggested.

Freya was silent, mind whirring, but unable to reach any meaningful conclusion. In the back seat, Roman growled under his breath. Behind that, Mr Fluffbum uttered intermittent, melodious wails to make sure that everyone in the car knew that he was not a happy travelling cat.

"Sorry, Mr Fluffbum," Freya called to him. "Not long now."

CHAPTER SIXTY-EIGHT

HOME AGAIN

It felt like a lifetime ago that Freya had last been to her home town, so close to the sea, despite her recent visit with Aisha and her family. So much had happened in a few short weeks.

"Will your family really let a were-wolf stay, Aisha?" Freya asked.

"We'll see. If they don't, there will be words." Aisha sounded grimly determined.

Roman made a whining noise in his throat, as though he wanted to say something.

"You can change once we're there, Roman. And talk, too. Just be nice to the cats and everything should work out."

Roman's ears went back, just a little.

"Don't look like that. Cats are the most important thing in my house, and don't you forget it," Aisha said.

Mr Fluffbum gave an affirmative mew from the boot, and everyone laughed, the tension dissolving. Even Roman's ears came up.

A light drizzle began as they drove down the road, which was only slightly worn about the edges from the previous year's storms and flooding. There weren't many cars here - few people earned enough to pay for the luxury of a private vehicle these days. A train whistle sounded nearby, causing Roman to flatten his ears completely. However, Aisha brightened, shedding tiredness in anticipation of home.

"Here we are," she announced, pointing to one of several identical brick houses.

They scrambled out of the car.

"I'll drop you off here," Kylie said. "No need for me to get in the way. Give me a yell when you're ready to go somewhere, Freya."

"You won't be in the way," Aisha protested.

"Between a cat and dog fight? No thanks. Call me when you need me, Freya," Kylie said. She jumped out and pulled a cord from the front of her car. "You can charge me up while I'm waiting, though. I'll need that to get home." She settled into her seat and drew out her phone. "I'll just be out here reading."

Freya wondered if it was only her imagination that made Roman look cautious, hanging back a little behind Aisha. She didn't have long to wonder, however, because Aisha threw open the front door, calling out as she did so.

"Isis! Mum! I'm back before schedule, where is everyone?"

The usual flood of cats appeared, including Isis the cafe cat. Freya turned to the car to get Mr Fluffbum out and greet her own cat properly.

Some of the cats immediately looked at Roman and hissed, turning tail. Other, braver cats paused in the doorway to assess the newcomer. Isis padded forward regally, and lifted her nose to Roman's.

"Look at that!" Aisha whispered to Freya, who nodded in appreciation of the significance of Isis's acceptance.

"You might be in with a chance after all," Freya said to Roman. "So long as you don't threaten Aisha, that is." Roman's furry forehead wrinkled in a disapproving frown. A few seconds after the cats arrived, Aisha's mother also reached the front door, where Freya, Aisha and Roman had paused to greet the cats.

"Aisha. This is a surprise, I thought you were on holiday for several more days. But what *have* you got there?" Aisha's Mum had spotted Roman - he was hard to miss, after all.

"Mum, this is Roman. He's a history professor. As you'll see if we can just let him into a bathroom or somewhere with some clothes. I'm assuming you'd like to meet him with clothes, anyway."

Aisha's Mum looked scandalised. Given the number of were-foxes in this town, and what Aisha had told Freya about Gareth the were-fox's involvement with the cafe business, Freya found this amusing. *Maybe Gareth doesn't get naked around his employer's family. All things considered, that's probably a good thing.*

"If I'm to meet anyone I'd prefer them to be clothed. But Aisha, that's a *were-wolf.* How did you get him here? And more to the point, why did you?"

"Oh Mum, it's a long story. Can we get in the house first? We've been travelling all morning. Besides, Isis doesn't mind, look."

Aisha's Mum did look at Isis, who was now sitting in apparent contentment beside Roman.

"Oh, very well. Excuse my manners, Freya. Come in, all of you." She turned and led the way to the house's natural gathering place, the kitchen. Once there, she bustled around putting on a kettle to boil and assembling an assortment of snacks. Freya was grateful for this automatic hospitality. Even if there were arguments later, at least they'd be fed now.

Aisha pointed Roman towards her brother's old room, ignoring her mother's frown.

"Grab some clothes from in there and get changed. There should be something that fits better than a sheet," she said.

"There had better be an excellent explanation for this, Aisha," said her Mum warningly.

"Oh, there is. Freya, you can tell her all about it."

Freya cast a dark look at her friend, but thought she'd better give her version, in case Aisha's was less flattering.

"Well, Mrs Tanoute, it all started yesterday when Aisha and I were walking on the moors..."

Aisha's Mum was still frowning by the time Roman returned. Freya broke off her explanation gratefully. No matter how she phrased it, she couldn't manage to put herself in a favourable light.

"Good afternoon, Mrs - Tanoute, was it? - and thank you for taking us in with no notice. My name is Dr. Roman Lykaios."

"I thought you said Dr Canid," interrupted Aisha.

"I said that was a joke," Roman muttered, before resuming his professional-sounding introduction. "As Aisha informed you, I am a history professor - although I must admit that I am between jobs at the present time."

As Roman set about trying to charm Aisha's mother, Freya pulled Aisha to one side. This was difficult to achieve without tripping over Mr Fluffbum, who was twining around her legs.

"I know, Mr Fluffbum, I missed you too." She patted the insistent cat, then realised that cat-food would probably answer better.

"What is it?" murmured Aisha.

"Are you going to want to stay here, if Roman gets to? Or will you come back to our holiday?"

"In demi-infested York? If you don't mind, I think I'll avoid the area for a little longer. We've only just gotten away!"

Freya stroked Mr Fluffbum again, who arched his back and seemed inclined to purr.

"It's just that I know I'll have to go back. Work, you know."

"I can see where you're heading, Freya, but I don't think I can be your backup. I just don't have any powers to cope with a volcano demi. Fleas and locusts don't cut it against lava."

Freya sagged. That was what she'd been afraid of. She couldn't blame Aisha, but she didn't want to return to York without anyone at her back.

"I'll just go out for a walk than. Maybe drop in on Mum and the kits, once I've fed Mr Fluffbum," she said morosely.

Aisha patted her shoulder.

"Good idea. Why don't you go find your Australian friend, too? Her car's probably all charged up."

CHAPTER SIXTY-NINE

Missing Tammy

Freya didn't go straight to her Mum's house. Instead, her footsteps took her to the crumbling cliff path, threatened more every year by the encroaching sea. It had been moved back another metre since her last visit, temporary fencing encouraging visitors to stay away from the edge. Up here was were-fox territory, but Freya was beginning to feel that she could handle a were-fox or two, if the alternative was an emotionally volatile volcano demi.

She made her way up the cliffs, then along and down to the cove where she'd found her nieces and nephews four years ago when looking for her sister. The wind was strong here, buffeting her as she clambered down the stairs. She stopped before she reached the beach itself. The tide was in, and she didn't want to get too close to the waves. Sitting on the midway stair, she gazed out over the grey ocean. Kittiwakes and guillemots screamed above her, arrowing in to feed their young, or squabbling over territory. It was restful, she thought, despite the raucous calls of the birds. Birds were so much easier to deal with than people. A wave crashing onto the beach below her sent sea spray flying high, a few drops reaching her. She shivered, though not out of cold, and backed up a couple of steps. She wasn't even sure why she'd come here. She'd spent the last few years trying to stay as far from the sea as possible.

"Are you out there somewhere, Tammy?" she murmured. Perhaps that was it. Coming home had reminded her forcefully of her sister's absence in a way that she hadn't been while she was inland gaining her qualifications. Unfortunately, there still didn't seem to be anything she could do about that. Tears trickled down her cheeks for a time, the blurring of the sea nothing to do with the movement of its waves.

Eventually she roused herself, stiff after sitting so long. Mooching around staring at the sea wasn't going to solve her problems. Somehow, she was going to have to do that herself.

Resolutely, she marched down the hill to find Kylie. She was going to need a lift to see the chilli king.

CHAPTER SEVENTY

ANGIE HAS BAD NEWS

Kylie dropped Freya at Angie's gate late in the day, saying she needed to get home to charge her car again. Freya burst into the living room. The door banged into the wall behind her, and bounced back without quite closing. Kylie had said she should check in on her landlady, but everything seemed normal here.

"Something wrong?" Angie asked, looking up from the romance novel she'd had open, the inevitable glass of wine on a table by her side. Freya couldn't help but notice that the pages were unusually dog-eared. Angie's hands continued to fiddle with the book while Freya spoke.

Freya was taken aback. The way Kylie had talked, she'd thought there must be something drastically wrong, but Angie seemed more or less as normal as she ever was. Thrown off-kilter, she started talking at random.

"I feel like I'm always trying to sort out other people these days. One day I need to figure out what I want instead."

"That sounds like my whole life, love. But that's the way I like it, really. It gives me a good feeling when I can fix other people's troubles." Angie's hands stilled and fell into her lap as she spoke. Freya wondered what she'd been anxious about, but put the thought aside to consider Angie's words.

"Really? It doesn't sound so satisfying to me."

"Perhaps that's because you're young. I wasn't so altruistic in my twenties either."

"I'm not *young*!"

"Compared to me?" Angie smiled serenely.

"Oh, all right. You're an ancient old woman, at least, ooh, ten years older than me?"

"More like fifteen, I should say. Fifteen years more wisdom."

"Yeah, sounds ancient. But nothing I've done lately is for me. I don't know why I thought growing up would be so good, people just turn to me to look after them instead of me looking after me."

"Too much babysitting over the weekend, then?" Angie asked.

Freya laughed shakily. She didn't feel up to describing the whole volcano god meets were-wolf debacle on the moor.

"It's not that. I enjoyed looking after my relatives, surprisingly. I just - thought that being grown up and looking after myself would have more meaning."

"Perhaps you haven't found your calling yet. There's plenty of time though."

"What if I never figure it out though? I've already spent years getting educated." *Which turns out to be not as useful as my demi-powers when it comes to defeating plant diseases...* "I could turn into an old woman and still not know how to find fulfilment."

Angie patted the book she'd put down, its cover a lurid depiction of a half-naked man holding a woman in a sweeping gown.

"That's what books are for, love. If life fails to fulfil, find the life you want between the covers. So to speak."

Freya had to giggle, her bad mood evaporating.

"It certainly looks like the main characters in that book will find fulfilment between the covers. Or possibly under them."

"It wouldn't be much of a romance if they didn't," agreed Angie amiably. "But I don't think those two are concerned about being covered, if you know what I mean."

Freya was struck once again by the solitary nature of Angie's life, visited only occasionally by the husband who'd brought her here.

"Do you ever consider leaving? Going back to the city, finding someone else?" *Maybe Angie has something in her attitude to life. It's certainly easier to deal with other people's problems than with my own. Like Mum. Or Stefan.*

Angie stroked the cover of her book again before answering.

"Of course, I do. But it's not such a simple thing to do. It's easier to stay as I am, despite the disadvantages. Maybe I'm just a coward. It would take something drastic to change that, I think."

"*I* don't want to get stuck in the wrong place, though. What if I'm doing the wrong thing now? How will I know until it's too late?"

"So dramatic! Here, do you want some wine?" Angie waved the cask at Freya.

"No, I'm fine. I don't want to follow in my Dad's footsteps, at least."

Angie sat taller, looking interested. Freya could practically see her ears twitching forward. Still, why not tell her? Angie was good at sympathising.

"Really? Why, what did he do?"

"Only left us when I was still a kid. He was a traveling wine salesman. You know what? Pass me a glass of that wine after all. It might not solve anything, but since I can't change the past, I might as well enjoy the present."

"That's the spirit. Or well, it's not, it's wine, but working on the present is better than raging against long-gone fathers." Angie fetched a glass for Freya and poured her a glass. "This one's from Kent. Didn't you say that's where you went for work?"

"No, that was Devon. Nice place. I wish we'd grown up there instead of on the crumbling coast."

"Plenty of crumbling coast in Devon. That's where the dinosaurs are found in cliffs, isn't it?"

"Probably. I've never been much of a dinosaur fiend as a kid, though."

"Interesting choices your family has made, by the sounds of it."

"Interesting is a good word for it, yes." Freya took a sip of her wine. "What about you, did you have an interesting childhood?" *It's far easier to hear about other people's lives, really. Maybe that's why Angie likes talking to people.*

"I had a very normal one, by the standards of the time. You know, a few years of off-and-on home schooling while the pandemic was on, then a few more years of being told to avoid people. Really, I think that's what made me like people so much, not getting to see them enough as a child."

"Sounds different. My Mum said she was out foraging a lot during those years."

"My family was in the city, so we were dependent on online deliveries. I don't think anyone in my family would have been able to identify an edible plant in a garden, let alone in the wild." She grinned. "That's why I look after people, not plants."

Freya laughed.

"I guess if you look at it that way, I'm in the right place. I would be terrible at looking after people. I never know the right thing to say. I'm not even a good babysitter, I get bored."

"Well, here's to being in the right place, after all," Angie smiled again, raising her glass in a toast.

Freya raised her own glass in salute, but after a sip she put down her glass.

"Are *you* in the right place?" Now that she'd calmed down a little, she was remembering Angie's restless hands.

Angie put her own glass down empty, and those hands clutched each other again. Freya noticed suddenly that Angie's pink-varnished nails were bitten to the quick.

"I just don't know, any more." She took a shuddering breath. "Here I am, preaching about taking the easy way, when I'm seriously considering my own options."

"Why, has something happened?"

"I got a call. From Will."

Freya nodded encouragingly. Will was Angie's husband.

"You know he's out on the road delivering fertiliser half the time. More than half, really."

"Yes. I've hardly ever seen him here," said Freya.

"Well. It turns out he has been doing one or two other things as well as that." Angie's round face crumpled. "Your Dad's not the only one who made bad decisions. Will's got another family, Freya. A wife and child. It's bigamy, of course. So, I could sue and get the farm. And I will. And then I'll sell it and move to the city the way I should have done years ago. That bastard has taken the best years of my life, and I've just been sitting here being a good little wifey keeping the home fires burning. I just can't believe I never saw it coming."

Freya rose and awkwardly put an arm around Angie's shoulders as the older woman sobbed.

"That's terrible, Angie. I'm sorry. I can't believe I was just complaining about looking after people, and here you are needing someone and I didn't even see it."

Angie patted her hand.

"No reason you should have. I just needed to have a bit of a weep and get over it." She took a deep breath, much as Freya had done earlier. "It seems it's quite the week for revelations, doesn't it? Here, pour me another glass, please. Else I'll sit here snivelling all day."

Freya obliged, though she felt the sides of her mouth pulling down. She felt like her own history was being repeated.

"Sounds like Will's no better than my Dad was, after all," she said.

Angie nodded, seeming unable to form a coherent sentence this time.

Freya wished she knew what to say.

I'm just not good at comforting people. I guess I haven't had much practice. To her relief, Angie took a sip of her wine, gave a deep shuddering sigh, and seemed to pull herself together.

"At least this means I can say yes to some of those invitations I get down the pub," Angie said, apparently consoling herself.

Freya rolled her eyes. It didn't sound like much consolation to her - but then she'd never gotten the hang of chatting to strangers in pubs. Angie would probably be a pro at it.

CHAPTER SEVENTY-ONE

STEFAN HAS GONE AWAY

Freya hadn't come up with any solutions for dealing with Stefan by the time she returned to work. She had braced herself to see Stefan when she entered the canteen at lunchtime, but there was no sign of him. She saw Phillip eating silently near Diana the were-polecat, and avoided sitting near there. She didn't want to deal with Diana looking at her as though she were a recalcitrant mouse, even if Phillip wasn't the bore she'd first imagined him to be. Swerving away, she saw a group that she thought were geologists, Stefan's colleagues. She took a seat at a table behind them. Kylie joined her there, holding a laden tray. She shook her head at Freya when Freya raised her eyebrows at the mountain of food there.

"I'm hungry, alright?" Kylie said defensively.

Freya didn't pursue the topic, however, because she heard one of the geologists mention Stefan's name.

"Lucky sod, getting a trip to Hawaii. I can't believe work paid to send him to a tropical island."

"Yeah, how come we don't get that sort of perk?"

"Because you don't have Stefan's magic touch with a rock hammer?"

There were derisive hoots.

"At least he won't be griping at us for a bit. He's always nit-picking."

"True. Enjoy the break. And anyway, he'll be dodging storms all the way there and back, that's no picnic."

Freya and Kylie exchanged looks. Apparently, neither of them would have to, or be able to, confront Stefan anytime soon.

CHAPTER SEVENTY-TWO

A VISIT TO THE CHILLI KING

Freya stood uncertainly outside the chilli king's house where Kylie had dropped her off. Although she'd meant to go straight from the coast to the chilli-king's house, Kylie had persuaded her that she'd need to check in with Angie first. Freya winced at the thought. Poor Angie had not been having a good time. Freya had felt she needed to stick around to support her. Then it had been so late she'd stayed home. She then had to go to work. Despite the time that had passed, puddles of water from the floods that had followed from the snowstorm on the moor lay between the road and the hedgerow, and a strong smell of mud rose from the surrounding fields. A pair of bullfinches chirped to each other in the hedge. There was no sense in standing out here; she'd have to confront Phillip sooner or later, and later would bring the risk of darkness with it. Freya raised a hand and knocked on the door.

Just as before, the chilli guy answered the door promptly. This time, his clothing was more than usually rumpled, and a smear of mud covered one side of his face.

"Ah, Freya. I was rather hoping you would stop by. There are some people here I'd like you to meet."

Freya's eyebrows rose. After she'd left his polytunnels awash in floodwater, thanks to quenching Kylie's accidentally-sparked grass fire with a summoning, she'd expected to be turned away on sight. She hadn't thought to be greeted warmly, even though she'd sent a message in advance of her arrival.

"Really?" It was hard not to sound surprised.

"Yes indeed. I've long had some correspondence with a most delightful woman who lives on the coast. I've sent her chilli sauce in the past, and she's been telling me about your mother recently," said Phillip.

Can I not get away from my mother anywhere? I'm trying to make a life of my own!

"Er, OK. I didn't realise you knew my mum," she said aloud.

"I was unaware of her existence prior to this. But I am exceedingly pleased to say that I have sent her a sample of my best seed lines, and she will be maintaining a backup seedbank for me henceforth. This will be most helpful in the event of further, ahem, accidents."

Oh great, now there will be chillis whenever I go home, too.

Phillip's eyes strayed towards his still-soggy polytunnels, barely visible from the front of the house, and Freya felt another twinge of guilt. Still, the snowstorm hadn't been due to her. Just the river-induced flood.

"Yeah. Um. Sorry about that."

"No matter, no matter. My plants will recover, which is more than they would have done had they been burned. And given that the heat wave continued well past expectations, I'm grateful for extra water. Now, come in, please."

Freya followed Phillip down the black-and-white tiled hall and into the conservatory again, feeling a sense of deja-vu. But this time, instead of groups of well-dressed lab workers, there was a hodgepodge of people in various states of disarray. Freya was immediately distracted from her plan of discussing Stefan with Phillip. She'd thought that the chilli king might well hold the key to a safe future around the unpredictable demi.

They look like they've been sleeping rough!

It was an unexpected sight in the chilli guy's well-appointed conservatory. Freya paused in the doorway, unsure of her welcome - or of her safety.

"No need to hover, Freya. These people are the mainstay of my little operation." He beamed at the assemblage, apparently oblivious to their appearance.

As she gazed at them, Freya began to notice long nails (though many were bitten short), hairy forearms, flared nostrils. Heads cocked in listening attitudes. The hair on the back of her head stood up of its own accord. Once again, she had walked into a room full of weres.

"Er - do you feed them?" she blurted out. She'd also noticed hollow cheeks and gaunt frames.

Phillip smiled at her as though she was his favourite chilli who had just won a prize.

"No, no, they feed themselves. I admit I did start out offering accommodation and board, but for some reason they informed me that they preferred accommodation alone. I don't understand it myself; I was offering them the same excellent cuisine I make for myself."

Freya smothered a grin. She could guess why these people had decided to cook for themselves after sampling Phillip's excellent cuisine. It was fine, so long as you didn't mind chilli in *everything.*

"So, they're all labourers on your chilli estate?" she asked. *Why would weres come here, instead of doing regular work like Kylie does?*

"Oh yes, they all work for me, of course. I cannot afford to run a charitable institution. But their work has enabled me to greatly expand my operations. And I do pay them. Of course, they often arrive in a rather poor state, so it can take some time for them to be fit for any sort of work. Most of the group in here have only been here for a short time."

"But - where do they all come from?" Freya wondered if Phillip knew he was housing several were-packs.

"I understand that many of them are refugees, or otherwise displaced. They are referred to me by those who form my chilli seed exchange network. An informal system, but effective, I believe."

"Why do you do it? It sounds like a big undertaking."

Phillip looked at her with his head a little tilted.

"I may seem like just another mundane human. But my brother was not."

"But that means-"

Uncharacteristically, Phillip interrupted Freya's comment.

"He and I visited Mexico largely for his benefit, although I certainly did not lose from the experience. My brother stayed in Mexico. I have not seen him in twenty-five years. But he communicates with me from time to time, and he has explained to me the difficulties facing weres and demis in this country. The simplest things may be made impossible without a birth certificate, for example. And if one is born in animal form, often no birth certificate is possible."

"I guess that's true..." Freya agreed, thinking of her nieces and nephews. They were found as fox-kits - did *they* have birth certificates? It wasn't something she'd thought about as a teenager when they appeared on the beach. "But can't you just apply online?"

"Alas, that is not an option in all cases. So, you can possibly imagine the difficulties faced by such a one trying to obtain tax codes, setting up bank accounts, even getting paid, without proper certification. There is a huge gap into which many non-mundanes fall. I help some of them, as I would have helped my brother, if he had let me. It is that simple."

Maybe that's one of Lio's problems.

"That's all very worthy, I'm sure." Freya was feeling nervous, in a room full of hungry weres. She felt like all their eyes were watching her. When she looked at them again, several glanced away - they *had* been watching.

"You seem to hold a special fascination for weres; witness Kylie and Diana homing in on you," said Phillip.

"I didn't realise you knew they were weres. Even I didn't, at first!" said Freya.

"I have had considerable experience over the years. And you are only young; no doubt you don't appreciate that an additional decade or two of observational practice does in fact help."

"I've had plenty of practice - more than anyone needs," said Freya defensively. *I hate it when old people get condescending about their experience.*

Phillip simply shrugged, and picked up a plate of sandwiches that was sitting on a sideboard nearby. He offered Freya a plate of biscuits.

"Come, help me serve afternoon tea, and then we can discuss your problem," said Phillip.

Freya took the proffered plate - there seemed to be no other option. She wondered if these biscuits were laced with chilli, too. They looked like innocent ginger biscuits, but she remembered the chilli orange juice, and decided that she would pass on them herself. Steeling herself, she approached the group.

"Biscuits?" She held the plate out at arm's length. While she knew from Kylie that not all weres were problematic, she hadn't really got used to the idea yet.

Someone giggled.

"Why is she standing so far away?" It was a child's voice, wondering.

Any minute now they'll start commenting on my smell, thought Freya. *I wish I'd applied perfume.*

She gritted her teeth and shuffled closer, hoping to forestall such commentary.

"Here. Take one, go on." Freya lowered the plate to child height, and immediately several dirty hands made a grab for the biscuits.

"Just one, Maisie. Listen to what the lady said," instructed a woman from near the back of the group. There was no indication that Maisie or anyone else listened to this injunction - all the visible hands disappeared with more than one biscuit. Looking up, Freya struggled to match the face with the voice. She decided it probably came from the woman with dark, tangled hair and gleaming eyes set in a dark face. What sort of were was she? After a second, Freya decided it didn't matter. All she was doing was trying to be nice, after all.

"Er - have you all been here long?" she asked tentatively.

"Arrived last night," said a gruff voice belonging to a middle-aged man with grizzled hair cut off roughly at chin-length.

"I didn't get here till this morning," said a lighter tone. A woman with dark brown hair and tanned skin, watching over a pair of thin children.

"Most of us arrive in dribs and drabs, see?" someone else commented - an older man with full beard and greasy-looking clothes. "No-one wants to be too obvious about it."

"Yeah, no-one wants the attention of the volcano demi. Unless they're stupid." Several people made shushing noises at this voice. Freya wasn't sure which one it had been, but she mentally called blessings upon the speaker. This was the first time she'd heard anyone talk about Stefan. At least, she assumed it was Stefan - it seemed unlikely that there was another volcano demigod in the area who was particularly bothered by weres.

"Do many of you encounter the volcano demi?"

There was a brief silence.

"You may as well tell her, now you've mentioned it, Brian." Freya was almost sure there was a muttered 'Idiot' following that sentence.

Brian appeared to be a scrawny young man around the same age as Freya, though it was hard to tell under the dirt and stubble.

He looked wild-eyed, but his voice was normal enough when he spoke.

"Some of my friends thought they would give him something to remember when they saw him on the moor. Seeing as how one of their friends had been done over by him."

"There seem to be a lot of connections in this story," Freya commented. "What did the original friends do to attract his attention?"

Brian looked away.

"They didn't say," he mumbled.

Perhaps they didn't say because they were working for Stefan.

"Don't know," Brian said. "Don't really want to know, either. Anyway, my friends happened upon him up on the moors, several of them and just him there. But it all went wrong somehow. They got hurt pretty bad. After that, word got sent around to avoid him. Before that... I guess two or three of us had bad encounters with him. He's pretty territorial, for a singleton."

Unfortunately, that account seemed to match Stefan's personality and declared interests. Maybe the attacks he'd spoken of, too. And that fight up on the moor. This visit was giving her answers to questions she didn't want answered.

There was a scuffling towards the side of the group. An argument had broken out over a tray of juice.

"They're not used to having things provided, see," explained one of the earlier voices after order had been restored. "Usually, it's hand to mouth. We just hope it will be better here."

Freya shrugged helplessly.

"I get the impression Phillip likes to be a good host." She glanced self-consciously to where Phillip had been standing earlier, but he had disappeared. Great. Now it was just her and the weres. Her worst nightmare revisited.

She gave herself a shake. These weres showed no sign of attacking. The worst that could be said of them was that they needed a shower. She suddenly wondered how sensitive were noses coped with the lack of showers that inevitably accompanied homelessness. Was that worse than the lack of food?

Her thoughts drifted back to Stefan. And from Stefan, inevitably to recent events she'd experienced with him.

"Er... so. Do any of you happen to know someone called Roman?"

The effect on the room was electrifying. Freya was no longer surrounded by gaunt, beaten people taking their first decent meal in weeks; she was in the midst of a growling crowd hairy, sharp-toothed gang of the scariest-looking were-beasts she'd ever come across. The fact that most of them didn't come above her waist was completely beside the point.

The hair on the back of her neck stood on end; she raised her hands placatingly.

"I'm not sure if you love him or hate him, but I'd really like to know why the strong reaction," she stammered.

Breathe, Freya. Surely Phillip wouldn't have asked me to try and get along with weres who would try to kill me.

It wasn't looking good, though. She took one step back, then another. The weres advanced as she retreated. There was a flurry of movement at the back, and Brian resurfaced, struggling into a ragged shirt.

"How do you know Roman?" Brian demanded.

"Er. Well. My friend and I helped him out, on the moors. He's recuperating at her place now."

Freya tensed for a reaction, clenching her fists so tightly that her nails bit into her palms. Was she going to have to fight her way out of a horde of weres? They were already toothed and hairy, what chance would she stand? She wouldn't even have time to summon the river-gods. The weres closed in, surrounding her with a smell reminiscent of unwashed dog. Freya braced herself for the first bite and closed her eyes a moment, attempting to draw strength to herself.

CHAPTER SEVENTY-THREE

THE WERES REJOICE

Paws and noses touched her. Was that a lick? Arms closed around her, hugging. Hugging? Freya opened her eyes. This wasn't an attack; it was an onslaught of affection. Half the weres seemed to be wolves, dogs, or other canines. The others were still in human form.

"I guess you like Roman then?" she choked out.

"He's the one who's kept us going for the last decade," said Brian, one of those who had stayed human-shaped. "Without him we'd all be dead in a ditch, or worse. Subjects for medical experiments most likely. But we haven't seen him for a few weeks. We've been dead worried. Especially with that volcano demi around. He's just bad news."

Freya must have made some noise of dissent, because the arms around her removed themselves, and cool air replaced the hairy bodies that had pressed close.

"It's not as simple as good or bad," she said, feeling obscurely obliged to defend Stefan.

"How is it not?" The speaker was an older woman, two small children clinging to her.

"No-one is just bad. Not even Stefan."

"Oh, you know the volcano demi, then?" The woman's voice was suspicious, a marked change from the hugs that had just been pressed upon her.

"Well, yes. He's... someone at my work." After their disagreement on the moors, Freya no longer wanted to be associated with Stefan. They'd seemed so close, and she acknowledged that she was still attracted by him - but his actions repelled her as well. *It's so confusing.*

The weres seemed to pick up on her prevarication.

"Just someone, eh? Maybe a bit more than a colleague?"

"Look, I don't know, OK? Yes, we were going out, but I've just had a horrible experience and I don't *know* anymore!"

"Leave her, Cassia. At least she knows where Roman is. We should get that address from her," Brian said.

Cassia must be the were-wolf woman, whose eyes were shooting daggers at Freya, even while her hands gently patted her children's backs.

"If you are his friends, I'm sure he'd be happy to see you," Freya said. "But you should know that he's staying in a were-fox town. And my friend isn't one of them. So, it could be... tense. You'd need to be careful."

"As if we don't know how things are in the world," someone muttered.

"I'm just trying to help!" Freya defended herself.

"You're obviously privileged then."

"You don't know much about my background if that's what you think."

"Don't know, don't care," the speaker replied.

"And I don't have to tell you where Roman is."

"Come on, Cassia, we need to know about Roman. Leave her be and we can have an adult discussion about Roman's whereabouts."

Freya backed away from the group, looking for the door.

"Hey, wait."

"Don't go yet, we'll be nice. Whoever your boyfriends have been," one of the weres called.

Freya paused. Roman had helped her and Aisha, and had expressed concern for his were-family. Perhaps he would welcome contact from these weres. She should probably try to overcome her own fears - after all, she'd more or less accepted Roman. And Aisha had actually left her precious cafe in the hands of a were-fox. Perhaps she was just being over-sensitive. She'd discovered that not all demis were happy, stable people - in a way she'd known that all her life. At the same time, not all weres were evil, slavering maniacs. Maybe not even most. She took a deep breath and turned around.

"Roman's my brother," said the woman with two wolf cubs at her feet, licking up biscuit crumbs.

Or should that be puppies?

"He's protected us for years. Now it's our turn."

"Alright. I'll take you to see Roman. But I'm not sending you without me, because that's not fair to my friend. And I don't have a car - not that you'd all fit in one anyway - so we'll have to go by bus."

The tension in the air lessened considerably, although there were some subdued murmurs about the cost of travel being prohibitive. Freya could certainly relate to that, having been in a similar position for most of her youth.

"I have a van which I am prepared to use to help you with this effort." It was Phillip, back from wherever he'd been. Perhaps he'd been listening in. Freya turned to him in some relief.

"Can it hold all of these… people?"

"It should suffice. I have had occasion to transport small groups in the past, and this one is no larger. It would be best to do so in the evening, however. There are still essential tasks to be done today, and in any case we will attract less attention travelling at night."

He smiled benignly at the puppies. "And those young ones will be able to sleep the trip away."

Really, the chilli guy is nothing like what I thought at first.

With all parties now in agreement, a trip to take the weres to see Roman was soon organised. Freya opted out of helping in the greenhouses to pass the time, explaining that she had the opposite of a green thumb. Instead, she wandered out into the garden, ostensibly to call Aisha and warn her of the descending crowd. Once outside, however, she did not immediately make the call, but stood indecisively by a large lavender bush that seemed to have lost half its foliage to some blight. Could she do something about that blight? She'd tried working on diseased plants a couple of times since Devon, but she hadn't had enough practice to be sure of her ability.

She closed her eyes for a moment, concentrating on the plant, humming a song under her breath, envisaging the internal flows of the bush open and healthy. One toothy frond at a time, the lavender regained its normal grey colour. She opened her eyes again, saw the restored plant, and smiled. No exploded, dripping trees this time. Maybe she just needed practice. The ability she'd discovered in Devon was not just a fluke. Maybe she could only work one plant at a time, but then again, perhaps her skills would improve. Even if it was only one plant at a time, maybe she could save the country's crops.

There was a scrape behind her. She turned hastily to see Phillip closing the front door.

"An impressive talent. I trust you will not be moving on too soon. I have some cultivars that are susceptible to blights, while still being very useful. Such as the one I use to dismiss unwanted river gods. I'd be interested in making use of your skills."

"Er. Yes. Great. That would be a good cultivar to keep going, certainly." Freya was discombobulated by Phillip's unexpected appearance. *He must have some were blood, if his brother is one. Perhaps that's how he manages to sneak about so quietly.*

"Yes. However, that is not why I came out here. I simply wanted to thank you for your willingness to work with today's group of weres. They have had a difficult time, and I believe it will be very beneficial for them to regain their leader, who I understand you have already met."

Unusually, he hesitated.

"They are just a few of many, you understand. When you do go out into the world, you may come across other weres who are hurting or in bad places. Will you be kind to them? Send them on here if need be, but a helping hand in place is often all that is needed. So often, you see, weres don't believe that demis can be kind. Show them otherwise, and the world will be a better place."

Freya nodded.

"So long as they don't attack me on sight, I can do that."

"I am pleased to hear it. And of course, you may use my special lemon chilli if they *do* attack on sight. Word will spread, you know. And as it does, you will also be less likely to be attacked."

So that's what his 'special chilli' is for. I may have to keep it on hand in future.

"Sounds good to me. I don't enjoy being attacked."

"Few of us do." Phillip smiled at her, the crow's feet around his eyes crinkling in a friendly way. "Now, I will leave you to make your phone call. I am sure that your friend would appreciate some warning of weres descending on her doorstep." He retreated into his house again, shoes clunking on the black and white tiles in his hall.

Freya shook her head in bemusement. She hadn't found the secrets she'd expected, but rather a treasure trove of potential allies - so long as she was brave enough to treat them as such. She lifted her phone. Time to call Aisha.

CHAPTER SEVENTY-FOUR

A VAN FULL

Freya was relieved when the van full of were-wolves pulled up outside Aisha's modest brick house.

At least on train journeys no-one objects when I ignore them for five minutes... of course, then I'm travelling on my own.

She tumbled out of the van ahead of the weres, and was knocking on the door before they started to emerge. That was all to the good, she thought - she hadn't been able to have a particularly free and open conversation with Aisha with all those were-wolf ears listening in.

However, it was Aisha's mother who opened the door. Freya tried not to let her disappointment too obvious - Aisha's mother had always been good to her, after all. But at times like this, Freya did wish that Aisha had a flat of her own, rather than living with her extended family.

"Is Aisha in? She's expecting me."

"Yes, she just told us a few minutes ago. Come in, your cat has been missing you." Aisha's mother's words were somewhat beside the point; there was a flurry of black and white motion while she spoke, and a cat landed on Freya's shoulder.

"Oh, Mr Fluffbum. It hasn't been that bad here, has it?" Freya patted her cat, who purred loudly in her ear while clawing her for balance. "Come down from there, you're needling me." She transferred the cat to her arms with only a little encouragement. "I've missed you too." She'd left Mr Fluffbum in Aisha's care while Kylie drove her back to York - just in case she ran into Stefan. She didn't want to put her cat in harm's way.

When she lifted her head from greeting her cat, Aisha's mother had disappeared and Aisha herself had taken her place.

"I hear you've brought Roman a few friends. He'll be pleased, he's been pining here with only cats and foxes for company."

"Hello to you too. Roman's welcome to his friends. After two hours of people time, I'm ready for some time by myself." She looked down at Mr Fluffbum. "Or with just a cat, that would do nicely."

"It's a shame about the gathering down at the pier, then," said Aisha in a suspiciously neutral voice.

Freya looked at her sharply.

"What gathering is that, and why can't I avoid it? You know I don't go near the sea."

"Oh, you know… just a group of weres and a few of their friends assembling to greet someone who's been missing for a few years. Her children will be there of course, but it will be a shame if her sister misses the occasion."

Freya stared at her friend, mind whirring furiously.

"Are you saying what I think you're saying? Because if you're making this up, I may never forgive you."

Aisha relented.

"You've got to come, Freya. Gareth tells me your sister is returning from the sea!"

At the waterfront, a familiar lorry was drawn up near the pier. In front of it lounged Nik. A small group of goblins, short and so pale their skin was almost green, scurried to and fro in hi-vis vests.

I wonder how they stay so pale all summer?

They were assembling railroad tracks, joining a line that ran up the hill towards the station and along the road to the end of the pier. Freya realised that Roman was there too, watching from a distance with a group of his were-wolf fans clustered around him. There were other familiar faces here too - russet-toned heads abounded in a large group on the far side of the pier. Lisichka, the were-fox matriarch, was prominent among them, apparently telling her clan where to stand.

Freya's Mum had evidently been called down too, for she stood slightly apart from the were-foxes. Freya's nieces and nephews bounded in fox form between the were-foxes and Danae, evidently hugely excited.

Freya walked over and exchanged a stiff hug with her mother before returning to ask questions of the most unexpected person present.

"Nik. What are you doing here? And what are those goblins doing?"

Nik shrugged nonchalantly.

"Improving my cousin's chances. Why not?"

Freya looked in bewilderment between Nik and the goblins.

"Are these friends of yours?"

"Sure, why not?" Nik gave the green-haired goblin who was directing operations a thumbs up sign.

Freya wasn't sure if that was a yes or a no, but she supposed Nik might have something in common with goblins - if only a penchant for differently coloured hair.

"And what do you mean about your cousin? Are you talking about Lio?"

"He's the only one of my cousins I talk to these days, so yeah."

"And the purpose of the rails is what?"

"Mostly it's just a means to make an offering, really. Did you know that iron is quite useful to the sea and its gods?"

Freya shook her head, wondering if Nik was quite in her right mind. *Mind you, I'm not sure anymore if I'd recognise that. I didn't realise Stefan was so... warped.*

"No need to look like I'm off my head. I got that info from the goblins here, but I looked it up and all, too. Seems it's one reason that reefs grow well on shipwrecks. Some places in the sea are iron-limited, so they only grow if they get extra. These rails are one hundred percent iron, no limitation at all. So, we give them as an offering to the crazy goddess-lady out there, while also getting on-side with those cringing were-foxes over *there* by fixing their pier."

Nik casually waved at the were-foxes, some of whom were indeed cringing when Nik looked in their direction. "And the cat-goddess folks you hang with are pleased too, since they root for the railway. All up, we get lots of pleased people, plus maybe your sister too."

Freya had never heard Nik so loquacious. She wondered if the time she'd spent in London had changed her so much, or if Freya had just met her at bad moments in the past. But...

"I don't see how all that gets Tammy back," she said.

"You can thank Lio for that. He's been negotiating for years. It just came together this week."

Freya felt her eyes bug out.

"*Lio's* been negotiating with Nehalennia? Really?"

She remembered him saying he had urgent business after the fight with Stefan. She hadn't imagined it had anything to do with her.

"Really. Cousin Lio has quite the silver tongue, you know."

"I've never found him particularly talkative," Freya said.

"He's probably too busy trying to impress you with his thunderclap."

Freya gave up the conversation. But she was prepared to wait around a bit if there was a chance that her sister might actually return. She looked nervously at the waves. Were they getting bigger? The tide was nearly high, and wavelets were slapping gently at the edge of the seawall which attempted to separate land from sea at this point of the town.

Nothing to fear yet.

There was a commanding yell from the green-haired goblin, and the stocky one nearest the end of the pier gave the spike he was hammering one last bash. The rails continued past him, over the edge of the pier and down into the water. He raised his arm to wave at green-hair. The remaining goblins appeared, pushing a small cart along the rails. When they reached the end of the pier, they gave it a final shove, and the cart swooped down the rails and into the water with a splash.

"What was *in* that thing?" asked Freya.

"That's an offering too," Nik said.

"I'm sure that won't help the shipping lanes," said Freya.

"Sure, it will," Nik said. She was now lounging on one of the bollards that prevented vehicles from going straight off the seawall. "Anything that makes the goddess happier will be good for shipping. And that cart is full of the finest selection of sea-goddess bribes money can find. Fish smelt, elvers, you name it. Some other things it's best you don't know. Besides, my goblin pals will no doubt retrieve that cart, they use it a lot back in London."

"I thought you were getting out of London, Nik? And whose money paid for goddess bribes?" Freya asked. She wasn't sure what to make of the idea of bribing a goddess with baby fish. Maybe it was just what a sea goddess wanted?

"I may be away from London for a bit, but that doesn't mean I didn't make friends there. It was just time for a change. These guys will probably head back when they're done here." Nik didn't answer Freya's question about money.

Sure enough, the cart was shortly reeled back in on a rope.

"Thanks Frodo. Thanks, Galadriel," called Nik. Presumably those were the names of some of the goblins, for they waved at Nik before trudging back up the hill, the cart behind them. "Now, Freya, if you're still capable of summoning, now would be a good time to call a goddess."

"Truly?"

"Yeah, go on. Get singing."

Freya looked around.

"There's not much vegetation round here. I need a thyrsis first. I mean, last time, I had to use a river as a go-between to even call Nehalennia," Freya objected.

Nik put two fingers in her lips and gave a piercing whistle. The green-haired goblin looked up.

"Vegetation for a wand, d'you reckon you can find something?" Nik called.

Moments later, Freya found her hands full of ivy, pine, fennel and more.

"Righty-ho, give it a go," Nik encouraged. "I don't think you'll need any go-betweens this time."

Taking a deep breath, Freya did so - under her breath.

"Put some effort into it, girl!"

She sang a little louder, still half-watching the goblins walking away. Freya was soon distracted from the goblins by the sea beginning to seethe, just off the end of the pier. At first, that was all that happened. After a few minutes though, coloured flashes shot out of the centre of the seething water in all directions. Those that hit the seawall bounced back to head further out to sea. It was a little like underwater fireworks. The next thing to happen had Freya backing up hill as fast as she could, breaking off her song. The small wavelets receded along with the sea, revealing the shelly shore awash with crabs racing for their burrows as their covering blanket of water disappeared unexpectedly. The sea drained as far as the pier's end, revealing all manner of detritus that must have washed there over the years. When it seemed that it could go back no further, the sea returned full force, a miniature tsunami pushing water back over the sea bed, and up and over the sea wall. The assembled crowds followed Freya up the hill, but the driving force of water followed them, piling people up against buildings and washing away ambitiously planted flower beds in the town square.

With horror, Freya realised that Danae and her little were-fox kin had not retreated fast enough to avoid being swept into the water. Her nieces and nephews didn't seem to be worried by the wetness however - and as Freya put a hand to her mouth, they *changed*. She wasn't sure what exactly they changed into, but they suddenly seemed perfectly at home in the water, still furry but with broader heads, and *flippers*, ducking in and out and circling Danae, who was making futile grabs at them in an attempt to rescue them from the wave.

A wet rushing sound announced the arrival of a second wave, overlaying the first. This one formed a sort of hump, with another beside it. The second hump split, white foam cascading away from it - and there was Tammy, Freya's long-lost sister. Freya rushed towards her, for once heedless of the water dragging at her legs. However, she stopped short when the first hump formed into a person shape made of seawater. Some of the coloured flashes from earlier sparked through the shape.

Great. Back to negotiating with sea-goddesses.

"Greetings, Nehalennia," Freya said to the sea-goddess. Maybe there *was* a right time to use that phrase. Then she couldn't restrain herself anymore. She dashed forward and hugged her sister. "Tammy, you came back!"

Tammy hugged her back, soaking Freya in the process.

"Good to see you too, Freya. You look like a proper grown-up, now!" Tammy released Freya, turned to Nehalennia and bowed. "Thank you for my time. I trust that our agreement stands?"

The sea-formed shape, Nehalennia, bowed in return.

"All agreements are kept. The sea remembers all."

Tammy nodded. Her ritualistic stance was interrupted, however, as her children, were-foxes no longer, came arcing through the water, splashing to a halt at her feet. She crouched and hugged all three to her. "Ah, my lovelies, I see you have learnt your new forms at last. I'm so happy to see you." Tongues appeared, licking at Tammy's face. "It's nice to see you too. But no licking, please. That's my number one rule." She stood, to the evident disappointment of the kits.

"It's quite the gathering here, Freya. I understand one of your friends is responsible for pulling everything together. You'll have to thank him for me." She grinned, and Freya saw a hint of the old Tammy at last. "He fast-forwarded things nicely, I hadn't hoped to be back on land for another five years at least."

"You've been at sea this whole time?"

"Do I look like a fish? Of course not, Freya. Nehalennia provided me with safe haven, by her standards." Tammy was dismissive.

I'd forgotten how much Tammy acts like she knows everything better than me.

"You've got to tell us more than that, Tammy. We weren't even sure if you were alive!"

Tammy shrugged. "I've been busy. It was pretty hard at first, having no-one to talk to, and then having to take the kits back. That was the worst." Her mouth turned down. "I don't like to think about that." She turned abruptly away from Freya, and bowed to Nehalennia. "Your powers are strong, ancient one," she proclaimed. "May they remain so."

There's a lot of bowing and proclaiming going on here, thought Freya. *I don't remember Tammy being so formal except when she was trying to get into the were-fox clan. She's changed.*

A giant wave swept in over the standing water, subsuming, or perhaps reclaiming, the hump of water that was the sea-goddess. Were-foxes, were-wolves and assorted demis grabbed for handholds to avoid being swept out to sea. Freya grabbed a niece in each arm and hooked her leg around a handy railing. She held her breath as the wave crested over her; the water stung the corners of her hastily closed eyes.

This is why I avoid the coast. I hope someone else grabbed the others.

She suddenly thought of her special chilli, safely tucked into a pocket. Hoisting a niece higher, she managed to pry a piece of the chilli out, releasing it into the waves. The wave rolled back immediately. Freya wasn't sure if she was imagining its haste.

After all, that's the anti-were chilli. I don't know if it works on sea-goddesses.

As the wave retreated, pulling at Freya's legs with a sucking feeling, she saw Aisha held one of her nephews and Danae the others. All safe and accounted for. She released her squirming nieces, who apparently just wanted to play in the remaining water. She had a brief flashback to the day she'd found these nieces and nephews on the shore.

I suppose they've been with Nehalennia and Tammy in the sea before, I needn't have worried. But I'd never forgive myself if I let one get lost, no matter what species they are.

Tammy bent and touched the heads of her foxy children. "Thanks for looking after them, Freya. Or was it Mum?"

"Mostly Mum. I had to go to university."

"Oh, you got away then. Well done, I didn't think you had it in you."

Tammy laughed when Freya glared at her.

"I thought you might stay, since you snagged that wind demi."

"I haven't 'snagged' any demi. Sure, I am friends with some. But anyway, demis have been making my life difficult recently. I met a volcano one, you know."

"So, was Mum right about them? I always thought she must be exaggerating their power." Tammy sounded intrigued, and Freya decided on the spot that no matter what happened in future with Stefan, she wasn't going to introduce Tammy to him.

"Plenty of power. But luckily, he's not here." Freya returned to the issue that bothered her. "What did you mean about a friend of mine speeding things up?"

Tammy laughed lightly, shaking her wet hair back out of her eyes.

She always did fit the image of a descendant of Freya better than me, Freya thought, noticing many eyes upon her sister. She quashed the now-unaccustomed jealousy. *No need for that, I have enough trouble with my own life without getting jealous of people looking at Tammy.*

"Oops, I don't think I was supposed to say," Tammy said, laughing lightly.

"You can't let go of half a truth and not tell me the rest, Tammy!"

"As to that, your wind demi has been negotiating with Nehalennia practically since I left here. He never stuck around when I tried to talk to him, but he's the one who managed to persuade her to return me. I believe his argument was that I could give her more than one litter if I returned to her mate." She made an expression of distaste. "As though I was a brood mare. I want children that I can keep. But here I am, back in Britain. I still can't quite believe it. But since I am here, it must be time to take over the reins of my pack once more." She straightened her shoulders and splashed regally over to the gathering of were-foxes.

She always did want a pack, I guess. This should be interesting. But what has Lio been doing out there? Why did he never say he'd seen Tammy?

To Freya's surprise, the were-fox matriarch Lisichka stepped aside at once when Tammy stood in front of her. She made a come-here motion, and Tammy's erstwhile were-fox partner sprang forward. It seemed he'd been held back by his matriarch's wishes, for he greeted Tammy enthusiastically.

That should keep Tammy happy.

Freya looked away, feeling a little melancholy. Who was here for her, in all this gathering? Stefan was volatile and not here anyway. Fortunately. Aisha was her best friend, but she was currently chatting avidly with the were-wolf Roman. Nik was an unknown quantity, as ever. And Lio had apparently been negotiating for her sister all this time - and he wasn't here either.

There was a distant rumble of thunder.

"Bastet lives, it's going to rain again," exclaimed Aisha.

"We could do with the rain, after the summer we've had," Freya said.

Though the heat has really eased off since Stefan left the country. Coincidence? I think not.

"Yeah, but I wanted to ease Roman away from those weres who're fawning all over him, long enough for a walk at least. It's harder to make the excuse when it's bucketing down." Aisha smiled demurely, only her twinkling eyes giving her away.

"Somehow, I feel sure you'll manage something, Aisha."

"Somehow, I feel sure you're right."

The rain started, pattering lightly down on the assembled heads. Freya turned her face up to it, letting her melancholy blend with the rain, trying hard not to feel sorry for herself. There was a flash of lightning, close enough to brighten the dull day. Thunder followed on its heels, and hands closed around her waist.

Freya's eyes flew open in fear and astonishment. But the face in front of her was not the one who'd been recently haunting her nightmares, but a kindlier one.

"Lio?"

"One and the same. I'm sorry to be late, there were a few things still to sort out with your sister's return."

He looked frustrated, Freya thought, hair more tousled than usual, lips pressed together.

"You don't look happy about that."

"Oh, I am beyond thrilled to have her back where she belongs and off my island. It's just that she let out the storm hounds as she was leaving, and I've had a right time of it getting them to heel ever since. I need to hand them over to Nehalennia, to complete our exchange. I had hoped to be here before she was, to let you know."

"Wait, my sister has been on *your* island?"

"Taunting my brothers most of the time, yes. It's been profoundly irritating. You have no idea."

"Actually, I think I do. I did grow up with her." Freya realised that Lio's hands were still on her, and thought of Aisha's advice. "Um. Is there something you wanted to tell me?"

"There are many things I'd like to tell you. But right now, I'd like to ask you something."

"Go ahead."

"Want a race to the sea? Last one there's octopus bait."

Freya couldn't help it. She laughed. *Is that Lio's way of asking me for something more in a relationship? I'll risk it, if so.*

"Took you long enough to ask!"

Epilogue

S tefan tramped moodily between the rivulets of lava from the latest eruption on Mt Kilauea. The magma might be the same everywhere, but the demi-gods were quite different. He didn't feel at home here at all, and he wasn't sure how anyone thought he could access geothermal power in this state. Not that his workplace realised how he achieved his goals. He'd have to figure out a way to connect with the earth here somehow, or the whole horrible trip, weeks on a boat as far from his natural habitat as could be imagined, would be wasted.

His thoughts returned to Freya, as they had done uncountable times before, and he frowned in irritation. He didn't want to be distracted by thoughts of her. She'd rejected him. She wasn't worth spending thoughts on. That was half the reason he'd agreed to come here at such short notice, to avoid having to see her. Nevertheless, her face presented itself to him again as he cast to and fro, trying to locate the most useful vent between the solid rocks.

"Jörð, don't torment me so."

He gritted his teeth. Something was going to have to be done about this lingering passion.

THE END

Afterword

I hope you enjoyed Freya's adventures. If so, please leave a review! It makes all the difference for independent authors like me. Book 3 is in the works. Meanwhile, you can sign up for my newsletter at www.melissagunn.com for updates and a free prequel story in the Weather Gods world.

ALSO BY MELISSA GUNN

Flash Flood

Storm Surge
Treescape {in Magic and Mystery: a Limited Edition Anthology}
Feels like heaven (in Aftermath: Stories of survival in Aotearoa New Zealand)

Acknowledgments

Thanks to the Auckland Writers Cafe Novel Writers Club, my awesome writing critique group and editor Julie. Moss and Sophie provided helpful comments and my family were encouraging. Thank you also to my ARC readers!

About the Author

Melissa always planned to write books, but waited until life was at its busiest to start doing so. She enjoys mixing fact with fiction as a change from her day job, where mixing fact and fiction is distinctly frowned upon. She also loves wildlife photography, but mostly finds that plants are her best subjects since they stay still to be photographed – most of the time, anyway.

www.ingramcontent.com/pod-product-compliance
Lightning Source LLC
Chambersburg PA
CBHW021132110726
47900CB00002B/312